IT WAS EVERY DRAGON FOR HIMSELF

Bazil looked away, sickened, barely able to believe what he had seen. A single lucky blow had destroyed the most graceful of the dragons of the fighting 109th. And rolling across the arena was a large metal box on heavy wheels, pulled by an army of slaves under the lashes of six imps. The door to the metal box crashed down. To Bazil's amazement, another dragon emerged, a wild drake of enormous girth and angry eyes. It vented a scream of rage and leaped forward, pawing the ground with heavy claws. Bazil's heart sank. He had no sword, and this beast outweighed him by a wide margin. He would fight but he knew it would be of little use, and the wild one would tear his head from his body. Then a great realization struck home. . . .

BAZIL BROKETAIL

MAGICAL ADVENTURES

BAZIL
BROKETAIL

Christopher Rowley

A ROC BOOK

ROC
Published by the Penguin Group
Penguin Books USA Inc., 375 Hudson Street,
New York, New York 10014, U.S.A.
Penguin Books Ltd, 27 Wrights Lane,
London W8 5TZ, England
Penguin Books Australia Ltd, Ringwoood,
Victoria, Australia
Penguin Books Canada Ltd, 10 Alcorn Avenue,
Toronto, Ontario, Canada M4V 3B2
Penguin Books (N.Z.) Ltd, 182-190 Wairau Road,
Auckland 10, New Zealand

Penguin Books Ltd, Registered Offices:
Harmondsworth, Middlesex, England

First published by Roc, an imprint of New American Library,
a division of Penguin Books USA Inc.

First Printing, August, 1992
10 9 8 7 6 5 4 3 2 1

 REGISTERED TRADEMARK—MARCA REGISTRADA

Printed in the United States of America

BAZIL
BROKETAIL

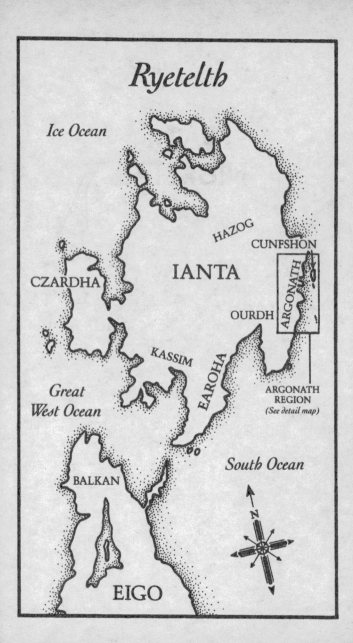

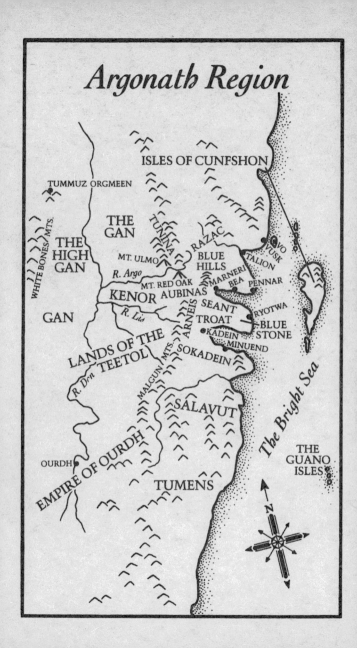

CHAPTER ONE

High and clear the clarions sounded the silvery cry of Fundament Day from the Tower of Guard of the city of Marneri. The old year was ended, winter was begun, soon there would be flakes of snow upon the air.

Already there was a chill in the wind at night that sent children indoors early, while mothers put more logs on the fires; but for now it was time for the greatest festival of the year. The harvest was in, the sun still held warmth; it was a day to mark the passing of the old and the beginning of the new.

Throughout the Empire of the Rose, from the Isles of Cunfshon to the western marches of Kenor, the people were as one on Fundament Day.

In the city of Marneri, sited at the head of the Long Sound, there was an additional significance to Fundament Day. The Greatspells were renewed, in solemn majesty, replenishing the strength of the city walls for another year. Drums and the sharp reports of firecrackers urged the folk out of their houses and through the massive North Gate to the Green Field beyond the city walls.

Today! sang the horns, today is the day of the Greatspell and every able witch must come. To make the walls stand tall, the height of fifteen men, with the power to resist all known assaults. To make the turrets firm and adamant! To give the gate spirits, Osver, Yepero, Afo and Ilim, their strength to resist the magic of the enemy.

From the corner towers floated the brightly colored banners of the high families of the Guard. Small balloons flew, carousels twirled upon the green. Folk in colorful silks danced the ancient steps of the Fundament dances.

The crowds were filled with people wearing blue and red Marneri caps. The men wore white wool shirts called "copa," and thick winter leggings of black and brown. Most of the women wore traditional cream-colored linen dresses, with the red sash of the Sisterhood.

By the tenth hour of the day the city was almost empty. The sound of the distant fireworks and horns and drums became muffled echoes around the stone-flagged courtyards behind the mighty Tower of Guard.

In the Stables of the Guard, where sixty horses made quiet chuffing sounds, the echoes of the distant fun made young Lagdalen of the Tarcho's heart feel hard and heavy in her chest. Sometimes it was awful to be well-born, a member of a High House, with all the privileges of that station and all the responsibilities.

The drums and fifes died down, and it grew quiet once more except for the sounds of contented horses. Lagdalen bent to her task again, mucking out the stables.

No matter how she looked at it, it still seemed enormously unfair. As if all the world were arrayed against her, from the Lady Flavia and the officers of the Novitiate to her own family. She was simply a young girl who had fallen in love, and as a result here she was muckraking on Fundament Day. While all the city was dancing on the green, she would be laboring for hours on this punishment detail which would take all day. And by the time it was done, and the feasting had begun, Lagdalen would be too exhausted to do more than bathe and go to sleep on her cot in the Novitiate.

Fundament was ruined, and all because of a mad infatuation with a boy, a silly boy, a boy she still ached for. A boy with the tiny green, triangular freckles on his skin that marked a bastard of the tree, an elfchild.

A boy named Werri, a boy from the "Elvish" race, who grew from trees in the sacred glades and loaned their skills to the aid of the people of Marneri and all the Empire of the Rose. A boy who worked in the foundry, forging steel by day, and who stayed in the elf quarter by night, caught up in their mysterious world of ritual and trance. A boy she had seen only a handful of times, a boy that she barely knew in fact; although this realization was new to her, and she had only come to it in the last few days.

The news of her downfall had brought no response from Werri. No romantic invitation to leave her life in the Tower of Guard and join him as an elf-wife in the quarter with its funny, narrow streets and crowded tenements.

Werri had behaved just as her father had predicted.

"You'll see," he'd said with the contemptuous foreknowledge of an adult. "He's only interested in wenching with normal folk. To him you're no more real than a phantom."

She burned with embarrassment now, for she knew in her heart that her father had been right. Even after the love she'd imagined between them when she'd gone to him, he'd barely acknowledged her, barely taken the time to say goodbye, before slouching off with his friends clothed in elf green to the quarter and the ale house.

In tears of bitter humiliation she'd gone back to the Novitiate with her romantic dreams shattered. Werri didn't want her in the quarter. Now that he'd had his way with her, he didn't even want to know her.

Grimly the Lady Flavia had prescribed the punishment: long and hard labor on Fundament Day.

Of course, Werri was a handsome young devil, in the way that elvish folk often were, with a long lean jaw, slender straight nose, and green-brown eyes that danced when he spoke. And long, green-blond hair that hung down to his shoulders and which he shook back from his eyes or tied back with a silver elf-band.

But those triangular flecks on his skin were the mark of the wild elf glen and of entry into the world through the womb of a tree. No woman could give birth to such as Werri, for the only product of such liaisons was the engenderment of imps, debased and evil.

And thus to be caught abed with such a one as Werri was a serious matter for a young witch in the Novitiate.

And for Lagdalen of the Tarcho they had high hopes; the Lady Flavia had said as much in prescribing the punishment.

"Normally for this sort of thing, I'd take the cane to your backside and set you a full Declension of the Dekademon, plus a month of service in the Temple to show you just how silly it is for a witch in the Novitiate to be infatuated with an elfboy, and to remind you of your place within our mission. But you are not just any novice, Lagdalen. Of you we have hopes of much achievement in this world. You are to go to Cunfshon, to the teachers there. If you continue your growth you will go on to a great career in either the Temple or the Administrative Service."

Flavia had frowned most thoughtfully then, while gazing into a white paper file upon her desk.

"So instead you will clean the Stables of the Guard on Fundament Day, and produce a full Declension of the Dekademon by the end of the week. Am I understood?"

Lagdalen's heart had grown heavy at the thought, for she loved Fundament Day beyond all other festivals and would willingly have endured the cane, though Flavia's was a notoriously heavy hand with it, instead of spending that day working in the stables.

Flavia had then said, "You must understand this, Lagdalen. The passions of the body are sent to torment us and to turn us aside from our historic mission. We must eschew all thoughts of love and family during these learning years. And, of course, it goes without saying that we must not have congress with the elvish. From such unions can come only imps and disaster. The elvish cannot understand the distress they cause in this behavior; we are playthings to them in this. But for a witch it is a deadly crime, a slip into abomination."

And thus had Fundament Day been ruined, although she had learned with considerable relief, at the medical examination which followed her interview with Flavia, that no imp had been quickened in her womb.

She had wept many, bitter tears since then. And rerun

through her mind again and again the awful humiliation of that moment when Helena of Roth, Lagdalen's most bitter enemy, had pulled open the door and shown the proctors what was going on in the little laundry room at the back of the dormitory.

Helena was a senior novice, and she took particular pleasure in disciplining the "little Tarcho brat." Lagdalen recalled, with a spine-chilling thrill of horror, the vindictive laughter with which Helena had greeted Lagdalen's arrest and removal to Flavia's office.

And now she drudged, mucking out the stalls of sixty horses. Of course the stable boys who normally did this work, but were excused on Fundament Day, had left all the dirt and straw down from the previous two days. They knew that on Fundament Day there was normally some poor wretch enjoined to work there all day for punishment.

She lifted another shovelful of manure and cast it into the barrow; the job ahead of her was mountainous. It would take her all day to rake it and shift it.

Wearily she filled the barrow, lifted it, and trundled it off to the composter heap. This was set in a covered pit just inside the Old Gate, under the looming walls of the tower. To reach it she had to leave the stables and negotiate the smoothly polished cobblestones of the Tower Yard, where the barracks troops performed their drill. This was the dangerous part of the passage, for not a drop of the contents of her barrow could be left on the cobbles for fear of old Sappino the Yardkeeper, whose obsession was the polish on his cobbles. Loud would be his complaints if she made a mess. Long would she kneel polishing the stones if Sappino complained to Headmistress Flavia.

Outside the stables, which were protected by a spell, the fat flies of summer still buzzed vigorously in the sunlight, and they soon discovered her cargo.

Lagdalen hated flies, and she quickly tried to cast her own fly spell. But it took two full declensions and a paragraph from the Birrak, and she made a mistake in the declensions. The flies continued to buzz, oblivious to the botched spell.

With a curse of woe, flies settling on her face, in her hair, around her eyes, Lagdalen pushed the barrow as fast as it would go over the cobbles of the yard to the compost pit.

A fly crawled up her nose. With a squeal of horror she stopped and brushed it away. The barrow tipped and fell on its side, cargo spilling over the stones.

Lagdalen burst into tears as the accursed flies settled with victorious, hot buzzing.

There was a triumphant peal of bright, merry laughter from her left. She looked up, tears forgotten in sudden rage. A youth, a ragged dragonboy, was visible at the door to the red brick Dragon House. He was pointing at her and laughing.

She felt a flash of intense dislike and reached into the pocket of her drab novice's overalls, pulled out a slingshot, and let fly with one of the round stones she always carried.

The boy vanished instantly, and the stone pinged off the wall and fell back into the yard. Lagdalen ran over and retrieved it for another try.

When she looked up, though, it was to find the grim figure of Helena of Roth looking on. Helena pointed a long white forefinger at her with undisguised glee.

"Possession of a weapon! Expressly forbidden! Use of a weapon against another human! You'll be whipped! Not to mention that pile of excrement you've dropped on Keeper Sappino's clean cobblestones. Wait till I tell him what you've done. I should think that when Flavia's through with you, you'll have accumulated another year's worth of drudge!"

With a scarcely contained cry of triumph, Helena wheeled about and marched off to find the yardkeeper, who habitually slept through Fundament Day and all other festivals, relieved of all concern for his polished cobbles on the parade ground.

Lagdalen looked back to the site of her disaster. Long

before she could shovel it back up and then sluice down
the stones with water, Yardkeeper Sappino would return,
and when he saw what she'd done he'd log an immediate
complaint with Flavia.

Tears renewed themselves in the corners of her eyes.
She seemed to be doomed to stablework for the rest of
her life.

She felt a nudge on her elbow. She turned, eyes blurry,
and discovered the dragonboy who had mocked her so
recently, standing just a few feet away.

He was no more than fourteen by the look of him, with
a raffish air and a cocksure grin. His dragonboy suit of
brown broadcloth was old and worn, his boots were
scuffed, and he wore his cap backwards. He was also
carrying a couple of shovels.

She resisted her first urge, which was to knock his hat
off and pull his nose. He gestured to her with a shovel.

"Use this shovel, we'll use ours. Baz here will fetch
some water. My name's Relkin, Relkin Orphanboy, at
your service."

Lagdalen gasped. Looming behind the boy was a battledragon, standing ten feet tall, with olive green hide
and big black eyes that fixed themselves on her most intently. It hefted a shovel with a blade more than a meter
wide.

She felt dragon-freeze begin to sweep over her, the
instinctive human response to full-grown dragons.

"I'm, I, I don't know what to say."

At this the dragon's huge head split into a wide grin
and the eyes seemed to gleam. The boy looked up and
snapped his fingers, breaking her out of incipient dragon
trance.

"Yes, I know, you're overwhelmed, girls often are
when we're around, but you'd better stop gawking and
get shoveling before that nasty girl wakes the yardkeeper."

"Why are you doing this?" she said at last.

"We talked it over. We decided we liked you and we
don't like that other one—that mean-spirited Helena of

Roth. We think it's rotten that anyone should be stuck here in the yard, working all day on Fundament Day.''

Lagdalen stared at him. He gave her a brief little grin and went to work with his shovel. However, both his and Lagdalen's efforts were virtually beside the point. The dragon wielded his own shovel and scooped up the mess in two huge strokes.

Lagdalen stared at the load, replaced in the barrow so quickly. Relkin took hold of the barrow and wheeled it across the yard to the alley and down to the compost pit.

Meanwhile the dragon sauntered over to a tall rain barrel under the eaves of the stables and picked it up as if it weighed practically nothing. With its contents he sluiced down the cobblestones in a trice. The water gurgled down the drain, leaving the yard damp but spotless.

Lagdalen used a cloth from the stables to mop it dry and shine it up once more.

"Thank you Master Dragon," she said when it was done.

The monster's face split into a terrifying smile, with two-inch fangs bared over a long green, forked tongue. It spoke with the characteristic sibilant hiss of dragon speech.

"Well, miss, you best call me by my name—Bazil of Quosh, at your service."

At which the dragon reared erect and stood to attention with enough energy to make the ground shake, while he snapped her a crisp legionaire salute.

Slightly stunned she returned the salute, hoping she was doing it properly. The boy, Relkin, had returned with the now empty barrow which he parked inside the stables gate.

"Always glad to help a damsel in distress," he said with a little bow, swinging his hat wide in an extravagant flourish.

Lagdalen smiled. In spite of her misgivings, there was something clownishly sweet about this young ruffian.

"Of course we should be grateful to know the name of our particular damsel," said Relkin with a sly smile.

"Why, thank you, Master Relkin Orphanboy. My name is Lagdalen, of House Tarcho."

"Lagdalen of the Tarcho, eh? Well, well." He grinned. Here was a useful ally. By the margin of blue on her sleeve, Relkin could see clearly that she was of the senior class in the Novitiate, and the Tarcho were one of the most important families in Marneri.

"That was a good shot, Lagdalen of the Tarcho. If I hadn't ducked you'd have given me a bump for sure."

"I'm sorry," said Lagdalen.

"Sorry for what? I shouldn't have laughed, I know it, but at first I thought you were someone else, a stableboy perhaps. There's one of them with brown hair cut like yours. We don't get on with the stable boys. They're all older than sixteen and suffer from overgrown heads, if you know what I mean."

"I think so."

"And besides, I like a girl who can shoot straight and carries a good pebble."

"Why, ah, thank you." Lagdalen didn't know what to say suddenly, charmed by this wild child of the dragon yards. A child with oddly calculating eyes.

He seemed to hesitate, as if afraid to say something, and then he blurted it out.

"And I wonder if it would be impertinent of me, to ah, ask the Lady Lagdalen of the Tarcho, if she would like some company for the evening feast of Fundament."

She observed that he was crumpling his cap in his hands as he spoke.

"Well, I don't know. I was supposed to be spending the whole day working in the stables. I won't be finished until dark, and I'll be exhausted, so I don't think I can . . ."

Relkin's eyes were bright.

"We'll help, won't we, Baz?"

She looked to the dragon, still leaning on his shovel. The dragon gave her that unfathomable crocodile smile.

"Be glad to help, Lagdalen of the Tarcho. I'll bring

over the dragon barrow; it'll hold a lot more than that little one you're using."

Lagdalen was stunned anew. She gaped at them. They really meant it. No one had been this nice to her in years, if ever.

"Why, thank you, Relkin and Bazil," she managed at last. "I do believe that if I can get the job done in time, Mistress Flavia could not possibly object to my attending the evening rites."

"Oh good!" exclaimed the boy. "I know how we can get some hot apple wine and good seats at the puppet show."

The dragon suddenly hissed.

"Someone approaches."

"Quick, we must hide," said Relkin. Lagdalen found herself being pulled through a postern gate into the huge, gloomy interior of the Dragon House. Inside was an odd, herbal odor and a stream of warm air that flowed from an interior gate that led to an unseen corridor.

Through a slit in the door, she watched as Helena of Roth returned with Sappino the Yardkeeper, who had been awakened with some difficulty from his morning nap. He was in an irritable mood as a result, and the sight of the clean yard sent him into a fury. He always suspected the sly young females of the Novitiate, always imagined they were out to trick and embarrass him. He turned and set off to find Headmistress Flavia.

"Perhaps a few stripes with the cane will cure your impudence!" he snarled over his shoulder.

Helena looked around wildly, eyes glaring. How could that little Tarcho brat have done this? There'd been a huge pile of horse dung right here. She could never have cleaned it up this quickly.

She heard laughter up above, and turned and glimpsed a round-faced boy grinning at her for a second before vanishing into a crevice in the wall of the Dragon House. Helena frowned, mystified and distressed by this sudden turn of events. After a quick look in the stables for Lagdalen, she gave up in disgust and headed for the gate, hoping to be able to stay out of Flavia's way for the duration of Fundament Day.

Later that afternoon, as she squirmed into a standing place at the puppet show, so far from the stage that the puppets of the Old Witch and the Little Child were hard to distinguish from one another, she noticed with considerable annoyance that Lagdalen was sitting in a much better seat, close to the front, with a boy in the costume of the dragoneers beside her.

Helena ground her teeth. If only Flavia could see this! But Helena was helpless. To report this crime meant she herself would have to visit Headmistress Flavia, which she knew very well to be an extremely risky proposition on that day. Flavia bore an intense dislike of old Sappino, and she would take vengeance on any girl who gave Sappino cause to enter Flavia's presence to voice his loud and eloquent complaints!

CHAPTER TWO

Later, when the moon rose to bring Fundament Day to a close, Relkin and Lagdalen joined the crowds that thronged the space outside the North Gate, where the High Witches were drawn up in two squares, as neat as troopers on parade.

Thousands of torches on ten-foot-high poles lit up the scene. The faces of the people were bright eyed, expectant.

It was the time for the renewal. The Greatspell was almost completed once again, the words whispered in perfect witchly unison, bringing the bond to full power. Many thousands of lines of declension, texts from the Birrak, paradigms of the Dekademon, had already been said, for the making of this spell took many hours of preparation. And the reciting of it required great powers of concentration, ignoring the firecrackers and drums and the cries of the populace at festival.

Now that the context had been laid down, the higher passages were begun, for under the full moon the majesty of the work was expanded and the power of the Great-spell increased.

The crowd was quiet now, with just the low buzz of occasional greetings and hellos as more people came in from the fields.

Relkin and Lagdalen watched from a spot at the rear of the crowd, where a hillock offered a better view over the heads of the people in front. They could both see the serried ranks of the High Witches, all clad in black with the badges of their Orders emblazoned on their right shoulders. The low murmur of the spell's words surrounded them.

They began to feel the rising power of the spell as the ancient art of Cunfshon witchery wove magical energies around the walls of Marneri once more.

This was the holiest moment of the year, celebrating the assumption of power in the lands of the Argonath by the colonies sent from Cunfshon to reclaim them. In those times the lands were afflicted by the servants of the enemy, the demon lords, Mach Ingbok and Cho Kwud, who ruled by terror where once the fair kingdoms of Argonath had flowered, before their bitter fall in malice and ruin.

The redemption of Argonath had been long and bloody, and was by no means a completed task. Six times Cho Kwud had brought his great host out of the north and surrounded Marneri the fair. Six times he had been defeated by the city's walls and forced to retreat by the advancing legions of the other cities.

A dozen great battles had been fought before the blue abomination, Mach Ingbok of Dugguth, could be destroyed. The lists of the valiant dead were long, their names were encoded into these walls. Marneri remembered the fallen, recalled the valor of their passing while simultaneously raising the standard of civilization upon the eastern margin of great Ianta.

A single note from a clarion sounded a short break in the spell-casting. Lagdalen and Relkin exchanged happy glances.

"Did you enjoy the day then, Lagdalen of Tarcho?" said the dragonboy.

"Yes, Relkin Orphanboy, I did. Thank you again."

"Actually, there is a way you could repay us, especially Baz."

"What's that? Anything within my power I will happily do."

Relkin leaned closer to her side and dropped his voice to a whisper.

"Actually we do have a problem. It's our papers. We don't have a discharge stamp from our former employer. We, uh, had a dispute with him, you see."

"I thought you were a newcomer," she replied, equally quietly.

"Well, we thought we could sign on with the New Legion they're raising here."

"And then I'll never see you again," she said mock mournfully.

"No, Lady Lagdalen, you will see us again," said Relkin. "But only if I can get a dragon stamp for Baz. Without that we can't join up."

"How could I help?"

"We have a friend in the Administrative Chamber who has the stamp we need. But he doesn't dare try to bring it out of the office. We wondered if you would do that."

Lagdalen hesitated a moment. "Well, I suppose I could."

"Good!" He accepted this with alacrity. "You will go to the administrative block shortly anyway, to get your birthday stamp—am I correct?"

Lagdalen was shocked. How did he know that? She felt her privacy invaded.

"Yes." Her voice rose out of a whisper. "I go tomorrow. I was seventeen last week."

"I'm sorry, my friend in the chamber sees that information all the time, so when I knew who you were I asked him to look up your file. I know it was wrong of me, but our situation is getting desperate. We don't have much money left, so we can't leave Marneri and we need to find work. You're our only hope."

"I am?"

"Look, Bazil is a premier battledragon, one of the best there is. Marneri needs him."

"He seems enormous!" she exclaimed.

"Actually he's only medium-weight for a leatherback. But he's terrific with a sword and he has great endurance. A lot of leatherbacks have tender feet, can't take the marching, but Baz is a trooper—he can stay up with anyone. He also likes horses, and not just for food, so he's no trouble with the cavalry."

"I'm sure he's everything you say, Relkin. But it is an invasion of privacy to do things like that. I think you should have asked me, to my face."

Relkin hung his head; he'd blown his chance, it seemed. And he'd been so sure that this girl would help them. He'd misjudged her, not thinking she would care to be asked her age.

"But I will help you if I can," she said.

"You will?" His hopes which had lain so obviously in the dust, sprang back to life. How could she say no to him?!

"Of course, I'll have to get past the scrutineers." Lagdalen was troubled by that thought. She had never before stolen or smuggled anything, and thus had never suffered the fear of discovery by the scrutineers.

"Ah, yes, but you are a Senior Novice. You can use a dissembling spell and walk past the scrutineers with no fear of detection."

"I can, but the scrutineers are said to always be attracted to the novice that dares to wear a cloaking spell in their presence."

Relkin accepted this with a resigned shake of the head.

"Well, yes, indeed this is the reason our benefactor in

the chamber won't smuggle the stamp out for us. He and the other workers in the chamber are always scrutinized very carefully when they leave at the end of the day.''

''Yes, I see.'' And Lagdalen did see. Relkin had aided her, it was true, but now he asked her to risk much in order to get him the stamp. What if he were a spy? There was much talk just lately concerning spies who had been sent to infiltrate the city.

The great enemy to the north was putting forth its strength once more. The dread shadow of the Masters of Doom lengthened across the world.

Then she reconsidered. No dragon would serve the evil Masters. The dragon race's hate for the Masters was undying and universal, the thing that bound them to the people. And if Bazil were not a spy, then how could his dragonboy be one?

Lagdalen shrugged to herself. Paranoia was abroad these days, and it was easy to fall victim to it when spy scares were so common and rumors so strong.

''Anyway, once I'm past the scrutineers, what am I to do?''

''Don't worry, I'll be watching outside the gates for you.''

''You just walk down the Strand and I'll contact you when I'm sure it's safe and you're not being followed.''

Horrors, what would that do to her reputation, already besmirched through her infatuation with Werri?

''But if they catch you, I will come forward and confess, this I swear to you by all my ancestors.''

She smiled. ''But Relkin, you don't know who your ancestors were. How can you swear by them?''

''Then I swear by my own conscience, which would never let me be should I betray you, Lagdalen.''

''Well, thank you, Relkin. I think that will do. Still, one other thing troubles me.''

''Yes?''

''The nature of this dispute you had with your former employer. What was that about?''

Lagdalen studied him carefully. This was crucial—she knew the killer's mark would show if it was there.

"We had a contract with the Baron of Borgan. Borgan, if you've never heard of it, lies near Ryotwa in the Bluestone Hills. The baron decided dragons were too expensive, so he bought maroon trolls—terrible things, they breed them out of elk and turtles."

Lagdalen blanched. "But trolls are forbidden throughout the Argonath."

"Funny how many there are, though. Baz and me have spent our lives fighting them, mostly down in the Bluestone country."

"But why?"

"They're cheap. They eat slop and they're easily contented. Give 'em weak beer and sex with farm animals, and they're happy."

Lagdalen was revolted. "That is disgusting!"

Relkin nodded. "I always thought so, myself."

"So what happened?" she said.

"When?"

"When this baron brought in these trolls."

Relkin half-closed his eyes and shrugged. "There was trouble."

"Trouble? What sort of trouble?"

"Well, the maroons get aggressive when they're drunk and the baron gave them too much beer. Eventually they challenged Baz, and there was a helluva fight and Baz had to kill one of the damned things and broke the legs on the other. The baron wouldn't pay us after that, and he owed us for six months."

"So what did you do?"

"Well, we thought about robbing him but we didn't want to be branded outlaw. We just wanted honest soldiering work, that's what we do best. So we broke our contract and slipped off into the hills and came up here. We heard about the New Legion they're raising, you see."

Of course, the New Legion had brought in recruits from far and wide.

Lagdalen stifled her fears. She detected no trace of deceit in his face and she was trained for such work.

"All right, Relkin Orphanboy, I'll help you. But if you've lied to me, I'll find out and then you'd better watch yourself!"

Lagdalen looked back to the lines of witches. Under the moonlight their hair was long and silver, their faces were etched with harsh lines and their eyes sunk in shadow. She knew that one day she would stand among them and recite the Greatspell. It was an idea with both attractive and frightening qualities. They seemed so grim, so purposeful, so far removed from the life she currently knew. She wondered if she could ever learn such patience and determination, ever be accepted among their ranks.

Close under the North Gate's looming towers, each sixty meters tall, a fire had been lit. The High Priestess Ewilra led the male choir of the Temple in singing the hymns of the Fundament, and many in the crowd sang along with them while the witches rested briefly, all the preparatory declensions, descriptions and convolutions having been uttered without a mistake.

The final declensions were soon to be said. Herbs were burned carefully upon the altar and the sweet smell of their smoke wafted out to the crowd.

Now the witches gathered themselves for the final utterances, ninety lines of power, forged from dekedemonic principle. The crowd's excitement rose to the climax.

The drums thundered and it began.

The lines came forth quickly and the power of the spell-saying rose until a field of tension hung over the scene like an invisible fog. The voices grew loud, the last lines were virtually shouted, with the crowd shouting along beside in a vast euphoric mass.

The fires flamed up brightly and the drums and cymbals crashed and it was done. The Greatspell was said. For a long still moment there was an absolute silence, not a cough, not a whisper, not even the sound of a bird broke that quiet.

Then the trumpets blared, the people cheered, and the music became loud and general.

Now in solemn march the populace set off behind the witches to pass in and out of each great gate and through the city streets between them. First they entered the North Gate, which was under the control of the spirit Osver.

"To Osver and his health!" they shouted, and broke out flagons of ale to toast the gate warden.

Then they passed into the city and down the broad expanse of Tower Street with the great mass of the Tower of Guard behind them and the graceful Tower of the Watergate ahead.

At the Watergate they toasted Yepero's health, and since her spirit also guarded the harbor they continued to cry her name as they marched to the west of the city along Dockside and Soundside.

Here the marchers were hailed by the sailors on the ships at dock and the merchants and their retainers, leaning out from the balconies of the tall white-fronted buildings that lined the street.

Ships from every port in the Argonath were there, along with the great white ships from the Isles of Cunfshon, and the merchants included representatives of every great trading house on the eastern shore of Ianta.

Eventually they reached the West Gate, where they sang the hymn to Ilim, the female spirit that guarded this gate.

From there the procession turned and went back across the city on the West Road and Broad Street to the Hinge and the plaza at Afo's Gate.

And here everything came to a sudden stop.

Cries of horror and rage erupted from the head of the column. The priestesses wailed and wept. The witches broke into declamations and began an immediate purification spell.

Troopers of the King's Guard came pushing their way through to the gate. They were joined by all the constables in the city. The hue and cry grew by leaps and bounds.

But the evil was done.

Over the center of the gate projected a beam with a lamp on its end. Hanging from the beam by a rope around its neck was the corpse of an older woman, much abused and tormented. Someone had placed it there unseen during the day when the city was virtually empty.

The woman's body was a horror. She had been most fouly used for the casting of an evil spell; something from the book of Fugash, perhaps. Her right hand had been cut off and shoved wrist foremost into her mouth, so that now the dead fingers projected like obscene tongues into the air.

To those with the deep knowledge of the evil art this was called the "Hand of Leotha," and was a sure sign of necromancy of the malign path.

The left side of her face had been peeled and the flesh gouged away to the bone. The right eye was missing and the left eye glared in death-fixed horror, its lids removed. In three places on her body the flesh was burned and charred where a red hot bar of metal had been thrust through very slowly. Her feet were nailed together.

Such an abomination on the day of the Fundament was a mortal assault upon the Greatspell.

Great Afo, the spirit that protected the gate from an assault from the outside was of course powerless to protect his fane from such an assault. Somehow the human guards had failed in their task.

With such abomination there would have to be lengthy purification spells recited that very night and the Greatspell itself would have to be resaid the next day.

Relkin and Lagdalen were far back in the procession and heard of the horror at the gate long before they could glimpse it over the shoulders of the Guards. As the crowd inched past, now silent, with drooping banners, they saw merely a limp form hanging from the lantern beam above the gate.

To reach this place the culprits would have had to enter the gate building and lean out of the window set directly above the beam.

When a search of the gate was made the body of a young guardsman was found, his throat slashed, tucked behind some chests in a storage room on the ground floor.

Relkin and Lagdalen were borne away past the scene and up Wrights' Street. Around them people babbled madly and the rumors grew wilder by the minute.

"Who would do this?" said Relkin, stunned by the evil apparition.

"We have great enemies here in Marneri, but we do not mention their name since it only adds to the shadow they seek to cast," replied Lagdalen.

Relkin knew at once who she meant, and he shivered. Down in the Bluestone Hills they'd had plenty of problems, but never anything directly connected to the Masters of Padmasa, those cold intelligences that sought to rule the entire world.

Since the destruction of their servant Ingbok and the fall of Dugguth, there had been relative peace and security in the coastal provinces of Argonath. The memories of the horror had faded.

"Ginestrubl, we call them," he muttered. "The undying ones. I am afraid they are more forgotten than remembered now in the Bluestone country."

"That is one of their names, and they are not forgotten here in Marneri."

"So they have their agents here, in the heart of Argonath."

"So it would seem, Relkin Orphanboy."

"What will happen? What will the king do?"

"They will search the city high and low, they will question everyone, but they will not find the evil person who did this."

"Why are you so sure?"

"Because this is just the latest of many outrages. And nobody has been apprehended for any of them."

"What happened?"

"Similar things to this, but only with animals."

Relkin shook his head. "The dark magic always requires life."

"It feeds on life. It destroys life—all life."

They turned onto North Street in silence and went past the narrow houses of the elf quarter. Lagdalen's thoughts returned to Werri and she blushed. It was awful to admit it, but her father had been terribly, terribly right. Werri never loved her; he was incapable of such emotion. It all seemed frighteningly clear to her now. The elvish folk were the allies of the people, but they were more distant than the dragons in many ways.

Back at Tower Square they separated after agreeing to meet the following morning outside the administrative block of the Tower of Guard. Relkin went on down the hill to the vast hulk of the Dragon House, while Lagdalen turned in at the near gate to the tall brown stone pile of the Novitiate.

CHAPTER THREE

The day after Fundament Day dawned grey and cold with a sharp wind from the west. The Marneri witches rose early—the Greatspell would have to be resaid, although now there would be no feasting and dancing on the green to distract them in the saying of it.

The city also arose and went about its business. Trading ships put in at the docks on the inlet. Smithies' fires flamed in the north ward, looms and spinning wheels hummed along Foluran Hill. But everywhere tongues wagged over the horror witnessed on Fundament night.

Grim faced, the witches went forth to recite the spell, and while they did so the constables, assisted by the priestesses, worked their way through the city sifting for clues.

The city of Marneri was now protected by walls in

which the great magic was steadily weakening, hour by hour. This somber thought dispelled the happy atmosphere that normally pervaded the city after Fundament Day. And yet the city was the hub for an entire region; its life and rituals had to continue, despite the sense of outrage and alarm that pervaded the place.

In the red brick Dragon House there was great bustle and commotion, for instance. For this day, the first of winter, marked the beginning of the contests among young dragons and recruits to win places in the New Legion.

In the stalls the dragonboys strapped on the great steel breast plates and helmets. They stropped and burnished dragon blades and shields. Only when everything was perfect would they allow their dragons to take their places in the stalls at the amphitheater. The final contests were begun.

Now with blunted swords and padded maces they were matched in bouts of one-on-one, twos and threes. From their performances in these bouts they would be selected for combat with the veteran legion champions at the end of the week. Much depended on this selection, and upon the performance given in that later combat when the recruits would go up against their seniors in exhibition contests before great crowds of city folk.

Dust flew, heavy feet stamped the flags of the floor of the amphitheater. Twenty-foot-long dragons clashed chest to chest, nine-foot-long swords swept and rang together. Heavy shields yielded splinters of metal with steely clamour.

Yet these were not contests to the death, although once in a while a great champion would forget himself and strike a little too hard and some young twenty-foot hoglin' would hurtle to the ground inert, only to be dragged away by a team of three cart horses. For the most part the injuries sustained were survivable. Nicks and bruises, broken talons, sword cuts and broken ribs. The dragon infirmary would be full all week, and dragonboys would be busy with linament and bandages, antiseptic and poultices; but despite the violence, deaths were very rare.

Among the hopeful dragons was Bazil of Quosh, now in his fourteenth year and a lean veteran of many small campaigns in the Bluestone country. Bazil was a medium-weight dragon of twenty-two-foot length from nose to tail, of the brown-green leatherback breed.

To compensate for his lack of heft, Bazil had been endowed with a natural skill with weapons. His movements were always deft and economical, and he had an uncanny knack for anticipating an opponent's blows. Fighting with a foil he was as quick as a man, something most unusual for dragonkind.

However, before he could enter the ring in Marneri he required a dragon stamp. This scrap of parchment, the size of a man's hand, was vital. The Dragon Laws were strict—dragons being such large and potentially rapacious creatures, each one employed in human service had to carry a stamp and to produce it on demand.

On the whole the Dragon Laws had preserved the peace since the two races had joined in common desperation to fight the dread enemy of Padmasa with its hordes of trolls, imps and weres, all bred in unholy ways from living animals.

To get into Marneri in the first place had required that Relkin talk his way through the watch at the Watergate. They'd come at the peak period in early morning and got passed on without having to show any stamp. It was a time when there were lots of dragons in the city.

But to enter the combat ring they had to produce the stamp, and Bazil's first bout was set for noon.

Relkin had been in the city only a few days and yet he had made a number of friends, including his contact in the Office of Administration who was also from the village of Quosh, although somewhat older than Relkin.

However, everyone in Quosh was immensely proud of Bazil and they had all been much distressed by the ill treatment accorded the Quoshite leatherback by the Baron of Borgan. The man in the Stamp Office was eager to help, but he could not bring the stamp out of the building himself. The scrutineers would inevitably discover him in the act.

And so Lagdalen of Tarcho awoke, breakfasted, and brushed her teeth in dread. Then she went out to meet Relkin at the appointed hour feeling most unhappy. She had never feared the scrutineers before, it was an increasingly uncomfortable experience.

They met outside the administration block and walked up to the North Gate together while Relkin apprised her of the situation and what she was to do.

Relkin was wearing a rustic, brown cloak against the wind, but at the North Gate this was not unusual since here was the live animal market and hundreds of drovers and riders from the countryside were at work.

Everything was ready, she was informed. The scrutineers of course were being especially cautious that day, but the same things that made it safest for Lagdalen to bring the stamp out in the first place applied even more strongly now. The scrutineers were looking for the guilty alien or a corrupted citizen. They would not look long at a novice from the Temple.

She was to enter the building, go up to the second floor and walk down a hallway where petitioners brought civil suits for registration and informal arbitration. The place was always active and people were constantly exchanging small scrolls, large scrolls, and even stacks of scroll.

A man in the grey tunic and blue trousers of the administrative clerical corps would approach her, they would meet briefly, and he would give her the stamp. She would then go on down the hall and out on the exit stairs.

The scrutineers were posted on the landings on the stairs and she would not be stopped.

That at least was the plan.

With a sinking feeling in the pit of her stomach, Lagdalen entered the building through the great, grey gates.

Inside she proceeded, as if in a dream, along the hallway, among a traffic of folk from all sectors of society, and thence up the marble stairs.

A portrait of King Sanker loomed above, made in his prime some thirty years before. He wore armor and the helm of a Legion Commander and the red robe that went with it. The king's eyes, by a twist of skill from Rupachter, the great painter of the age, possessed a *trompe l'oeil* effect and seemed to follow the viewer below, as if his majesty was examining one and forming a stern judgement. Sanker watched all!

Lagdalen felt terribly unworthy at that moment. She was about to do something that violated the spirit, if not the substance itself, of her vows.

Worse still, she felt certain she would be caught.

And then what?

She would try to explain to her father that following the debacle with Werri there had come an entanglement with a dragonboy, a wild, feral youth from far away. And that for this boy's sake she had risked her future in the Sisterhood.

Her father's face would crumple with repressed grief. Solemnly he would send her away from his presence. Her mother would break down into hysterical weeping.

Lagdalen would almost welcome being sent away, to do military penance on the frontier in the army. There was a woman's brigade in the Legion; it had been used as a threat to discipline the young women of Marneri for many years now. She could imagine herself serving there, growing coarse and hardened over the years. Eventually perhaps she would settle on that frontier and become a peasant. Her illustrious family would of course have long since disowned her.

Her feet carried her on, and once she was past the portrait of King Sanker XXII, the stairs brought her to the second floor. Dignitaries in robes of office and of foreign lands were gliding past on a separated gallery built a few feet above the main passage, but not connected to it except through a guarded and hidden entrance. This was the magnates' walk, from which they could communicate, barter, trade with the public but still maintain a distance.

Both the walk and the much larger passageway around it passed into the long, rectangular Hall of Plaints.

Here Lagdalen proceeded more slowly. The large oval room was occupied by several dozen people in conversation. Clerks towed small trolleys laden with scrolls. Large scroll readers were set up along the walls and most were in use.

Suddenly a plump man in a grey tunic appeared in front of her.

"Ah," he said. "You must be a friend of Bazil of Quosh."

"Yes," she whispered. Were they listening? Were there scrutineers scattered through this hall?

"He is a very special dragon. Everyone in my village is following his career very closely." The plump man rubbed his hands together and beamed.

"Your village raised him, I take it."

"From the egg, and he was always a hungry spratling. He could eat ten chickens at a sitting by the age of five."

"Goodness," she said.

"Yes, it is very expensive for a village to grow a dragon, but since it obviates legion taxes for the entire village it makes sense when there are good harvests."

If there were scrutineers they were all doomed, she concluded, and this Quoshite from the Stamp Office was an idiot. They would send her to the legion or even into exile.

Noticing her anxiety, however, the plump fellow leaned close and said in a quiet voice, "It's perfectly all right. Nobody tries to monitor this place—it's a madhouse. The only danger is on the stairs, but you're in novice blue, so they won't even look at you."

"I wish I were so confident," she muttered.

"All will be well, you will see. Here is the stamp."

Here it was, the moment of culpability.

She took it from him, a little thing, rolled up and stuffed in a tube made from a dried symony leaf.

She tucked it into her sleeve pocket.

"Remember, the village of Quosh has its hopes pinned on you!" said the man.

He turned and left her and headed away, through a group in loud discussion of water rights on some city-owned land.

Lagdalen licked her lips and headed the other way, toward the exit and the scrutineers.

The dread returned. Damn the village of Quosh—her own future was on the line here. This they would never forgive if they found out.

The stairs going down were crowded, however, and the first scrutineers seemed disarmingly unconcerned, observing the passing crowd quite impassively.

On a ledge overlooking the stairway two heavyset women and an older man with white hair sat in easy chairs watching the people going by. They were in continual conversation and seemed quite detached from the proceedings.

Lagdalen skipped down the stairs and avoided even glancing in their direction as she passed, although she wanted to look up desperately hard. It was almost as if they were willing her to look up, to bring herself to their notice.

Lagdalen passed the first landing. The scrutineers receded behind her.

Still she was sweating freely as she went on and no command to stop came from above.

The second set were younger and all male. They did scan every face with great intensity and Lagdalen felt sure she was blushing as she went past them and down the stairs.

And yet no call came, no constable appeared to take her away and a few moments later she was back on the street, with the illicit dragon stamp safely in her sleeve and her heart beating furiously in her chest.

She walked almost blindly across Tower Square and down the Strand.

Relkin caught up with her at the corner with Bank Street, and as they walked along she gave him the stamp.

He swore undying devotion and gratitude to her and then vanished. He would just have time to register Bazil in time for the noon bout.

CHAPTER FOUR

In the first combat Bazil was drawn one on one against Smilgax, a taller dragon, a "hard green" from the county of Troat.

Smilgax had a reputation for sullenness and a dislike of learning. He was resting in the bottom tenth of the cohort in tactical skills and lore. Consequently he needed a great performance in the combats if he was to remain in the running for a place in the legions. Only the top two-thirds of the cohort would be inducted, the bottom third would go home to their villages to aid the agricultural effort, a worthy if unexciting prospect.

"Good luck, Baz," said Relkin with a final pat on the leatherback's shoulder before he slipped down from his perch on Bazil's back and took his place in the front stalls, behind the protective barrier of rough-hewn logs that surrounded the wide amphitheater floor.

"He's big," said Bazil, quietly fingering the straps on his shield. When standing on his hind legs, for combat, Baz was just under ten feet tall. His opponent was six inches taller and somewhat wider as well. The unofficial rating on the bout had Smilgax as favorite with odds of two to one. Bazil's odds for victory were an unflattering nine to one.

"Oh well, big doesn't necessarily mean clever. Otherwise trolls would own the world," Baz said to himself. He handled his sword Piocar in its well-worn sheath.

They entered the ring and moved towards each other,

Smilgax giving his sword great play in the open space while uttering ferocious snorts and roars. Baz remained quiet, unmoved by this display, and merely stared hard across the space between them.

Smilgax circled, with drawn dragon blade before him, nine feet of gleaming steel. Bazil drew Piocar, handed down for many generations by the dragons of Quosh. The gong sounded and the bout began.

With a surge they moved together, both swinging, and their sixty-pound blades rang off each other with fat sparks aflame.

They circled. Smilgax wore a helm of black steel with paired horns that jutted forth in front. Bazil wore a steel pot of more conservative appearance, with no horns and just a single spike.

Smilgax began an assault, sword whirling, crashing, lunging.

Bazil defended, gave ground, used his shield with good effect and then swung his tail mace into play with a roundhouse sweep that cracked hard on Smilgax's helm and left his defensive countermove far behind.

Smilgax fell back, his head ringing. He snapped his own tail and flourished his mace.

"All right, Quoshite, I'll see to you now," he snarled.

Smilgax renewed his attack, his great sword swirling in heavy cuts and thrusts. Bazil used sword and shield to blunt them and turn them aside.

Once again Bazil made play with his tail, but this time Smilgax was quicker with his own and their tail maces rang together in a minor key as they thrust and grappled and shoved shields against each other.

Smilgax was unable to gain an advantage. With an oath he pushed Bazil away, and once more their swords rang together. This time, however, instead of backing off, Bazil ducked and dipped inside and brought his sword up from below and caught Smilgax's forelimb and knocked it aside. Bazil swung the blade back and caught the hard green a cut below the breastplate, low down on the left side.

The gong rang to announce the point and Smilgax gave ground with a vicious curse concerning Bazil's parentage and the entire village of Quosh.

Bazil merely smiled in reply and his eyes flashed.

An old champion, Margone, called from the stalls. "Now, now, Smilgax, temper tantrums won't get you into the legions!"

There was an appreciative murmur in the stands, where sat a dozen or more heavyset champions, like Great Vastrox, the four-ton Master of the dragon school.

Smilgax snapped his jaws and attacked once more. This miserable Quoshite oaf would not be allowed to stand in his way!

The swords rang, whined off shields. They clashed belly to belly for a moment, and Smilgax used his superior mass to force Bazil into retreat. Once again the swords swung, Bazil defending desperately as Smilgax attacked with renewed vigor.

Smilgax caught Bazil's shield with his own and pulled it aside from his body. Smilgax feinted with his sword, Bazil turned to counter, and Smilgax thrust out a leg and kicked the leatherback on the thigh.

Such kicking was regarded as poor technique, since if countered the blow might result in the loss of a foot. But this time Bazil was taken by surprise and sent tumbling.

Smilgax pounced, his sword swinging high. Bazil dodged a decapitating blow. Smilgax was in a fury and would hold nothing back.

Piocar was almost struck from Bazil's grip in the next moment, and the Quoshite was forced to roll ignominiously across the sand to avoid the next attempted death-stroke.

Smilgax's tail mace, however, connected several times with his head and shoulders, and when he recovered his footing a moment later, Bazil received another blow right on the helmet that rang in his ears and sent him reeling.

Smilgax charged, Bazil defended, Piocar catching the next huge overhand slice, and Bazil turned inside the bigger dragon and tried to elbow Smilgax in the throat.

Smilgax dodged, their shields clashed, and Bazil swung Piocar low and forced Smilgax to jump.

Tail maces rang together, Smilgax danced backwards and tripped over his own feet and went down with a crash that shook the place.

Bazil stood over him but deliberately refrained from a killing stroke.

As Smilgax regained his feet there was a ripple of applause from the human observers in the gallery above. Such honorable qualities were much appreciated. And the rally between these two young drakes had been quite spectacular.

But Smilgax cursed most horribly and rushed forward again. Once more their blades clashed, their shields smashed together with all the force of their two-ton bodies behind them. Smilgax continued to snarl curses; he spat at Bazil and tried to trip him, a most dishonorable tactic that brought boos from the gallery as they broke apart.

Bazil went on the offensive, swinging Piocar from side to side in great measured sweeps that kept Smilgax moving back, with no time to maneuver or do more than counter.

Smilgax reached the wood wall, then ducked away to the side and Bazil caught him with the flat of the blade along the rump. The smack was embarrassingly loud, and Smilgax jumped as if stung.

The hard green's eyes were now rigid in rage. Smilgax jumped forward, swinging with all his might.

Piocar met his swing and deflected it. Smilgax staggered and almost lost his footing. Bazil shoved him hard with the shield, then moved in with Piocar once more, hewing from side to side, keeping the other on the defensive, until once more he was forced to the wall, turned and received another swat on the rump.

Applause erupted in the gallery above. The champions shouted approval.

Smilgax was maddened to a dangerous level. Once more he approached, and they grappled and he spat and hissed and attempted a throw that Bazil, off balance, was forced to spin away from. Then Smilgax brought up his heavy knee and caught Bazil a low blow to the groin.

Bazil gasped, ducked aside, and dodged the sweep of the sword that followed. He spun off balance and Piocar knocked away Smilgax's illegal stab at his back.

A chorus of boos broke out in the crowd.

Frustrated and enraged, Smilgax slashed with his sword at Bazil's tail and sliced off the last two feet and the flexible tip that gripped the small mace.

Bazil fell back, stunned by the loss. The crowd in the gallery rose to their feet with a gasp. There were more boos and cries for a disqualification. However, the rules were inflexible on this issue. There could be no stoppage to a combat except by limit of time or the surrender or loss of consciousness by one or another opponent.

Grim-mouthed, the champion dragons now watched as Smilgax set to destroy Bazil of Quosh in the remaining minutes of the bout.

Bazil did not give up. He fought stoutly and well, Piocar keeping Smilgax's sword away, his shield work still deft and strong. But without a tail he was unprotected from Smilgax's own tail mace, and again and again it whirled in and struck him about the head and shoulders.

Bazil survived, grinding out a draw by sheer endurance and a stubborn refusal to give up. When the final horn was blown, he was still on his feet, unbowed. Smilgax gave a violent curse and stormed from the ring, with boos in a crescendo beating down from above.

Bazil maintained his dignity and staggered into the Dragon House, keeping his feet until Relkin could lead him into his stall, whereupon he collapsed and gave up consciousness.

CHAPTER FIVE

Bazil's tail was a disaster. The surgeons in the dragon yard did their best. Medicine in Marneri had attained a high standard of skill and cleanliness, but the reattachment failed and the last two feet of the tail soon began to mortify.

Relkin was forced to remove it at last and cauterize the stump with a sulfur poultice. Bazil sank into a terminal gloom.

Relkin faced the future with dread in his heart. It would be a drab future. Crippled dragons always returned to their village to aid the agricultural effort. Relkin would go with Bazil—such was the law for the dragonboy, wedded at six to his two-ton charge.

Still Relkin grasped at every straw, as it occurred to him.

"You'll face Vastrox in the final combats," he announced cheerfully after seeing the postings on the notice board.

"Oh wonderful, my pail runneth over at the prospect. Vastrox will handle me like a bantling."

"But Baz, think of the honor they do you. Vastrox knows that you were winning before Smilgax committed the foul. Everyone knows that."

"It will matter little. Without tail mace I can never join the legions. Face the truth, fool boy! We are going to be working with a plough for our suppers pretty soon."

Bazil was hunched over, lost in despair.

But Relkin would not give up. He went out to search for a magical remedy. They needed work, their money was running out, and this New Legion presented a great opportunity. A new start, patrolling the frontier in Kenor. A hundred silver ducats a year for them, and the village of Quosh would be free of the Argonath military tax for every year they served. The village would be well repaid for its efforts and for giving an orphan boy a chance in life.

The legion term was ten years, after which troops could retire or sign up for further service. Older active legionaires provided the engineers, the transport command and dozens of other essential components of the overall military effort that was being made by the Ennead cities of the Argonath.

When they retired, legionaires, including the dragons, were encouraged to settle in the colonies and become free farmers, owning their own land, working it for themselves and paying only a tithe to the colony to help support of the legions and administrative services provided by the Ennead cities.

They were also seen as the nucleus for resistance in the event of raids into the frontier by the savage Teetol or fell parties of raiders from the dead lands of the Tummuz Orgmeen.

In retirement, Relkin foresaw a farmstead, maybe two hundred acres, out in Kenor. He and Bazil would work the land together. Relkin would still be a young man and would take a wife from the frontier people. Bazil would apply to the Dragon Propagation Board and would be given the opportunity to fertilize an egg. Later when they were rich they would hire others to work for them, and they would lead whatever lives they cared to.

But now this bright shining future was about to be snuffed out. Instead of colonial freedom they would go to Quosh as agricultural laborers.

Relkin flung himself out of the Dragon House and down to Tower Square. Goats were being sold, and wild drover boys with skinny arms projecting from goatskin shirts and shorts were running between the pens.

Relkin wondered what life might have been like if he

had grown up in a family that herded goats. Would he have been happy in such a life?

He crossed the square. It was pointless to speculate. He'd been born an orphan, his parentage unknown; his future lay before him, he could only go on. This he had learned at an early age. His father was unknown, possibly a soldier from the garrison in Ryo. His mother had left the village in disgrace and her family had refused to take him in. He had never known any family until the day they gave him Baz.

He turned onto North Street and went on down it, with the elf quarter beside him on the left. Here the elf houses, cramped three-story tenements lacking in straight lines, jammed together along narrow lanes. Elf children, boys and girls in smocks and breeks, sprang through the lanes in play, their high voices raised in happy song.

On the south side of the street were tall terrace houses with whitewashed fronts and high, shuttered windows. Occasional servants could be seen at work in an otherwise sedate scene. These tall white houses, belonging to prosperous merchants, seemed to frown across the street at the untidy squalor of elfdom.

Further on, past the drapers' row at the junction with Foluran Hill, the buildings became more haphazard, with shops of many kinds at street level.

He turned down Sick Duck Street and entered the shop of Azulea, a medicine crone who dealt in love philtres, curses and their removal, plus arcane medicaments for unusual ills. She had been recommended to him by another dragonboy, name of Gath, who already belonged to the New Legion and knew the city quite well.

Azulea heard Relkin out. She rustled through a spell book and a directory and then informed him that she had nothing that specifically addressed the problem of regrowing a dragon's tail. She had a good dragon liniment that would cure the pox and a great tonic for a piqued dragon that was made from mandrake root, but neither of these would do much for a severed tail.

However, she did have a spell and the recipe for an

unguent that would grow new branches on a tree, and she offered to try it on Bazil for six Marneri ducats.

Relkin said he'd think about it. He went out and strolled on down Sick Duck Street, stopping to look into a few more shop windows. The old buildings here were made of wood and lathe covered in white plaster and roofed in black slate. The walls bulged and curved in near organic disorder. Many of the shops were very old, run for decades by their current proprietors.

Six ducats! He had scarcely two left in the world, and he and Baz needed to eat. Baz had been good, but he was tiring fast of the horses oats that were the free ration in the Dragon House.

On the corner with Hag Street, Relkin stopped in to see Old Rothercary, a country *brujo* with a million herbal remedies and potions in bottles and tubes in the back of his narrow shop.

Rothercary was an enormous grey-haired man with ruddy cheeks and a big red nose. He roared with laughter at Relkin's request and rummaged around in the back parlor before producing a small bottle containing a tiny quantity of a viscous red fluid.

"This'll do the trick!" he pronounced. "The blood of a Cunfshon steerbat that's been warmed nine times to boiling by the concentrated light of the moon. The price is ten ducats."

Relkin's jaw dropped at the sight of the small phial of dark red fluid.

"But what does it do?"

"Do? Why it, grows things back, like the limbs and sex organs and so on. It's very popular among the castrati in Cunfshon, they say, though whether it really works on that area I cannot report for sure, but I've sold it a few times to unfortunates here in Marneri. Just paint it over the stump and in a matter of days there is fresh growth. It's wonderful stuff, which is why it's so expensive."

But ten pieces of silver was an impossibly huge amount.

Relkin went back to the Dragon House rubbing his chin, lost in thought.

At the notice board he found a special note. A rematch in the first combat had been sought by Smilgax, in protest at the awarding of a draw in his fight with Bazil of Quosh.

The rematch had been granted. Bazil would have to fight Smilgax again, on the morning of the day of the final combats. The winner of the bout would then perform against Vastrox.

This negated Vastrox's noble attempt to give the dragon from Quosh at least one moment of glory, by taking him on, even without a functioning tail tip, before the big audience of the final day.

Instead Smilgax would grab that opportunity. Smilgax's action was contemptible, but apparently the hard green did not care about opinion. All that mattered was getting into the Legion, even if he had to trample over his own honor and the Quoshite leatherback in the process.

Relkin reeled along the passageway to the infirmary and collected fresh supplies of liniment, disinfectant and talon restorer. Then he went on down to the stalls and their temporary home, a stall with a worn stone floor, beam and plaster ceiling and heavy curtain instead of a door across the front. There was a small, potbellied stove, a human cot and a large oak beam crib for a dragon set across one end.

Bazil was sitting on the crib, attempting to shave a damaged claw with a knife made for human hands. Relkin winced at the sight of all the bandages and abrasions on his dragon's head and shoulders. Smilgax had done evil work with the mace in his effort to capitalize on his ill-famed lucky blow.

"Give me that," he said, snatching the paring knife out of the big dragon's paw. Baz barely seemed to respond. Relkin sensed the profound dragonish woe that enveloped his huge, leathery charge. The eyes, those immense yellow and black saucers, seemed milky and opaque, decidedly unfocussed.

"You fought well, Baz, and you'll fight again. We're not going to let this thing beat us."

The eyes blinked, cleared.

"Humpf! What are you talking about? I have no tail—how can I fight dragons without a tail? The legions won't have me now. It has all been a waste."

"I have a plan."

"Oh, do you? Well, keep your plans, fool boy! We will be in Quosh by midwinter. Harrowing and hauling, breaking ice on the mountainside, oh what a life it will be."

Relkin noted all the five classic signs of a "sulky" dragon.

"Roll over. I have to get to those cuts on your back."

"Ah me, ah my, now for the sting and the smart. This is a grand life, did anyone ever tell you that? Getting chopped up in the arena and rubbed with stinging juice in the night."

Despite the complaints, Bazil did roll over and present his five-foot-wide back, with the huge shoulderblades and the thick arches of muscle that met along the spine.

Relkin wetted a swab with the liniment and started disinfecting the bigger cuts.

As the liniment soaked in, Bazil shook and cursed in sibilant dragon speech, ancient terms that fortunately had no meaning in human tongues.

Relkin decided the time had come to bring up his scheme, concocted on the way back from Old Rothercary's shop. "I was at Rothercary's shop on Hag Street this afternoon."

"And what would you be wanting from a brujo? That sort of thing is frowned on as you well know."

"He offered me some blood from a Cunfshon steerbat. For ten silver pieces."

"What? We don't even have *two* silver pieces between us."

"I know, I know, but there might be ways of getting some."

"You contemplate a life of crime now? Think again,

boy. This is Marneri—the witches find out in no damn time at all. Then you be for it.''

Baz cringed as the swab got close to an infected cut. As Relkin swabbed it, the big dragon hissed loudly for a second or two, then resumed human speech.

"Anyway, what's the point of blood from a Cunfshon steerbat, and what the hell *is* a Cunfshon steerbat? I can't even say that, it sounds so horrible.''

"I don't know, I never heard of it either, but Rothercary swears that it will regrow lost limbs, even tails.''

"Bah, what does Rothercary know about dragons? When has he worked here in the dragon yards? His potions are meant for humankind, not the dragonfolk.''

"No, listen, I believe him. We will get ten pieces and we will buy the blood of a Cunfshon steerbat. Then we will regrow your tail.''

"Bah! I will probably grow a donkey's tail. I am not going to rub the blood of anything from the witch isle on any part of me.''

"I can't believe it will hurt to try. You have to get your tail back. You have to be able to defend yourself. Smilgax has demanded a rematch.''

"What?''

"Yes, he has called for a rematch, in protest at the awarding of a draw in your bout. He will fight you for the right to meet Vastrox.''

Bazil groaned, long and low.

"We are done then! The hard green will beat me to death and go on to glory in the legions. You will bury my ashes in the graveyard and they will give you another dragon. I have failed. You will be free of me, Relkin.''

"Nonsense, Baz. I will buy the blood of the Cunfshon steerbat and we will regrow your tail in time for the combats.''

Bazil yawned. This whole idea would fail on the most obvious fact.

"How will you get ten pieces of silver? You own nothing but the clothes you wear. You are dragonboy, homeless orphan. In the village the law said that unblooded dragon not allowed to own any damn thing, dragonboy not allowed to own any damn thing either.''

Relkin clenched his fists in determination. ''I will get it! You remember when I climbed to the top of the palace tower and saw the garden of orchids? I will gather some of those orchids and I will sell them outside the opera. There is a performance of *Orchidia* tonight, they will be gone in a flash.''

''That will be stealing, dragonboy. You will get caught and take a thrashing.''

Relkin shook his head. ''They'll not catch Relkin. And the window is not guarded, nor are orchids heavy to carry, so I'll just bring them down in my satchel.''

Bazil turned a gloomy dragon eye upon him. ''Farewell, Relkin Orphanboy. I ask only that you place my ashes in an urn of Quoshite brick.''

''They won't catch me, Baz. You'll see, have faith in Relkin now.''

But the dragon remained beyond consolation.

''The thrashings are administered by the drubbing women, a dour, broad-shouldered lot. You will not survive their ministrations, Relkin. I will miss you.''

CHAPTER SIX

As night settled in across the white stone walls of Marneri, a cold wind arose from the north. The tocsin began to ring as the stars glittered in their courses, the moon had not yet risen.

A sudden disturbance echoed in the stairwell of the Tower of Guard. Shouts, secretaries running ahead. A guard holding back the door to the restricted rooms. Two women in the grey cloaks of priestesses of the Temple came hurrying across the landing to the double doors of the anteroom to the royal bedchamber.

"Awake the king," said the shorter of the two, a round-faced woman who wore the red surplice of an abbess. "We must speak with him."

The guards sent for the Lord Chamberlain, old Burly of Sidinth.

Burly and Plesenta were old antagonists. The chamberlain's ancient crusty face soured at the sight of the plump abbess. It soured further on considering her companion, a tall, grey-haired priestess with no badge of rank, Viuris of the Office of Insight.

"What is it now?" he said testily. "It's damn late, you know."

"An urgent matter for the king. I require his permission to use the Black Mirror."

The chamberlain looked as if he'd been bitten by a snake, then with a convulsive shake of his head he led Viuris on into the royal bedchamber.

King Sanker of Marneri was not happy to be awoken so soon after he had been put to bed.

He was even less happy to be told that a passage through the Black Mirror was requested.

"Damnable thing! I wish I'd never agreed to let them use it."

"Your Majesty, it has not been used in three years. Only on a matter of grave urgency would we make this request."

"And what is this matter?" His peevish eyes snapped. Servants assisted him in rising to a sitting position. Angrily he brushed them away when they sought to arrange a coverlet about his scrawny frame.

Viuris hesitated, then bent forward to whisper in the royal ear: "The investigation of the desecration on Fundament night."

"Mmf, won't find anything, know that before you start. Damned stuff and nonsense."

"Someone comes from Cunfshon itself."

"Long way to come, must be hellishly dangerous."

"It is dangerous, but she is a mighty traveler."

"Damned dangerous. One mistake and we could lose the entire city."

"We must open the mirror, Your Majesty."

"I don't like the idea, not one bit."

The abbess had an idea. She leaned forward and whispered in the other royal ear.

"Your Majesty, the Princess Besita will be required to serve at the mirror's side. She has the duty for this week."

King Sanker's face was transformed suddenly.

"Besita has to attend, eh?"

"Absolutely, Your Majesty, it is her duty on this night."

He scratched at the white stubble on his chin.

"Sounds wonderful. You have our permission—you may proceed."

"Thank you, Your Majesty." They genuflected and departed swiftly, two contrasting figures cloaked in grey, Viuris tall and lean and Plesenta, short and plump.

On the way out to the central stair, Viuris whispered to the abbess, "What changed his mind?"

"Ah, Viuris, you have not been in Marneri long, but you must know how much Sanker hates his daughter. In fact he denies that she is his daughter. He claims that her mother, Queen Losset, had relations with dozens of lovers. It all happened long ago, but Sanker is an unforgiving man."

"Now I recall the matter. Yes, of course, I see."

"Perhaps you also see why Prince Erald cannot be allowed to sit the throne here in Marneri."

"He's a halfwit, of course."

"The king refuses to acknowledge this."

"I see, the king has a somewhat perverse view of life."

"One way of putting it. The Royal House of Marneri has been increasingly difficult to deal with in the past two generations, both Sanker and his dreadful sire, Wauk, have been quite capricious."

They came to the great doors to the outer world beyond

the royal apartments. They passed the guards and headed quickly up the stairs to the uppermost floor.

There they found no sign of the Princess Besita.

"Where is she?" said Viuris.

Plesenta sighed. "Besita is a woman of the flesh. She is more of a political priestess than a spiritual one."

"I understand. The practice is widespread in the Argonath cities."

"And you have little experience there."

"My service has been further afield, Abbess."

Plesenta knew that Viuris was not just the traveling Sister of the Benevolent Mission that she appeared in her grey robe, white surplice and complete lack of adornments. When the Black Mirror was used it always involved the Office of Insight. Viuris, even with her inexperience in the Argonath, was clearly one of those Sisters.

"Well, I will send her a note. Perhaps that will bring her."

"Let us hope so, Abbess, for the message was urgent—someone crosses the deeps even as we speak. If we do not open the mirror in time there may be a disaster."

"There is always such danger with the mirror."

"I know, Abbess, and you must compose yourself to face it. I have experience, this is all I can say, and if I sense the worst I will shut the mirror. We might lose our passenger but that would be better than to lose the city."

Abbess Plesenta snapped her fingers at a page.

"Run quickly to the Princess Besita's apartment and tell her that the abbess awaits her on a most urgent matter in the chamber of the Black Mirror." The youth left at a run, bounding down the stairs. The abbess turned to Sister Viuris.

"She will come, she knows that it is her duty. You see, Besita was never allowed to marry. Sanker wanted no young pretenders to the throne of Erald. You have to remember that Sanker put Losset to death for her adulteries."

"So Besita depends on the Sisterhood for survival, is that it?"

"More or less. She could not be wed, she could not enjoy the favor of the king, and she could not leave Marneri. Sanker remembers that his father had to put down two rebellions on behalf of pretenders to his throne. So she joined the Sisterhood."

The wind was whistling around the upper part of the tower. The door to the turret in which the Black Mirror was kept was locked both with metal and with a spell. Plesenta stepped forward and pressed her hands to the gate and unsaid the keeping spell. Then she produced the key and unlocked the door.

"I pray the princess will be in time," said the grey-eyed Viuris. How different things were here in these Argonath cities. Here the local culture had permeated the Sisterhood and the discipline Viuris was used to had broken down. In the distant missions of the Office the outside world was entirely hostile. Discipline was strict because without it survival was impossible.

In the outer lands Viuris had seen things that she knew would have frozen this plump abbess to her marrow. That was part of the distance between them.

Plesenta, for her part, pursed her lips and suppressed her urge to end this farce and ask Viuris openly about the Office of Insight. She had so many questions bubbling inside her head.

It was such a mysterious body, said to be closely allied to the Imperial Family in Cunfshon. Had Viuris ever been in the imperial presence? How Plesenta longed to ask about the emperor and the empress. Were they as beautiful as the portraits made them out to be?

"She will hurry, won't she?" The grey-eyed Sister could not hide her mounting anxiety.

"Yes, Viuris, she will hurry, do not fear."

Plesenta wondered what it must be like to be in the Office of Insight, constantly moving from city to city, pursuing rumors and intrigues, hunting for enemy spies, never having a place to call one's home. Plesenta was glad that she was allowed to remain in one place, in her beautiful city of Marneri, secure behind great walls.

Viuris's agitation grew apace as they waited. "Where is the woman? The call was urgent, very urgent."

"She will come, Viuris, be calm."

They waited and Plesenta hoped Besita would not be overlong in responding. Besita was getting to be awfully indolent these days, and she was probably terrified of the duty of the Mirror's Side.

In fact, the page with the message from the Abbess Plesenta had actually caught Besita at a most inconvenient moment. A handsome young magician, Thrembode the New, who had been sending the ladies of the court into swoons for a month, had finally been seduced into her bed. He was a dark, virile man of passion and fire. Besita was in the process of enjoying herself enormously.

So she ignored the knocking at her door for as long as she could stand it and then finally bade Thrembode to desist, while she rose, flushed and flustered, to investigate. Her maid passed in the message. Besita read it and voiced a loud, vulgar complaint, but there was nothing to be done.

"An emergency has arisen, my dear Thrembode. I must go. I promise I will return as soon as I can."

Thrembode's face registered shock and masculine outrage.

"What? Besita, will you abandon me now? In this aroused state! Can this duty not wait, just a few more minutes even?"

Besita shook her head unhappily.

"I am afraid not. I am compelled to attend the abbess in the chamber of the Black Mirror!"

Thrembode's eyes snapped wide; his demeanor changed, however, and he softened his complaint. "Someone traverses the deeps tonight?"

"I cannot say, but the call is urgent."

Besita dressed herself hurriedly in a purple smock and grey robes. She wore the black and gold surplice of the Office of Purchasings to which she nominally belonged.

"Will you wait for me, sweet Thrembode? I should be back here within the hour."

"Possibly," he said with an ill-natured shrug. "I dislike being jilted in this fashion."

"But Thrembode, someone crosses the deeps. I must go!"

"I won't let you! Come back to bed, let someone else worry about the Black Mirror."

"No, darling Thrembode, I can't do that. I must go."

"Besita, you are most vexing."

"Thrembode, darling, please be kind. Forgive me. Stay, I will be as quick as I can."

Besita rushed forth, the door closing behind her ample posterior with a soft thud. Thrembode cursed vilely and pulled sheets around his body and strode from the bed. Damn the woman, how could she leave him like this?

He stared out the window, looking over the North Gate to the elf quarter and the walls of the city. Beyond the walls the green field was grey with night and far away the lights of villages twinkled on the hills.

Who crossed the deeps? Thrembode's curiosity was awoken. Someone dared the dangers of the darkness on an urgent, unscheduled crossing. He wondered whether to wait until Besita returned or whether it would be better to leave and allow her to entreat him to return later that night. Either way he would have it out of her, that much he was determined upon.

He congratulated himself—the little horror show at the East Gate of Afo had done its work. The imperial interest had been drawn to investigate. Good, it would keep them busy while the real work went on.

After a moment's indecision, staring at the distant lights of villages in the Marneri hills, Thrembode turned and started to dress. Besita would be more enjoyable next time if she had to beg a little.

He pulled on his scarlet magician's leggings and fastened his green velvet doublet before throwing on a heavy cloak in black fusgeen and heading out of Besita's apartments.

Outside the tower he pulled the cloak close around himself and headed down into the city; the wind was chill, a reminder of the winter that was approaching. Thrembode had lived most of his life in warmer climes, and he dreaded the onset of the cold.

The thought of cold, as an abstraction, always sent a shiver through him that had nothing to do with the temperature, or the wind, but with the memory of his abduction to the freezing vault beneath the marrow of the Black Mountains. A terrifying place where the Masters had examined him and made him their own.

Uncomfortable with these dreadful memories, he drove thoughts of the cold out of his mind by sheer will and then turned and sped quickly down the hill on Tower Street. At the corner of Foluran Hill he paused to purchase a penny cup of hot cider from a vendor before continuing on, down the hill, past Broad Street to the Dockside where he entered a courtyard that was a maze of drink shops and hostels for sailors and travelers.

In the chamber of the Black Mirror, Besita finally joined Abbess Plesenta and another priestess who Besita did not know. Plesenta was unhappy, the other sister, introduced to her as Viuris of the Benevolent Mission, was plainly anxious. Her voice almost broke as she urged the maximum celerity in the declensions as they began to weave the heavy, complex spell that would ignite the mirror once more from the nothingness in which it was normally hidden.

Besita absorbed some of this anxiety. Her own heart began to thud in her chest. Whatever was going on it was probably terribly important. Besita felt vaguely frightened at the thought. She also felt alarmed at the prospect of being by the side of the mirror. One read such horrifying stories.

Set into a circular piece of black stone four feet across, the mirror was now cool and opaque. It seemed like clouded glass, giving back nothing but reflections.

"Come, we must make haste. Our traveler risks everything for us, we must be on time!" Viuris trembled.

Besita hated to be rushed in declension and almost ruined the primary spell twice. She was sweating profusely, and hating herself and Viuris by the time the spell was completed. Finally a spray of rosemary was burnt over the mirror while the three priestesses joined hands around it.

The power built quickly in the room after that and finally with a sizzling sound, as if a dozen hen's eggs had suddenly dropped in a frying pan, the Black Mirror opened. The reflections were gone; instead there was a view was if through a window onto a world of whirling grey chaos. Dark shapes fled past, twisting and tumbling like clouds or waves.

The mirror itself suddenly crackled with red energies, sparking and hissing. Besita saw one spark leap out and burn a spot in her robe. She shivered; this was the most dangerous service of all. The stories they told about deaths around the mirror were spine chilling. More sparks flew in. A smell of ozone and sulphur filled the air.

Viuris was watching her, Besita fought down her fears. Viuris sought to reassure her.

"It will not last. She places a sensing spell, she has our location now."

"My new robe is ruined!" Besita wanted to scream back, but didn't dare in front of Plesenta. The abbess had such a wagging tongue, one had to be so careful around her.

With hot red sparks spattering occasionally around them, the three women continued to hold their position and keep the door open into the chaos of the dark.

Quite soon the sparking died away completely, although lightning continued to fork within the mirror, seeming to draw further and further into the reflection world.

A figure appeared, tiny in the distance, buffeted by the winds of the dark. Speeding through the tunnels of chaos, burrowing between the worlds, it flew towards them.

Travel through this nightmare region was done at great risk. Here grew the mightiest terrors of the enemy, including the dread Thingweights of Void. This was their home.

The tiny figure grew in size, but slowly. Chaos raged around it.

"There's a force tracking on her, I can feel it," cried Viuris, who possessed great sensing strength.

"Yes!" exclaimed Plesenta, "I can feel it too. It's closing quickly, it has a sourcing on her."

The figure continued to grow, getting closer to the exit point from the realm of chaos. But something enormous was coalescing behind it now, something with the breadth of a mountain, the mass of an ocean.

"It's coming in quickly, it knows she's there!" Viuris muttered in a desperate voice. "I don't know if she knows how close to her it is."

To the mirror she cried, "Hurry, Lessis, hear me and hurry! There is little time—a Thingweight tracks you through the ether of the dark."

"Lessis?" cried the Abbess Plesenta. "It is Lessis herself who crosses the dark?"

"Yes," said Viuris. "It is Lessis herself. She has crossed more often than anyone still alive."

Their companion had meanwhile grown very pale.

"Did you say a Thingweight was tracking her?" said Besita in a faint voice. Besita was already terrified about the dreadful things that could reach out from within the dark chaotic region. But of those things none compared with a Thingweight, the ruling predator in that darkness. No witch that had been taken by a Thingweight had ever returned, except in an evil form as a servant of the darkness.

Besita's plump lower lip began to shake. "Shouldn't we break the contact? We must not allow one of that dread breed to draw a trace on this Black Mirror, sourced here in the city of Marneri."

"Hold on," said Viuris, "Lessis comes!"

And Lessis could be seen clearly now, approaching

fast, floating in a vertical posture, as if she were standing on solid ground somehow, her garments flapping in the hurricane breeze of the subworld. Behind, onrushing like some gigantic locomotive of shapeless cloud, came the vastness of the Thingweight.

"We must pull out, we must not let it discover the mirror in active use!" screamed Besita, white-faced in terror. There was a swelling roar, a shuddering vibration building in the subworld, the gross textures of the surface of the Thingweight were growing clearer. The mirror sparkled with renewed energy, small white-hot bolts of it stabbed out at the walls.

And then Besita lost her nerve and tried to pull away, to break the triune of their clasped hands, but Viuris would not let go of her wrist. Besita tried the other hand, but Plesenta held on and snapped an order for her to desist.

Besita shuddered and tried to scream, but found her tongue held by a spell from Viuris.

"Damn you, witch!" Besita wanted to shriek at her, but could not and the triune was held.

Viuris returned the hate in Besita's eyes with a blank neutrality that was unnerving after a second or two. Finally she hissed, "Besita, desist, all will be well. Do not fear, Lessis is the greatest of all the dark riders. She will win, you will see."

Viuris, however, was at that moment far less certain of this than she would have liked. The Thingweight was terribly close, much closer than was safe. A forerunner limb might twitch against the mirror at any moment. A moment after that they might all be seized and drawn into the monster's pouch.

The mirror was alive with alien energies, sparks of white and blue were exploding from its surface. Besita yelped as one ignited against her foot like a firecracker. The roar was swelling, as if a storm had ignited in the room. The air was shaking and a sulfurous smell was getting fierce.

Abruptly there came a great flash of reddish light, and

a human figure in grey-green robes burst through the mirror and tumbled off the dias to the floor with a gasp of breath as if she'd surfaced from a deep ocean dive.

Viuris and Besita rose and broke the triune and closed the mirror. A second or so later the searching tentacles of the monster in the dark groped past the mirror's location in the overworld and blundered on, losing the trace for good.

Besita then sank down to the floor herself, shaking all over, positively wet through with perspiration. Unable to speak, she stared up at Viuris and then across to the slight form of the grey-haired woman kneeling on the floor.

This was Lessis of Valmes?

She saw an exhausted, haggard woman in middle age, still struggling for breath. Catching Besita's stare, the woman gave her a quick little smile and pressed her hands together as she took a deep breath before speaking. She had a wide face, high cheekbones and large, luminous eyes.

"My goodness, that was a near thing, I thank you all for holding on." Her voice was quiet, melodious.

Lessis struggled to her feet and Besita noticed that Lessis's right foot was bandaged and stuffed into an oversize slipper. Lessis hobbled over and helped Besita rise from the floor.

"I think we certainly shaved a whisker from the face of father fate that time! Sisters, I thank you, you showed the courage one expects of Marneri witches."

Besita saw that Lessis's cloak was stained and muddy, and the boot on her left foot was worn and cracked. She looked anything but a high agent of the rulers of Cunfshon.

"Lessis! Oh, my dear," Viuris could not restrain herself. With tears in her eyes she clasped the frail figure.

Lessis withstood this embrace stoically, then disengaged gently from Viuris's arms and trapped a lank lock of grey hair and tucked it away beneath her hood. She drew a deep breath and set her shoulders. She had yet to complete this business, and there were many things to do.

"Thank you, Viuris, you and your colleagues here. I had to hurry my spell. It leaked rather badly, I'm afraid. I must have been detected at the beginning of the crossing. If you had not hung on, I would probably be entertaining one of the terrors of the deeps right now."

She paused for another breath, then continued wryly. "Of course, you shouldn't have done that. You put the city at risk."

Besita could not restrain a venomous look at Plesenta. Then she caught Lessis's eyes upon her and felt instantly low and unworthy. Besita blushed with embarrassment.

"But," said Lessis, raising a finger, "this time it was for the best perhaps."

They moved towards the door, and when they were close Lessis coughed harshly for a moment. She leaned on Besita who embraced her tenderly. She was so slight, so little, Besita felt a pang of tenderness.

"Thank you, brave Besita. Your courage has served us well."

Lessis knew her name? Besita was stunned and proud. Unconsciously she stiffened, felt her chest inflate, as if suddenly a spotlight was upon her.

Lessis of Valmes had that effect on people. Besita did not know it, but she had absorbed two small spells in the space of three seconds. Her sense of duty and patriotism had never been so inflamed.

Lessis limped to the door, continuing to lean on Besita.

Outside the door Lessis finally left Besita's side and proceeded down the hallway with Viuris, apparently quite fit enough to limp along unaided. They turned down the stairs, lost in hushed conversation.

Besita and Plesenta followed at a distance. Plesenta spoke in a conspiratorial whisper: "I never know what to make of them, these Grey Sisters. They go hither and thither, even into the places of the enemy. And then they use the Black Mirror. It's true what she said, we did risk the whole city. We risked our lives—another moment and we would have been snatched into hell.'' Plesenta was still shaking from the memory.

Besita stared at her, seeing only a grumpy vindictiveness in the abbess's tone and words.

''Abbess, theirs are the secrets, theirs are also the deeds done in obtaining them. Viuris was right, Lessis did outrace the Thingweight.''

Abbess Plesenta stared at Besita in an odd manner.

''Are you all right, Besita?'' she said.

''Perfectly all right, Abbess, perfectly.'' Besita gave her an even smile and headed for the stairs.

CHAPTER SEVEN

Two hours past dusk, when Relkin scuttled along the battlements of the wall of the Chapterhouse that stood behind the Tower of Guard, a great golden moon was suspended in the eastern sky just above the horizon.

But the brightness of the moon gave no warmth, and the north wind easily penetrated Relkin's broadcloth jacket and shirt. He was shivering when he reached the juncture of the battlement with the outer wall of the tower itself. Here he had found a few handholds in the chinks where the mortar had fallen out, and on his first night in Marneri he had climbed the tower to look down on the city and get a sense of it from above.

Now he gazed across to the roof of the Chapterhouse. There were warm lights beckoning down there, comfortable rooms with fires in the grate, and yellow lamps lit. There were soldiers there relaxing in the warmth around the supper table.

The wind wailed faintly; he shivered again and reached

up for the first handhold. From this point the tower soared straight up more than forty meters to the first battlements and setback.

Relkin had found his handholds easily enough—the tower was no longer inspected regularly. Nor was it even primarily a military installation. The families of well-placed persons in the legion and the administration were given apartments there. Windows had been cut in the great walls. Cracks had begun and been allowed to grow.

Relkin was an agile youth and good at climbing. Soon he was passing the windows of apartments, shuttered close against the wind. He moved quickly past these floors and eventually reached the battlements where the tower's setback occurred. Here the tower shrank to one half of its former width and soared another fifty feet to a conical roof, becoming the tallest structure in the city of Marneri, overlooking all else, including the great dome atop the Temple.

A quick glance around showed no sign of the guards.

Relkin skipped quickly across the stones of the battlements. He crossed the tower and looked down upon the southern face. Here there were elaborate balconies cut in the wall. On these balconies were heavy tubs bearing shrubs and small trees. Amber lamps were alight in many windows. Here lived many of the most important people in the city: administrators, estate holders of rank, and members of the Council of Guard.

Relkin had spied on the guards. They usually patrolled the perimeter in pairs, once around every half hour. Since none were in sight, he had time to put his plan into action.

When he reached the point that he knew offered the easiest descent to the balcony he sought, he climbed back over the battlements. The south face of the tower had been remodeled with ornamental stone borders to frame its gates and windows. It was child's play to a nimble burglar. Relkin was soon clambering onto the wide balcony of one of the uppermost floors, where there grew a garden of orchids in a small, circular greenhouse with an unlocked door.

There were a pair of lamps lit within the glass paneled doors of the apartment. The curtains were drawn aside and Relkin could see into a sumptuous room filled with heavy pieces of dark brown furniture. There was no one in sight inside, however. His way was clear.

He paused a moment to take in the view from the balcony. The moon rode low on the horizon and the stars glittered in the sky. Spread out below, stretching down to the dark water of the sound, the white city sprawled, suffused with the warmth of yellow lamplight. On the mole stretching out into the dark water was the Marneri lighthouse, its great lantern sweeping around every two minutes as it was pulled by a team of trained Cunfshon monkeys.

Relkin felt his hopes for the future rising once more. With a few of the fabulous flowers he could earn at least ten pieces of silver from the wealthy folk who would attend the *Orchidia* at the Opera House. Then on the morrow he would buy the magical blood of the Cunfshon steerbat from old Rothercary and they would regrow Baz's tail.

There was no lock, the owner had never imagined that anyone would climb the tower like this to steal her flowers. The greenhouse door opened easily and Relkin slipped in. A brazier's heat kept it steamy and tropical inside with the curious peppery scent of some black liver plants that grew in a tank on one side.

On the other side were the orchids. And what beauties they were! Long, pendulous-lobed petals bore exquisite shades of yellow and pink, now dusted pale with moonlight. They were the most beautiful blooms Relkin had ever seen.

He opened his satchel and began to pull the orchid plants out of their pots. Keeping a small amount of the moist matting around their roots, he wrapped each plant in a tissue of mattaleaf and thrust it into the satchel until he had a dozen or more. He closed the satchel, swung it over his shoulder, opened the greenhouse door once more and stepped out.

All was as it had been with one exception. He was no longer alone on the balcony. An ape dog wearing a thick-spiked collar was sniffing along the area of the balcony rail that he'd climbed across.

Relkin tiptoed quickly in the other direction.

The balcony came to an end. There was a long jump to the next one. The ape dog began a horrific howling and barking. Relkin could hear its claws skittering along the stones as it charged. He panicked, jumped awkwardly, and slipped on the neighboring balcony rail and almost fell to his death. Only the fact that his legs were astraddle the balcony saved him, and he landed with punishing force with his feet on either side. The breath went out of him, but he managed to topple inside the rail before fainting.

He returned to consciousness too soon. He was still struggling to breathe, his testicles ached. It was hard just getting to his knees. Even harder to gather up his satchel.

Before he had achieved that much, however, he was interrupted. The doors to the balcony opened and a figure stepped out. Relkin stared up into the face of a slender woman with lank grey hair and exhausted eyes, wrapped in a brown blanket against the cold. In her right hand glittered a foot-long knife which she kept pointed at his throat.

For a long moment she simply stared at him. Was this a harmless child, or some deadly thing from the enemy?

"What do you do here?" she said at last, using the witch voice that would compel his answer.

"I stole orchids from the greenhouse," he said. His reply astonished him with its sudden frankness.

"Why?"

"To sell at the performance of the *Orchidia*. To get the money for a magic to regrow the tail of my dragon."

"A dragonboy?"

"Yes," he said, not knowing quite why he answered so simply and truthfully. There was something about this haggard-looking woman that compelled honesty from him.

She also held the long knife in a manner that suggested that she knew how to use it. The steel glittered; he watched it, entranced.

"Come inside, you'll sit while I decide what to do with you."

Relkin felt something lift off his mind, almost like a heavy cloak. His urge for self-preservation surged to the fore.

"Ah, wouldn't it be much simpler if I just carried on and climbed down the wall?"

She turned to stare at him; her eyes were most peculiar, they seemed to bore into one's head.

"Inside! I'll not have common thievery wreaked across the tower. The flowers must go back to the person who has taken such pains to grow them. It is difficult to grow these tropical blooms in the northlands."

Relkin looked to the balcony rail and calculated his chances. The woman looked up, saw him and snapped her fingers twice. Relkin followed her inside, walking as if he was in a dream. He sat in a chair in a room suffused with an amber light and furnished with heavy bookcases bulging with tomes wrapped in deep brown leather. He still felt distinctly nauseated, but the pain between his legs was ebbing slowly.

The woman rang a silver bell. A guard appeared and received instructions.

She turned back to Relkin. "Now, tell me exactly what it is that's wrong with your dragon."

Relkin tried to speak, but his thoughts were filled with fog and he was unable to articulate.

"Come along, young man!" she said. Then seeing his trance-struck eyes she caught herself.

"Oh, silly me. I'm sorry." She snapped her fingers a third time and broke the declension. Relkin's mind cleared from the spell for obedience.

"Now," said the lady. "What's wrong with your dragon?"

"His tail tip was cut off by a sword."

"And what is this dragon's name and of what breed is he?"

"Bazil is his name, Bazil of Quosh. He is a Quoshite leatherback, brown on the back, green on the belly and strong in the shanks."

"I'm sure he's a beauty. Well, I'll be just a minute. Leave the flowers you stole upon this table. I will have them returned to their rightful owner at once."

Glumly Relkin removed the flowers from his satchel. Now he would be punished and later Bazil would fail the battle tests, and they would be sent to Quosh to become farm labor for the rest of their days.

He waited for a minute or so and the guard returned, now accompanied by a pair of monitors, young seniors from the Chapterhouse who assisted in the maintenance of order in the Tower of Guard.

The guard pointed to Relkin.

"A thief. Take him down to the crypt and deliver him to the disciplinarians. I recommend perhaps a quick dip in the sound."

"He'll need a dip once the drubbing women have finished with him," said one of the monitors, a pinch-faced youth with weaselish eyes.

"They're in a fettle tonight!" added the other one. "We've had three drunken apprentices and a pickpocket already," he said in a cheerful voice. "It's the full moon, of course, happens every month—and the drubbings! Oh my, oh my, what a night we're having."

The fellow's good cheer did not hearten Relkin a whit. He was pulled to his feet, his hands were cuffed before him and the monitors prepared to lead him away, when the door opened and the pale lady with the tired eyes returned.

"One moment. Before you take him away I have something for him."

She pressed a small packet, a brown envelope folded tightly, into his shirt.

"Here, Master Relkin. Boil the contents of this packet

in a pail of water and give it to your Quoshite leatherback to drink. He'll hate the taste, I can guarantee it, but it will help his condition as you described it."

Relkin had barely time to thank her before he was pulled through the door and down the stairs to the crypt in the cellars.

On the landings he was led through the various crowds of servants, novices, guards and occasional notables. On the lower floors the landings were larger and broad corridors ran away in three directions.

On the ground floor Relkin passed a party of female novices scrubbing down the marble flags. The girls giggled to themselves as he was pulled past them towards the stairs leading to the crypt.

"Guess who won't be walking so insolently later tonight!" said a voice. Giggles resounded.

"Give him a dip in the sound, that'll cool them down again!" said another voice.

And then he was tumbling down the stairs to the guard post. He was logged in and sat on a bench outside the small gymnasium used for peremptory punishments. Several other youths were already sitting there. Mostly they were apprentice boys, rounded up for fighting. They sat there sullenly, silent and fogged with alcohol. A smell of sour beer and sweat emanated from them.

His handcuffs were removed and the guards logged him in with the disciplinarians, who emerged briefly from inside the door to collect the next young criminal. From within the doors there came briefly the cries of pain associated with the place. Relkin shivered to himself. There was nothing to be done about it as far as he could see. This anteroom was locked even though the guards now left him.

The inner doors opened again. A middle-aged woman in the shapeless grey robes of the Discipline Order came in. Her heavy arms were wrapped in gold bracelets of rank. Wordlessly she pointed the way for the first of the young louts. With ill grace he got to his feet and went inside ahead of her. Relkin glimpsed the stocks set up inside, with seats for the Recorders of Justice in rows in front.

The doors closed again. The other youths stared at the floor; they made no effort to converse.

Relkin was left with his own naturally gloomy thoughts. Ahead lay the hope of curing Bazil's condition, and for that he was grateful. Before that, however, he faced an uncomfortable period.

A key turned in the lock to the outside corridor. The door swung open and a face slid into view. He stared at it dully, for a moment and then snapped to attention.

"Lagdalen!"

"Ssh!" she whispered, and bent down beside him. "Come with me, I know a way out of here."

The others barely looked at her—she wore the grey robe of the Sisterhood with a novice's blue borders. She endeavored to look as official as possible, walked over and pushed open the door into the gymnasium. A punishment was in progress and the apprentices looked down, intent on their own thoughts.

Relkin followed Lagdalen inside and together they slipped past the backs of the Recorders of Justice, who were intent on the stocks and never turned to look at them. A few feet further on and they entered a narrow stairwell that opened at one side of the room. It led to changing rooms filled with equipment for the gymnasium's primary usage.

"Quickly, we don't want to be caught in here," said Lagdalen in an urgent whisper, pulling him through the dark room and into another passage. They came to a window that looked out on a narrow alley.

"That passage leads out to the kitchen. If you keep straight on you'll come out by the stables."

Relkin was momentarily overcome with gratitude. He told Lagdalen about the woman with the pale, lank hair and the packet she had given him.

Lagdalen's eyes widened.

"What floor was this woman's apartment on?"

Relkin shrugged, did it matter?

"Near the top of the tower, maybe three floors down."

Lagdalen bit her lip and shook her head. "You are lucky, Relkin. Those are powerful people's apartments. She might have turned you into a frog for your troubles."

"But she didn't. She was kind, I think."

"Probably one of the High Witches. Again, I say you have been very lucky. You should be more careful, orphanboy, next time I may not be around to get you out of trouble."

"Thank you, Lagdalen of Tarcho."

"Well then," she said nervously, pressing her hands together. She would have to return the key to the guardpost, before its absence was noticed.

"Why did you save me?" he said.

"I was passing on the landing and I saw you and I just hated what those other girls were saying and I knew that I had to try and free you if I could."

"You have risked a drubbing yourself."

"I don't think anyone who could recognize me saw me enter. The boys there were too depressed to notice."

"I thank you again, Lagdalen of Tarcho."

"Goodbye, Relkin, try to be more careful."

"Goodbye, Lagdalen, until we meet again."

CHAPTER EIGHT

By midmorning the witchbrew was ready and Relkin's patience was stretched to breaking point. Relkin had a very sulky dragon on his hands.

"This damn tail hurt too much." Baz inspected his tail in the ray of sunlight that fell into the dragon stall through the roof ducts.

"Of course it does. You wouldn't leave my poultice on it for long enough."

"Bah, what good is human poultice? This is dragon flesh, fool boy."

Relkin sighed. Sometimes dragon-tending could be quite a trial.

"All flesh is corrupted in the same way, Baz. By the tiny things of the air and soil. Everyone knows that. Even dragons get infections."

Bazil grunted and continued to examine the sore, corrupted tail stump. The infection had now spread back a full inch from the wound.

Relkin dabbed the wound with iodine disinfectant again. Bazil gave a yelp and emitted the weird hiss of the dragon in pain. The big eyes glowed.

"This better help," he growled. The narrow dragon ears were laid back and the thick slate-colored lips tightened to bare two-inch fangs. It was not a reassuring sight on a beast weighing more than two tons.

Relkin adopted his most soothing tone of voice.

"I know it hurts, Baz. I'm sorry too, but if you'd just drink the magical brew I've made for you, all this would soon be done with."

"Drink that stuff? No."

"Bazil!"

"It's disgusting."

"It's magic, it won't hurt to try it."

"It makes my stomach heave to even contemplate drinking it."

"You must try."

"I have a delicate stomach, as you well know."

"Baz, in three days you must fight Smilgax. You must win so you can go up against Vastrox in the finals. Without the witchbrew you haven't a chance against Smilgax. You'll be out of contention for the legions."

"How you can expect a dragon with a stomach like mine to drink that foul mess, I do not understand!"

Relkin squared his shoulders in anger.

''Now I know why they called you such a 'sleepy' dragon! You're just being idiotic about this.''

The big eyes glowed, the hiss increased.

''Fool boy, can you not smell that stuff? I don't know what it is, but it stinks something powerful.''

''You want to go back to Quosh? Join the other 'Sleepies' around the village. Haul a dung cart, pull a plough, day after day!''

The hiss stopped abruptly. Bazil gazed at the tall black pail, filled with the witchbrew.

''I will not drink anything that smells like cat feces, I don't care what—''

''It may not be pleasant, but it isn't that bad.''

''So speaks a human boy with a human's useless nose. Bah, what do you know about smell. No human can smell his way out of a brewery unless he has a light to see by!''

Heavy dragon arms were folded at this for emphasis.

Relkin refused to give up.

''It wasn't until your ninetieth day in the egg that they got tired of waiting for you to hatch and they opened the egg for you.''

Which was true. Bazil had been one sleepy little leatherback when he was first brought into the world. Baz shot him a look of outraged dignity.

''What has that to do with this, fool boy?''

Relkin continued in a mournful voice.

''You were just curled up there, waiting for them, they said. You didn't know any better. You thought that's what the world was about, just waiting until somebody came along and opened your egg for you!''

Bazil turned himself away with a big grunt. The tail flickered oddly, the two-ton torso expressed hurt and outrage. He looked back to Relkin.

''Now you're just being nasty and I don't have to take any notice of you.''

''Drink up that pailful of magical fluid. The witch promised me it would work.''

Bazil gave a dragony sniff of disdain.

''Nasty smelly stuff. No thanks.''

"I would remind you that I risked a lot to get that stuff for you. The least you can do is try to drink it."

"Ecch!"

"Bazil! Do you really want to go back to Quosh and haul a barrow for the rest of your days?"

The dragon emitted a small sniff. Peeked back with one eye, turned away when confronted by Relkin's angry stare, hands hunched on hips.

"You know what it'll be like in the village. Soon as you do something silly, get too drunk, knock over a haystack, you know, they'll have you down to the blacksmith's and get out the gelding irons."

Bazil grunted, looked away. By the Ancient Drakes, it would be a boring life to lead. As sedate as that of the cattle in the field.

"They won't allow a boisterous dragon in the village."

Bazil gave a vast sigh of unhappiness. For a moment he hissed softly to himself in the sibilant speech of the dragonfolk. Then with a groan and a big shake of the head he turned back to Relkin.

"Trouble is, Relkin boy, you are right. Pass me the pail."

Relkin knew better than to waste the chance. He pressed the assault mercilessly.

"Just imagine pulling a plough all spring, Bazil. We'll do well at that, won't we? After a while you'll be so plump and happy to please you probably won't care much, I suppose."

Baz groaned.

"You know how to get to me, fool boy! Pass me the pail!"

Bazil took hold of the pail of evil-smelling brown liquid. It was thick, with a shiny viscosity that made it look slightly like beer in the early stages of fermentation— cloudy, dark brown, with a yellowish scum at the top.

Bazil didn't know whether he dared to believe boy Relkin's story. On the face of it, it was crazy. A powerful witch with a chamber in the High Tower had taken the time and trouble to concoct a potion for Relkin Orphanboy. In exchange for a few flowers he was carrying and a few sexual favors.

Bazil certainly didn't believe the parts concerning the beauty of this witch and the nature of the sexual favors. He knew boy Relkin's boastful little mind too well. But he couldn't seem to shake the boy on the witch herself, or on her being the source of the potion. It was inexplicable, on the face of it.

He lifted the pail of evil-smelling fluid. It was hideously rank. His nostrils wrinkled shut in disgust. He put it down again.

It made his stomach jump and twitch, just at a whiff of it.

"It smells like the droppings of a sick cat!" he roared.

Relkin simply stared back.

With a weary groan, Baz lifted the pail, then tried a quick slurp. Maybe he could get most of it down before noticing it.

It smelled like cat droppings and by the gods it tasted pretty much as Baz had always imagined cat droppings probably tasted.

He set the pail down and gagged—the stuff wouldn't go down! It was simply too awful for his throat and stomach to accept. Bazil clasped his big jaws shut and tried to swallow. It took an enormous effort.

As the stuff slid its viscous way down his throat, he told himself frantically that the witch had promised that it would work.

The stuff was like warm slime, the stink was horrible.

He was struck by a dreadful thought. What if the "witch" had simply been a lady happy to play a trick on an unfortunate dragon?

Such things were often rumored.

The first gulp was down. He shuddered and sucked in a deep breath.

"That was awful. That was truly horrible."

Sweat beaded his muzzle and forehead. The long muscular stubs on his back, where wings had once grown in his ancestors, began to itch.

Relkin was pitiless.

"Finish it, Baz, now you've started."

He eyed the pail. Could he? Could he really get that muck down? He lifted it quickly and poured a hefty gulp into his mouth, he swallowed, half of it went down, then he choked and gasped and spat the rest out in a spray of brown foam.

Relkin dived for cover behind the weapons rack, then peeked back. Bazil gazed at him with eyes filled with the infinite sense of agony that only dragon eyes as big as saucers can convey.

Once again Baz lifted the pail and poured a gulp into his mouth. He shivered and gagged and swallowed.

"By the Prime Egg, this stuff had better work!"

Relkin was awed. The stuff smelled every bit as loathesome to him as it did to Bazil. He knew that his dragon was performing a quite heroic act. In fact, it was a mystery to Relkin that the dragon was keeping the stuff down. Baz had a notoriously finicky stomach, like a lot of leatherbacks.

But Relkin knew that the stuff possessed a potent magic of some kind. Of that he had no doubt, not since he'd boiled it up.

In fact it was incredible stuff. When he'd taken out the packet and opened it, there had been a small amount of brown powder and half a dozen twigs with a few tiny yellow leaves, but once he had begun boiling it in the bucket of water it had changed—astonishingly, becoming a thick, evil-smelling sludge that bubbled to itself long after it was removed from the heat.

Baz paused, fighting down the nausea; he belched and almost lost everything. He recovered after a moment. Swallowed and took a deep breath. Then he passed a huge hand over his eyes.

"Perhaps it would not be so bad to live in Quosh after all, Relkin. In fact I was never unhappy when I lived there in my youth."

"That was then, Baz, but now you'd have to work full time for your food. You know how it is. To get started you'll have to take on a lot of heavy labor. But there'll be a nice stall, and regular meals and a stove to keep off the winter's chill. And in the spring there'll be ploughing, and in summer hauling and in autumn harvesting—you know, the peaceful bucolic life.''

"Alright, alright, I'll try again.''

Baz made a great effort and raised the pail and drained the rest of the witchbrew. He put the pail down with a clang and leaned back against the wall of the stall. His head was swimming.

"I feel awful,'' he said. "I think I am going to die . . .''
The nine-foot long torso sagged, the big hind legs gave way and Baz slid down the wall. He gave a huge shudder when he reached the floor, and curled up to sleep with his battered tail tucked inside under his neck.

Relkin watched anxiously for a minute or so. Had he poisoned his dragon? They'd hang him if he had. What if the witch had been wrong? Or made a mistake in the process of assembling the spells?

Baz began to snore, loudly. Relkin pressed a finger to the big artery behind Bazil's ear; the dragon pulse was slow but steady. He examined the inner lining of the ear; it was a healthy pink. The nose tip was cool. Baz didn't exhibit the usual symptoms of poisoning.

Finally he felt the skin along the wingstubs below the shoulderblades. They were normal. A sick dragon always ran a temperature there first.

The minutes lengthened, Baz continued to snore peacefully. Relkin tiptoed away and began to work on Bazil's armor and shield; both had taken a beating from Smilgax and still required work.

Baz slept on. Indeed he remained asleep for a straight twenty-nine hours before awaking again, in late afternoon the following day. Then he came back to life with an enormous appetite and a new tail tip, a little shorter than the old one and bent at an odd angle so that it appeared broken.

But it was a tail tip, and quite flexible and controllable after a few practice efforts.

Relkin gave a whoop of triumph and danced around the stall. Baz stared at the new tail tip—the horrible potion had worked, although he was not sure he liked the look of the result.

"Oh, well," he said sadly, "I will always have an ugly tail now."

The tail tip was grey and contrasted oddly with the olive green of the rest of him.

Relkin just whooped.

Experimenting, Baz picked up a pail with the tail tip and tossed it up in the air and then caught it and threw it against the wall. It was as if he'd used it all his life!

He gave a happy roar, and reached into the weapons rack with the tail and pulled out a dragon mace. He whipped the mace about in the air with the tail, gave the exercise bag hanging in the corner a few hearty thwacks. Relkin dived for cover.

"It worked, Relkin boy! It damn well worked!" The mace thwacked the bag with vigor.

Baz threw back his head and gave a great roar of delight.

A few hours later, Bazil, already nicknamed "Broketail" by onlookers, practiced vigorously in the gymnasium, his new tail a wonder to behold. He actually found it an improvement on the old one in some ways, since it had a subtle grip on a small sword hilt. He thought he might become good with the tail sword, the most difficult of the dragon combat arts and one that had never been a very strong part of his repertory of skills.

Finally he gave in to Relkin's pleas and stopped. It was time to take a splash in the pool and then get some dinner. The crowd of onlookers drifted away, except for a tall, green-hided dragon.

"Greetings, Smilgax!" said Bazil, recognizing his foe.

"Bazil of Quosh, you will serve the empire well, as a farm dragon of course. I will go forth to the legions, you

will return to the dunghill. It is the way of things, is it
not?''

"I don't know about that, Smilgax. I'll be ready for
you in the final combats. I have a renewed tail tip, and I
can wield mace and shield with ease."

Smilgax gave a mournful laugh.

"That mutant tail you've grown will not help you when
I attack, cutting and slashing with the blade from Vo,
'Blue Murder.' ''

"My sword from Quosh, 'Piocar' will meet you. And
my new 'mutant tail,' as you so rudely term it, will enable me to defend against tail mace and small sword. As
you recall, Smilgax, when we met before things did not
go all your way."

Smilgax seethed.

"That disgusting thing you have for a tail now will not
save you, Quoshite! Once I am in the ring a few strokes
will suffice to lay you on the dust."

The tall, hard green was staring, twitching.

"You seem very confident, Smilgax! But look, see my
tail, I will be ready for you."

Bazil swung the tail up, whirled the mace, threw it into
the air and caught it cleanly on its way down. Then he
gave Smilgax a contemptuous look before tramping off
to the plunge pool.

Smilgax stared after him with burning eyes. As Relkin
sidled past, Smilgax turned to glare at him. Relkin saw
an unreasoning rage in Smilgax's eyes. He knew that the
hard green was under rules in the Dragon House after a
couple of outbursts in the past few days. He had badly
hurt his dragonboy in the last incident, breaking an arm
and shoulder with a careless, angry blow.

Relkin kept going, refusing to run, though he felt
Smilgax's presence hot and strong behind him. With a
snarling, crackling hiss, Smilgax turned and stalked mo-
rosely back to his own stall.

An hour or so later Relkin was surprised by the appearance of a stranger in the door of his and Bazil's stall.
The stranger was a man of medium height with dark hair,

flashing black eyes and an extravagant moustache. The black cloak parted to reveal scarlet pantaloons and boots in bright green leather.

Bazil was asleep on his slab, slow gentle snores echoed in the stall.

"Greetings," said the stranger with a little bow. He set down a black leather bag.

"Allow me to introduce myself, I am the veterinarian Herpensko, famous in Kadein and Monshago, well-known in Minuend and Karpensaka, in fact I have treated patients in every southern city. I am visiting friends here in Marneri, and when I heard that there was a dragon that had lost a tail tip I had to investigate."

Relkin bristled, instantly disliking the fellow.

"Actually my dragon is perfectly well now, and resting, so I'm afraid you've wasted your time."

"Ah, the time will be well spent, believe me. Besides, I haven't touched a dragon in a while—I need to give myself a little refresher course. I will not even dun you for the costs. There, isn't that a generous offer?"

The stranger darted into the stall and paused over Bazil's tail.

"What a strange tip for a dragon's tail. I cannot imagine how it healed thus."

Relkin came up off his cot. His hand hovered close to the knife in his belt.

"Please keep your voice down. My dragon is sleeping, he needs a good rest today. Tomorrow is the day of the final combats and he needs all his strength. So, if you don't mind, I must ask you to leave now. Unauthorized visitors are not allowed here anyway."

"So you say," muttered the stranger who gave an odd little shrug and fluttered his long fingers in front of Relkin's face. Relkin gagged. He found it hard to breathe.

His knife was out; he swung at the man but missed.

Then the man had an arm around his throat and was pressing a pad laced with a strong-smelling chemical to his face.

Relkin struggled, but when he took a breath everything seemed to move far away. His struggles weakened.

The man was standing in front of him. He had taken away the knife. He was saying something in a low, harsh voice.

Something like a vise seemed to close on his chest— Relkin gasped, and then it was gone.

Completely befuddled, Relkin got up, wandered out into the hallway and stood staring down the line of doors and stalls. Some dragonboys were kicking a football around in the distance by the gate to the dragon yards. Relkin stared at them stupidly and wondered who they were.

Meanwhile the stranger had returned to his bag, from which he produced a red sack. With a knife he cut open the sack and produced a bright green fruit which he placed on the floor in front of Bazil. In a second the fruit began to wither and shrivel. The stranger pronounced a few words of power and the enchantment was complete.

Then the man chuckled and took up his bag and left the stalls. He passed the witless Relkin staring down into a rain barrel at the reflections, and disappeared out the door.

CHAPTER NINE

The tocsin announced sunset once more from the Tower of Guard. Windows were already shuttered across the city against a gusting wind, the forefront of a storm system that was leaving snow on the heights of the Blue Hills. The white trees along Foluran Hill were shedding their brown leaves and the wind was whipping them down and around the dominating mass of the Temple in the plaza at the bottom of the hill.

Evenings were the preferred times for funerals, and in the main chamber of the Temple the services were being performed for a merchant, Tahik of Bea, who had succumbed to a sudden fever in his eightieth year in his house on Ship Street. A crowd of relatives, sea captains, merchants, and bankers, was gathered there to pay their last respects.

And while the ground floor was thus occupied, a small but important meeting was taking place in a secret room in the crypt below. In this room, entered through a closet in the senior priestess's vestry, were gathered the Insight Committee of the City of Marneri.

The texts of the Weal of Cunfshon lay open in the center of the table, a guide to the rules of argument, if they were required. And after twenty minutes of argument there was a good possibility that they might be. Appeal to the texts was rare in such a situation, but tempers were already frayed to the breaking point.

The Insight Committee was drawn from the highest ranks of the civil and military services in the city. Its job was to exchange information with the Office of Insight itself, which was run from Cunfshon. The committee also formed a useful forum for arguments between groups that normally lacked a place for venting complaints or presenting ideas to each other.

The forces in contention were set along the usual lines; the Legions, run by men for the most part, against the Temple, run by women almost exclusively. The royal Administration Services and the representative for the commercial and merchanting houses were set between the two extremes of Legion and Temple, torn in different directions by each strand of the argument.

Across the wide, circular table Generals Hektor and Kesepton glared at High Priestess Ewilra, Abbess Plesenta and the Princess Besita. The Chamberlain Burly sat to the right of Kesepton with Police Warden Glanwys on his right. Opposite them sat the merchants, Javine and Slimwyn, a pair of very stout gentlemen dressed in suits of black and green wool. Finally there was Lady Flavia of the Novitiate, included because of the renowned strength of her intellect and her innate common sense.

Despite her complete lack of a power base, it was to Flavia that many decisions were passed, usually by deadlock among the others. Princess Besita, included because she was in fact the High Priestess of the Charitable Effort in the dominions of her sire, often set up these deadlocks by abstaining from the debate. Besita hated making decisions.

At this moment, the High Priestess Ewilra had risen to counter criticisms of the security failures of the Day of Fundament made by General Hektor.

"The Greatspell has been reknit, the city walls are safe once more. Your words are an unjust calumny upon our Temple."

General Hektor was unmoved; he barely blinked.

"I give thanks to the witches of Marneri for their skillful work," said Abbess Plesenta hurriedly to ease the silence.

"But how did someone perform fell magic inside the city during Fundament Day?" pressed the general.

"They killed the guardsman there, and everyone else was at the festival."

"There are supposed to be five guards at each gate," said Merchant Javine.

Ewilra grew flustered and sat down.

"Exactly," said Hektor. "Things have grown lax in Marneri. Instead of five there was one, and he was slain."

Glanwys fought down an angry retort.

Burly, the chamberlain, shrugged angrily. "I resent the attempt to put the blame on the king's guards. These are the finest men in the city."

"Enough, Burly, we know the quality of the Guard. The fact is that four of the complement from the Gate of Afo were absent and this allowed the evildoers to do their vile work."

Ewilra glared. "Men are weak-willed creatures governed by crude passions. Men can be bought for little more than a few pieces of gold and silver."

Generals Kesepton and Hektor exchanged glances. "Men" was it? Ewilra was clearly feeling defensive today.

"It seems to us that enough is spent on the police function and the Temple witches to ensure that such things cannot happen at all," said Hektor.

"And I would like to add," said Kesepton, "I have always been a strong supporter of the police function in this city. Have I not, Glanwys?"

Glanwys gave him a weak smile. Ewilra bristled again.

"And who is this telling us that too much is spent on the policing of Marneri?" Ewilra was furious. "I'll tell you who. It's the general that spends forty crowns a head on his legionaires for beer at the last Fundament festival. You dare to criticize the Temple finances when you waste our farmers' hard-earned wealth every day of the year!"

Hektor rolled his eyes. "My dear High Priestess, I was not criticizing the Temple finances, only—"

He was cut off as his senior, old Kesepton, rose to reply in barely suppressed fury. "By the treaties that bind together the realms of the Argonath it is stipulated that Marneri shall keep two legions under arms. In addition it must keep them from starvation. The wages for the men of the First Legion have been slow to reach Fort Dalhousie. Why is this? Why are the men expected to do without, while all around them in the colony cities they see men and women living in prosperity."

"They are given enough!" said Plesenta. "And it is important for you to realize how much it costs to keep our forces in the field. The legions are not our only contribution. Marneri keeps eight great ships, half of them at sea at all times, suppressing piracy in the Bright Sea."

Hektor shrugged with visible impatience.

"Look, you've got it all wrong. First of all, it was forty crowns between the legionaires on duty that day. I mean, think about that for a moment will you? Forty crowns per man! Beer sells for a flagon a penny. There are one hundred pennies in a crown. How much beer do you think a legionaire requires? Enough to bathe in, eh? How

can you believe in such nonsense for long enough to repeat it? Forty crowns bought four thousand flagons of
beer for the brigade on duty. That's four flagons per man
for the whole day!''

Plesenta was amused, Ewilra flushed with embarrassment. Hektor ploughed on, determined to hammer home
the point.

''Kesepton is absolutely correct, things have reached
a scandalous point. The legions have always been given
just enough to keep body and soul together. It's been a
scandal, but it never attracted much attention here because our hungry men are in Kenor, five hundred miles
away. The men have put up with it, dragons and horses
have gone hungry. But now the funds are coming a full
three months late. The legions in Kenor are actually
starving this month.''

High Priestess Ewilra responded with considerable
passion in her voice. ''We have had a difficult season,
there have been outbreaks of banditry all over the Blue
Hills. Bandits that the legions have been slow to act
against! Seek no further than your own indolence in this
matter!''

The generals glared at her with rigid eyes. They spluttered in indignation: ''Indolence!''

Flavia of the Novitiate sighed inwardly. This was going to be a difficult session of the committee. And they
had yet to hear the bad news from the distinguished visitor.

Flavia noted that Besita was being unusually quiet.
Normally Besita would have been at the forefront of the
attack on the legions. But today Besita had her eyes on
the door. Waiting for the arrival of their mysterious guest.

Flavia was well aware of the importance of this visitor,
who doubtless brought them more bad news from the
depths of the continent.

The door opened. Lessis of Valmes, wearing a plain
grey sari, entered the room accompanied by Viuris of the
Office of Insight, who also wore plain grey without
adornment.

"Greetings, Lessis, on behalf of everyone here may I welcome you to our council," said Besita.

Flavia looked up again in surprise. Besita was rarely heard to praise the expenses of the Offices of Insight. Indeed, she was one of those who often bewailed the entire practice of the offices in their secretive war with the enemy, behind the scenes, out of public view.

"Thank you, Besita," said Lessis in a quiet voice, which nonetheless was clearly heard by everyone present.

Flavia felt again that extraordinary sense of presence or immanent power that enveloped Lessis like an invisible aura. This quite ordinary-looking woman, who dressed in the simplest costume and, it was said, owned nothing of her own whatsoever, was one of the three greatest adepts in the Empire of the Rose. A Great Witch beyond the rest, with high rank within the Temple hierarchy of Cunfshon itself.

Once more she puts us under her spell, thought Flavia as Lessis charmed them, exerting her spell of attraction with practiced ease. Appearing in her simple grey sari, her head covered, she seemed as if she were no more than a perfectly ordinary, poor woman of middle age.

"Greetings to you all." Her eyes glittered, reflected in Flavia's. "I won't waste time with formalities—we know each other do we not?"

Oh, Flavia knew the witch well—too well.

"I have a great deal to tell you, and therefore I'll get on with it right away."

Lessis took her seat. She moved, as always, with an easy compact grace. Flavia could imagine her as a dancer, or a gymnast. Flavia imagined the woman was deadly with a knife as well.

Lessis continued speaking.

"It has been a year or more since I was last here, too long I'm afraid. Always do I love to return to the white Queen of the Bright Sea." She paused, and seemed to contemplate something most distasteful before continuing.

"But once again I am here, and I bring the most appalling news."

Ewilra seemed to shudder. Always, always, the Grey Sisters brought bad news. Everyone shifted uncomfortably in their seats.

Ewilra could not hold it back.

"As usual, when the Sisters of your office come to Marneri they bring bad news."

"And with the news some urgent need of money, it is always the same," agreed Chamberlain Burly.

Lessis turned upon them a simple smile. They protected themselves from what they knew was a subtle spell. Burly merely closed his eyes and thought of sex. Damn witches! But sex always worked for him in keeping the stuff out.

Damn witches!

"Alas," murmured Lessis, in apparent total agreement. "It is true that the Sisters of my office bring bad news most often, when they bring news at all. It is our task to discover the plots of our enemies before they can be hatched. Thus do a small number of us keep vast forces of the enemy ineffective, even inert. Through intelligence operations we are able to nip many an enemy thrust in the bud."

"Or so it is claimed," said Burly. "But these claims are difficult to substantiate in every case."

"Inevitably. The Sisters of the office work far from the safety of any desk where proofs might be manufactured. But would you have us cease to operate? Would you feel safer, Burly of Marneri, if the Sisters went not forth into the secret places of the enemy to seek out the evils hatching in those terrible shadows?"

"Bah, of course not," grumbled Burly with a dismissive gesture.

"No, of course not," murmured Lessis. Then her tone shifted to something sharper, which demanded their deepest attention.

"Listen to me, listen well, for I have recently returned from a major operation that we conducted in the depths of the subworld beneath the city of the skull, Tummuz Orgmeen.''

Horrified dread rose in everyone's heart at that name, and they swallowed and stared back at her.

''In that hell upon the world, there are several hundred captive women. They are confined in grim holding pens, twenty to a cell, bearing imp after imp, until death releases them.''

There were visible shudders.

''How have so many been taken?'' said General Kesepton.

Lessis shrugged sadly and seemed to convey the sadness of an entire world.

''Many have been bought from the Teetol, taken as captives from the frontier colonies. Others, sadly, were bought from the south, from Ourdh.''

''As before,'' rasped Ewilra, ''the Ourdhi sell their own women to the enemy. They are an ancient people with cruel, inhuman ways. They sell their own mothers to the enemy for a few pieces of gold and silver.''

Lessis refrained from comment. The problems in the ancient Empire of Ourdh were many and most resistant to solution. Lessis was always thankful that she was not attached to the effort made in Ourdh by the Office of Unusual Insight, the super secret service that Lessis actually worked for. The work in Ourdh was thankless in so many ways, for it dealt only with people, and the Ourdhi masses were quite intractable. Through countless aeons they had endured. Dynasties rising and falling endlessly down the centuries. This had bred a certain eccentric warp to their societies. Their cynicism and fatalism were extreme, their love of cruelty seemed bizarre to travelers from the other parts of the world. It was common for men in the villages to sell children to wealthy city folk who used them as they wished. The practice of eating the family pet, at least once a year, was widespread. The most popular sport among the poorest was rat fighting.

The tide of muttering concerning the Ourdhi subsided. Lessis spoke up again.

"In the cellars of Tummuz Orgmeen, the Blunt Doom is raising a great army of imps. It has also recruited a legion of fell men, renegades of the most evil spirit, who will happily do its work in subjugating and destroying other men. There are also many trolls, more in one place than I have ever seen before. I would expect the armies of the Blunt Doom to number twenty thousand full-grown imps by the spring. There will be more than two thousand trolls and many other monsters. The Blunt Doom has been experimenting with the codes of life. New horrors fill the vaults."

They stared at her. Appalled. These names were writ in blood in an ancient book, one that these fair folk had not seen in their generation. These were horrors from the elder days, which had been held away from the Argonath for a hundred years by the power of the legions.

"Twenty thousand? Did I hear you correctly?" said Burly finally, in a voice reduced to a croak.

"Yes, and it may be an underestimate. We have no reports from further into the Hazog."

"They will overwhelm us," exclaimed Kesepton. "Our half-starved men will be swept aside."

Ewilra licked her lips nervously. "How can we be sure? How can we know that their force will be that large?"

"We have managed to penetrate the underworld of the enemy. Tummuz Orgmeen depends on the labor of an army of slaves, many of them older women beyond childbearing age. We have a few willing agents among them— to the last one they hate their masters. So these are not estimates, these are head counts from the bearing pens."

Ewilra blanched.

Hektor leaned forward. "This is grievous news indeed, Lessis. Where do you think the blow will fall?"

"Towards Kenor will the main assault come. They will first seek to force the Argo Valley and reoccupy Dugguth."

"We must be ready for them," said Kesepton.

"We must. But this will be the feint, for some five thousand imps will be pushed across the Oon and up the valley of the Lis to attack Fort Teot. When we respond, which they expect us to do with all the forces we have left along the Lis, the treacherous Teetol will raid in towards Fort Picon and seize as many as a thousand women from the new colonies."

There was a stunned silence.

"And it would work too!" said Hektor. "We would have been forced to concentrate much of our strength in the Argo Valley. Then when the second army marched on Fort Teot, we would have been forced to commit the brigades from Fort Picon. Necessarily Picon would be shorthanded as a result. If the Teetol came in after that they could not be resisted, and they could come quickly, because it is less than two days march to the villages of the Teetol from Fort Picon. In contrast it would take at least three days for fresh units to reach Picon over the High Pass. If there were any fresh units available. Most of our strength in the Malgund forts would have already been ordered out and committed to the defense of the Argo."

"Hektor is right," said Kesepton. "And in addition we should remember that it would take as much as eight or nine days before any sizable relief force could be sent to aid Kenor. As it is, Kenor has the bulk of the active legions present at any one time."

"I have always said that it was a mistake to colonize Kenor," said Ewilra in a deathly tone.

Lessis grew mildy impatient at this. In a gentle tone she remonstrated. "Now Ewilra, that's so silly of you to say. It is the mission of the cities of the Ennead to oppose the enemy. We cannot shrink from the task, for the enemy will only grow more powerful if we do and eventually become irresistible."

"We can withdraw all women from the frontier again!" snapped Ewilra.

Lessis agreed, reluctantly. "We may yet have to do

that. Kenor is vulnerable, especially to treachery from the Teetol.''

Abbess Plesenta broke in with another complaint. ''Long ago the legions should have purged the Teetol. They have betrayed our trust again and again. Now the tribes contemplate this fresh treachery. I say the legions must act against the Teetol.''

''Then they will have to be paid!'' said General Kesepton hotly.

''There can never be enough to satisfy you!'' replied Plesenta.

Lessis turned to Plesenta. ''My dear Abbess, all this will be extremely expensive whichever way it goes, no matter what we decide at this meeting. If we do nothing for instance, and the Blunt Doom succeeds in seizing a thousand more women, then we will have to face an army of twelve thousand fresh imps within the year. The cost of that I hardly need go into, I'm sure.''

Nonplussed, Plesenta stared at Lessis.

As usual Ewilra sought to place all the blame on Ourdh.

''This is catastrophic news. How many women are they buying in Ourdh? How can the Ourdhi not see that this is the doom of everything if they sell our enemy his most powerful weapon, the power to bring imps and fell fruit to term?''

Lessis shrugged sadly. In Ourdh the ancient ways of extreme patriarchy had continued from early times.

''They buy what they can from Ourdh, and they will seize many mothers and daughters from the farms of Kenor, if this deadly plan is allowed to take fruit.''

''It must be stopped,'' Plesenta said with fervor.

''Yes, Plesenta, it must. But it will take all our strength and ingenuity.''

''Knowing their plan is the best weapon of all,'' said Besita, still showing a naked admiration for Lessis that brought stares from Plesenta and Ewilra.

Lessis smiled at the princess.

''We will prepare defenses in the Argo,'' said Kesepton, "and then catch their smaller force and destroy it to the last imp."

"Or we might set the field of battle to our advantage and take the larger force in the Argo and destroy that," said Hector.

Lessis nodded; Kesepton and Hector's instincts were in the familiar direction of the legions. Theirs was the way with the sword, the decisive battle, the big campaign.

The Sisters of the Office of Unusual Insight, on the other hand, believed in preventive action wherever possible.

"Indeed, if we have to accept battle. Generals Hektor and Kesepton are right, we will have to set the field of battle to our advantage. On the other hand, we have the winter months to act in. What if we move suddenly on the Teetol in midwinter to take Wishing Blood, and probably Death Whisper and Red Hands too. They are all in the lodges of Elgoma, the high chief of the Northern Teetol."

Hector grunted in admiration. Kesepton nodded.

"It makes sense, though we will have to field a well-fed legion. Kenor in midwinter is a harsh land."

Plesenta was nodding to herself. Once again she was amazed. How did the Sisters know anything of what went on in the harsh, isolated, male-dominated world of the Teetol tribes? It was true what they said; the Grey Sisters had ears everywhere, their eyes saw everything. Breathe a word and they would know it.

Plesenta wondered idly which of the others on the council was the secret spy for the Office of Unusual Insight, the super secret power that worked within and without the greater Office of Insight itself.

Who could it be? Long ago she had thought it to be Flavia of the Novitiate. Then her focus had shifted to Glanwys, the chief of the police function within the realm of Marneri. But for Glanwys to be a spy broke with precedent and was far too clumsy. So suspicion had shifted to the generals. Hektor was a hothead, Kesepton too cautious at times. Plesenta could not make up her mind as to which would be the choice for such an informant.

"An expeditionary force of three brigades, given winter conditioning and training, must be assembled," said Lessis. "It will move against the Teetol when they are in the lodges in midwinter. They break the treaties they have with us. They must be made to see that this will cost them dearly."

"Three brigades! Too much, surely?" said Ewilra, determined to prevent any further taxation being levied on the farmers and estates of Marneri.

"Three brigades is an essential minimum. We should properly send two full legions. But I realize how expensive it would be. Still the Teetol need to be taught a sharp, bitter lesson. We will fight in winter if we have to—they cannot."

"Where will we find three brigades that we can spare?" said Kesepton.

"There is the New Legion, now being raised here. Take the best two brigades from that and bring down a brigade from the Blue Hills to stiffen them. I believe Marneri has the famous Fourteenth Brigade in winter quarters in the hills. Activate them. That way there will be no warning from movements along the frontier where the enemy has so many spies."

"The New Legion was not to move from Marneri until next summer," wailed Burly. "It will cost thousands of crowns, thousands we have not budgeted for, if it is to go so soon."

"That is understood. But the alternative is to have the Teetol attack us next summer with Wishing Blood at their head, rather than in a jail cell at Fort Picon. Without him the unity among the northern Teetol tribes is fragile. The Shugga Teetol have good reason to rethink their commitment to fresh war on the front with Fort Picon there."

"We can destroy the lands of the Shugga in a single summer if we have to," said Kesepton.

"Exactly, and without Wishing Blood to bind them

they will not march on Picon at the behest of any ambassadors of the Blunt Doom.''

''The Doom takes the women of the Teetol, too.''

Lessis nodded gravely. ''The Teetol are a complex people. Their history is writ in tragedy. But if we strike at them this winter and do enough damage, and take Wishing Blood, then we can prevent their attack next summer.''

''In which case, what will the enemy do?'' said Hektor.

''We can only hazard educated guesses. The Doom may throw his entire army at us in one force. It will be more than twenty-five thousand strong with two thousand trolls.''

Kesepton responded quietly. ''By next summer we will have sixteen thousand men and a thousand dragons in the field.

''And so it will be a very close thing. This will be the battle of our era, and upon its outcome will hang everything that has been wrought here in the Argonath in two hundred years of sweat and blood.

''Thus we must be certain that we take the field when we have every advantage available from the terrain. Should we close with the enemy and suffer a defeat, the consequences would be devastating. The enemy might seize thousands of women, and with them produce a vast host of imps with which to assault all the cities of the Argonath shore. Once more Marneri could be ringed round with the hordes of the enemy.''

Plesenta stared at Lessis. Defeat in Kenor, hundreds of miles away, would lead to the doom of the cities? The abbess didn't want to believe that. She refused the thought.

''Impossible,'' she snapped. ''The legions will hold them—they must.''

Lessis shook her head gravely. ''At present the Argonath keeps eleven legions, of which six are inactive. Three patrol the frontier in Kenor, one is stationed at Kadein to guard the southlands, and the other is broken into brigades that shuttle around the cities and other postings all over the Argonath. It would take a month or more for the cities to put the inactive legions into combat shape. It would take them several months to get to Kenor. What would happen if we lost two or three of the frontier forces, or had them damaged so badly they could not contemplate further action for months? We would be left with a few brigades scattered among the cities until we could ship up the legion from Kadein. In that time, the enemy could do anything it wanted. We must remember this; our enemy can accept terrible defeats. It always comes back. We cannot accept defeat—for us it would be annihilation.''

"Help would come!" said Ewilra. "In extremity the Motherhood of the Isles will stretch forth its wings and protect its children of the Ennead."

"Thank you, Ewilra," said Lessis, "but that help would come too late to save some of the cities. And even with all the strength of the isles, we would have not more than twenty-five thousand effective troops. In such evil circumstances as I have outlined, that might not be enough. So, you can see that we must spend the money now that will enable us to take urgent action to prevent this catastrophic attack from being launched."

"But how?" exclaimed Besita. "The Teetol we can attack, and Wishing Blood can possibly be captured. But how can we affect what happens in the tower of the Blunt Doom?"

Lessis smiled again.

"If Marneri makes sure of the Teetol, that will be enough for the white city to contribute. As for the rest, we will have to see, Besita of Marneri. We must have a commitment from every city to activate another legion by the spring. We must be ready to put a reserve army into battle if we have to, and we must increase our forces in Kenor. After the winter campaign against the Teetol I would hope the New Legion could be sent in its entirety to the Argo."

Lessis sighed as if contemplating a tremendous amount

of work ahead. "Meanwhile the Sisters of my office will be busy through this winter, keeping track of our enemy's plans. But despite all our efforts we can be certain of this, that by the spring the Blunt Doom will be able to field a large force. There will be war along the march of Kenor—we must be ready for it."

The council sat in silence for a while, brooding on this terrible news.

It had been three years since the last bout of fighting in Kenor. In the raids of 2127 Marneri had suffered more than a hundred casualties in the First Legion, then on duty at Fort Picon. Now it seemed there was a penalty to be paid for that lull. Their enemy, brooding in the fastness of the black lands of the Na-Hazog, had produced an enormous army. The following summer would be one of full-scale war. It would be enormously expensive and unpopular, and the public would complain bitterly of the premature activation of legions. Taxes would go up during the leanest season of the year, before spring warmed the lands of the Argonath and brought fresh green to the fields.

But there was no choice, and thus with grim faces they agreed to act upon the information they had received. Lessis of Valmes was thanked for her efforts and the council ended its meeting.

Lessis and Viuris now accompanied Burly to a private audience with King Sanker in the small Palace of the Kings, set within the Tower of Guard. As they walked through the streets, Burly studiously avoided conversation. He was sunk in gloom. The future ahead was suddenly filled with dark, ominous clouds.

CHAPTER TEN

King Sanker the Twenty-Second was only in his sixtieth year, but he was close to death and he knew it.

Steadily he grew weaker, and steadfastly refused to listen to the doctors. He was addicted to wine and rich foods. His heart, his liver, his digestion all were ruined by a life of excess but he refused to change his habits.

Most days he consumed two or three flagons of wine, and occasionally drugged himself with batshooba, a foul narcotic grown widely in Ourdh.

As he grew more ill he grew more petty and unreasonable. He continued to wear the clothes that were fashionable in his youth—tight breeks of satin, shoes with the two-inch high heels, tightly tucked silk jackets with ruffled lapels.

Unfortunately what had been romantic at twenty-six was repulsive at sixty. His stomach protruded like a grotesque balloon, swaddled in silks. He tottered on his shoes and fell over occasionally when he had been indulging in wine.

Lessis of Valmes had met Sanker three times previously. Once when he was fifteen and crowned king, once when he was in his forties, at a time of great crisis, and once the previous year when she had come to badger him concerning his son and heir.

To Sanker her visits had been unwelcome. He regarded her as a bird of ill omen that flew into his life only to bring him tragedy. This latest thing was in some ways the worst of all.

The damned witches wanted him to put aside his son

in favor of the bastard daughter of Losset. Erald was an idiot, and worse, he was a spoiled idiot with a big ego, but he was Sanker's son. He would safely pass on Sanker's royal blood to the generations beyond him. Besita on the other hand was nothing but a pure wedge of usurpation.

It brought up unwelcome memories of the time they had come to Marneri and pressured him into giving over control of the armies back in 2114, after the disaster at Fort Redor when the Teetol had massacred the First Legion. It was a moment of grave crisis. Sanker was then deeply involved in the military affairs of the legions. He had ignored the efforts of his advisors to make him withdraw from this involvement. He rose to the occasion, making decisions with swiftness and a steady heart.

And then Lessis had appeared from Cunfshon with "advice" from the imperial wizards of war.

He had resisted her at first, but it was very difficult. She was always right, and always informed with matchless intelligence. It was next to impossible to win an argument with her. He had humiliated himself twice in public by trying to overwhelm her with his knowledge of war.

He had spent three summers in his youth tramping the mountains in Kenor with the First Legion. He had witnessed some fighting, including the end of the battle of Shashion, which ended the career of Dead Legs the warchief of the eastern Teetol. All this had given him the belief that he was a naturally gifted general of troops and armies.

Lessis let him embarrass himself in front of witnesses. He had suffered an agony of humiliation and had withdrawn from the military command circle and stayed aloof from it thereafter.

His only connection with the legions for the last sixteen years had been formal appearances at reviews, giving out honors, standing in the uncomfortable royal regalia as a figurehead for the devotion of the men. There were times when Sanker thought back to that time, six-

teen years before, and his regrets made him hate the
memory of Lessis of Valmes.

Then they had the gall to send her again, just a year
ago, to express concern on behalf of the emperor concerning the succession in Marneri.

Sanker had lost his temper several times and had refused to listen to any plea on behalf of Besita, who he
condemned as a "bitch-bastard out of that greater bitch,"
by which he meant her mother, Losset, and which Lessis
also took to mean all the women and the witch-power of
the Isles of Confshon. There was a lot of anger in poor
Sanker of Marneri.

To be a king in Argonath was to exercise a constitu-
tional role, fettered by the laws of the empire. Royalty
naturally chafed at this, and both kings and queens found
themselves frequently opposed to all the vast, conniving
powers of the empire, the Temple and the various offices
of the administration.

Sanker stared at her gloomily. Lessis knew what he
was thinking: *Now Lessis of the Insight is back, with some
new tale of woe.*

In fact such thoughts had already run through his mind.
He was instead pondering the way her appearance never
changed an iota from decade to decade. She looked exactly as he recalled her from sixteen years before, or
indeed from forty years ago, on the day of his corona-
tion, when she had appeared mysteriously in his room
and had spent an hour or more talking to him. It was an
old but prominent memory, and yet he could not recall
what it was she had asked him or what he had replied. It
remained a mystery, something that he had gnawed on
for the rest of his life.

And of course she would want money, of that he could
be certain. Always these Gray Sisters wanted money,
enormous sums. Five thousand ducats here, ten thousand
there; they were incredible in their demands.

"Your Majesty." Lessis bowed low and then stood silent, hands at her sides, a half smile on her face.

"Lady, you are back so soon? Just a month ago it

seems you were here. Much do we see of you in these evil days. Burly says you are the 'warbird.' Is this so?''

"Your Majesty, I was here one year ago on another matter, if you recall; the question of the succession."

"I remember, damn it! You want me to abdicate in favor of my daughter! You want women's rule here in Marneri where it does not belong! Know you this—the next king here will be Erald."

Lessis refrained from saying anything, although her smile grew sad.

"I expect you are right, Your Majesty. However I am here on another matter. Burly has the details, so I will spare you those. Essentially we face a massive attack next spring from Tummuz Orgmeen. When our forces are completely committed, the Teetol will raid in and abduct hundreds of women from the frontier provinces."

Sanker's lined faced crumpled into a scowl. "I have always said that there should be no women allowed on the frontier."

She nodded gently. "That is a legitimate point of view, Your Majesty. However imperial policy has been to take the broadest view of the situation. There must be women so that there are children, young people that will grow up in Kenor and belong there. This is the only way to reclaim land from the enemy. It takes a generation or more to get the foothold, but then we are anchored there."

He continued to scowl, but less resolutely.

"But now we must spend a fortune to protect those women. You will want to reactivate legions, will you not? That means a new tax."

"I fear it must be so, Your Majesty."

"Tell me this, woman; when were taxes last raised on the isles? Why are we paying so much and they so little?"

"I must dispute these claims, Your Majesty. The isles maintain the great fleet, these keep the seas clear of piracy and make the coasts of the Argonath safe and productive. What tax money is left over from that effort is sent to aid the Argonath, and it is as much as any two cities here.''

''Then where does it all go? Why are we left in this situation?''

''Your Majesty, the colonization of the Argonath is an ambitious undertaking. We face a most dread and powerful enemy, and the fate of the whole world lies in the balance here. If we can check the enemy's expansion in the east then we will hearten its enemies elsewhere. There is no room for defeat; we cannot allow the hordes from Tummuz Orgmeen to break through the Malguns and sweep down to the coast. We could lose all the Argonath in a few seasons as a result. We must rise to this challenge, not descend to penny-pinching complaints. Burly has all the figures—he knows whether the wealth of Marneri is well spent.''

She turned to Burly seeking an answer.

''Chamberlain, has the price of wheat from the isles risen this year? The harvest in the Argonath was poor. Exploitation of this could be expected.''

Burly shook his head. ''No lady, the price has held stable despite the shortage of supplies. The emperor be praised for his actions.''

Lessis turned back to Sanker. ''There is a cost to this. Prices in the isles have risen and thus people there are suffering with you from the poor harvest. The empire spreads out the burden of our difficulty and makes it easier for all to bear it.''

Sanker shook his head as if to clear it of cobwebs. Damn these women—they were so slippery, so full of themselves, so, so impossible!

''Alright, alright, the empire's strength protects all of us, I know, I know. So what is the price? What is it going to cost me now?''

Lessis pursed her lips momentarily.

''We need to bring forward the activation of the New Legion. It is largely recruited now, and the men are in training for the winter. We want you to take the best two brigades and send them into the Teetol country on a raid.''

Sanker exploded. ''What? Put two brigades of raw recruits into the midst of those savages? They'll end up in the cookpots. Why are we to sacrifice these lives so wantonly?''

''No sacrifice is intended, Your Majesty. The new brigades will be accompanied by a veteran brigade currently resting in the Blue Hills. The Teetol do not fight well in winter. It is difficult for them to put numbers in the field at that season.''

''It's hellishly difficult for anyone to fight in the winter,'' said Sanker.

''But easier for us than for them. We will take some of the war party leaders captive and sow dissension among their ranks. Next summer they will not move against us.''

Sanker wavered. It was an excellent scheme—bold, swift and decisive. He wished he had thought of it himself.

''It sounds like an enormous gamble. What if we fail to capture the ones we want?''

''Then we will face serious difficulties next summer and we will have to reactivate all the legions of the Argonath. We may face several years of war; we may even face complete destruction and the loss of the cities.''

Sanker stared at her. He knew she was telling him the unvarnished truth, and yet he hated to accept it from her. At last he agreed with a heavy sigh.

''I will do it.''

''Burly will have all the details, as I said.''

The king was not finished. ''And know you this, woman—I will leave the throne to my son. Erald will be crowned king after I am gone.''

''As you say, Your Majesty, Erald will be the next King of Marneri.''

Sanker was slightly mollified by this. The discussion shifted to other subjects briefly, and then Lessis left with Burly.

In the chamberlain's private office Lessis divulged her other mission while she was in Marneri.

"Lord Chamberlain, there is another matter."

Burly rolled his eyes heavenward.

"I knew it, I knew it, these visits of yours are never so simple as to be restricted to a single thing."

"I will be frank. We are convinced that there is a spy, quite recently planted here, at work in the upper echelons of Marneri society."

"Connected to the evil on Fundament Day?"

"No, that is simply a distraction, the routine work of the enemy's agents. No, our spy is more clever than that."

"We are always plagued with the fear of spies."

'We should fear them, especially now as we enter this critical period."

"Ah, the succession. Well, Erald will be king."

She smiled, nodding agreement. "And you will advise him?"

"At first, but I am old, I will pass on and another will take my place."

"You imagine you will be able to control the selection of that person?"

Burly chuckled. "I will have some say in the matter."

"But Erald will be king. He will be able to make decisions on his own authority if he decides to. He will attract women, some of whom may not have the welfare of Marneri in mind."

Well, it was true, but any chancellor worthy of his salt should be able to see off grasping females.

"And you think Besita will be more amenable to wise control?" purred Burly.

"She is a silly goose, we both know that. But she is also forty years old and has learned a few things about the world. With wise advice, either from yourself or from the Sisterhood, she will avoid the truly catastrophic mistakes we foresee from Erald."

"She has never shown herself much interested in the throne."

"You are recalling conversations you had with her when she was much younger. She was a foolish girl. We believe she will make a surprisingly good sovereign."

"Advised by the Sisterhood?" That was rich, the woman would be a puppet for the machinations of the Grey Sisters.

Burly spread his hands. "Well, so what? The decision will be made by Sanker and none other."

"Yes, that is true. In the meantime we need to find the spy that lingers on the margins of the royal family."

Burly crossed his fingers on his ample stomach.

"What do you expect?"

"Someone to maneuver close to Erald. Or Besita. Or both."

"I will check—as you know I monitor these things as a matter of course, Besita less than Erald, however. The heir's chief interest at the moment has been a young woman named Wassmussin, a very pretty little thing of nineteen from Troat."

"She is beautiful I hear."

"Very, and Erald is much taken with her. However the prince is the son of his father and the grandson of Wauk the Great. He may be an idiot, but he has an enormous ego. There is little room in his heart for love of anyone else."

She made a wry face.

"This itself is too little upon which to base the security of Marneri for the next decade or more."

Burly raised his hands in a gesture of frustration.

"Besita will never be queen! The king has a positive hatred of her. It all derives from her mother; you must remember that he was cuckolded, made a fool by Losset. He is convinced that Besita is not his child."

"Erald's mother drank wine throughout her pregnancy. She drank to excess frequently, she died eventually of liver disease as a result. Erald was damaged in the womb by the effects of drink. He has all the classic symptoms and the look of such victims. We know that he will never improve and that he cannot grasp the simplest things about the process of government, yet he possesses a child's ego and a degree of cunning. He can make no real emotional attachment, but he is torn by emotions that he has little control over. This is too dangerous a mixture for the throne of the white city by the Bright Sea.''

"Nevertheless, that is the king's wish.''

"It is not unknown for dying kings to want to bring down their kingdom with them. In this case the king's wish must be overridden by a higher authority—he is bound to the emperor.''

Burly shrugged. ''Well, madam, you are correct. As always you have excellent sources of information. I doff my cap to the Sisterhood once more. I have detected this tendency in His Majesty's heart more and more recently. He is dying young, much younger than he need have, but his family has a fatal weakness for drink. He is bitter and he has come to hate the world.''

"Then, Burly, you must remember your oath; you are bound to serve the imperial interest in this matter, not just the word of your king.''

Burly smiled at this. ''I do of course remember my oath. I also wish to serve Marneri, and I know that that service must stretch beyond the life of my lord the king. Come then, lady, what do you wish me to do?''

She seemed pleased and relieved.

"I always did believe that you were still stout and true, Master Burly. I am glad to find that my faith in you has been rewarded.''

Her voice took on a quality as of a recitation, and he felt his heart tugged upward, by some mystery of magic, to a higher plane. A plateau on which the fate of nations was decided.

'' 'Tis upon men and women such as yourself, Rodro Burly, that our great enterprise rests. They are barely a handful in the multitudes, but a handful that can think beyond the parochial concerns of their position and place. You know that we face the most terrible enemy in the history of the world and that any mistake might lead to utter catastrophe.''

She paused to search his face, her eyes were magnetic.

''As for what the office would ask of you, I can only say this: try to ease the king's mind concerning Besita's parentage. And keep your eyes open for new faces in the circles around Erald and Besita.''

Burly nodded slowly. ''I will do all that I can. As I said, the king hates his daughter, he will not want to hear praises of her sung by me. However there may come a time when I can attempt to present a better side of her.''

Her warm smile was back.

''Burly, I'm sure you will exceed the emperor's expectations in every way. I offer you the thanks of my office.''

Then she was gone and Burly heaved a sigh before ringing for an assistant and beginning a review of the Princess Besita's current amours.

Besita was a sensualist, in this she shared her mother's primary characteristic, but she was not addicted to wine. It was instead her passion for younger men that marked her as the child of Losset.

She was kept away from most of the centers of power in the city and most decision-making. She sat on the committee, but she was a lightweight, given only to cantankerous complaints about taxation. Young men passed through her bed fairly frequently, but she never kept them around for long.

On the face of it she made a worthless target for a spy. Easy enough to get to, but she lacked the king's favor and knew nothing of the inner knowledge. Thus Burly was inclined to dismiss the thought that a spy would try to use her to reach the king. But it would cost him little in time or effort to investigate and the Sisters would be grateful. So he would get Lessis a complete report.

A thought struck him. Perhaps the Sisters intended to remove Erald themselves. It was often rumored that they had poisoned King Adalmo of Kadein and had killed the twin sons of King Ronsek of Ryotwa to pass his throne to his gifted daughter, Queen Vladmys.

All the rulers of Argonath lived with the same sense of unease. They were grouped by treaty within the empire, centered in Cunfshon. They provided legions to an army much greater than anything they could field as individuals, and thus they had survived and prospered despite relentless assault from their enemy. But they were ruled discreetly by the emperor through the Sisters and the Temple. Royal power was subtly circumscribed, always through "negotiation" and agreement. And on the occasions that an Adalmo arose to trouble these delicate arrangements, an accident happened and the source of the trouble vanished from the scene.

It had happened to Rugash of Talion, carried off by a strange wasting disease after he had murdered his son Valins. It had taken Pondenso the Magnificent of Kadein who had slain most of his own family during a reign of terror and was found barking mad one morning after consuming tainted wine.

Yes, the Sisterhood was constantly at work thus, pruning the royal trees to keep them strong and healthy. Burly was well aware of this. And he was glad of the opportunity to befriend such a power as Lessis of Valmes.

CHAPTER ELEVEN

When Lessis finally slipped away from the lord chamberlain, the Temple bells were ringing for the hour before midnight. A chill wind blew down the hill into her face as she walked up the Strand to Tower Square.

At the Old Gate Lessis bid Viuris good night and sent her off to the Novitiate for some supper and a warm bed. Lessis went on through the old yard to the tower entrance and then up the main stairs, through the huge draughty hallways, to the apartment put aside for her use during her visit.

As she climbed she mulled over the events of the meeting. All in all she was satisfied. She had done her best to stir them up, and now Marneri would move to check the Teetol. As usual, Marneri's example would shame the others, even wealthy Kadein to the south, into improving the position of the legions. By the summer campaigning season along the River Don, the legions would be ready.

Yet Lessis's heart was heavy following her conversation with the king. Sanker was filled with bitterness. His son Erald was a cretin, damaged in the womb by excessive drinking on his mother's part. That Sanker should exhibit such a fixed preference for Erald indicated the depth of his degradation.

Lessis feared that unless Sanker's preference was changed there would have to be action from her office. Lessis also feared that she would be the one chosen to execute that action. Sanker of Marneri had been hers to manage throughout his tortured life. She had known Sanker since he was a little boy. He had been a good king for Marneri, and when the great crisis came he had stood aside when required to, although it had hurt him deeply that his views on military strategy could not be accommodated.

It would be distasteful in the extreme to be the one ordered to kill him. Lessis shook her head. It was a wearying world, and this staircase seemed longer than ever!

"My lady," a voice whispered urgently to her from the dark on a high landing.

Lessis turned. A girl in the uniform of the Novitiate was standing there, her hands clasped together.

"Yes, my dear. What is it?" Lessis's practiced eyes studied the girl for signs of an enchantment or the wispiness of an illusion generated by the black arts of the enemy. There was none, this was just a novice in the Temple Service.

"My lady, I'm terribly sorry to bother you, but I have

to ask your aid for someone you know, someone who is in great trouble.''

Lessis frowned. What was this?

"You see, my lady, I have a friend—a dragonboy. He said he met you once, that you were very kind to him.''

Lessis nodded at once. "Yes, yes, I remember him. Relkin Orphanboy, I believe is his name. Comes from Quosh, down in Bluestone.''

"Yes, milady, that's it.''

"Well, what is it now?''

"My lady he's been entranced, and his dragon too. They're a pitiable sight, you have to come and see.''

"Entranced? How? By whom?''

"I don't know. Some say that a man visited them in their stall, a man with a black cloak and a physician's bag.''

Lessis' ears pricked up at this.

"Mmmm, and then?''

"Relkin has lost his wits—he doesn't respond to anything with more than an empty smile. His dragon is terrified of everything, even his own shadow. He cowers in a corner, shuddering with fear, it is quite unlike him. I knew that Relkin had spoken with you the other night, and that you had helped him, so I dared to come here and trouble you.''

Lessis stared at the girl. Who would do this and why? And how would they bewitch a dragon?

"The tail of this dragon, what condition is it in?''

"Well, my lady, that's another strange thing. The dragon had an injured tail until today. But today his tail has healed. It's still bent a little, but he was using it earlier today—I watched him in the amphitheater.''

Lessis heaved a sigh. "Yes, yes, very odd indeed. Well, it sounds like I had better take a look into this. Lead me to the boy and the dragon.''

Shrugging off her weariness, Lessis followed the girl back down the steps.

"Tell me, my dear, what is your name?''

"Lagdalen of the Tarcho, my lady.''

"Lagdalen of the Tarcho, eh? An honored name. I know other members of the Tarcho kin, Lord Mahjuk of the Susuf for one."

"I have never met the lord, my lady. I have never traveled further than eighty leagues from Marneri."

"Yes, my dear, of course. But one day, perhaps, you will. Perhaps you will travel far and wide."

"Only the mariners do that, my lady, and I will not be one of them. I will live here in Marneri all my days I expect."

Lessis smiled. The girl's smug certainty about her future aroused something in Lessis, something unfathomable, almost an urge to mischief.

Lagdalen led her down the stairs and out into the courtyard of the tower. They passed the stables, where sixty horses stood quietly in their stalls. Ahead loomed the mass of the Dragon House. At the gates the two women in the garb of Sisters of the Temple aroused no interest in the guard. They passed on down the wide corridors of the main floor. Here were housed the champions, those great dragons retired from the legions who lived in Marneri to train the young drakes from the countryside.

They reached a wide door into a less exalted passageway and passed the stalls of the apprentice dragons. These stalls were smaller, barer, with walls of wood and floors of stone. Dragonboys sat in the doorways, at work on armor and weapons. Small lamps glowed within the stalls.

They reached Bazil's stall. Relkin sat on a stool by the wall, a couple of other boys crouched down beside him. The dragon was slumped in a vast heap, shivering beneath a blanket on his crib.

The boys beside Relkin looked up in alarm.

"He ain't done nothing wrong!" exclaimed one of them.

"It's alright, Meekil, the lady has come to help us," explained Lagdalen.

Lessis had turned her attention to Relkin, who indeed

appeared to have completely lost his wits. His eyes were vacant, his mouth slack-jawed.

Instantly she felt the spell surrounding him. A harsh evil structure, its components feeding on the boy's life-force, destroying him to keep him in this state of oafish stupor.

It was crude but effective sorcery. Lessis exerted her sensing power and absorbed a little of the mark of the evil spell. Enough so that she would know any other spell laid by its creator.

From the trace she detected many things. It was the work of a man, of that she was certain. The spell had the body and linear strength of a spell from a masculine mind. But a relatively crude mind, and one that was inflated with its own self worth.

Lessis nodded to herself. She spoke a rapid-fire stream of syllables and passed her hands across the boy's face.

Relkin gagged and choked; the evil was well-lodged, it was hard to exorcize. Lessis rolled up her sleeves. Relkin began to shake and shudder and sweat profusely as she worked deeper into the knot tied around his spirit.

It took time, but after a long struggle Lessis succeeded in lifting the spell from the boy. Relkin promptly fell back upon his cot and went to sleep. The boys at the door along with Lagdalen were still there, staring in awe at the witch.

She turned her attentions to the dragon.

Dragons were not her specialty, but she could tell that Bazil of Quosh was in a weird funk from the way he shrank away from her as she pulled up a corner of the blanket to look at him.

"Bazil of Quosh, do not fear me," she said.

The dragon gave a vast groan and rolled over on his side.

Lessis stood back. She noticed a shriveled brown seed of some kind on the floor in front of the dragon's crib.

On impulse she picked it up and examined it. A faint scent of exotic fruitiness lingered there. She felt the hairs rise on the back of her neck.

A fell fruit, a blood-grown bulb of the yamumba fungus.

"It's alright, this is just a drug of some kind. Dragons are too resistant to magic for any but the most powerful intelligence to have any hope of bewitching them."

The boys at the door continued to stare at her.

"What can we do?" said Lagdalen.

Lessis thought for a moment, then remembered the name she sought.

"There is an old woman apothecary on Sick Duck Street by the name of Azulea. Do you know her shop?"

"I think so. It has a whitewashed front and a stuffed cat in the window."

"The cat is not stuffed. It sits on the margin of life and death forever, and thus cannot move anymore. Anyway, that is her shop. I want you to go there and give her this." Lessis handed Lagdalen the shriveled fruit.

"Ask her to make me an antidote to this particular bulb. Azulea will know what kind it is—she knows all the lore of the plants and fungi. Tell her that you are on an errand from me, Lessis of Valmes. She will recognize the name."

Lagdalen ran through the Dragon House and out onto the square and down North Street.

Lessis sent another dragonboy back to his stall to fetch her cold compresses for Relkin, who was now running a fever. She stood there looking down but not seeing him; instead she concentrated on the threads of this odd incident. Someone with great power, and the skills of the dark, had interfered here most rashly.

This was no red herring, Lessis felt certain.

Turning to the other dragonboys, still crowded in the front entrance of the stall, she asked them who Bazil faced in the next combat.

"Smilgax of Troat, who cut his tail for him in the last," said the first youth to reply.

"But Bazil was winning until that point. It was a foul, but it wasn't called," said another.

"And when is the combat between them scheduled to take place?"

"Tomorrow morning."

Lessis nodded. A picture was forming in her mind.

"And who will the winner of this fight face?"

"The champion Vastrox, on the following day."

No young dragon could hope to best Vastrox. That could not be the target.

Then she realized with a start that King Sanker and Erald would be in the royal box for Vastrox's bout, in fact for much of the final afternoon of the combats.

CHAPTER TWELVE

The stall in the Dragon House became a storm center as Lessis unleashed a blizzard of actions to counter the threat she had laid bare. There was no doubt in her mind now that the green dragon from Troat, Smilgax, was part of some plot against the crown of Marneri.

Dragonboys with messages ran hither and thither between the Dragon House and the Novitiate and the Tower of Guard. Two more youths were sent to fetch a stretcher and then to carry the unconscious figure of Relkin over to the Tower of Guard, and thence to Lessis's apartment high above.

The spell was lifted but there would be lingering aftereffects, and Lessis wished to observe him carefully. Messages went to the lord chamberlain and to the Novitiate. Marneri was to be roused to watchfulness.

Viuris rose at once when the message came for her. She dressed and, shaking her head to clear away sleep, she hurried to the tower. Meanwhile young Lagdalen had aroused the old crone Azulea in Sick Duck Street.

Azulea cursed her roundly for her impudence until she heard the name "Lessis of Valmes." Abruptly her demeanor shifted.

" 'Tis for Lessis herself that you run this errand?" said the hag with wide eyes, obviously awed.

"Yes, 'tis for the Lady in Grey."

"Then come in and don't waste any more time. We must get to work at once."

Lagdalen entered the shop and carefully scrutinized the tabby cat in the window. It stared outwards, unmoving. Azulea caught her glance.

"You'll not wake up old Thusela, girl. He's concentrating on higher matters."

"I'm sorry, I always thought he was simply dead and stuffed."

"Dead? Old Thusela? That's a good one. Hah hah! I will tell him that some day, if he decides to wake up again during my lifetime. Dead? Hah!"

Lagdalen followed the crone into the rear of the shop. There Azulea studied the withered fruit. She broke off small flakes and examined them under a microscope from the great firm of Feshdorn in Cunfshon.

Lagdalen had only recently learned the significance of that name when in her classes in the Novitiate they had begun to study the small-scale structure of natural things and the teacher had brought out a much smaller microscope, also made by Feshdorn, and informed the class with pride that it was a genuine "Feshdorn optical instrument—they are the best in the known world!"

And looking through the magnifying tube had shown them all such wonders that Lagdalen's entire view of the world had been changed.

After studying the bulb for twenty minutes and making a number of careful drawings on a sheet of white paper parchment, Azulea leafed through an enormous book that she pulled out of a shelf of similar tomes.

"Well, we know enough to guess that this is a Swinebane, the question is which one. They are a widespread family and though most are noxious, I have not heard of one that was particularly evil for dragons.''

She pursed her ancient lips and turned more pages.

Lagdalen watched with great interest.

''Swinebane, swinebane, here we are.'' She marked the spot with a long finger.

'' 'Tis a favorite vegetable for the evil stews required for the dark arts.''

Lagdalen felt her mouth go dry. This was the work of the enemy. Right here in Marneri.

Azulea was still muttering.

''There's a venom in all of them, of course—they're all the most incredibly poisonous little things. Let me see, there's False Ginger, that's properly known as the Gold Gall Swinebane. A small pinch of that will kill a man, a teaspoon will kill a horse. But dragons? Dragons are such resistant beasts. It takes an intense poison to have much effect on them.''

She turned another page.

''Ah, now this is closer. Purple Swinebane, Vermillion, and yes, this is it. Viridian Swinebane. Oh, what an evil little thing this is. It is toxic to humans but not always so, and in dragons it can produce mental instability, paranoia, a fear of shadows, that will last for life.''

Azulea looked up and shook her head grimly.

''Poisonous to horses and elephants, too. Very nasty.''

''Is there a remedy?'' said Lagdalen, appalled at the thought of the dragon left in this state of paranoia for the rest of his life.

''What?'' Azulea seemed lost in her thoughts.

''A remedy?''

''Yes!'' Azulea returned to life with a snap. ''Yes, there is, I'm sure, but with all Swinebane poisons there is a risk of death from the antidote. One in fifty I'd say. But most important of all, the dragon must not sleep for at least six hours after taking the antidote.''

Lagdalen stared in wonderment now as Azulea busied herself with mortar and pestle, crushing some brittle black leaves. These she mixed with a white powder and then stirred into a small pot of heated water that could be sealed tightly.

This she gave to Lagdalen at last.

"Take this and give it to the dragon to drink. It will purge him of the poison. But he must keep in motion or another kind of poison will form in his flesh, and that will kill him."

At Lagdalen's expression the crone shrugged.

"It is the only possible antidote! You tell Lessis of Valmes what I said, girl, you understand?"

Lagdalen gulped as she returned to the cold night air. She pulled her cloak around her and ran back to the Dragon House through the dark streets as fast she could go.

A few minutes later she stood, struggling for breath, red-faced from the exertion while Lessis examined the small pot and its contents.

Getting the antidote to the Swinebane was one thing, getting it into a reluctant dragon was another. Try as they might, Lagdalen and Lessis were unable to persuade the hallucinating Bazil to swallow the contents of the small pot.

Eventually Lagdalen took a message to the mighty Vastrox himself. In it Lessis asked for assistance from the Dragon Champion.

Vastrox was asleep and rose reluctantly to attend to this emergency. Grumbling in dragon tongue, the giant marched down into the lower Dragon House at Lagdalen's heels.

He found the plucky young leatherback he'd seen go down gallantly, fighting tail-less to the end two days before, now reduced to a shuddering heap under a blanket. It was a disturbing sight.

After a moment the champion noticed a slender woman with pale hair and simple grey robes.

"I seek Lessis of Valmes," he said in a threatening rumble.

"I am she," said the woman.

The giant dragon was surprised.

"You do not dress like most important humans."

Lessis smiled. "In my work it is usually best not to make a show of oneself."

Vastrox eyed the woman carefully. He had heard something of this Lessis of Valmes, but he had had little contact with the Sisters of Insight and was unprepared for the sight of someone of such drab appearance and indeterminate age. Still, she gave off an unmistakable aura of authority.

"What has happened here?" said Vastrox.

Lessis explained briefly and Vastrox lifted a corner of the blanket. Bazil emitted a weird wail and cringed back against the wall, where he suddenly switched modes to a snarling, hissing, cornered beast.

With a whistle of disgust, Vastrox stood back. He called in dragon tongue to the heap under the blanket. The heap shuddered but made no reply. Again Vastrox called. The heap replied, "I won't be fooled like that! Go away. Take all the blue worms with you."

"Blue worms?"

"This is what he said earlier," said the woman. "Everything is crawling with blue worms."

Vastrox sucked in a breath. He called again.

Bazil writhed and snarled.

Lessis was concerned that Smilgax would learn of the discovery of the plot, so Vastrox sent at once for Gerun, Talbo and Fencinor to join him. These were the senior champions of the legions and closest to Vastrox in ability.

Quickly he briefed them and sent them to apprehend Smilgax and keep him under restraint, in chains if necessary. Lessis accompanied them—there were some questions she had to ask the young dragon and they could not wait. She instructed Lagdalen to stay with Bazil and to inform her when he had been persuaded to take the antidote to the poison that had addled his wits.

When they were gone, Vastrox returned his attention to the young drake from Quosh.

It took time; it was at least an hour before Bazil calmed

to the point where he would respond to Vastrox's questions. Then he finally consented to drink the antidote.

The stuff in the pot tasted vaguely herbal, but was not unpleasant. Once ingested it went to work swiftly, purging the poison throughout Bazil's blood.

Soon Bazil was freed of the hallucinations and the terrors. He broke out into a heavy sweat and shook his head repeatedly as if to clear it of vapor.

"Where am I?" he mumbled at last.

Vastrox clapped him on the back and bade him rest for a day or so. The final bout would be postponed; the champion would see to it.

Meanwhile, Smilgax was under arrest and the bout with him would be canceled. Bazil shook his head in wonderment at this news. He remembered nothing since the end of the fight with Smilgax and the loss of his tail tip. But at least the blue worms had vanished along with the nightmarish fog that had filled his thoughts so recently.

Still he shivered and ran with sweat.

Lagdalen caught his attention.

"Sir Dragon, you must keep moving. I was told by Azulea, the apothecary who made the antidote to the poison, that if you don't keep moving around a new poison will form in your flesh and kill you."

Bazil gave a groan. "Oh, that is great news. And I feel ready to sleep for a week. What happened to me? I remember nothing."

Suddenly his throat felt dry and harsh. He coughed.

"Water!" he gasped.

The girl took off the lid of the dragon pot. Bazil hefted it and sloshed a few gallons down his throat.

Water had rarely tasted so sublime. He leaned against the wall and shivered some more. This was about as bad as the worst case of scale fever he'd ever had.

The girl still stared at him with eyes like saucers. Something about her made him snappish.

"What is it girl? Where is my dragonboy?" Baz did not sound like a happy dragon, not even to himself.

The girl was struck dumb for a second, then she recovered herself. "Sir Dragon, I am here because, well, the lady told me to keep watch over you. Your dragonboy is in her care; he was bewitched and you were poisoned."

But Bazil had discovered his new tail tip. It was a greyish color, quite different from his usual olive green. He held it under his disbelieving eyes for a moment, then gingerly touched it. It was bent at an odd angle. It looked broken, as if crushed under the wheel of a heavy cart.

"Your tail was regrown, do you not remember?"

"No. No memory of this." The tail tip was weird. It felt strong and flexible, it curled and snapped straight again with ease. And yet it looked quite broken.

Bazil was licking the air with his thick, forked tongue.

"Sir Dragon, you must keep moving. The poison will form in your muscles otherwise."

"Yess, yess, yess." Bazil rose and strode out of the stall. "No room in there to walk. We go and walk outside. The cold will keep me awake. I stay in here, I sleep."

Lagdalen pulled her cloak around her and followed him out. Together they paced up Dragons Walk towards the Tower of Guard. As they went Bazil plied her with questions.

When he inquired about Relkin she told him that the boy was in the tower, where the Lady had had him removed for further observation.

"But boy Relkin is alive? You know Relkin?"

"Oh yes, Sir Dragon. Relkin is very dear to me."

"Ah hah! So fool boy is addled by some wandering wizard who then tries to kill an honest leatherback from Quosh."

The boy bewitched, the dragon poisoned. Bah! It was just as the old tales told it.

"Why did this wizard do these things?"

"I do not know, Sir Dragon. I am only a novice in the Temple Service."

A memory pulsed back to life. A novice and a pile of horse manure in the stables.

"Yess, I remember now, you are Lagdalen. You help us get the dragon stamp. You good friend of Bazil of Quosh."

"Thank you, Sir Dragon."

The big eyes shuttered momentarily.

They'd reached the top of the Dragons Walk beneath the battlements of the Chapter House. The mass of the Tower of Guard loomed just beyond.

"We can walk up to the gate. I will wait outside while you go in and find out how my dragonboy is doing."

"Certainly, Sir Dragon."

CHAPTER THIRTEEN

"More of the red wine, my darling Thrembode?" gushed the Princess Besita.

He nodded. "Of course, it goes excellently with these ribs, and this sauce! Mmm, but it is magnificent. Not even in Kadein have I had a sauce that was better."

"How wonderful," said Besita happily.

The Princess Besita was having fun. What a night it was turning out to be!

First she had captured the dark, handsome Thrembode the New and taken him from Lariga Tesouan's evening party at the Tesouan house on Tower Hill. Besita knew that Lariga had designs on the dashing Thrembode herself, and to have scotched her rival while at the same time obtaining the company of Thrembode for the rest of the night was a triumph to be savored.

Next she had prevailed upon her servants to produce a marvelous supper, largely from the kitchens of the Blue Pike Restaurant, it was true; but nonetheless, it had put Thrembode in a terrific mood.

She was sure he had quite forgiven her for the horrible interruption they had suffered two nights previously.

She was wearing her most revealing evening gown, a green silk confection cut in the saucy Kadein style with a deep decolletage, a tight waist and a snug fit over the hips. Dancing across her breasts was a string of pearls, a family heirloom, and from her ears hung pendulous clusters of pink and blue pearls, further pieces of her inheritance from Queen Losset.

She poured the wine into his goblet and their eyes met once more. Forthrightly she stared him down.

"Oh, impious man!" she giggled as his eyes roamed down her body very, very slowly.

"My princess!" He raised the goblet and sipped the wine.

Damn, but it was good wine, he thought to himself. From Kadein, he expected. Marneri wines were all white, all hard and steely with the chill of the north. They couldn't make red wine worth drinking this far from the southern sun. Something about being on the wrong side of the continent, no warm currents. It got too cold in winter and froze their damn vines.

Drinking Kadein wines made him long for that great city of the sun. He'd take Kadein over Marneri any day. Hell, he'd take Kadein over any city he'd known, and he'd lived in six.

Ah well, there was no point in wallowing in regret. At least he'd been posted in the Argonath once again.

He looked at the wine in his goblet.

Damn, it was a lot better than anything you could get to drink in the lair of the Masters! But then the Masters frowned on all the pleasures of the flesh. Cold water, served at "room temperature" in their ice-cold cells— that was all they ever drank.

"You have no princess in your distant homeland?" asked Besita in a mock little-girl voice.

He chuckled. It was not entirely a pleasant sound.

"No, there are no princesses for me there."

Indeed, the very idea of such a thing as a princess in the cold dark world of Padmasa was a laugh in itself.

"Then I am your only princess?"

"You are my only princess."

"Good." She wriggled back onto her chair. Thrembode imagined her large, soft posterior in his hands and felt himself harden. Curious how he could be attracted to such a northern dumpling. Admittedly this was business first and not pleasure, but still he was oddly aroused by this fleshy, pale creature, so unlike his usual favorites—Ourdhi slave women.

The smug look on her face informed him that he was expected to stay the night. By the cold bowels of the demon Uruk, these northern women were sexy enough but hellishly arrogant. Especially these trollops of Argonath. What airs and graces they gave themselves. The Masters would take pleasure in humbling such overweening pride. All of them would be given to the imp breeders in time.

A part of Thrembode actually felt sad at the thought. They were good for tumbling and he would miss their sheer, exuberant enthusiasm for sexual pleasure. Ourdhi slave women were submissive to the point of boredom sometimes—there was no resistance there, no will to stir one's juices.

"It is so wonderful to have you here, my darling Thrembode," whispered Besita in a husky voice.

"Mmmm," he said, while his eyes lingered on her cleavage.

However, while he knew that she was itching to be seized and carried into the bedroom in his strong, virile arms, at that moment he was more concerned with her mind than with her voluptuous body.

Their conversation had touched upon the Black Mirror incident that had sundered them so unsatisfactorily two nights before. Trying not to seem too overeager, Thrembode had closed in on the subject.

"You know, I am still filled with fascination for this mirror business. As a professional magician you must understand that these things, these great works of the witches, are enormously interesting. I look upon them as the greatest works of an art in which I am, alas, but a simple journeyman, tricking out the juggler's act.''

Besita squeezed herself back onto her seat.

"Well, it is a secret, you know. Really, I shouldn't have told you anything about it. . . .''

"Oh, my most beloved princess," Thrembode began in his most humble and ingratiating tone. "You know that I am a loyal subject of the empire. I would never dream of repeating anything I heard from your lovely lips.''

"Am I really your most beloved?" she said at once, her eyes alight.

"Of course, my dear. But tell me, who was this person who came through the mirror?''

She clucked at him. "Silly you, I didn't think I'd have to tell you that. Everyone knows that! It was Lessis, the Grey Lady of Valmes.''

"Oh my goodness," he said. "Well, better not say any more. I had no idea.''

The Grey Lady, the great hag herself! Oh, but that was a mighty name. The hair on the nape of his neck rose involuntarily.

Once, not long ago, he had almost fallen into a classic trap that had been set for a network of agents in Kadein. By great good fortune Thrembode had been late in making contact with the circle, who were all arrested and interrogated by Lessis herself. She had been behind the penetration of the network, and with the knowledge gleaned from it had discovered the base system itself. The controllers of the two other nets in Kadein were also taken as a result.

Thrembode had slipped out of Kadein that same day, taking a salt fish junk to the Guano Isles. Six months he'd spent there, in the frightful stink of the guano mines, before he dared ship back to Argonath.

He'd landed in Bea and immediately received orders to proceed to Troat to observe the dragon Smilgax and

see that it went to Marneri. The plot against King Sanke
was ripening quickly.

Thrembode was immensely relieved to learn that the
debacle in Kadein had not rubbed off on him. Other
agents had not been so lucky. They'd been ordered back
to Tummuz Orgmeen for "review." He shuddered at the
thought of what could happen then. The Blunt Doom was
sometimes capricious but always cruel.

Still his brush with the Grey Lady had given him the
worst fright of his career. He finished the wine and con-
cealed his shiver of fear.

Besita's expression had changed meanwhile, happy lus
replaced by a positively fatuous look of heroine worship

"Do you know that when the Lady came through the
mirror I felt that a great truth had been opened to me?
A truth that had lain unnoticed for most of my life."

"Really?" said Thrembode.

"Yes, she made me see, by her example, that our cause
is the cause of all that is just and good. And she made
me realize how big a thing it is, the empire I mean. The
building of the Argonath is like one of the great epics o
the ancients."

"Well, of course," murmured Thrembode. Yegods
The simplicity of the woman!

"I have never realized before, for some reason, that
was just so caught up in all our petty little local troubles
That the world is so much more important."

He whistled to himself. It was pure propaganda, like
that recited by children in the Temple indoctrination
classes.

"So what if we have to negotiate a reduction in tax
rates?" she burbled on. "All those things must be har
monized and made simpler. Increasing trade in the Ar
gonath is a necessity—it is important for the whole
empire."

The happy stupidity in her voice grated on his ears and
he imagined the likely end of all these people in the Ar
gonath once the conquest was completed, and he heard
the dread laughter echo within him.

Fools! They were doomed. They were grains to be ground between the millstones of much greater powers. The Masters were the mightiest of all and in time would lay claim to all the world. It was forewritten in the stones. The Masters represented a full Rook on the Sphereboard of Destiny; they would move soon. Worlds would tremble beneath their sway.

But he betrayed none of this, keeping his bland smile in place and nodding to encourage her rambling.

And Besita loved the sound of her own voice, especially after a few glasses of wine. Eventually he slipped a question into the proceedings.

"What I can't imagine is why the Grey Lady would take such a dangerous route to come to Marneri."

Besita swallowed her wine. "Oh, there's going to be war next summer. In Kenor."

She blurted it out so easily it might have been anything but a state secret. She seemed quite unaffected by the thought of war. But then Kenor was a long way away and he doubted she thought it could ever involve her. Fools! Such a casual attitude to security. Give her a secret by noon and the entire world would know it by two in the afternoon.

He cringed mentally at the thought of what would happen to someone who blabbed thus and was caught within the labyrinth of Padmasa.

They'd be fed to a Thingweight. The feeding from the dark, the withering, the agony of it, oh yes, he'd seen it. A teacher from the sophistry school, plucked out one day and taken away. The fellow was put up in a cage, not far from the school gate, and one could watch him as he was consumed from within over the next couple of weeks. Such were the ways of the Masters with those who weakened or betrayed them.

But this was important news. No doubt of that.

"War? With whom—the Teetol?"

"Yes, and the enemy, the great enemy again. Long had we thought that menace stilled forever. But now we learn that the Doom is at work out there somewhere, and it promises bloody war upon the colonies in Kenor.''

Thrembode made a face. This sounded like news that should be sent at once to Tummuz Orgmeen. If the filthy grey hags knew there was to be fighting in Kenor next summer, then the Doom should be told.

He fluttered his hands like a helpless artist.

''Oh my. I think I will take myself back to the southern territories in the spring, then. I am not one for war—a nasty, brutish business. I do not recommend it to you, my princess.''

''Thrembode.'' She extended a pudgy hand for him to kiss. ''You care about your princess, don't you?''

She wore three ruby rings on her fingers.

''Of course, of course.''

He kissed the rings.

''Well, Thrembode, the war will be a long way off, I mean Kenor is a month's hard riding away. The war will not affect how we live here. So you can plan on staying for as long as you like. Don't you want to stay with your beloved princess?''

''Mmmm, you know I do.''

She was leaning over the table once more, her heavy bosom very close to his face, her eyes shining.

''My darling Thrembode,'' she said in a husky voice.

''My beloved princess.''

She glanced toward the bedchamber. She could scarcely wait, he thought.

Later he recalled that the Temple bells were ringing out for midnight when he laid her on the bed.

Besita whispered, ''Now I want to make full amends for what happened last time,'' and then she pulled him down beside her. She was insatiable, or so it seemed for a while, but eventually she slept, exhausted with pleasuring.

He lay back against the mounded pillows and crossed his fingers over his stomach. He was well satisfied with himself. The big day was upon them, the Smilgax mission would be completed and it would be time to move to the next phase. The bewitching of Erald.

Erald should prove easy enough. He had already shown a taste for somewhat extreme sex practices. Thrembode knew such regions well; he would find the perfect bait.

He looked around to see if there was any wine left. There was. He poured it into his goblet and returned to bed and balanced it on his chest. All was well with the world.

Far away below he heard a distant slam. Then the sound of a gate being opened. An officer said, "Quick march!" and a squad of men tramped past, below Besita's window.

Thrembode's ears pricked up at the sounds.

What was this? It was past one in the morning. The smug, comfortable feeling faded. Lessis was in Marneri! That in itself bred danger. It was the most grievous misfortune that she should turn up here when the mission was about to reach its climax. If all went well, he would shortly be at the ear of the new king of Marneri, the witless Erald.

Already he had made good friends with Erald, who appreciated his lewd jokes and obscene pictures. Thrembode had some little cards that he'd bought in Ourdh that showed the most amusing positions!

He had the measure of the young man. He knew the mission had tremendous potential. He would be a section leader before this was over. Perhaps a new posting to Kadein, or to the far west, to the mysterious lands of Endro. Where the leash was longest and the control from Padmasa the weakest. Everyone said there were fabulous places out there, where cities floated and elf gardens were common.

But now Lessis herself was in Marneri. The slightest thing might arouse her formidable suspicion. He felt his pulse thud and his mouth dry out. Those poor bastards in Kadein. They'd been hanged in private after their interrogations. That was always the way with these hags.

Another squad was marching out and going in the other

direction! Many men were in motion. It was an unmistakable sound: feet thudding on stairs, armor, shields clashing. Doors opening and closing. The noise from the Chapterhouse across the way grew louder. More men at arms were standing to the alert.

He slipped out of the bed and cracked the shutters an inch. A freezing wind blew in, but down below he saw a squad of men go marching out of the postern gate and into the square.

A small figure came running through the Dragon Arch from the Dragon House. Then there came another scuttling into the dark towards the postern gate.

And now, looking over to the bulk of the Novitiate, he saw several young women come running down the stairs and off towards the Dragon House.

Something was up! Something important enough to waken the center of the city in the middle of the night. He licked his lips. It was cold out there and the wind was chilling his belly, but he kept watching.

More figures were running through the arch that led to Dragons Walk. There was a distant uproar that was swelling in volume. Dragon voices! Nothing else could be so loud.

Somewhere, a dragon was screaming!

A chill went down his back. The plan was uncovered! It must be! But how? How had they done this? How had they penetrated the plot? He cursed and slammed the shutter tight.

It was that damned hag Lessis. The legendary ageless horror from the witches' isle.

Thrembode had an uneasy feeling that the squads were heading for the gates of the city. Wall patrols would be stepped up, and from here on leaving the city undetected would depend entirely on smugglers' tunnels.

He pursed his lips. It was obviously time to move on. Of course they could not detect Thrembode's hand in this. He had dealt personally with the dragon from Quosh and that boy, but who would remember him? And how would they ever get information from his victims?

Meanwhile Smilgax himself was under a complex lifetime spell. He could tell them little about Thrembode. They had met only a couple of times, and that but briefly. Smilgax would remember more about the man that had raised him up in Troat. That man they would seek out.

Thrembode chuckled drily to himself. Of course the fools would not find the dragon handler, unless they wished to visit him in Tummuz Orgmeen!

But Thrembode was in deep trouble anyway.

The Doom would be most displeased to learn of the loss of Smilgax. That was a weapon that had been most carefully bred and handled. It had taken years to mature, and would have led to a significant advance in the struggle to control Marneri through its ruling family.

The agent who lost such a thing could expect punishment. Possibly to swing in the dark of the deep pit for a year and a day, possibly worse, much much worse.

To make up for the loss of Smilgax, therefore, Thrembode needed a coup of some kind—something quite extraordinary.

More men went tramping past, heading for the postern gate.

His glance fell on the plump features of Besita. In a moment he was at her side and began a swift incantation. He took up a candle and struck a match. Then he took some of Besita's hair in his hand and burned the ends a little.

Between his finger and thumb he snuffed out the flame. Besita did not stir, a soft snore continued.

The burnt smell rose in the room as he continued the dire syllables while he cut his forearm and dripped blood onto more of her hair. This, too, he burned.

Besita's eyes opened soon after that and she sat up on his command. She noticed that he was using a scrap of her fine silk sheet to bind a wound on the back of his wrist.

"Besita, where would Lessis of Valmes be if she was sleeping in Marneri tonight?"

She would know this, of course!

"Lessis has an apartment here in the tower," said the trollop. "It is directly above my apartment, three floors up."

Ah ha! Easier even than he could have hoped for. At least something was running in his favor!

He strode back to the window and pulled open the shutter once more and looked up, examining the route he would have to take. He was quickly reassured. There were balconies and he was confident he could climb it quite easily.

He shivered nonetheless—it was damnably cold out there. Once more he drew inside and closed the shutters.

He gave the docile Besita a series of instructions and had her repeat them line by line. She was to dress and order her carriage brought around at once. She was to go down and order the driver to bring the carriage to stand in the passage between the tower and the Chapterhouse. She was to wait there until Thrembode joined her. If she was questioned, she was to say that she was acting on orders from the Grey Lady. That would keep them off!

The screaming was renewed from the Dragon House. Huge voices were shouting somewhere, dragons bellowing. Thrembode's worst suspicions were confirmed; there was nothing for it but to improvise and seize the only opportunity that remained. He dressed quickly and tightened his cloak around his waist with the inner straps.

Besita was dressing. Without a word to him she went out and rousted her maid from her bed, bidding her to take a message at once to the coachman in his room at the Chapterhouse.

Thrembode made sure the message was given clearly and the maid despatched into the night, and then he returned to the window. He thrust open the shutters and went out onto the balcony.

CHAPTER FOURTEEN

Helena of Roth looked around herself at the apartment and sniffed. The place was as barren as a dormitory for novices. What few furnishings there were were meager, hand-me-downs, worn out and scuffed.

Helena of Roth was not impressed. Helena prided herself on her expensive taste in furnitures and rugs, and for her knowledge of all the intricacies of proper style and design. Her room in the Novitiate, though small, was well set out with Kadein rugs and Talion oak furniture. Without breaking the bounds for what would be appropriate for a well-born junior priestess, her room was impressive.

Yet here she was in the rooms of Lessis of Valmes herself and they were utterly inconsequential! The woman had no sense of taste. It was a shocking discovery.

The rooms themselves were sufficient, for tower rooms. They were too big to keep warm, but they had nice moldings around the high ceilings and there was a window in each room. Indeed, from the balcony there were excellent views over the river and the city which seemed spread out like a map below.

But the blue stone floor flags were unpolished and there was dust in the corners. The walls were bare, the cots in each room were covered in the boring blue blankets issued by the Novitiate. And there were hardly any rugs! How could someone as important as Lessis of Valmes live like this?

There was a single table in the front room, an old monstrous thing of dark wood with drawers set in one side. The chairs did not match it, nothing went with it and it was much bigger than anything else. It was a horror, done out in a heavy style that had been out of fashion for a hundred years.

What rugs there were were old, faded things that should have been thrown out long ago. Indeed, the only thing in the place that looked cared for was the bookshelf, which fairly groaned with heavy tomes.

Helena imagined the apartment if she was allowed to fix it up. On the walls she'd have some of the latest paintings from Kadein, *trompe l'oeil* exercises that were simply marvelous fun. Then for furniture she'd put in a complete set of Talion oak work. With the blue stone floor flags polished up and some nice Marneri rugs set on them, the place would come alive.

But that was dreaming. It would be a long time before she would be able to obtain rooms in the tower. These apartments were only for the highest ranks.

Her room at the Novitiate would soon be a memory too. She would be moving on to the rank of junior priestess, and that meant transferring to the Temple.

She shivered. There was nothing comfortable about the Temple. It was freezing cold all the time and juniors were housed four to a room.

Gloomily she traced her fingers along the bookcase. There was a full set of the Birrak, all thirteen volumes, plus several copies of the Dekademon and commentaries. There was Ruting's *History of Veronath* and the complete *Poems and Lays of Mistress Worthy*. It was all so hideously boring.

Just like the Birrak! It was just so tedious to memorize all those lines of declension. Helena hated the memorizations. She was just not cut out for that kind of mental effort. But she knew where she was going and what she would do. She would transfer to the Commercial Administration after her first year as junior. With her family contacts she was sure she would get in. And in the Commercial she would never have to bother her head with the Birrak or any of the rest of it.

However, the bookshelf did contain some things that

aroused Helena's interest. In addition to the boring old
Birrak there were a dozen black tomes in leather sheaths
that were securely locked and sealed with thick leather
straps.

Their titles were written in the Cunfshon script and
Helena could barely decipher them; however, she knew
that one was definitely titled *Small Spells, River En-
chantments, Tree Songs.* Another had a word that she was
sure was "death," but that was the only one of six she
could identify.

It was so frustrating! Even after three years of studying
the ancient tongue of Cunfshon she was quite hopeless
with it. And the use of the tongue was something she
would need when she went over to the Commercial.

It was so boring to have to learn it, and there was so
much memorizing involved, but just being able to touch
these exotic, powerful books gave Helena a thrill. This
was the real power. These were books of the great magic,
filled with the most awful secrets. How to turn people
into frogs and rats, how to avenge any wrong and wreak
malicious woe upon one's enemies.

Helena tried all the locks once again, but they were
solid and quite proof against any lock-picking techniques
that she might possess, which she had to admit were non-
existent. But then the picking of locks was not something
that well-bred ladies did, and Helena was first and foremost a well-bred young lady.

Of course she had already tried the drawers set into
the rim of the rickety old table. Unfortunately they too
were firmly locked. She turned back to the bed and
sighed. There was no way to gain access to the forbidden
secrets.

On the bed lay the boy, a dragonboy recovering from
a black spell, an actual casualty in the long war with the
great enemy. A boy who had been enchanted by an unknown agent of that enemy, who had penetrated right
within the walls of Marneri.

This was more exciting as an idea than as a reality,
unfortunately, or so Helena had discovered.

When Flavia had asked for a volunteer from the senior class, Helena had been glad to be selected; it was a mark that Flavia had forgiven her in the matter of the fuss caused by the awful Sappino on Fundament Day.

And when she'd been climbing the stairs of the great tower and entering the rooms and listening to Lessis give her instructions, well, it had still seemed exciting. After all, how many girls got to speak alone with Lessis of Valmes?

But now?

The boy slept, snoring lightly. He was a pretty boy, with a nice nose and a broad forehead, but Helena was impervious to the charms of boys from the lower social orders. To her he was just a dirty little dragonboy and she had to sit there, for hours it seemed, and do nothing but look at him.

She didn't want to. She wanted Lessis to return from the Dragon House and let her go back to her bed in the Novitiate. It was late, way past bedtime. It was time for this adventure to be over.

After all, this boy was perfectly fine. He looked quite normal. If he'd been half turned into a frog or a rodent, then that would have been something to tell the others in the morning, but as he was he was totally boring. In fact she didn't understand why anyone had to look after him since all he did was sleep.

Restlessly she turned in her chair. The fire was burning down; she would have to put another log on pretty soon. And even with the fire the room was not very warm. It was just as everyone said about these tower apartments; they had good rooms for summer, but they were iceboxes in the wintertime.

So far she had managed to keep the really big temptation right out of her mind, but now as boredom set in she found herself thinking obsessively about the bag, lying on the bed in the other room.

It was a very plain bag, covered in a coarse grey cloth. It had no fastener that Helena could see and seemed wide open for a little stealthy exploration. However, it was undoubtedly Lessis's personal bag and this gave Helena pause.

What if it had a spell upon it? Such was the way of the Great Witches. Everything about them was magical, from the way they looked to the objects they carried around with them. They never aged, for instance. They had peculiar familiars, cats that could speak, birds that could speak, even dogs that were perfectly loquacious. In addition, of course, they were the absolute mistresses of booby traps and snares.

The bag that lay there so still and enticing might easily turn out to contain some unpleasant guardian: a viper or a biting rat.

She pushed all thought of it out of her mind again and studied the damned boy. There wasn't anything else to look at, that was for sure.

It was too cold to look out the window at the view, and it was night anyway, so there would be little to see except the stars, which Helena was not interested in. When she was very young her grandmother had informed her that only the lower classes were knowledgeable about things like stars and winds and waves. People of her class were expected to be informed on other matters, primarily commerce and finance and trade.

She shivered and hugged herself and wondered what might be in that bag! And then, almost without consciously thinking about it further, she rose from the chair and went into the other room and stood looking down at the bag.

It lay there mutely on the pale blue blanket that covered the bed. A grey cloth bag with a simple cloth strap. It was stuffed with unknown items.

How she wanted to look at them. What fascinating treasures there might be. Maybe a homonculus. Maybe a radipterous. The Great Witches always carried such things with them, it was well known.

She examined it from several angles. It was plain, it was boring, and it evidently had some things in it. Without touching it she could determine no more.

Eventually she could stand it no longer. Prepared to leap back, jump out of the room and slam the door if a biting rat materialized, she reached over and flicked the bag open.

It wasn't even fastened!

There were clothes inside, just boring clothes. No biting rat, no viper, nothing in fact appeared to protect the bag.

Having gone this far she could not stop now, so she pulled out a smaller bag that lay inside at the top. It contained a few crude toiletries and some tiny pouches filled with herbs.

Then there was a lightweight robe, of black silk, and a set of woolen underthings. Helena was utterly absorbed by now.

A shirt, very plain in white cotton, and a pair of matching leggings followed, and then three pairs of woolen socks and a black-handled hairbrush.

A pocket version of the Concise Birrak came next. It had the look of a book well used for many years. Then there was a skirt of black cotton and a pair of leather sandals. And then, right at the bottom of the bag, she found a brass box, the same size as the Birrak. It had a keyhole on the front and it was locked tight.

She shook it and felt several things moving around inside.

What might it contain?

Now this was exciting!

This must contain some powerful talisman of great magic. Something she would never be privileged to learn about since she would never graduate to the elite classes.

Abruptly her excitement was cut off with a slice of dread. She heard a noise in the other room and started up with a gasp of horror. Her blood turned to ice in her veins.

Lessis must have returned! And Helena of Roth would be caught red-handed, pawing through the Grey Lady's things. Helena dropped the box from her nerveless fingers. It bounced on the blanket and fell to the floor with a clatter.

Helena groaned inwardly and stooped to pick it up. Now she was done for; Lessis had ears of legendary keenness, and she must have heard that noise.

She assumed an utterly submissive posture and waited by the door. Long seconds passed but no Lessis appeared. The apartment was silent once more. She hesitated and then, scarcely daring to hope, she crept out of the room and went down the corridor to the other one.

There was cold air in there, and something else—a slight scent, almost as if of sweat. She looked around the room, but it was empty and untouched.

The boy continued to sleep, undisturbed. Perhaps he had rolled over and made the noise that she'd heard.

She went over and examined him more closely. No, there was no sign of movement. The wretched boy continued to breath evenly and slowly, a slight snore fluttering up with each inward breath.

So what had caused the noise she'd heard?

And then a heavy hand came round and clamped across her mouth, and she was jerked backwards and another arm came around her body and held her still.

She had completely neglected to look behind the door!

Her assailant had powerful fingers hooked into her throat, and now he lifted her smoothly off her feet and began to strangle her.

Helena felt the blood pounding in her head; there was a roaring in her ears. She twitched frantically in his grasp and kicked hard. He had to shift his grip and she was turned towards him.

She saw a dark, narrow face, filled with fury. Black eyes glared at her with hate and triumph mixed. The cruel mouth had a fierce smile on it as she choked and thrashed. There was nothing she could do to stop him.

His eyes terrified her. Not being able to breathe was even worse. And then a red darkness fell over her and she knew no more.

Thrembode hefted the body into his arms and carried

it into the other room and tossed it on the bed. He covered it carefully with the blanket.

From the disarray on the bed it was obvious that the little slut had been going through the private things of the great Lessis. Thrembode smiled. Snooping came early to witches.

Among the rags there was a little brass box. He looked at it carefully. Such things could be dangerous. What if it recorded his activities and transmitted them somehow to Lessis's ear? He needed to investigate more carefully.

He relaxed his mind into the Padmasa pathways and repeated the syllables of power. The room became invisible; the walls of the tower melted away.

On a level of perception that was of a different order from the normal, Thrembode saw the pulses of living beings as plasmas in the dark. Even the little mice in their holes shone out like bright little stars.

The boy glowed nearby, and so did the figure of the little slut. She was near death but not yet dead; her glow was an orange color, cooling to yellow at the edges. Well, he chuckled to himself, let her live if she would. She'd never forget this night's work, that was for sure!

On this plane of consciousness the brass box was invisible, but the contents were not. Four perfectly smooth spheres of energy glowed in the dark like yellow and pink pearls. Thrembode recognized them as gaming pieces in the witch's game, "Pinti." He gave a snort of amusement, so the hag had a weakness for games, had she? Thrembode would show her some games!

He broke the trance state with a harsh set of deep breaths and rubbed his face to clear his head. He replaced the Pinti pearls in their locked box on the bed. Now he would conceal himself and wait for the arrival of Lessis.

He wove a dissembling spell that would conceal him in the corner of the inner room. When Lessis entered he would strike. He slid his knife from its sheath. It was an Ourdhi blade, made for the assassin's trade. A straight stabbing blade, eight inches long with a hollow tip that could be filled with poison.

The Ourdhi, who were the masters of this sort of thing, would use the venom of the spitting cobra, or sometimes that of a certain scarlet tree frog. Thrembode however preferred the blade without poison; a single good blow with it in the upper back was sufficient.

For a moment he reflected on the sad bits and pieces scattered on the blanket. Perfect bait. It would distract the hag for a precious second when she first entered the room. She would not penetrate his spell. She would reach down to touch her things, so brazenly interfered with, and he would strike, the blow passing right through her chest. The work of a fraction of a second and then the great hag would be no more.

She would never even set her deadly eyes on him!

Looking at these small, wretched possessions he could not help but agree with the common wisdom. These witches really thought they were better than the rest of the human race. They thought they owned it all so they didn't have to bother with possessions of their own. If they saw something they wanted, they simply took it. Of course they were so haughty that they would own to wish for virtually nothing, at least nothing made by man. And that of course was the worst of it—the arrogance of them because of their exalted femininity.

It was enough to give him the shivers, just thinking about being a man on that island of theirs. Run by women, ruled by women, controlled by the damned hags and their mouthpieces. Speak out of line and they shut you away in one of those prisons of theirs. Strike a woman and they castrated you. Rape one and they hanged you. The place was utterly oppressive.

What a horror it must be to grow up as a man under that regime. Thrembode would never have stayed; he knew he'd have found some way to get out.

There was a knock at the outer door. Thrembode froze. The knock was repeated and then someone worked the latch. It was unlocked. Someone entered the other room.

They crossed the room and sat down. Clearly it was not Lessis—why would she knock at her own door?

Thrembode fidgeted with impatience. It would not do to have a witness present when he killed Lessis. Perhaps he would have to finish this one as well.

He waited.

She remained in the other room.

With a curse he broke the dissembling spell and slid into the other room on the balls of his feet.

It was a girl, about the same age as the other one.

He slipped the knife back into its sheath. This little chicken he would take in the same manner as the other one—a quickly wrung neck would do the job and leave no blood spilled for Lessis's keen eye.

The girl was holding the boy's hand and whispering to him. Little fool! The boy was unconscious—he wasn't hearing any of this. What was the point of wasting breath on him, especially when they were the last breaths she would ever take?

Thrembode felt the excitement of the kill take over again. He enjoyed this kind of work sometimes. He stepped towards her and accidentally brushed against the table. The slight sound startled her, and she swung around too soon.

His hands missed the death grip. But he caught her shoulder and snatched her up close. Then things began to go wrong.

The girl emitted a wild shriek and clawed at his face. One finger scraped his eyeball and he flinched from the sudden pain and shock. To his astonishment she kneed him, hard, in the crotch and broke free as he doubled up.

He emitted a scream of rage and dove at her, but she succeeded in putting the heavy table between them, and he slammed against its corner and almost fell.

Then she had the poker from the fireplace in her hand, and she struck at his ankles with it as if it were a sword.

He jumped to evade the blow, and she caught him a smart rap against the ribs with it as he came down on his feet. If it had been a sword, he realized, it would have taken his life. Damn these witch girls!

He shoved the table across the floor and pinned her to the wall, but she slipped down beneath it and slid out across the floor.

He was upon her then, a single bound, his hand out to get a grip on her. But the rug he landed on slipped beneath his boot and he came down with a crash and slid past her.

She was up then and at the outer door. In a second she was through that door and out in the hallway.

Disaster!

The girl was out the door.

He stood there aghast.

The damned little slut had got away; he could hear her shrieking as she ran for the stairs.

Damn!

There were guards out there a few floors down; he couldn't kill the girl without them noticing. And he probably couldn't kill all of them before the hue and cry would most definitely be aroused.

Nothing to do but get out and get out fast with whatever he had to hand.

He went back out to the balcony and over the side and down the tower. He went fast. Fortunately, climbing like this was something he was good at, even if he didn't seem to be able to bring off an assassination when everything was stacked in his favor. By the black guts of Gozubga, he hated to fail like this!

At least he still had the princess, and that might be enough to save him if he could get her back to Tummuz Orgmeen alive. He would have to hope that it would be enough—the alternatives didn't bear thinking about.

CHAPTER FIFTEEN

From the edge of the ramp that led to the main entrance to the Tower of Guard, Bazil of Quosh looked up to the stars and shivered against the cold wind.

He easily identified Zebulpator the Red Star, the centerpiece of the Dragon constellation. Above it glittered Hasades and Kelsab, bright white points that marked the Dragon's eyes, and then beyond these the seven bright stars of the tail.

He recalled nights on the hills of Quosh, when he was but a few years old. In the summertime old Macumber, his handler from when he was fresh from the egg, would sit out under the stars and drink wine and sing ancient songs of the Macumber clan. There had been Macumbers in Quosh from the earliest days of the revival of the Argonath. The Macumbers even recalled the days of mighty Veronath and the kings of the Golden Throne.

And between songs, Macumber would identify the stars to Bazil and give him the stories behind their names and their naming.

The stars, young Bazil, were named by dragonkind who first learned how to use them as a guide for travel at night. Dragons were abroad in the earliest days of the world.

How did human folk learn the names?

In the earliest days there was no conflict between man and dragon. They shared the world and there was plenty for both. It was then that the dragons shared their names for the stars with men.

But the numbers of humanity grew and swelled out

across the world, while the number of dragons remained steady and then shrank. In the end the dragons fought to save themselves but were exiled to the distant northland, where they lived apart from men until the founding of the Argonath.

And of course Macumber even had stories about Dragon Home, that fabled land of wyverns and wild beasts. Bazil had enjoyed those stories more than anything else: *The Story of the Bald Bear, The Song of the Lonely Tiger, The Wolf Tales.*

He remembered them well.

Baz wondered how old Macumber was now. Was he still fit enough to tramp in his beloved hills? Was he telling those tales to another young dragon, hatched to replace Bazil of Quosh?

Had Macumber heard about the disaster in Borgan and their flight to Marneri? Did he know that his pupil had been disgraced?

It was impossible to know. With heavy heart Bazil watched a squad of guards tramp out the postern gate and head off to the eastern gates. The cold wind whipped around the tower's mass and sent dead leaves skittering past the entrance to the Dragons Walk. Bazil saw the guards' heavy cloaks and wished he had one of his own.

Then he scoffed at himself. He'd spent too many years harnessed to the human life! This was not cold. In Dragon Home, now that was cold. He thought of the ancient song.

There was a land of ice and snow
With skies pale blue and the midnight sun
And a legend of old in every dragon run.

But of course Bazil was an Argonath dragon; he had no wings nor the fiery breath of the ancients. He had been born and bred in the mild climate of Quosh. He had never glimpsed the frozen wastes of Dragon Home.

Standing there he noticed that his scales were itching,

especially along his spine. It felt as if he hadn't had a
good dust in months. He rasped them with his heavy
thumbclaws and decided to walk. An itch like this could
be a sign of sluggish blood. The gods of dragondom alone
knew how long he'd been lying there polluted with poison, so it would be no surprise if his blood had grown
sluggish.

Below the ramp to the tower's entrance lay a kidney-
shaped space that had once been the bailey for the
original Tower of Guard on this site. That tower had
withstood several assaults by enemy armies in its day
before it had been replaced by the current tower.

Now the bailey was used for the thrice-weekly flower
and herb market, which attracted people from all over
the region. Along the wall were stacked the folded market stalls.

Baz passed the postern gate. The guards gave him a
careful inspection. They were unusually alert this night.
The horrible murder on Fundament Day and now the
news of a plot to assassinate the king had put everyone
on edge.

Great events were stirring in Marneri and tongues were
wagging as they hadn't for many a year. Among other
things it was now common knowledge that the Grey Lady
of Cunfshon was back in the city. Everyone knew that
when she came to visit, trouble was close behind. Her
visit in 2114 was still legendary. Then had the citizens
roused themselves to meet the challenge of the Teetol in
the great crisis. Then had they put forth their strength
and broken the host of the enemy at the ruins of ancient
Dugguth. Then had they buried more than four thousand
dead, a tenth of the population of Marneri.

Yes, they remembered Lessis very well.

Now she was back, an omen of war and uncertainty.

And thus the guards would have challenged Bazil, except that one of them noticed his tail with its odd bend
at the tip. Bazil's tail was already famous in the Guard
and Dragon Corps, so the sight of it terminated one set
of speculations among the guards and began another.

"It's the Broketail," said one.

"Funny-looking thing ain't it?"

"Now how the hell d'yer think that happened?"

"The grey witch is in the city, what else?"

He left the gate behind. More stalls were stacked along the inner wall here, all empty now, awaiting their owners on the morrow, when the market would be open with furze and heather from the Blue Hills and coriander and dzook from the tropic isles.

At the north end he paused to rub his back against a stone abutment and wish that Relkin were back at his post.

That thought brought up an image of Relkin on the point of death in some cold cot up there in the tower. Bazil prayed that his boy would be well, that he would recover completely from the evil wreaked upon him.

Things were bad when his boy could be bewitched in his own stall like this. And the dragon poisoned! It was just like the bad old tales.

He heaved a sigh. This was a moment of great importance in his life. If Relkin died here, or was left a witless invalid, then Bazil knew not what he would do. To join the legion with a new dragonboy was not to his taste.

But a footloose dragon would be urged to migrate to Dragon Home, and that would mean adjusting to a very different kind of life.

Ach! He cursed under his breath; by the shades of the ancient drakes, they appeared to be accursed. Victims of a persistent ill fortune. Perhaps the Baron of Borgan had paid for them to be cursed by some adept of the powers. The baron was vindictive enough, Baz was sure. Or possibly they had somehow, unwittingly, offended some local sprite or demon during their flight northwards. The lands of the Argonath were troubled by many such manifestations of the old powers.

Ach! All in all it was a troubling business and this dragon was heartily tired of it.

With an effort Baz tried to look on the brighter side of things. The quiet of the night had finally fallen over the

Dragon House. All that screaming and fury and bellowing had been hard on the nerves. Dragons are jumpy beasts, highly strung for creatures so large.

Bazil felt a deep sense of regret for poor Smilgax. From what he'd learned, it seemed the hard green from Troat had never had a chance. He'd been raised under the fell hand of evil men in the service of the enemy.

Now he was suspect, a possible rogue. There would be a Dragons' Court and Smilgax's fate would be determined, but at best it would be service on a farm somewhere. They would not trust him with dragon blade and shield again.

A sound turned his head. A closed and shuttered carriage clattered across the stones and rolled up to the postern gate.

The guards exchanged a few words with the occupants, who Bazil could not see, and then the coach passed on and headed across Tower Square.

Bazil strode back to the gate. Glancing through it, he saw the coach disappear down Tower Street.

The guards gazed at him uneasily.

"It's the Broketail one again," murmured one of them.

"Good night to you, Sir Dragon," called another.

Bazil nodded to them and strode on.

The fresh air had made him rather peckish all of a sudden. A vision of potato pie and butter biscuits floated up into his mind's eye. A couple of pies with a crock or two of ale would serve just about right.

He neared the entrance to the Dragons Walk once more. A pair of figures came towards him, walking swiftly. The grey robes were blank and nondescript, and they had their cowls up against the cold.

They drew abreast of him, and suddenly one reached out to touch him on the forearm. He jerked back, nervous at the touch.

"Bazil of Quosh has no need to fear me," said a soft, gentle voice.

Bazil saw her pull back her cowl. A woman of slender

features and pale grey hair was revealed. Her eyes were peculiarly piercing.

"You have me at the disadvantage, lady. I do not know you."

She smiled. "But I know you, Mighty Bazil. I am Lessis of Valmes. You do not remember of course, but we talked at length only two hours ago."

Bazil felt a green flush rising up his neck.

"My apologies, madam. I was not in my right mind."

"Of course not. Yet you seem hale and hearty enough already. You are a strong one, Bazil of Quosh—you have a stout spirit."

Bazil was touched.

"Well, lady, I believe I owe you great thanks over another matter. My boy informed me that you saved him from a life of crime quite recently."

Lessis grinned. She'd heard that dragons were proprietary beasts but had not spent much time in their company before. Now she could see that the tales were true.

"I doubt if I was that successful, but for the moment we have perhaps strengthened his resolve to obey the laws of Marneri."

Baz nodded as if sadly convinced against his better judgment. "He is a wild one, I admit it."

"But that is not your fault," she said.

"I should have restrained him, he's so impractical sometimes you see, but I was so caught up in my own troubles that I let him out of my sight. And look what happens? Thieving, magicians, poisonings!"

Lessis marveled at all this. Dragons were most peculiar beasts, so she'd been warned and so she was learning.

Baz stared up at the tower with soulful eyes. Where had he gone wrong with that boy? When he looked down again Lessis had enjoined the other woman to pull back her cowl too.

She was very much like the Grey Lady, except that her eyes lacked the instant power that Lessis's carried. She bowed and bobbed her head.

"I am Viuris of Ufshan, Sir Dragon."

"I am honored to meet you, Viuris of Ufshan."

Then before Bazil could ask them anything concerning the fate of poor Smilgax, there was a sudden disturbance in the main gate of the tower. A figure was running down the steps, shouting at the top of her voice.

"Ah, Lagdalen," said Lessis with slight resignation.

Lagdalen arrived breathless—her first efforts were choked off by her need to suck in air.

"Sir Dragon . . . Lady . . ."

But finally she managed it.

"In your rooms, my lady, the enemy. He has slain Helena of Roth I believe, but not Relkin. He would have slain me but I heard him approach."

Lessis looked up sharply.

"Arouse the guards, Viuris." She whirled on Bazil.

"How long have you been here, Bazil of Quosh?"

"All the while Lagdalen has been in the tower."

"Did you see anyone leave the tower."

"No, but a carriage left through the gate but a minute ago."

Lessis was transformed. "Quickly, after it. Which way did it go?"

"Straight across the square and down Tower Street."

And to Bazil's astonishment the figure of Lessis bolted through the gate, calling on the guards to follow her, and ran pell-mell across the square.

Lagdalen and Viuris followed with the guards. Bazil shook his head and set off behind them.

CHAPTER SIXTEEN

A charging dragon has the speed of a racehorse over the first one hundred yards, and Bazil soon left the others behind as he picked up speed and headed down the steep hill of Tower Street.

Fortunately, at this hour scarcely anybody was abroad in the streets of Marneri, for anyone in his path would have been flattened. On this slope and this surface Bazil could not have stopped.

He was rapidly catching up on the object of the pursuit, however. At Foluran Hill he caught sight of the carriage and saw it swing into a side street.

Bazil desperately tried to slow down, his big claws skittering on the cobblestones, but it was useless. He hurtled on, crossing Broad Street and speeding past the side street. He saw the carriage, but was helpless in the grip of his momentum.

Now the hill was at its steepest, right down to Dockside. Bazil fought to stay on his feet, but he was getting less and less traction on the cold stones. Disaster soon overtook him. His hind legs went out from under him and he slid ignominiously down the hill, across Halfslope Street, to the astonished gaze of a late-night drunkard reeling back from the dockside taverns. He went on sliding down towards Dockside, fetching up at last on the corner with Wright's Street, crashing into a great pile of empty beer kegs set out behind the city's chief cooperage awaiting collection in the morning.

Bazil flew through the kegs and over a ledge into the cooper's delivery yard. Fortunately, the kegs had slowed his pace somewhat, and he fetched up with a bone-jarring, but not bone-breaking, thud against a stone wall.

The building shuddered from top to toe and a slate fell off the roof and crashed down into the street. Bazil could hear things falling off shelves inside and smashing on the floor. It was things like this that gave dragons a bad name in human cities, he recalled.

Several windows opened and heads peered forth.

Someone yelled something about the barrels, which had been scattered like billiard balls down the street. Other voices took up the cry. It looked as if he'd succeeded in waking this whole quarter.

Bazil shook his head. It was ringing from the final crunch. He distinctly heard bells. But he could not wait for his head to clear. He had to follow that carriage. Thus he emerged from the yard just in time to see it going past on Ship Street, then across Wright Street on a heading for the harbor.

Bazil glanced back up the hill on Tower Street. His belly was sore. He was bleeding from a number of scratches. By the roar of the old gods, he'd slid a long way. His body was going to hurt on the morrow.

But Lessis and the guards were catching up; he could see them running across Broad Street in his wake. He gestured towards Ship Street and lurched down to the corner and stuck his head around.

Less than thirty yards down the street, the gates of the Blackbird Inn were closing. Nothing else was visible, the street was empty.

Bazil went on down Ship Street and paused outside the Blackbird. This was not an inn that catered to dragonfolk at all. There was no wyvern's entrance, nor did there seem to be room for a dragons' drinking den.

The gates were firmly shut, but he heard footsteps inside the court. A horse whinnied, maybe smelling dragon. Unless they were habituated to dragons, most horses reacted with instinctive terror to the smell of them.

Bazil looked back up the street. Lessis and Lagdalen rounded the corner, still running strongly. Bazil was surprised at how quickly the woman Lessis ran. She seemed so faded and quiet, yet here she was coursing like an athlete.

In a moment they were by his side. Following them came two guardsmen, sweating profusely under armor plate and helm, then Viuris, gasping for breath.

Lessis seemed the least affected by the running. After just a couple of deep breaths, she took stock of the situation and made her decision.

"We must enter the inn. Bazil of Quosh, will you wait here and watch these gates? Let no one leave."

Baz nodded. "Glad to, my lady."

Lessis let the guardsmen take three more deep breaths before she knocked on the front door of the inn, which was shut up and completely dark. Her knocking died away.

Above their heads the sign of the Blackbird creaked in the wind. Lessis turned to the girl at her side.

"Young Lagdalen, you will remain here with the dragon. Viuris, you will come with me."

Lagdalen groaned with the disappointment. Of course, she'd expected something of the sort would happen once they reached the most exciting part. They always sent the novices to the rear—it was just so unfair.

Still, Lessis's knock brought no response. She tried again, then motioned to the guardsmen, who hammered with their spear butts on the stout door.

The inn remained dark. A voice from across the street cursed them for disturbing the peaceful sleep of honest folk.

Lessis told Lagdalen to break a window on the upper floor. In a second Lagdalen had her special stone in her sling. She never questioned how the Grey Lady knew she had a sling. Little did she know there had once been an inveterate young novice in the city of Valmes who had been very good with a sling.

Lagdalen's stone flew true, as if she'd been saving it for just this mission. A small windowpane shattered and pieces fell into the street. *That ought to do it*, thought Lagdalen with satisfaction.

But the inn continued to maintain a stubborn silence. With a sniff of exasperation Lessis stood close to the door and placed her hands flat upon its surface.

No spell lay upon the door, but she sensed that it was locked with bolts top and bottom, and thus could not be opened quickly by any spell.

She turned to Bazil.

"Sir Dragon, I must needs call upon your strength once more. I fear the innkeeper must be dead or taken captive."

Bazil examined the door. It was of oak, burnished a deep black from generations of polish. It was a simple door that opened outwards onto the street. It was locked on the right-hand side and set into stonework. The handle was fat and heavy and it was wide enough to get a dragon paw inside. Bazil gripped the thing and tensed and pulled. The door groaned in its position but did not give.

He stood back and took some deep breaths while he sized it up. Then he took hold of the handle once more with both huge hands squeezed in and brought a massive leg up against the wall to increase his leverage.

The door groaned and shuddered. He increased the pressure. The thick muscles in his upper body and forelimbs stood out like steel ropes.

With a terrific screech the door handle pulled free of the wood, nails and all. Bazil sat down, hard, with the handle in his paw. The ground around him shook.

He picked himself up, muttering the while in dragon tongue. Now he was aroused. He vented a heavy hiss.

All the humans took several steps back at the look in his eye. Then he charged the door and put his full two tons behind his shoulder.

The door broke out of its hinges under the impact and went down. Bazil hurtled through and crash-landed in the tap room, putting a dent into the main bar and splintering furniture wholesale.

The echoes of the crash died away. With a loud groan,

Bazil rolled over again and started to sit up. His body the next day would be more than sore, it would pulsate with aches and pains.

Lessis and the guards were already scrambling up the stairs. The guards' heavy-shod feet thudded down the passages. The landlord was found cowering in his wife's wardrobe. He babbled about the dark man who was down in the cellar and begged for mercy.

Meanwhile, in the courtyard, Viuris had discovered the carriage with the driver stabbed through the heart, slumped over in his seat.

" 'Tis the Princess Besita's carriage," said Lagdalen after a quick examination. "There are her arms on the door."

Lessis was appalled. The enemy agent was abducting the heir to the throne of Marneri. He had to be stopped!

The cellar door was pulled back. Stone steps led down into a dark hole. Viuris thrust forwards a torch. The odors of beer and yeast were strong, but there was something else—a sour earthiness that Lessis immediately recognized.

"A troll has been here, may still be here."

They all smelled it now, a stench of mold and sweat curdled with an ancient evil. The guardsmen's eyes went very wide. "A troll? Here in Marneri?"

"I smell it, be careful, men, be very careful now."

Now Viuris led the way again with the torch held high. By its light they saw barrels stacked along the wall with mash tuns and brewing vessels at the far end. Through a narrow, well-worn doorway lay another room half-filled with sacks of barley. They reached the bottom of the steps.

Lessis already feared she knew why the enemy agent had gone to ground here. The Blackbird was an ancient inn, and there was probably a smuggler's tunnel from this cellar leading out and under the walls.

The question was, where was the entrance to that tunnel?

And where was that troll? The smell was stronger by

the door of the barley room. Lessis motioned to Viuris. Together they slid up to the door. On the count of three Viuris held the torch inside and cast its light into the room while Lessis examined it for signs of the enemy.

Sacks of grain were stacked along the walls with empty spaces at the corners. In the center was a cleared space, beneath a pair of folding doors set into the ceiling.

Viuris pointed upwards to the doors. ''They must open into the courtyard.''

Lessis nodded. In the corners were ominous pools of shadow. The smell of troll was stronger than ever in this room. She felt the hair on her neck rise, an instinctive response to the presence of a creature that ate human flesh.

She glanced up at the doors in the ceiling, then she started back to the stairs to tell Bazil to lift them up.

The guards stepped into the room, their spears at the ready. One of them suddenly grunted and shoved his spear into a corner.

He made contact, then his spear was jerked out of his hands and in an explosion of sacks of barley a huge figure erupted out of the corner space.

The troll stood eight feet tall, blue-black, with skin as tough as the bark on trees. It had the rough shape of a man, except that it was far too massive, built more like a bear. The head was surrounded by a thick mane of black hair and dominated by a pair of blazing red eyes. A mouth filled with sharp teeth opened wide and a bellow of rage filled the room. A battle axe with a huge blade appeared in its hands.

The guard that had jabbed him, Durkin by name, drew his sword and held it before him although it seemed puny by comparison, a mere toy. His legs wobbled.

The troll snarled. Its red eyes focused on the guard and it swept the space he stood in with the giant axe. He escaped by leaping backwards.

The others scrambled back, too; Lessis meanwhile frantically putting together a spell, a lethargy spell for the troll. She knew she could not stop it altogether. Trolls were almost as resistant to magical influence as dragons.

Steel rang on steel as the guardsman Durkin struck at the troll and hewed against its axe handle. Durkin bounced back and recovered, but with a swift, canny move the troll rapped the man on the top of his helmet with the butt end of his axe handle and toppled him.

Before their horrified eyes the huge axe came down and split Durkin in half as cleanly as a lobster on the block.

Lessis spat words of power, conjured swiftly and hurled her spell at the troll, but she could feel her spell fail to take root. Her heart sank. The damned troll had been especially conditioned against magic on top of its natural resistance.

The huge axe whooshed through the air again, and they scrambled to the door and escaped back into the barrel cellar. On the way the other guardsman almost lost his head to a vicious cut of the axe in the doorway, and fragments of wood and stone flew through the air. The troll was snarling a steady stream of vicious curses in its thick-syllabled tongue.

Lessis tried the lethargy spell again, and this time used a corkscrew effect that she'd learned long ago from a withered old woman in far away Noldaf.

This time it took. The troll moaned and hung there in the doorway. She breathed a sigh of relief—the thing could be reached! She had it paralyzed there. But not for very long, for to her horror it soon resumed struggling, moaning louder, and the spell could not hold. The troll stepped through the door.

The guard hurled his spear from close range and saw it sink into the troll's belly a good three inches.

That got to it! It emitted a whistling shriek of rage and jerked the spear out and threw it back at them, missing wildly and sending the spear deep into the side of a mash tun.

Still venting a shrieking cry it leapt at them. They dodged away, the guard only just getting clear to the foot of the steps. He looked up wild-eyed—he was on the verge of running.

"We can't do nothing to it!" he screamed, and ran up the stairs.

"Tell the dragon to break in from above!" shouted Lessis after him.

The guardsman cannoned into Lagdalen, who was hovering at the top of the steps, drawn by the sound of the fight.

"Get out of the way, stupid girl!" shrieked the guard, almost unmanned by his fear. "There's a troll down there—it killed Durkin like he was a chicken."

Lagdalen was tossed aside against the wall and the guard bolted out the door the next moment. She rolled down the steps and ended up on the floor of the cellar. Lessis and Viuris were working to keep the troll off balance, undecided as to which it should strike first.

Lessis had pulled out a knife that glowed faintly in the dark, for it had been forged by Cir Celadon himself and it carried a bane to all things of the dark force—in their presence it shone. Now it glittered between the frail woman in grey and the towering monster.

At the sight of Lagdalen the thing snarled and then raised its huge axe and rushed forward. Lessis didn't wait for it but gave a shout and darted in on an erratic, twisting path. The huge axe blade swung but missed her, and then she was past the monster and behind it.

The axe reversed, Lagdalen screamed, and Viuris ran in and dashed the torch into the troll's face. It gave out a huge bellow and staggered back off balance. Its free hand swung out and by ill luck caught Viuris's robe on its fingertips.

It pulled and she was yanked from her feet and taken up into the huge hand that fastened around her head. Viuris's scream cut off as her head was crushed like a rotten melon in that giant fist.

"Noooo!" howled Lessis as she hurled herself forward. The axe scythed towards her, but she dodged it and was beside the monster for a split second. Her glittering blade lanced in and she was away before the troll could slap her like a mosquito against its thigh.

The troll was stung! It bellowed and whistled in agony. It trampled Viuris's body for a moment and then charged Lessis.

She evaded another sweep of the axe and it buried itself in a big lagering tank. The troll pulled it free, and beer under pressure came foaming out in a shower of suds. The torch on the floor went out, leaving them in almost complete darkness. The troll's red eyes looked down to Lagdalen again, crouched, paralyzed with fear at the bottom of the stairs.

It lurched towards her, a huge hand reaching out. A scream froze in her throat. Desperately she tried to move her legs to run back up the stairs, but she could not get her muscles to obey.

And then there was a tremendous noise above them and something huge dropped into the barley room. The whole structure shuddered.

The troll's head turned.

"Get up girl, get up those stairs!" hissed Lessis.

Lagdalen's legs finally came back to life, she bounded up, two at a time.

But before she reached the top, the doorway to the barley room was abruptly enlarged. Something big and green exploded through it in a shower of wood and plaster.

And now there was very little room at all in the cellar with a troll and a dragon confronting each other.

The troll snarled, but with a much different timbre, for if trolls ate human flesh, so dragons ate troll flesh, and the only living thing that a grown troll would fear was one of the wyvern kind.

The axe swung, but Bazil was carrying a heavy steel ladle from the inn kitchen and he parried the blow and then struck the troll with an immense green fist, bouncing it hard against the wall.

It came back as if it were made of rubber, and Baz caught its axe arm by the wrist and held that steady while they traded blows with fists and knees. They grappled at last and it tried to sink its big canines into his shoulder, so he picked up the ladle with his new tail tip and rapped the troll hard over the head a couple of times with it to make it desist and back off.

The axe flashed and Bazil barely lurched back out of range. He was trapped against the wall now, no room to maneuver. The axe rose again and Lagdalen, from the top of the stairs, fired a stone with her sling that bounced off its head.

Distracted for a moment, the monster snarled and looked up—Bazil sprang from the wall. While he held its wrists, he hammered away with his tail tip and at last was rewarded with a deep groan from the troll as it sank into unconsciousness.

Lessis gave a cry of triumph.

"Well done, Sir Dragon! That was very well done. But now we must find that tunnel and catch our villain."

The dragon looked up the stairs to the girl with the sling.

"And my thanks to you, young Lagdalen of the Tarcho. That was a close thing there."

Lessis picked up the smouldering torch and blew it back to life. Then she went back through the shattered doorway to the barley room. She examined the entrance to the tunnel. It was wide enough for a smuggler's cart and pony, which was why the troll had been able to get through.

More guards had finally arrived, and now Lessis led a party of six into the tunnel. Unbidden but not forbidden, Lagdalen slipped in at the rear.

The tunnel was dark and well built and probably very old. After one hundred yards it suddenly split into three tunnels. Lessis sent a pair of guards into the right- and left-hand side tunnels, and then went on down the central one herself. Lagdalen followed her, discreetly.

Her heart was still pounding from the fight with the troll but she was suffused with excitement. Nothing had ever happened to her like this. Then she thought of poor

Viuris again and felt sick to her stomach. She was enjoying this, but Viuris was dead. She felt a sudden wave of shame.

Still she kept on, following the torch in Lessis's hand. After many minutes of tramping through the dark they suddenly came to a halt at the foot of a steep ramp.

Lessis noticed Lagdalen then.

"Ah, young Lagdalen of the Tarcho, not content with combat with trolls you wish to confront agents of the enemy, eh?"

Lagdalen had nothing to say. Her mouth had gone dry. Lessis managed a smile. "It was not your fault, girl. Viuris would not have blamed you either."

Lagdalen felt tears welling in her eyes. Lessis frowned.

"She would not have wept either, nor condoned it in you. Now get up this ramp and keep your wits about you. I will need you to run messages."

"Yes, my lady."

The guards sent down the other tunnels came running to report no sign of the fugitives. Then they climbed the ramp which spiraled up a complete turn and found themselves in front of a pair of heavy oak doors shut from their side with a solid beam.

The guards lifted the beam free, pulled the doors open, and they emerged into the lower part of a pump house built alongside the sound, a good eighty meters distant from the Watergate.

"Perfect smuggler's location, eh?" said the sergeant of the Guard.

"Perfect—the water to the side, the road to Bea just beyond that door. How long has it stood do you think?" said Lessis.

He shrugged.

"Well," she said, "our quarry did not come this way. Come on, we have to go back."

"You mean the beam. They could not have closed the doors behind them like that."

"Of course."

They retraced their steps to the point where the tunnels diverged and explored the left-hand one, which led out to a cellar in a house built along the Bea Road about two hundred meters beyond the wall.

No trace could be found there of the fugitives, either.

Finally they tracked through the left-hand tunnel and found that it opened onto a subterranean dock, cut into the land under a prosperous merchant's house on Dockside, inside the city.

Lessis examined the dock. Small boats could come and go easily, exiting through a tunnel that she was sure would emerge beneath the piers of the docks.

Lessis ordered an immediate search of all shipping currently docked at Marneri, some thirty vessels in all. The search went on through the night, but not a trace was found.

By the light of morning Lessis knew that she had failed and that her enemy had escaped, probably in a small boat, and had abducted the preferred heir to the throne of Marneri.

Two ships put out at once, plus several boats, with orders to scour the sound for a small boat, but Lessis knew that nothing would be found.

When she reported to King Sanker later that morning, he was struggling to suppress the joy he so obviously felt. Later there was a brief funeral ceremony for poor Viuris, after which Lessis returned to her rooms, and after seeing that Relkin was recovering quickly, dropped off into an exhausted sleep.

CHAPTER SEVENTEEN

On the morning of the fourth day following the battle with the troll in the cellar of the Blackbird Inn, Lagdalen was summoned to Lady Flavia's office.

She received the message in the hospital where she was visiting Helena of Roth, who had recovered consciousness only the day before.

Helena would be in bed for a long time. It was suspected that her neck had been broken. Her face was bruised and swollen, and she was barely able to speak. Lagdalen winced at the sight of the cast on Helena's neck and mumbled something about hoping Helena would get well soon. Their eyes met then and Helena's were filled with surprise. Lagdalen of the Tarcho was the last person she would have expected to visit her.

Especially now that the little Tarcho brat was supposed to be a big hero!

So what was this? One heroine visiting another? Helena had awoken to discover that she was a heroine herself for having survived the attack of the enemy agent.

They had already tried to question her about him, but of course she had barely seen him. All she remembered was that dark, narrow face and those blazing eyes.

And then a nurse had brought Lagdalen a note from the Lady Flavia and the Tarcho brat had left. Helena wished it was Lagdalen in the hospital bed, while she was out in the air soaking up the adulation from the people. Life was just so unfair!

Lagdalen meanwhile had left the hospital at once and headed up the hill toward the Novitiate. It was a sunny day, warmer than it had been in a week or more. The city was bustling and alive, quite unaware of the terrible danger it had been in only four days before.

A troll inside the walls! Even now the thought of it was startling to Lagdalen. And when she recalled her own part in that adventure her hair rose, her skin went to goosebumps, and she tried her utmost not to remember the death of poor Viuris, or the body of the slain guardsman.

But Lagdalen now knew for certain that she lived in a time of great adventure and excitement. She had never felt this alive before. Each day was a wonderful day, like the greatest holiday she had ever had.

And how crowded these days had been.

First there had been the funeral for the Lady Viuris. She was buried in the Martyrs Cemetery down near Soundside. Lessis had given the oration, wearing a simple white gown, with her head bare and tears visible on her cheeks.

Abbess Plesenta had read from the Birrak, and then the Last Prayer had been lead by Lessis. The body, wrapped in a shroud of grey cloth, had been lowered into the narrow, plain grave.

The stone read simply: "Viuris of the Insight."

Lagdalen hadn't known Viuris very well, but she did know that she was a brave woman and a companion of Lessis. Anyone who worked for Lessis had to be an extraordinarily unusual and wonderful person.

After the ceremony Lagdalen had seen Lessis by the gate leading to Water Street. Lessis's eyes were grim, the tears were still wet on her cheeks. She'd nodded to Lagdalen and given her a long look before going on. It was as if she had just then decided something that had troubled her for a long time.

Lagdalen had waited for Abbess Plesenta to pass by, with her assistants around her, before she too slipped out into the street.

Since then she'd heard nothing of Lessis but rumors. Ships had been dispatched to the other cities of the Argonath. The counties had been raised right across Eardha. Search parties were covering all the north roads, and Lessis was said to be in the midst of innumerable wild and improbable adventures.

Of course Lagdalen's part in the episode of the troll had become known and she was famous in the Novitiate for it. And she had struggled not to feel proud as a result. But it was hard, for it was wonderful to be noted by everyone, and for being brave and at the center of things for once and not for being caught out with an elfboy in a cupboard. Even the seniors, who ordinarily wouldn't have acknowledged the existence of a junior, would nod to her and whisper behind her back. Some even said hello.

And yet she knew that her own role had not been particularly heroic. She had watched, legs frozen in terror, as the troll had come after her and she had done nothing. There'd been nothing she could have done. When she felt guilty she knew in her heart of hearts that it was she who should have died then and not Viuris.

Through the old Novitiate building she went, skipping up the well-worn stone steps. She reached Flavia's outer office and was directed through the inner door by the secretary.

For good reason she always felt a sense of dread when she was in this office, and she recalled at once the last visit here, just before Fundament Day.

It was a place of white walls and dark wooden furniture, in a stout, straightforward style known as "early colonial." On the walls were portraits of previous directors of the Novitiate. Flavia was waiting, looking as grim as ever. And in a chair to one side sat Relkin Orphanboy.

Lagdalen's eyes widened.

"Hello," she mouthed.

Relkin flashed her a look of warning, and she turned away at once.

"You sent for me, Lady Flavia?"

"I did, Lagdalen."

Lagdalen had heard that Relkin and Bazil had been

inducted into the New Legion. But she had not seen them for days.

"I summoned you because I have grave news for you. I am afraid this news will cause your father and mother great pain. And I am also afraid that it is you who will have to take the news to them."

Lagdalen felt her breath catch in her throat. What could this be? Was someone in the family dead? But why would they ask her to bear the news?

"It has come to our attention, you see, that the celebrated Broketail dragon, Bazil of Quosh, came here without a full dragon stamp."

Lagdalen felt her chest freeze. Flavia rolled on, unstoppable. "As you might imagine, the discovery of the treachery involving poor Smilgax of Troat brought a great deal of scrutiny to bear upon the offices involving dragons. The matter of the faked stamp for Bazil of Quosh came to light. Your colleague in crime over there has admitted his part in the matter."

Flavia glanced coldly in Relkin's direction and then back to Lagdalen. "He has implicated you. He has begged me to show leniency in your case and claims that he pressured you into breaking your vows and the laws of Marneri."

Lagdalen felt as if a heavy stone had replaced her heart in her chest. Of course! The Smilgax affair would have had them turning over every record in the Dragon Office. She was sunk. And she would have to tell her father! It would kill him.

"I have listened to his story very carefully and I have sifted through the evidence. There is no doubt in my mind that you broke your vows as a witch of the Novitiate and then broke the laws of this city as well. There is also no doubt that you did this as a personal favor for a friend. Such behavior is utterly unacceptable from someone in your position.

"So I am afraid I have no choice in the matter—the penalty is laid down very clearly. You are to be expelled from the Novitiate at once. You may apply to join the

New Legion's female auxiliary if you so desire. You will take this news to your parents for me and repeat it to them.''

Flavia had passed the sentence of doom. Lagdalen sagged in her seat. It had all been for nothing, all those long years of her education in the schools. All that time and effort spent to win a place in the Novitiate, and now she'd thrown it all away.

She avoided looking at Relkin Orphanboy. She thought if she did she'd burst into tears, and that she would not do in front of Lady Flavia. Lagdalen swallowed, fought back the tears.

"I am sorry, Lady Flavia. I thought it would only help if Bazil of Quosh could join the New Legion."

Flavia sighed, the poor child had a good heart.

"The Broketail dragon will do well in the legions, and you did not do wrong in thinking that. But what if it had been another Smilgax and this young rogue here was just another agent of the great enemy? Then you would have paved the way for another piece of great treachery. Our rules are what we survive by and if we break them we threaten our survival. This has to be understood by every novice of every class and every priestess of every rank.''

"Yes, m'Lady."

Flavia swung her fierce gaze across to Relkin.

"As for you, young man, I hope you understand as well. I must uphold the rules that bind together our mission. Without them we are poised for destruction. You have ruined Lagdalen's career in the Temple, and she was on her way to a great one.''

Relkin did at least appear genuinely contrite.

"I am sorry as well," he mumbled. "I did not think this would happen."

"Indeed," sniffed Flavia. "Well, you belong to the legion now and there's no point in raking this matter up. We are assured that there is no taint on either you or your dragon, and since you are shortly to be in Kenor we see no point in trying you in the city courts."

Relkin licked his lips nervously.

"Now you may go."

He got to his feet and tried to make eye contact with Lagdalen, but she refused to look his way and in the end he mumbled something inaudible and sidled out.

When the door closed behind him, Lagdalen felt tears welling up and was forced to dab them away with quick moves of her hands.

"I am sorry that it has come to this, Lagdalen of the Tarcho. A few days ago I thought that I might have finally gotten some sense into you, but it does appear that you are unable to grasp the fundamentals of our life in this institution."

Lagdalen stifled a sob. Flavia knew when to cut these things short. The girl was a trier, but she just could not submit to the sort of discipline that was necessary in the mission.

"You may go now, child. I think it would be best if you went at once to your parents and told them. Later you can collect your things."

Lagdalen went back out into the bright daylight but could hardly see a thing for the tears that were brimming in her eyes.

A touch on her shoulder turned her head.

A simply dressed woman in a grey robe was there. She was not much taller than Lagdalen herself and very slight.

Lessis!

She wore a grim little smile.

"Lagdalen of the Tarcho, I do believe you've been thrown out of the Novitiate, haven't you?"

"Yes, my lady. I broke the rules. I . . ." She trailed off.

"Good, you strike me as the sort that doesn't mind going around the rules. I have something to say to you, and you will have to make a great decision. The remainder of your life will rest upon it."

Lagdalen looked at her blankly. The tears were drying. She hated to seem weak when Lessis was talking to her.

"Look, we need your kind of spirit in the Office of

Insight. To be more specific, I need your kind of spirit. I want you to become my assistant.''

Lagdalen gasped. Was she dreaming? Suffering delusions?

"Would you be interested in this sort of life? One thing I can assure you, it will not be an easy one. Nor will it be dull.''

"I, my lady, yes, I would,'' Lagdalen stammered.

"Good. Then we'll go and see your parents together. You have your news for them from Lady Flavia, and I need to obtain their consent for your new posting to my office."

Lagdalen had to shake her head. One moment it was as if her life was over and lost in total failure, and now she was redeemed and offered the best opportunity she could ever have wished for. It was almost too exciting to believe.

CHAPTER EIGHTEEN

The winter was over, a hard one filled with snow and rumor of war away to the south in the land of the Teetol. Now fresh green clad the slopes, and though the streams still thundered with the snow melt, they were diminishing daily while the greater rivers rose downstream.

The little white flower called the snowprince by the colonists had already blossomed and gone, and now bluebells and scarlet amydine cloaked the glades and clearings.

In the woods the deer fed eagerly, replenishing themselves after the lean months of winter; the rabbits had their young, as did the foxes, and the migrating birds were back from their southern sojourns. The thrush's song was loud in the hemlock-clad valleys, and the too-whit was active in every hedgerow and farmer's field.

And with the spring came war. Raiders from the cold lands beyond the Oon, small armies of imps and trolls, under the command of fell men clad in the black uniform of Tummuz Orgmeen, came coursing through the forests intent on slaughter and the capture of women.

And to protect the villages of the colony lands came the legions of the Argonath.

In the lands closest to the Oon and the flat wastes of the Gan, the legions went in strength—brigades, even full legions on the march—each with five hundred horse and fifty dragons in support.

In the lands further east, where the colonies had been set firmly for fifty years or more, the patrols were made by smaller units, and often these units were under strength and the patrols themselves seen as quiet duty, handed out to units that had seen active service in the winter.

And thus the weary dragons of the 109th Dragon Squadron found themselves in the magnificent country of the Upper Argo, marching past lush pastures and wide forests.

After the long campaign in the winter snows against the Teetol the 109th was reduced to six dragons, six boys and two dragoneers. While replacements were sought they had been assigned to a patrol along the relatively tranquil zone of the Argo Valley between Mts. Ulmo and Red Oak.

Leaving Fort Dalhousie as the snow melted, they had marched east and south along the Razac road as it wound into the hills. As they climbed higher, the bends of the Argo became magnificent meanders carved into the mountains with vineyards perched on their steep slopes.

Now they were resting high above a serpentine bend of the river, not far from the town of Argo Landing. It was a warm sunny day, and from their position on the flank of Mt. Red Oak they looked out across a wide view of the lands across the river. The vast forest of Tunina

was flushed with fresh green, and on the east great Mt.
Snowgirt bulked up against the sky with rocky Mt. Raptor thrust out in front like a bent claw. On the west Mt.
Ulmo raised a great snow-covered dome high above the
land.

Around the dragons were the jumbled ruins of an ancient place, a temple from bygone Veronath, now lost in
the red oak woods.

Unfortunately this timeless peace was illusionary. Everyone knew that the ugly rumors they'd heard in Wide-
field and the lower valley were turning out to be true.

Raiders had been seen in Tunina. Now a party of imps
and trolls had crossed the Argo and caused massive panic
around Argo Landing. It looked as if the weary 109th
was going to be in the thick of fighting before long.

As they had marched into the country of the Upper
Argo so the stories had grown and magnified. Now they
had been confirmed. Sergeant Duxe had come round only
an hour earlier and warned everyone to see to swords and
helmets, shields and plate. The dragons sat back and
groused, while the dragonboys worked feverishly on
equipment.

Two men came around with the water jug and filled
their canteens. A single canteen was not enough for hot,
thirsty dragons and they went down to a nearby creek,
still running with snow melt and drank their fill before
plunging in and submerging themselves as far as was
possible in three feet of water.

They emerged refreshed but hungry, and it was hours
before the cookpots would come out and noodles were
boiled.

They returned to the laboring boys in better spirits but
complaining about their hunger. However, they complained in a cheerful ritualized way that told the boys the
great beasts were basically in a good mood. It was a
funny thing, but the prospect of combat always seemed
to arouse them, no matter how tired or worn.

Bazil found Relkin at work on Bazil's small tail sword;
he had the blade laid out on his lap while he honed its

edge with an angle stone. Behind the boy loomed the ten-foot-high head of some long-shattered statue. The head was upside down, where it had rolled and caught in a gap in the tumbledown wall of the ancient temple. A skeleton tree had grown over the head and put down snakelike roots all around it, but the eyes were still visible, staring out upside down at Mt. Ulmo and the lands to the north from whence had come the enemy that had destroyed the carvers of those eyes and thrust down their temples and their gods.

The dragon shifted and sat down on his haunches. From the way his tail flicked to and fro, and the happy hissing sound coming from the huge chest, Relkin knew Baz was relatively content although hungry.

Relkin finished with the blade of the small sword. It was sharp enough now to drive through anything once Bazil was wielding it on the end of that strange "broken" tail of his.

"The water was cold enough for you?" he said absently.

"Water damn fine cold, turn boy blue in seconds."

"Hmmm."

Relkin was examining his crossbow, an elegant little Cunfshon bow made from steelreed and bracken wire. It was light but strong and easy to wind up with the cunning little Cunfshon gears. A deadly weapon at forty yards and easy and quick to reload.

"I need some fletching. I'll be back in a few."

"Boy need many arrows since so few ever hit target. You go, get as many as you can carry."

"Mmmm."

But instead of seeking out the armorers, Relkin went down the line to the comissary wagon and called in a favor from Wilbry, the cookboy, and obtained a couple of loaves of unleavened bread. He split them in half and Wilbry smeared them thickly with "akh," the preferred flavoring on foods that were not meat but were intended for dragon maws.

Akh was prepared from onions, garlic, ginger and fermented sowberries; it was palate-numbing to humans in anything but the tiniest of doses, but the wingless dragons of the Argonath ate it with everything.

He sneaked back to the upside-down head and found Bazil examining his long sword Piocar, head bent over it while he hissed some rhyme in wyvern tongue.

Carefully Relkin slipped one loaf down behind a rock and then walked in with the other.

"I thought you might want this—we've had a long march today."

The dragon eyes fastened on him for a second, then the nostrils detected akh and the eyes switched down to the loaf, split and thickly plastered with the gummy brown sauce. Petulance was abandoned in an instant.

"Boy, you damned good sometimes, you know that?"

The loaf vanished in a matter of seconds, however. Relkin resumed the inspection of his arrows while watching Bazil out of the corner of his eye.

The dragon was fidgety. There was akh in the air, nearby, and it was enough to make a leatherback salivate. All at once the dragon brain reached the logical conclusion. Boy Relkin was playing his games again.

The dragon would have to ask, then beg, then promise something in return, before that second loaf, all thick with akh, would be given up.

Bazil sniffed. Unless, that is, he could find it simply by smelling it out. But of course he would have to do it in a dignified way; it would not do for a dragon to go crawling around looking for a loaf of damn bread and akh.

At least not while the boy was watching.

Relkin however seemed completely preoccupied with his bow. Bazil tensed himself to rise silently and move to his left where he sensed that the loaf covered in akh was hidden.

Relkin looked up, smiled blandly at the dragon and looked out over the river. A movement in the air caught his attention.

"Look, Baz!" He pointed.

A pair of hawks swung in lazy circles over the valley. They moved away and were joined by another pair. The four birds circled above the forest of Tunina, Mt. Snowgirt rising above the treeline.

"Snowgirt still has plenty of white on him, right down to the shoulders," said Relkin.

"It would be cooler up there in those north woods. But we must stay here and wait to fight imps and trolls. Such is a dragon's life."

"Not forever, Baz. Someday we retire. Maybe we could go and live in the forest there, in Tunina."

"Bah, elf forest! Infested with tree people and who knows what creatures; not right for dragons."

Relkin gazed out at the forest, a huge expanse of green. What might it be like to live there, as a forester, wild and free?

The woods teemed with deer and squirrel, wildfowl at the lakes and watercourses. The winters were harsh perhaps. One would have to get by on nuts and stored tubers, but it would be a free life without the daily constraints of a career in the legions.

Of course the elves did still rule in Tunina, so one would have to get along with the folk of the trees, but Relkin didn't think that would be too difficult. He had always found the wood folk to be easy to please and quite generous to those they deemed kind to their trees.

And what wonders might one glimpse, when the moon was full and the elf groves were alight with rituals and dances. Then their strange music would waft across the forest and enchant the ears of all who heard it, and the gross eyes of men might gaze upon the glories of elven life.

Bazil's long neck was strained to his left—somewhere over there was a loaf. The dragon stomach rumbled. One loaf was not enough.

Bazil looked back and the boy caught his eyes. Trapped!

"Boy, you have hungry dragon on your hands." An open admission was the only way out now.

"I know, I know, and this dragon is a weary dragon, too weary to lift a sword and hack down a few boughs for a dragonboy to sleep on, oh no, not when there's good hard ground for that boy."

"I was tired, very tired. You know how far we march yesterday?"

"Oh yes, I do, and I know which dragonboy kept some extra water and carried it half the day just so his dragon could wet his long, dry throat."

The dragon was contrite. "Alright, I admit it was wrong. In future I will always cut boughs for dragonboy to lie on, terrible to think of dragonboy resting his precious bones on cold, hard ground."

"Thank you, Bazil. Uh, there's a loaf with akh on it just over behind that broken pillar to your left."

The loaf was seized in moments and chewed enthusiastically. Damn dragonboys—they always knew how to get to one!

A crunch on the gravel behind them turned Relkin's head. Kepabar appeared out of the brush with his characteristic heavy tread while walking upright. Old Kep was the heaviest dragon in the unit now, a full "brasshide" with the armor plates of horn and bone that were typical of his breed. On the march, unlike the others, he frequently went down on all fours.

Behind him came Tomas, his dragonboy, a blue-eyed boy from the hardscrabble hills of Seant, across the long sound from Marneri.

Between old Kep and Bazil Broketail had grown up a dragon bond of friendship. They had fought side by side in the winter battles, and were now teamed with the freemartin Nesessitas for the left side of the squadron's formation.

They greeted each other with heavy slaps of the forepaws.

"I'm getting hungry enough to draw flame," grumbled Kepabar.

"Long day, walking and walking and no food for dragons," responded Bazil.

Well, almost. Bazil avoided looking at Relkin. Fortunately Kep had a dullard's nose and could not detect the faint odor of akh still in the air.

"Word is we're to move out again," said Tomas.

Relkin groaned—his legs ached from the five leagues they'd already covered that day. Tomas was agitated; he was always nervous before a fight.

"Are we going to fight today—that's what I'd like to know," said Tomas. "I hate to eat before a fight, it always makes me sick. But I'm really hungry now, and if we ain't going to fight then I need to eat something or my guts'll be rumbling all night."

Relkin had never suffered from this particular problem, but he tried to be sympathetic.

"Sergeant Duxe said to be ready. I think we'll fight."

"You do? That's depressing news, everyone's so tired."

Relkin shrugged. It had been a long day and he would have liked a good meal and a ten-hour stretch in his blanket, but if they had to fight then fight they would.

Relkin had seen a lot of fighting through the winter. There was a thread of steel through him now that had not been there before the campaign in the Teetol country.

"Well, Tomas, I guess it's just whatever-will-be, you know?" Whatever-will-be, the patron saint of the ordinary soldier. Tomas grunted unhappily, then pointed to the huge head.

"Who was that, do you think?"

"I don't know, but it looks very old."

"Ancients knew how to build," commented Bazil gruffly.

Kepabar stretched his limbs, one at a time, working the kinks of each muscle group in turn.

"Your feet hurt, Broketail?"

"Of course they hurt. We walk twenty days now. But at least we don't walk in snow. Do you think we're going to fight?"

"I don't know. I wish we could get some meat for

supper, though. It's been noodles and dumplings for days now.''

"If we fight there'll be troll to eat," said Bazil.

"Disgusting stuff, only in the last resort."

Bazil shrugged. "If you're going to be that finicky I don't know what we can do for you. Troll not that bad—you got to make it tender. Beat it with a flat sword, then grill it and have it with akh and wild onions.''

"Quoshite!" snorted Kepabar. "They taught you to eat all sorts of weird stuff down there, didn't they? Like fish. I bet you even ate fish." He said the last word with a peculiar tone of disgust.

Bazil guffawed. "Fish is good, very good especially roasted over hot coals, or baked in an oven. Mind you, I like it raw, too.''

Kepabar slapped a huge forepaw against his big belly.

"Ugh, you know they are right when they say that Quoshites are not like others.''

"Bluestone is the most beautiful land in the Argonath," said Relkin proudly.

"Ach, dragonboys!" grumped Kepabar. "Grilled troll for dinner, providing we fight.''

"We will, I think. I can feel it," said Relkin.

"Feel it? Can't count on feelings, boy Relkin.''

"I always get this feeling though, before we fight. I know it'll happen.''

"There are raiders out there. That much we do know," said Tomas.

Bazil gestured around them at the tumbled stones of the ancient temple. "Maybe this place of war god, eh? Maybe war god know that we will fight today. Maybe war god tell the boy, eh? You know boys are susceptible to these things.''

"Mmm." Kepabar looked at Tomas, who grinned back.

"I don't know," said Kep. "Some dragonboy have heads of wood, so I don't see how they could be susceptible to anything. Maybe Relkin is different.''

Tomas ignored this.

"I bet Marco will know who this place was built for."

Relkin nodded, "Possible, definitely possible. Marco grew up in the Argo country." But long before they saw Marco Veli, dragonboy for freemartin Nesessitas, the order to move forward came once again. With a collective groan they got to their feet, shouldered packs and gear and set off. They tramped through the tumbled stones of the ancient temple. Mysterious pylons, carved with the heavy runes of Veronath thrust up from the stones.

Then the temple was behind them and they moved on into the forest of oak, pine and hemlock that cloaked the mountainside at this elevation.

They came to an outlying piece of the temple, a small fane, with bas reliefs cut into the stone blocks. Sergeant Duxe, tall, pale and hard bitten, came by, marching at his habitual double stride, with his second in command, Poulters, breathing hard to keep up.

"Pick it up there," he demanded. "Go down this track until you see Lieutenant Weald. He will direct you to your places."

"We'll be fighting then, today, Sergeant?" said Tomas.

"You'll be fighting in less than twenty minutes, I'd say. Get moving. We've got our work cut out for us. There's a party of the enemy coming up the mountain and they're coming fast."

Standing by the fane, Relkin adjusted his quiver and looked up into the cold eyes of a face, carved long ago. War god? The face seemed fierce enough to Relkin. Would the god aid them in the upcoming fight? And if it did, how would they know? This was always the problem with the mystical realm for Relkin of Quosh. The signs were so subtle that one might easily mistake them for the actions of pure chance.

Of course there was always magic, and that was real enough, but Relkin was ignorant of the mystical background to the great art. Bored by the memorization of the Birrak he had shirked his few classes at the little temple in Quosh.

The fane fell behind and they went on down the track that led through the woods to a wide meadow.

CHAPTER NINETEEN

The raiders had first been spotted in the forest of Tunina, a mob of imps, squads of trolls, the whole under the direction of fell men on horseback.

First they were seen in the northern woods, crossing the Thun at the shallow ford of Riunna. Then they had come south along the flanks of great Snowgirt and rocky Raptor.

There, not far from the Argo itself, four hunters were surprised in their tents at night and taken. After questioning, three were eaten by the trolls. The fourth man escaped and ran all the way to the outposts at the landing.

Within hours the news sent tremors of alarm up and down the Argo country. It had been many years since such a large raid had reached this far back of the frontier.

The raiders had evaded the patrols of the militia and crossed the Argo somewhere upstream from the landing. They passed through the farm of the unfortunate Hansert Kapel. His body was found nailed to a lamppost at the crossroads, horribly mutilated.

Why the trolls had not eaten him was of course the major mystery to most. But even as they pondered this they got out their wagons, hitched up their mules and set out for the fort at Argo Landing.

When a party of girls aboard a coach was chased into the landing by a dozen imps, a general panic set in and the small towns along the Argo began to empty as their inhabitants went north to Dalhousie or south over the pass and into the Razac.

Farms were abandoned, cattle and pigs left behind to the ravening trolls, so great was the fear. It began to look as if the season's planting would be given up, and thus there would be no crops from the Upper Argo this year.

And then down the pike from Dalhousie came Captain Hollein Kesepton and his command, appearing in the nick of time. With him young Kesepton had seventy-eight men from the Marneri 13th Regiment, twenty-three troopers from the Sixth Talion Light Cavalry, and the six survivors of the 109th Dragon Squadron with their officers and handlers.

And of course this raid was the last thing Kesepton had been expecting. This patrol on the Upper Argo had been meant to give his small force a well-earned rest.

And thus young Hollein Kesepton faced an immediate crisis in his career as a full captain. Newly promoted during the winter, this was his first rank command in his own regiment. During the winter he had been a volunteer, seconded to a regiment in the New Legion, raised in Marneri the previous year and sent against the Teetol.

It had been a harrowing campaign with many casualties on both sides, and in the end the raid had failed to catch Wishing Blood, the war chief of the Shugga Teetol.

Hollein had proved himself in the assault on the Lodge of Elgoma. First he had steadied the men of Marneri who were on the verge of breaking under an intense assault from Teetol bowmen, and then he'd led them to rout the archers and drive them from the forest and into the killing ground outside Elgoma's walls.

And so here he was, the grandson of the great General Kesepton, now with his first real command, a battered company from that same New Marneri Legion, along with some Talionese horse who had also seen the winter out in the Teetol country.

To add to his difficulties he had the insubordinate Sergeant Duxe to run the 13th Marneri and the completely impossible Subadar Yortch in command of the Talionese horse.

Liepol Duxe was a dour, hard-nosed fellow contemptuous of weakness in others, a sergeant of the old school, quick with his sword and just as quick with criticisms. He had come up from the ranks of the Marneri First Legion and had seen action in ten years of fighting on the frontier.

Unfortunately, Duxe resented Hollein's swift rise to captain. Liepol put it down to the influence of General Kesepton working on behalf of his grandson. Liepol, like his men, had not been involved in the winter campaign and knew little of the young Kesepton's success at Elgoma's Lodge.

Hollein understood the sergeant's feelings and wished he could tell him that he was absurdly mistaken. If Duxe knew the general, he would have known that old Kesepton would never show the least sign of favor to a relative. The general was also a soldier of the old school. Alas, nothing could be said; Duxe would only take it as a sure sign of weakness, and that could not be allowed.

Furthermore, while Duxe was a handful, he was at least a known quantity. Subadar Yortch, on the other hand, was as close to impossible as an arrogant Talionese braggart could be. All pride, ferocity and stupidity, the subadar was two years older than Hollein and convinced that he, rather than this jumped-up half-captain of infantry, should be the commanding officer of the patrol.

Yortch had been a full subadar of light horse for three years and he found it hard to take orders from someone younger than himself.

Kesepton had ended the subadar's initial refusals to obey orders by announcing that he would place Yortch under arrest if he did not immediately obey. He would then be sent back to Dalhousie to face court martial. A great silence had fallen. Yortch had struggled with himself for thirty seconds while Kesepton and Lieutenant Weald had watched with fascinated eyes before he capitulated.

Reined in but still surly, Yortch exhibited all the baffling qualities of Talionese arrogance. Young Kesepton did not relish having to undertake a fight with Yortch as his cavalry arm, but he had no choice. Their mission to the Argo had plunged them into the thick of a bad situation.

The sheer presence of the men, the huge battledragons, the dust of their column had helped to calm the panic to a degree. But even as they marched around the bend of the Argo the smoke of burning farms on the hillsides began to rise into the sky. Gangs of evil imps were abroad, trolls had been seen eating cattle.

All day they had climbed the flank of Mt. Red Oak, passing through near deserted villages, with those smoke columns rising ahead of them above the trees.

In the mid-afternoon they were finally given a halt, and they rested among the ruins of the ancient temple not far from a broad meadow that extended far up the side of the mountain.

It was clear that they were getting close to the enemy now. The nearest smoke columns were less than a mile away. Kesepton sent out the Talionese to reconnoiter in the woodlands ahead, further down slope.

The troopers vanished into the woods and were gone. Half an hour later Kesepton heard the loud sounds of a running, slashing fight in the forest in front of them.

Warned by the sounds of combat from across the meadows, he ordered the men and dragons out of the temple and brought them forward to deploy in a line along the forest margin, men on either flank, dragons in the center.

Before it was done a lone rider came galloping back across the meadow with a message from Yortch.

The captain scanned it and conferred briefly with Lieutenant Weald. ''Yortch says we've got at least one hundred imps coming up the trail toward us, and more somewhere behind them.''

''Trolls?''

"No sign, yet. But they're out there—remember the report from Tunina."

Weald nodded gloomily. "Right. Well, we'll be formed up very shortly."

Kesepton looked across the meadow. It would be best if he could disengage the cavalry and pull them back for a mobile flanking force. He was outnumbered, heavily by some reports; it might be essential to keep the horsemen for a reserve element. Of course it would be difficult to get Yortch to disengage, however. He scribbled instructions on the reverse of the parchment and sent it back to Yortch. The rider thundered away.

Kesepton looked along the lines. Arranged just inside the margin of the forest, the men were set out in pairs, with bows and spears ready. On the order they could close up in a defensive phalanx or an offensive skirmishing line. In the center the dragons were massed, a solid bulk of thigh and sinew.

There was the sudden sound of horns, across the meadow, and a huge shout went up. The horns blared again—dull, heavy horns, not the cornets of Marneri or the bugles of Talion. These were the large brass horns of the enemy.

And there began the infernal yipping of charging imps.

Kesepton cursed under his breath. Too late now it seemed. What was Yortch doing?

There was motion now on the far side of the meadow; figures on horseback were galloping back. Arrows seemed to rain around them as they came, but by great good fortune none were hit and they continued to close up rapidly on Kesepton's line. Now behind them emerged a dark mass with horsemen in black uniforms at the front. The shrilling of imps grew very loud.

Weald was back. "Looks like more than a hundred to me, sir."

It looked that way to Kesepton, too.

"Damn those Talionese. I don't need a skirmishing line, I need a flank force."

"They're coming, sir. Looks like the subadar got into more of a fight than he bargained on."

A horse went down in that moment and the imps uttered a shriek of delight and rushed forward, nocking fresh arrows to their bows as they came.

An officer galloped back and snatched up the man and escaped with him clinging to the back of his saddle just ahead of the first arrows.

"They're brave enough these Talionese, they're just too damn difficult to work with," said Kesepton.

"Aye, sir," agreed Weald.

Now the Talionese began to thunder into the lines, passing through the men and then slowing in the underbrush and bunching up on the paths.

Yortch appeared last, with the unhorsed trooper on the back of his saddle. He paused beside Kesepton, who greeted him with upraised hand.

"Good of you to turn up, Subadar. I thought we'd lost you for the day there."

Yortch was aroused, his face flushed, his breathing hard. His wild corn-colored hair was escaping from beneath his helmet.

"My apologies, but we were detained by the enemy— they thirsted to taste our steel and we were forced to oblige them."

Kesepton sighed inwardly but bit back his reprimand.

"I want you to form your men up and keep them together behind the line now. Let them rest—we'll be needing them soon enough."

For once Yortch made no protest. He nodded his leonine head. "Yes, that's the best thing to do, I think."

Kesepton chuckled tightly and looked to Weald, who simply wore a resigned frown. "Carry on," said Kesepton. Yortch spurred his horse away. Hollein turned back to the meadow.

He immediately saw that which caused his heart to sink. Behind the imps came a party of tall, massive figures.

"By the blood," he murmured.

"Doesn't look good, sir—at least a dozen. Maroons, I'd say."

"Have the drags seen them?"

"Looks like it, sir."

And indeed there was a stir within the clump of dragons. Massive figures moved purposefully through the woods, big heads on long reptile necks craned to get a good view of the approaching trolls.

"We'd better brace these lines, Weald. I'll take the left—meet you back here shortly."

The officers turned their horses and moved away beneath the canopy of the forest.

CHAPTER TWENTY

With black pupils slitted, the dragons of the 109th watched the enemy surge forward across the meadow in a great dark mass, their high yipping war cry floating ahead of them. Great hands tightened on the hilts of swords, heavy muscles knotted in anticipation of the fray.

Then the imps slowed, sensing something amiss. The men they pursued had ceased their flight. With their sensitive feet the imps could tell that the horses had pulled up somewhere in the woodland ahead.

The treeline made a natural line of defense. Imp leaders, some as much as five and a half feet high, cast anxious looks ahead. The rest of the savage mob looked to the leaders for reassurance but found none.

The leatherclad men on horseback urged them forwards with oaths and threats. Always this was what the men did—the men were so cruel, so casual with the lives of imps. The very imps they depended on to do their fighting.

The imps threw up sharp complaints; in frustration they bashed their cutlasses against their heavy, square shields.

The men were adamant—they unsheathed their cat-o'-nine-tails. Urgently they swished them about.

The imps advanced, but they went at a tentative pace. As a result the long-legged trolls soon caught up and would have passed through their line but for the harsh cries of command from the men.

The imps complained again. Always the bloody trolls were kept safe from harm, always the imps were the ones that had to do the dirty work. The big maroon trolls snarled back things about the flavor of imp when cooked in certain ways, and the imps made scornful references to the lack of sexual organs among troll kind.

The men laid about themselves with their heavy whips to instill order and push the imps on while holding back the trolls until the enemy's dispositions were understood. Then the trolls would be sent in, to smash through the enemy line and break up their formations and open them up to the swarming attacks of the imps.

The waiting dragons rumbled with excitement, their fatigue completely forgotten. Their ferocious natures had bubbled to the surface once more, they were eager for battle.

Relkin had seen this war lust several times now, during the Teetol fighting, but it still made the hair on his neck rise. It was such an elemental thing, a surge of crazed energy. The dragons had gone into themselves, into a state where they wielded weapons with merciless energy and slew everything that stood before them.

The natural human instinct was to run away at once from these huge, dangerous creatures. Their wild cousins ate human beings, along with anything else they could catch, and in this battle mood they gave off a terrifying potential for carnage.

Driven forward by the harsh shouts of the men in black, the imps finally drew close to the defensive line. Suddenly the air was thick with arrows as the men of Marneri fired a volley.

Burly imps went down with shrieks of complaint. The imp majors lashed them on, the heavy horns blared. The imps stood their ground. They had little desire to go forward and receive more arrows. There was death in those woods for them; their coarse features were bent in frustration and rage.

But the cat-o'-nine-tails cracked down upon them and they knew that much worse awaited them if they did not obey. Their frustration built to a peak. Suddenly the mass of thick-limbed figures vented a shout and broke into a charge.

Across the remaining distance came a mob of muscular grotesques of more human form, most less than five feet tall, waving heavy cutlasses above their steel pot helmets.

Relkin sucked in a breath and raised his crossbow. This would be the true test for the 109th. Out beyond those imps stalked the trolls, brazen-skinned monsters nine feet tall. They had never fought trolls before. In the winter campaign they had faced simply the Teetol, and the Teetol for all their prowess as warriors were only human. Trolls were what battledragons were for.

Imp arrows came whistling through the leaves. Relkin pressed himself close to the tree. He glanced to his right. Bazil was waiting crouched over, with Piocar in hand. With his tail tip he held his small sword. Over his left arm he carried his shield, a buckler five feet across, made of triple-lapped steel and hides.

At the sight of Bazil Relkin's fears vanished. They were the fighting 109th, their foes would soon find out what that meant!

And then the imps were upon them.

A dozen or more of the squat shapes broke in on the dragons' front. The great wyverns rose up and long swords beat down on the imps, with flashes of steel and sparks of flame imp helms were sundered and bodies clove in two.

Aghast at this violence, the imps sprang backwards with the cry of "Gazak!", a most deadly word in their rough speech. Yes, filthy great Gazaki were waiting in these woods.

More imp shafts filled the air, and the heavy leather joboquin jackets worn by the dragons sprouted with arrows like a weird form of plumage. Kepabar, just beyond Bazil, uttered a thick curse as one arrow found a chink in the leather and pierced the flesh of his shield arm shoulder.

Tomas leapt up the mighty brasshide's flank and cut the shaft free. Kepabar growled with rage the whole time.

The imps had become cautious on this part of the line. Elsewhere they had crashed into the men with a thunder of steel on steel and successfully pressed them back with vigor, although the men fought with iron determination and soon would yield no further ground. Imp bodies piled up in front of them as the swordsmen engaged each imp to his front, while the spearsmen leaned past to jab and impale the thick-bodied enemy.

From the center the word went back to the men on horseback—filthy dragons are in the woods, they have killed five good imps!

The men conferred swiftly and then sent the trolls in fast. Half the trolls carried the heavy spear, the dragon lance. The heads of these were two-foot-long wedges of sharp steel, forged in the bowels of Tummuz Orgmeen. The other trolls bore immense axes, weapons that could cut a man in half as easily as a sword cutting through a rat.

Arrows flew, studding the trolls and eliciting moans of rage from their dull throats. They strode forward and crashed into the dragons waiting for them under the eaves of the forest.

The leading trolls attempted to spear the dragons, who defended with shield and sword and sought to clear the spears away and close with the trolls. Great swords flashed in the late afternoon sun, and treelimbs and brush flew around like chaff under the flails.

Bazil and Kepabar were in the center of the dragon mass. Four trolls, two armed with the long lance and two holding heavy two-handed axes, came up against them.

The imps gave way with shrill, exultant yipping but the trolls thrust forward with their lances and the dragons yielded ground, moving back between the larger trees, swinging their immense swords to cut away the lance heads.

Now four imps dashed in through the underbrush, seeking to hamstring the dragons hemmed in the thickets. As they came Relkin and Tomas loosed their crossbows and brought a pair down, bolts through the throat and eye. The remaining pair came on and met the swords of the dragonboys.

Relkin faced an imp that was shorter than himself but twice as broad. He ducked and darted and kept his sword flickering in the creature's face while it sought to reach him with its own heavier weapon. It was dangerous going, hampered by the trees around them. Relkin had a couple of close escapes before he managed to blood the imp with a thrust into its arm.

It shrieked its rage at him and lunged forward. Relkin tripped going backwards and went down with a thud right in the imp's path. It gave a triumphant bellow and raised its sword.

And then with a shrieking whistle Bazil's tail sword swept down and crashed full upon the imp's iron pot with a flash of bright sparks.

The imp went down in a heap and lay still.

Relkin jumped to his feet and drove in to distract the other imp as it fought with Tomas. It turned to block his thrust and Tomas at once jabbed his own sword into its side. It gave out a groan of despair and tumbled backwards. Tomas caught it another lick across the back before it was out of range.

Meanwhile, Kepabar had sundered the lance of one troll and was engaging one of the axe trolls. Kep's sword, "Gingle," slashed wide at the troll and buried itself in the side of a tree. With an oath the great brasshide struggled to remove it. The troll gave a gurgle of delight and swung the axe high, intending to cut Kepabar's arms at the elbow. But Relkin's arrow lodged in the side of its head and distracted it and the axe fell wide, thudding into the ground and sinking deep.

Kepabar abandoned his sword for a moment and drove a huge fist into the troll's midriff, which set it down on its haunches. It tore at the arrow in its head and succeeded in pulling it free. A gush of black fluids ran down its face and neck. Kepabar yanked Gingle free and charged. The troll barely scrambled back in time.

Elsewhere Bazil crashed chest to chest with another troll, and then wrested the dragon lance from its grip. The troll squealed with rage and kneed the dragon in the belly.

Bazil felt as if he'd been kicked by a stallion. He reeled back, but clutched hard on the dragon lance.

The other axe troll sought to reach him but was deterred by a slash of the tail sword. Then Kepabar's Gingle swung high again and clove the axe troll from shoulder to waist.

Without a sound it toppled and crashed to the ground.

The remaining trolls fell back with groans of dismay. Everywhere they had received stern punishment from the filthy Gazaki.

Two of their number were dead, for Nesessitas had disemboweled another with her swift sword "Mercuri." The rest had bruises and cuts aplenty.

Seeing the loss of enthusiasm among the trolls, the men sounded the dull horns to call off their forces. The imps and trolls disengaged and fell back, loosing more arrows as they went, until they were out of bowshot. And in truth they were as eager for a respite as the men of Marneri.

At once Hollein Kesepton moved up and down his line, heartening the men and reordering their positions.

There were three dead and a dozen wounded. Barely a fifth of the enemy's casualties but still enough to trouble

Kesepton. Among the dragons, Chektor and Vander had taken slight wounds from imps harrying at their legs.

"We held them, sir," said Weald, who had a small cut across the ridge of his nose from an imp cutlass.

"Aye, Lieutenant, we did, but they will come again. And now they know our strength and dispositions."

"It will not be easy to get those imps to charge again like that. They're damned unstable troops."

Kesepton smiled grimly. "Perhaps we can make them even more so." He turned his horse and threaded his way back through the trees to find Subadar Yortch.

He found him kneeling beside a wounded trooper, whose arm had been bandaged from wrist to shoulder.

"Your men fought well," said Yortch, getting to his feet.

"An experienced unit, Subadar—experience makes all the difference."

"But I disagree with the disposition. You should put two dragons at the ends of the line. The men were pushed back by the first shock—you need to anchor them."

Kesepton's mouth tightened. Did Yortch not see that that would leave the center open to a charge by the trolls, who would smash through and kill men and dragons in the resulting rout?

"I'll not be discussing my tactics with you, Subadar. Just assure me that your men can be mounted and taken out to the right flank. On my signal I want a flank charge, behind them when they come again. I want you to engage their leaders who hover there, out of bow shot."

Yortch nodded, thoughtfully. "Yes, it sounds good. I will do it."

Kesepton felt a vein in his temple throb. He fought to keep his voice under control.

"As quickly as you can then, Subadar. I expect a second charge any moment now."

Yortch nodded again. "Of course." He whistled and a man brought across his horse. He swung up into the saddle and gave Kesepton a mocking salute.

"And thus farewell, my Captain, for we go forth and

we may not return, I and my gallant band from Talion. Give good reckoning on us if you survive and we do not.''

Kesepton shook his head, and then laughed. ''Of course, Subadar, your courage had already been noted. Now drive that shock home when the time comes, harry them, and let us get to grips with them without their leaders being able to watch it all in calm repose from the rear.''

Kesepton wheeled about and galloped back to the front beneath the trees.

The enemy had formed up into two thick clumps, each with trolls in the center. The horsemen were yelling at them in their harsh tongue.

Liepol Duxe emerged from the brush on his right.

''What are they doing, do you think?'' said Duxe.

Kesepton shrugged slightly. ''They will charge, but this time in two divisions, seeking to concentrate their efforts on our flanks. They know they outnumber us.''

''The men are ready for them. The dragons also by all accounts.''

As if by magic Dragoneer Tetzarch appeared beside them.

''I heard that, Sergeant Duxe, and I can assure you that the 109th will be ready.'' Tetzarch was a tall, rangy fellow with premature grey hair and pale hazel eyes.

''The dragons fought well, Dragoneer,'' said Kesepton.

''No more than they would expect to, sir. They've become a seasoned bunch.''

''But this was their first taste of troll, I believe.''

The Tetzarch smiled. ''Actually they're discussing their first real taste of troll right now, and quite a lively discussion it is too.''

Kespeton and Duxe exchanged glances.

''Oh yes?''

''The Broketail says troll is best when marinated in wine and herbs. Kepabar won't agree, while Vander wants his raw and Chektor wants it boiled.''

Duxe's hollow laugh was rarely heard, but now it rang out sharp and distinctive and the men of Marneri looked up and were heartened. If Liepol Duxe thought the situation was that funny, then it could not be as bad as they had supposed.

CHAPTER TWENTY-ONE

Once more the horns brayed and the whips rose and fell. The imps thrust forward arrayed in a phalanx with spears leveled and shields raised and interlocked. Above them echoed their shrill war cry, adding to the din of horns and drums.

At the edge of the woods the men of Marneri met them with steel and shield, and once again the clang of metal resounded through the trees.

Kesepton gave the bugle cry to set Yortch in motion, and moments later the Talionese broke from the woods on the right and thundered towards the leather-clad horsemen behind the trolls.

In moments they were among them, and a snarling cavalry fight developed that moved away across the plain in a chaos of slashing swords and flying hooves.

Behind them in the thickets the fighting grew desperate. The imp majors knew that the men of Marneri could be easily flanked, and now parties of imps swung round and began to come in on the left and right.

Kesepton and Weald hurled themselves into the struggle on the right and beat back a dozen imps seeking to roll up the line.

On the left things held for a while, but then a dozen more imps broke in at the rear on the extreme end of the line and quickly produced a collapse. Kesepton got there just in time to rally the men and make a stand to hold back the onrushing imps, now baying through the brush.

For a few moments it was touch and go, but Sergeant Duxe killed the trooper leading the attack, and a few seconds later they broke and went streaming away under the trees.

Kesepton leaned against a small tree and took a deep breath. His sword arm already felt as heavy as a piece of lead, and he'd taken a solid blow to the ribs from a shield that sent waves of pain through him every time he moved.

"A well-struck blow, Sergeant," he said, nodding to the body of the enemy trooper. Duxe stood there, breathing hard, trembling slightly from the exertion and the stress.

"So much for the easy patrol they promised us in Dalhousie."

"So it seems," agreed Hollein. Duxe recovered himself and began sorting out the survivors of the flank party.

Weald had brought the horses up. The lieutenant had a cut on his forehead that had bled heavily and stained his face and breastplate red.

"Word from the center, sir."

Second Dragoneer Heltifer, a pale, slender youth with dirt all over his face, came up. He had terrible news. Sorik was down, a troll's lance in his guts.

A little frisson of fear lanced down Kesepton's spine. A dragon down already, reducing his small precious force of wyverns to just five effectives? His small force was overmatched here already—they could not afford many casualties.

What if they could not hold them? Could they last until dark and make a getaway then? With foreboding in his heart he worked his horse through the thickets back to the center and the dragon's position.

The place certainly looked as if a battle had been fought there. The first thing he saw was a very dead imp, impaled on a sapling. A little further on the brush was all chopped down and bloody.

Dragoneer Rosen Jaib was lying there, bleeding to

death from a severed artery in the neck. Hunched beside the boy was the dark mass of his dragon, mighty Vander. Wordlessly Kesepton and the great dragon exchanged looks and then Hollein went on, a great sadness in his heart.

And then beside a pile of dead imps lay Sorik, the stricken dragon. The vast bulk was propped against a tree. Dragonboys were attempting to staunch the blood-flow, but the lance had been well thrust home and was buried in the dragon's gut. Inflammation and infection would kill him if the blood loss did not.

Two of the other dragons, Nesessitas and great Kepabar, the brasshide, were crouched beside their dying leader. Kalstrul, Sorik's dragonboy, sat next to them, weeping.

Kesepton went close.

Dragon eyes turned on him with a blankness that was frightening.

"How is he?" Hollein managed to mumble.

Nesessitas heaved a vast sigh. She had been wounded too; there was dried blood encrusting her forearm.

"He dies."

"I am sorry. He was brave and a great fighter."

The dragons nodded faintly; none would disagree with such sentiments concerning great Sorik. Kalstrul wept but made no sound. Kesepton squatted beside him for a moment and put a hand on his shoulder. No words were necessary or possible, fortunately.

Dragoneer Tetzarch appeared out of the thickets.

"Captain, you should come and take a look on our front. Something is happening."

What now? thought Hollein Kesepton. The day was already black enough. He followed the dragoneer through the smashed brush, stepping over a dead troll which lay like a felled tree trunk in the midst of the tangle.

At the edge of the woods, Dragonboy Relkin was waiting; he pointed across the meadow.

It was hard to make things out at first, there was a

haze and the late afternoon light was deceptive, but then he realized what he was seeing and his heart sank.

"More of them," he groaned softly.

Another mass of imps was pouring out of the forest on the far side of the meadow, under the direction of a small group of horsemen. With them came more trolls, three at least.

"Where are Yortch and his men?" said Hollein, grasping for straws.

Tetzarch gestured down slope to the left.

"Somewhere far down there, pursuing the defeated foe." The Marneri man's contempt for the Talionese was plain.

Hollein cursed. Yortch was off on a wild cavalry jaunt, forgetting the main battle entirely. Possibly he had even decided to take his men out of it, back to the landing with the news that the Marneri unit had been annihilated and the Talionese were the only survivors. With Yortch anything was thinkable.

With an effort he controlled himself and muttered quietly, "Let's hope they get back here in time."

With grim faces the men of Marneri watched the new mass of imps join the first. The imp majors called for another charge and soon the mob came on, their infernal yipping cries rising high above the shock of battle.

And now it was very grim, for the flanks were bent back and back into a U and soon, Hollein knew it would be a circle and they would be completely surrounded. Meanwhile the trolls were back to full strength and the dragons were having a desperate time of it.

Men were going down here and there, and the imp arrows were coming in from all directions.

Hollein realized that the position was untenable. He convened with Duxe and Tetzarch. Weald joined them a moment later.

"We don't have much choice. We must retreat, pull back to the ruins of that temple and try to hold them off there."

"We cannot leave our wounded."

"Of course not."

"Some cannot be moved—they must not be left."

"Troll meat if we do," said Weald.

Hollein's mouth was dry, his pulse was racing. The imps were all about them, readying for another charge. Any time now they might break through and then it would be doom for all of them.

He made his decision.

"We cannot hold here, we must pull back. Give the orders. Ready the men for the cornet, on the third note we move as one. Detail men to bring those wounded that cannot walk."

"And Sorik?"

"Sorik is dead," said Tetzarch.

"Damn, that is bad news. To your stations—remember, on the third note we move."

Hollein ordered one badly wounded man lain over his horse, and then he gave the bridle to Kalstrul.

The cornet blew and the men and dragons moved back in skirmishing formation, lurching through the woods until they found the temple ruins once more, where they dug in and turned at bay.

"Here we stand and here we triumph or die," Hollein told Weald and Duxe.

Weald licked his lips. Death too soon was all he could think. He had had a long life ahead of him, ten years service in the legion and then retirement and a farm in Dalhousie. And now instead of that dream, a terrible death loomed with the subsequent ignominy of being devoured by trolls and imps.

Liepol Duxe merely straightened up and then spat on the ground. "We'll hold them. We have to," was all he said.

Kesepton concentrated the men on the corners of the temple dais with the dragons in the center. Anxiously they awaited the onslaught.

Suddenly huge rocks began landing among them. The trolls were pulling stones out of the outlying ruins and lobbing them into their position. Frantically the men huddled against the ruined wall for shelter.

The dragons moved for safety too, but not before poor Kepabar was struck on the helmet by a stone block and knocked senseless.

And now the horns resounded around them in the forest and the imps came piling in. Bazil and Relkin, with Nesessitas and Marco Veli, found themselves back beside the upturned head of the long forgotten god. The head lay between them and the enemy like a wall.

The enemy was coming, the yipping and drumming rising to a frenzy. But Relkin found himself floating beyond fear. An extraordinary calmness had come over him. Smoothly he loaded his bow and placed three other quarrels handy on the stone beside him. Then he turned to Marco Veli, an overeducated youth if ever there was one among the dragonboys.

"So Marco, who was this temple dedicated to?"

Marco laughed, for he had studied much of the lore of ancient Veronath.

"That's easy, this is one of Asgah's temples. He was the war god of the kings of Veronath. This very head is from one of his statues. In those days Veronath put fifty thousand pikemen in the field under Asgah's banner. Now he is a forgotten god."

"Bazil thought it would be a war god. We ought to dedicate the corpses of the enemy to old Asgah."

Marco chuckled mirthlessly. "Asgah, dead god of a dead world, if you hear us know this, the imps we slay here we dedicate to you!"

Marco looked to Relkin. "There, if he lives still in the shades, then he will know what we do here in his ancient place and he will approve."

And then the imps were upon them, running out of the brush with cutlasses waving above their heads. Behind them came the trolls, and Bazil and Nesessitas lurched out and met them head on.

Bows sang, arrows flew and a couple of imps crashed to the ground. The rest came on in a hurrying horde.

Huge swords whirled and clanged off troll shields and helms. Bazil evaded the thrusts of two trolls with lances and Piocar snapped back in their faces. Then a third troll swung a heavy mace at him and missed by a hairbreadth and struck the huge head of the long dead god.

The head wobbled alarmingly as if it might roll over. Relkin jumped back—if it rolled it could crush them like grain beneath a millstone.

And now a troll clashed up against Bazil, their shields rang noisily on the first clash and the troll was knocked back.

The troll pushed its helmet more tightly on its head and surged back to the attack with a snarl.

Piocar sang in Bazil's hands, but both behemoths were restricted by the stone walls around them, limiting their swordplay. Bazil did get in a solid blow to the troll's shield however, and knocked the creature to its knees for a moment.

Then it recovered and brought its axe round in a whirling slice that would have sundered Bazil's neck had he not pulled back sharply.

An imp ran in, his sword out, looking to slice the dragon's hamstrings, but Relkin was there and he met the imp with an arrow at close range that suddenly sprouted from the imp's right eye.

Bazil struck the troll again it wobbled backwards, almost trampling on some imps hemmed in behind its bulk. Arrows flew from both sides. Bazil had three sticking out of his right shoulder in a moment.

Relkin shot another imp and then the troll was back, joined by a second. Bazil exchanged snarls with them and then they were at him.

He was protected by the stone head of Asgah and dodged a lance thrust. Piocar swung in a massive overhand cut and clove the nearest troll's shield in half.

That troll staggered away with one arm half severed at the elbow. The one with the lance drove in again and Bazil only just put his shield up in time to deflect it.

The troll clambered over the tumbled stones and grappled with the dragon. Bazil was hampered by his shield and was jerked off balance for a moment. A huge maroon fist slammed into Bazil's tender nose.

The Quoshite bellowed with pain and jabbed his sword hilt into the troll's face. It stumbled backwards, roaring. The other one was getting back on its feet. Relkin put an arrow into its chest with no visible effect. Then the imps surged back around the trolls and climbed the wall. Men pushed past Relkin and engaged them at the crest. Relkin strung another arrow and loosed it into the packed mass of imps.

Bazil struck with Piocar and again steel shrieked in complaint and great sparks went sizzling over the heads of the hurrying imps.

More men came up, surging forward to stem the tide of imps. Two more trolls appeared, and while one engaged Bazil again the other hammered at the men, knocking them down with stunning blows from a giant mace.

Relkin ducked under the enormous sweep of that mace and thrust with his own sword at the creature's knee.

It bellowed in pain and black blood spurted. A hand swung down surprisingly swiftly and caught Relkin a glancing blow that was enough to send him staggering back against Asgah's head.

All the breath was knocked from his body. He could barely move. An imp closed in, its sword swinging, ready to take his head.

And Bazil's tail mace struck backwards and smashed the imp across the back and knocked it flat.

Relkin got to his feet, slowly, and dodged back out of the way of an imp with a spear. The spearhead sank into a small tree with a crisp sound. Relkin used his sword to deflect another spear and tried to slice the imp wielding it but missed.

A soldier beside him suddenly staggered under an arrow through the throat, and before he could move again an imp thrust a sword through his belly and he went down.

Relkin parried the next thrust from the imp and saw Cowstrap, the company smith, knock its shield aside and hack it across the belly.

A troll crashed to the ground on the other side and Relkin jumped. The troll's head rolled away from the body, severed by Piocar. Bazil stood over the troll's body and swept Piocar as if he were scything tall grass and hewed through the imps in front of him.

Relkin looked past the Broketail dragon and saw Nesessitas throw down another troll and then end its life with her sword. But dozens more imps were coming and were jammed up on the far side of Asgah's head.

Bazil felt a sudden inspiration. Another troll had clambered over the wall and leapt upon him. Bazil dropped his sword, knocked the monster's axe with his shield and got both hands around the troll's waist.

With a quick heave he jerked the surprised monster off the ground and lifted it over his head. The troll gave an odd cry of dismay—trolls fear any dislocation between themselves and the earth. Then Bazil swung the creature and dashed it against the upside down god's head.

The troll collapsed, all the fight gone out of it, but the huge head wobbled and then rolled over onto the massed imps on the far side.

With shrieks of dismay they were crushed and milled and the head kept rolling until it had resumed an upright position once more, the face of ancient Asgah staring back at the dragons and boys with a sneer of cold command that had once been well-known to his worshipers.

"Asgah!" yelled Marco Veli, and his cry was echoed by the other boys.

Asgah had heard their call!

There was a breathing space now on their front, although elsewhere the fighting went on, hard and heavy. Some trolls were now attempting to climb the ruined wall and get in among the exhausted men of Marneri.

With little sobs of effort, Bazil and Nesessitas roused themselves and staggered into the fray, huge swords whirling.

Bazil was immediately lucky, his first stroke took the arm off a troll and stopped its charge. The next one behind it was encumbered with the first and unable to do more than defend itself for a while.

Nesessitas was not quite so fortunate. The troll there had already gotten over the top of the tumbledown wall; it jumped down and dealt her a massive blow on the shield that almost toppled her. Then the troll axe swung hard at her head and caught her a glancing blow on the helmet. Nesessitas was rocked backwards, stunned momentarily and unable to fight. A gap was opened in the line.

Men ran up and hewed furiously at the monster and succeeded in distracting its attention. With a snarl of fury it swept its axe through them like a scythe through corn, chopped two men in twain and scattered them.

Grim-faced the other men held on, refusing to flee, their swords slashing into the troll's flesh from left and right. Black troll blood flowed among them, making the stones slippery, but still the creature stood firm while another was already climbing over to join the first.

Then great Vander swung in and stunned the troll with a terrific overhand cut to its helm that sent blue sparks flashing over the men's heads. While it was motionless Nesessitas recovered herself and smashed it across the side of the head with the flat of her sword and sent it sprawling. The men finished it off with their swords and knives.

Vander was already engaging the next troll.

But now the imps were coming back, in greater numbers than before, and there were only a few desperate men, the dragonboys and Dragoneer Tetzarch to face them.

Tetzarch called out a great cry to rally them and then collapsed as an arrow slipped through a gap between his chest plate and his heavy belt. When they turned him over, he was dead.

Then the imps were upon them. Relkin fired an arrow, then dropped his bow and drew his sword. An imp swung at his head; he ducked and jabbed the creature in the leg above the knee. It dropped its shield and drove at him and he was pushed back by its superior strength and almost overthrown.

He clung to his balance by the thinnest of margins and then struck down over the shield and caught the imp on the side of the head and knocked its helmet free. The imp threw him off the shield and cleaved the space where he'd been, but Relkin had darted sideways and now repeated his trick, jumping to greet the shield, leaning over and striking down on the imp's bare head. It went down with a groan.

There was no time to feel any sense of triumph or revulsion at the deed for the next was upon him, and behind it were more, many more.

The end loomed for all of them, for it was the same on every side. They were less than fifty and they were surrounded by three hundred or more enemies.

On the other flank Hollein Kesepton exchanged exhausted looks with Duxe and Weald. They all sensed the approaching end.

And then floating over the tumult of the imp drums and their infernal battle cries came the sound of bugles and cornets, high and silvery. And then with time a great shout as if half a legion were there.

"We're saved!" shouted Weald.

"A relief column," said Duxe. "But how?"

The cornets sounded again; one, two, three, four of them. And there was another shout.

"No time for questions," said Hollein. "Blow the cornets, we will charge. Now!"

"Charge? But we've got less than fifty men on their feet and only four dragons."

"Doesn't matter—the enemy is wavering, listen."

And it was true, the drums had ceased, the horns no longer brayed. And once more came the clamor of bright cornets, the clarion of the legions.

Kesepton grabbed up a cornet and began blowing the charge. Duxe ran down the line and shouted to the men, and someone else took up the other cornet and blew it too, and the men reached down into themselves for the last fraction of their strength and came up with a great shout. They stormed over the ruined wall and hurled themselves upon the foe.

The imps were irresolute, terrified of being taken at the rear, and now came the men they had ground down to the point of defeat, flying at them with steel and fury in their eyes. With a collective shriek the imps broke, suddenly, completely, and ran streaming away through the trees as witless as rabbits, dropping weapons, shields and anything that might impede their flight.

And after them came the survivors of the 13th Marneri harrying them all the way out onto the meadow, where by a stroke of fortune, Subadar Yortch and his weary horsemen were just then returning from routing the enemy riders.

Yortch sent his troopers into the fleeing imp horde at once, and they never regained their formations and fled in a panicked mass all the way to the Argo where many drowned as they milled about at the fords.

Only the trolls remained, and these had to be surrounded and shot full of arrows until they finally gave up the ghost and fell to the ground and lay still.

At which point, Hollein Kesepton rode briskly across the meadow in search of the reinforcements, whose horns had saved the day but who had not made an appearance.

He entered the woods. There was no sign of a legion or even a company. No sign that there had been anyone at all.

Baffled, he rode further on. They had all heard it; the damned imps had heard it and run. So where were they, those who had blown those wonderful horns?

The sun was setting and throwing somber, reddish light across the field as he returned, a puzzled frown etched on his forehead. Weald met him, his helmet replaced by a large bandage.

"Well, sir, where are they? What happened to them?"

Hollein shook his head. "There's no one out there, Weald, no one at all."

Lieutenant Weald stared at him with startled eyes, then looked over to the woods.

"The men were talking about the dead god Asgah, did you hear?"

"No. Asgah?"

"Veronath god of war. That was his temple. They say his fallen head rolled over and crushed a dozen imps at one point."

Hollein snorted in disbelief.

"You think it was Asgah blowing the cornets we heard?"

"I don't know, but if there's no one out there and we definitely heard the horns, then . . ." Weald's eyes probed the murk over the field.

Hollein Kesepton shrugged, at a loss for an explanation. Could the old gods still live? Weren't they all dead and gone, replaced by the Great Mother? Hollein was not a great believer in gods or even the goddess, but now he was sorely perplexed.

At length he mumbled, "Gods or human, I don't know who it was and I guess I don't care, but they damn well saved our lives. Without that threat I don't think we'd have lived to see this sunset."

Weald had an odd smile. "The dragons are going to burn the trolls on Asgah's temple floor, they think he might appreciate them as a burnt offering."

"That's going to make a stink fit for a god, alright."

They rode back towards the campfires.

CHAPTER TWENTY-TWO

By the time the very last rays had fled from the field, the survivors were counted and organized into burial parties.

Of the seventy-eight men of the Marneri 13th there were nineteen to be buried and another twenty with wounds ranging from cuts to sword thrusts through the belly. The medics were sure that at least three more would die in the night.

Of the Talionese horse, seven men were missing, presumed dead somewhere between the field and the distant Argo, to which Yortch had pursued the enemy horsemen. Another five bore wounds that would keep them from active duty for the rest of the season.

And of the 109th dragons, there were but four fit for duty plus poor Kepabar, whose head was still ringing from the rock that had laid him out cold.

While the men buried their dead, Yortch sent some troopers to round up wagons from the nearby farms to carry the wounded down to the landing. Meanwhile, the dragons and dragonboys cut brush and piled it up to form a vast bier upon which the dragons then laid the body of Sorik.

As dusk faded, Relkin and Tomas lit a small fire with which they set several large torches ablaze. The dragons then thrust these into the great mound of brush and set it alight. At first there were just clouds of smoke, but then quite suddenly the flames took and presently a great blaze roared up, with sparks whirling high into the air.

Now the blaze threw a harsh red light over the scene and sent spectral shadows across the meadow from the mounds of dead imps and trolls that had been piled up nearby.

Local people began to arrive, bringing wagons with food and ale, supplies that were much appreciated by the both the men and the dragons. Soon the cookfires were lit and cauldrons of polenta and pasta were bubbling.

The dragons drank beer at their usual frightening rate, and then began to sing the low, mournful dirge for the dead. The huge, heavy voices of the great wyverns rang off the rocks of Mt. Red Oak and carried away into the valley and were heard miles off, where people stepped out of doors and stared up towards the mountain with wondering eyes.

However, when the first cauldrons of noodles arrived the great reptiles ceased their song. Like everyone else in the legions the dragons subsisted on wheat, most commonly in the form of pasta. No other food was as immune to spoilage and so light and durable. Dragons spiced up their noodles with akh. Humans spiced theirs with milder preparations.

After they'd eaten their usual prodigious helpings, the dragons took up the beer kegs again and resumed the dirge. More locals had arrived by then, and there was quite a crowd gathered on the field by the time the dirge came to an end.

And now the dragons laid themselves down to sleep, each beside his or her dragonboy, with the light of the huge bier throwing somber shadows across the field.

There was however no sleep yet for Hollein Kesepton. After some extensive persuasion he had induced Yortch to send out scouting patrols. With their reports and those of the local people, who were coming in thick and strong now, he knew that the bulk of the enemy force had fragmented and fled down to the bottomlands along the Argo. Some had crossed into Tunina and disappeared into the great forest. Others had been rounded up by posses of those farmers who had stayed on their lands.

The enemy riders had also been dispersed. Six had been captured and were held in the stockade at Argo

Landing, another had been killed in a fight at the cross-roads south of the landing. The rest were across the Argo, scattered through the great forest.

Still there was the possibility of more raiders at any time, and Kesepton found himself surrounded by anxious farmers who were demanding protection for their properties. With only thirty-nine soldiers, four dragons and eleven cavalry troopers at his disposal, Kesepton could not protect very many farms. Indeed his entire force was in a state close to collapse.

If more raiders showed themselves in the next few days, he doubted very much if he could offer battle without reinforcements from Dalhousie.

Hollein had never been to Argo Landing, but from what he knew of the dimensions of the fort he would need more than fifty men just to man its fortifications. Of course the townsfolk would help, they were already showing themselves to be bold enough now that the main enemy force had been broken and driven from the field. But for the farmers with their tales of fear and woe he had nothing to offer. Privately, Hollein was wondering just how long it might take for reinforcements to reach him. If he sent a message by trooper to Dalhousie in the morning, it would get there within three days, providing the rains didn't make the road impassable. After that it might take anywhere up to a month before help could reach him. At any time during that period his force could be overwhelmed if the enemy came again. It was not a reassuring prospect.

The huge funeral pyre for Sorik was still blazing high, and the smell of incinerating dragon flesh was spreading in a great plume on the winds, borne to the north and west.

Kesepton struggled to keep his temper during a half dozen further passionate appeals for immediate patrols to particular farms where it was feared that imps might be hiding. His men were exhausted; nothing more could be expected from them that night. At last Lieutenant Weald relieved him and he waved aside the farmers.

Weald spoke quietly in his ear.

"We're set up on the other side of those cookfires. Your tent is up and there's some food set aside for you there." And so Hollein finally sat down, just outside his tent, and ate and drank and tried to relax with a second mug of ale.

Slowly the battle tension was leaving him. Whatever might happen in the next few weeks, there was going to be no more fighting tonight or tomorrow. He could allow himself to sleep.

But before sleep could finally claim him, a sentry gave a call and shortly afterwards two slim figures in the all-grey robes of the Sisterhood appeared before him. He struggled to get to his feet. A woman with a cool, gentle voice spoke quickly.

"Captain, you have given all your strength today, do not stand for us. Let us sit with you. We have things to talk about, you and I."

He looked up at her for a moment and saw a woman of some beauty, with delicate features, a wide face and high cheekbones. She was of indeterminate age, but not young, and though very pale not colorless. It was her eyes that gripped him, however; they were large and luminous and a soft grey.

Her companion was much younger, a mere girl, and quite beautiful with reddened cheeks and lively brown eyes.

"Welcome to you both, Sisters. Sit by me, tell me what news you bring."

The Sisters, old and young, sat without ceremony and immediately investigated the cook pot.

"Army noodles, I've always loved them," said the older woman.

"I'm afraid that's all we have to offer."

"I thank you, Captain, and we will accept gladly."

The younger Sister filled a couple of small bowls and tipped a little of the local sweet and sour sauce over them before handing one to the older Sister.

"Where have you come from?" said Hollein.

"From the south, climbing old Red Oak all day."

"Ah ha," said Hollein. "Perhaps you can help solve our mystery. We heard the horns of some troops in that direction, just an hour or so past, but we have yet to sight them. Did you perhaps pass them on your travels?"

The younger Sister stifled a giggle and looked down into the pot of noodles. The older one shrugged.

"No, we did not. We have been in the thickets. Possibly we were even lost."

"Hah, now that I won't believe. The Sisters in Grey are never lost."

She smiled. "I thank you for the compliment and I wish it were as true as you so confidently proclaim it."

Hollein, though tired to exhaustion, felt inexplicably cheered by the presence of this woman.

Witch! he thought to himself. *She has cast some spell here, but my ordinary senses were too crude to detect it.*

"Let me introduce myself, Captain. My name is Lessis, and this is my assistant Lagdalen of the Tarcho."

Hollein thought he had heard that first name somewhere, but he could not place it immediately.

"Hollein Kesepton, lady. And over there somewhere is my lieutenant, Sandron Weald. We are the Thirteenth Marneri with elements of the Sixth Talion Light Horse and the 109th Dragons."

"You fought long and hard today, Captain."

He swilled down the last of the ale in his mug.

"Damn close thing it was, too close. I wish I could find the other force that's out there somewhere. I just don't understand it—they never made contact."

Lessis smiled again.

"Perhaps what you heard was not made by soldiers."

"What? But we heard the cornets. Some say it was Asgah, some ancient war god that used to rule these parts, but it sounded real enough to me and no ghostly apparition."

Lessis cocked her hands to her mouth and suddenly blew into them. Crystal clear, the sound of a Marneri cornet signaling the charge rang out.

Hollein stared for a full three seconds. Then he slapped his palm on his knee and roared.

"Well, I'll be. So much for Asgah! You were the relief force! Just the two of you."

She nodded. "I'm afraid so, Hollein Kesepton. We saw that you were in need of assistance, and fortunately the enemy was fooled long enough to enable you to rally your men and dragons."

He nodded. "Damned right. We cut them to pieces after that. But we were fighting back to back before then."

"Granted." She smiled again. "But then our entire enterprise in the Argonath is a close run thing, and we must needs rise above ourselves time after time to defeat our great enemy."

Hollein's sense of wonderment overcame his disappointment at there not being a relief force out there in the woods. Just these two Sisters, and one of them a young girl, and they had helped turn the tide of the battle.

"No wonder we couldn't find anyone! But tell me now, how did you get lost? You must have been close by to hear us fighting in the first place."

"We were delayed in coming on. I had to find a messenger and teach it how to speak."

His eyebrows rose of their own accord. Witch-speaking!

"Well, I won't ask you more about that!"

"It is not as difficult as you perhaps think," she murmured.

At that moment Weald came round the cookfires and joined them.

"Duxe has posted sentries, and we have a half dozen farmers with horses riding down to the landing to bring in more reports."

Hollein nodded acknowledgment of this news and then gestured to the two Sisters in grey.

"Prepare yourself for a surprise, Lieutenant."

Weald looked up, his sand-colored eyes alert.

"Surprise?"

"This is Sister Lessis and Sister Lagdalen. They were the ones who saved our skins a couple of hours back."

Weald goggled. "They what?"

"They can blow their own cornets."

Lessis blew another short cornet note in her hands.

Weald scratched his head. "Well now I've heard everything."

"Hardly, dear sir," said Lessis. "But let me congratulate you on your performance today—you all fought extremely well."

Weald recovered. "My lady, we fought well because we would have been annihilated if we had not. We came close to ending this day as troll meat, all of us."

"Well do I know that, Lieutenant Weald."

For a moment they fell silent, the men astonished, Lessis mulling over her next approach.

"Well, I have a feeling that you want something of us, lady," said Kesepton at last.

She nodded and seemed to consider her words very carefully.

"Indeed I do. I am going to ask you to accept a most hazardous mission and to render service far above the call of duty for I don't know how long. You will be exposed to dangers that may even make this grisly day seem pleasant by comparison."

She said this so clearly and flatly that for a moment the men just stared back.

"Well," began Hollein, swallowing heavily. Now what was he getting into? His native caution was roused.

"No, you must hear me out, Captain." She raised a slender hand.

With a feeling that he was going to regret this, he sat back and listened.

"First I must explain. We are in pursuit of a most dangerous agent of the enemy. This agent has abducted the heiress to the throne of Marneri, the Princess Besita."

"She lives then?" said Hollein, surprised. "We had heard that she was dead."

"No, she was abducted by this man. All winter we have chased him through the cities of the Argonath. Finally we sprung a trap in Talion, but he was forewarned by a traitor and escaped us. Now he approaches the forest road through Tunina. We must intercept him there."

"What strength has he?" said Hollein.

"He will meet with a force of imps and trolls that lingers in the shadows of Mt. Snowgirt. That is why we need your assistance."

Hollein nodded. The winter campaign, then this terrible battle, and now more fighting in the ancient forest of Tunina. There was no respite.

"We are much reduced in strength and barely fit to march, let alone fight."

"I understand that, Captain. However, you are the only force within range that can be brought to bear on this enemy before he gets past our defenses and escapes onto the Gan. Our chances of capturing him there and recovering the princess are very slight. And once she has been taken into the City of the Skull she will no longer be fit to rule in Marneri."

Hollein shrugged. "So Erald will be king, as is the king's wish now. Everyone knows it."

"Erald is a willful cretin; he is young and playful and to an extent quite vicious. He cannot be allowed to sit the throne of Marneri."

Hollein bit his lip before speaking. "Should not the will of the king and his people be respected?"

"Of course, but in some cases the people are ignorant of the truth in such a matter. Erald has been made popular by distribution of largesse, by his father's manipulation of opinion. On his own Erald would soon be overwhelmed by his advisors, and these he will never choose wisely. I know that the men of Argonath resist the guidance of the empire in these things, but for now that guidance is necessary. All we have achieved still lies in the balance and our great enemy rouses itself once more.''

"The men of Marneri have no wish for women's rule. Else they would go to Cunfshon and accept the yoke.''

Lessis snorted and looked down.

"The men of Marneri have survived by their strength and their guile. What little rule there has been from the isles has surely not caused any great harm.''

Hollein nodded. "No, you're right. But I bristle at the idea that the witches will so casually interfere in the succession of the throne.''

Lessis sighed and shrugged. "It would be better if we did not, I grant you that. But in this circumstance it would be a disaster of the first rank if we allowed Erald to become the next King of Marneri.''

"There are some that would say I commit treason by even speaking to you concerning this.''

"Indeed, but they would be wrong, as you know.'' She spread her hands. "Come, Captain Kesepton, be honest with me. Surely the best interests of the city of Marneri and thereby of the entire Argonath would be served if a rational, sane person sat the throne there, rather than a confused child who will be preyed on by the corrupt and ambitious.''

Hollein shrugged. "Well, yes.''

"Then will you accompany us into Tunina?''

"I'll need orders concerning this. My current orders restrict me to this side of the Argo.''

She pursed her lips. "Of course, I understand that. We will send my messenger to Fort Dalhousie tonight and tomorrow he will return with your orders.''

"Dalhousie is three, four days ride from here.''

"My messenger does not ride upon the land, Captain.'' She cupped her hands again and blew, but this time, instead of the bugle call of the Marneri cornet, there came a curious hoot. A few moments later with a soft flapping of enormous wings a great owl flew in and landed on the top of Kesepton's tent pole.

Lessis blew again and held up her staff. The owl gave a flap and landed beside her.

"This is my messenger, Chinook of Red Oak. He has an active mind but one that is hard to reach with human concerns."

Hollein stared at the owl. It was enormous. Suddenly the head swiveled and the huge eyes stared back at him. What kind of understanding lurked within those ferocious orbs? Hollein was impressed.

"Well then," he said. "Dispatch him and let us see what the authorities in Dalhousie have to say about this."

How an owl was going to communicate with General Hektor was something Hollein remained curious about.

Lessis spoke to the owl in little mews and hoots and whispers while she scribbled a note on a scrap of parchment and tied it to the bird's leg with a piece of string. It shifted uneasily and lifted its foot and pecked at the parchment but did not dislodge it. Lessis spoke some more and passed her hand over the huge eyes, and it blinked then stretched its wings and flew away on huge, soft wing beats.

Lessis turned back to Kesepton. "We will have your orders by tomorrow, but we cannot remain here and wait upon them. We must move across the Argo tomorrow morning. We have a long way to go to reach the intercept point."

"You ask much of me, Sister Lessis. Without orders I cannot do this. I would face a court martial."

"You will have orders, Captain, from myself. Believe me when I tell you no one will challenge you on this."

Hollein whistled. "To the contrary, I think it would mean the end of my career in the legion."

Lessis tone became steely.

"Captain, do not mistake me in these simple grey robes. I am a direct representative of the Imperial Council. In legion rank I would be a general officer, do you understand? You will be operating under my command from here on."

He swallowed again, this promised to be more trouble than any battle. His command to be given up to a witch?

What would Liepol Duxe and Yortch have to say about this?

Lessis was speaking again. "We must move tomorrow because we have an appointment with my friends in the forest."

"Friends?"

"Yes, the elves of Matugolin. They have scouted the road and will have news of the movements of the enemy."

Hollein felt his blood cool. "The elves of Tunina are no friends of the Argonath, a wild strange breed, hostile to all."

Lessis accepted this with a weary smile.

"Alas, the folk of Matugolin have been much abused over the years. These good people of the Argo have not behaved well towards the elves. As a result the folk of Matugolin are cursed and reviled; that is the guilt in people coming to the fore. But I can assure you that the green folk are still ready to fight the power of the enemy."

"You speak as if you know them well, these wild elves."

"I do." She said it simply, and he believed her.

He saw that the younger Sister was looking at him with a gleam of interest. She was an attractive young woman. Hollein could not resist looking at her more carefully. She blushed then and looked away from him.

She lingered in his thoughts, however. How young she seemed. And yet she was an escort for this Lessis. And with Lessis Hollein knew well that he was in the presence of one of the Great Witches, a legendary force. Such witches were very few in number but their influence was enormous. This girl was thus made privy to great secrets. She was being groomed for that world of spies and agents and mysterious errands through the netherworlds that went on somewhere just beyond the perceptions of the rest of the people.

Hollein wondered if she would survive the challenges ahead of her. Would she be a Great Witch someday?

"Well," said Hollein, "I must see some proof that you are who you say you are. I know that you control the great magic, but so does our enemy."

Lessis's eyes sparkled with fire for but a bare half second. When she spoke she remained quite calm and unconcerned.

"Of course, young Captain, and you will have it. But do not think that the enemy controls the great magic. The enemy's arts are of the false magic—they trade on fear and superstition. There is no reverence, no feeling for life. Their charms and tricks are always cold and painful. They give no nurture."

"I am happy to be rebuked then, such matters are not my province. We in the legion follow a more linear, restrained mode of thought."

"Indeed, and so it should be. You are soldiers not spies. Believe me when I tell you how much the emperor and all his council value your courage and skill in war. You provide us with the rapier by which we puncture each of our enemy's greater designs. What we in the Sisterhood do is to provide a shield, so each of us serves in an essential way."

She paused, exchanged a glance with her assistant and then turned back to him.

"And now, Captain, I think we should go down to the surgeon's tent and lend our skills to the doctors. There are many badly wounded men."

Hollein would have gotten to his feet to bid them farewell, but they both reached out to touch his arms.

"Do not get up, young Captain," said Lessis. "Save all your strength for the morrow."

Lessis and Lagdalen moved away from the captain's tent. When they were safely out of earshot, Lagdalen spoke.

"Can the bird really cover that much distance so quickly?"

"He can. He will be hungry afterwards, so I tremble

for the squirrels of Red Oak, but he will be back tomorrow. Rassulane can speak the tongue of the owls and she will bear my message to General Hektor. A relief column will be here within the next week or so.''

CHAPTER TWENTY-THREE

The dawn came bright and chilly on the high slopes of Mt. Red Oak. Relkin awoke to find brilliant sunlight all about him while the camp slowly stirred to life.

He discovered that Bazil had already gone off to drink and wallow in the stream. There was time to get the sleep out of his eyes and take some breakfast. The smell of griddle cakes and katlu, the dark coffee of Ourdh upon which the legions of Argonath depended, was coming from the cook pit.

He stirred himself. His body was sore, especially his shield arm, which had taken a pounding the day before. When he walked he found his right leg had an ache in the thigh and a very tender ankle.

Beyond the camp the great funeral pyre for Sorik had burned down to a mound of smouldering embers. The sound of men digging came from the meadow. There were a group of local gravediggers at work creating a communal grave for the enemy dead.

A few legionaires were up, taking breakfast or lining up at the field-smithy to repair weapons, helmets and shields, all of which had taken a beating the day before. The smith had several fires going and the sounds of the bellows whooshing mingled with the clang of hammer on metal.

Relkin's first priority that day was to rebandage the cut on Bazil's shield arm and to get the shield itself repaired.

The smith would not be looking forward to that job. But Relkin realized that all the dragons must have taken damage to their shields and weapons. Yesterday's fighting had been the hottest they had seen since the assault on Elgoma's Lodge. The smith and his assistants would be working until well past nightfall for the next few days.

A group of men were standing by the cookfire eating wheat cakes and gulping down hot, black kalut. As they ate they chatted. Relkin's ears pricked up as he heard what they were saying.

Two Grey Sisters had come in the night, and Kesepton had given orders that what was left of the command was to accompany these Sisters across the Argo into the great forest. There was the likelihood of more fighting in the near future, too.

Relkin took some rolls and some polenta cake, plus a mug of the hot brew. He ate quickly, listening to the men complain about being suddenly thrown into danger again, with more miles of marching ahead. Everyone felt much too worn down for this. Another battle was out of the question. They were barely more than a third of a company, how could they be expected to fight without reinforcement?

When he'd finished Relkin went back to his sleeping place. Bazil's weapons were stacked there along with his shield, helmet and armor.

Piocar was too long and heavy for Relkin to work with easily, and by common consent Bazil took care of his own sword. The big leatherback had a mystical communion with that blade anyway and spent many hours polishing and caring for it. But the tail sword, the mace, the helmet and all the rest, they were Relkin's to keep repaired and ready.

He had pulled out the most damaged things, other than the shield, and was about to head for the smith's fires when a figure stepped in front of him.

He saw the grey robes and the brown eyes, heard his name and felt his heart leap.

"Lagdalen!"

"Relkin Orphanboy, greetings to you, mighty warrior."

She was smiling, amused and pleased at the same time. She had grown since he'd last seen her, back in Marneri. Her voice had changed, sounding much less like a girl now. He noticed other things, there was a sense of maturity about this Lagdalen. She was a woman now.

"So you were one of the Grey Sisters I heard talk about this morning."

"Yes, we got here late last night. The Lady Lessis was in deep discussion with your commanding officers for a while. Indeed it was a busy night."

"Well, we had a busy day of it yesterday. Bazil was very fierce with the trolls, killed three himself."

She nodded. "We have been up with the surgeons through the night. There was much work to do, it was pretty grim."

Her eyes seemed to pierce him then. He shivered—he never liked to see the surgeons at work, it was indeed most grim.

"Yes, I'm sure it was. We all came close to ending as meat for trolls yesterday."

"But the victory was yours," she said with a smile. "The enemy were swept from the field."

At which point he remembered the end of the battle. Where were the reinforcements? He looked around but saw no regimental banner other than that of the 13th Marneri. It was quite mystifying.

"It was confusing, I still don't understand."

She was giving him that piercing gaze again.

"And you have become a fiercer fellow than the Relkin I knew in Marneri."

He returned her gaze. "And you have grown up, Lagdalen of the Tarcho."

She giggled and looked for a moment like the girl he remembered.

"It seems an age has passed since we were in Marneri together," he said. "What happened there after we marched out?"

"Not much," she said. "It does seem as if it was years ago, does it not? But that's because we've been so busy ever since. I have been to every city in the Argonath now: Bea, Volut, Kadein. Oh, how I loved Kadein. The women there dress with the most wonderful taste; the city is so sophisticated, compared with Marneri. Someday I would like to live there, I think."

Women always loved their first visit to Kadein; Relkin had heard this a dozen times or more. Well, at least Lagdalen seemed to have forgiven him for his role in her expulsion from the Novitiate.

"And what brings you to old Red Oak here in Argo?"

"We are on the same business. All winter we have been chasing Thrembode the magician. He still has the Princess Besita, but the Lady Lessis thinks we have him trapped at last. Your dragons are going to come with us into Tunina, where we'll head him off and capture him."

Relkin whistled. "I'm afraid this lot of dragons won't be worth much for a while. We took a beating yesterday."

Her face had become grave. "We will have to find a second wind, Relkin, all of us, for we cross the Argo this morning."

Relkin stared at her. "It can't be true."

"Oh but it is, there's no time to waste. We must meet with the elves of Matugolin today. We will fight tomorrow."

"Oh, Lagdalen, you have indeed become a Grey Sister. Already you bring tidings of woe to us. We ache and must bind up our wounds, all the equipment is notched and cut, and you tell me we have to march this morning."

She seemed unaffected. "Alas, there's no alternative, my friend. We must make one more effort and save the princess."

Shortly after that she excused herself and left on an errand for the Lady Lessis, with a promise to meet with him later to tell him all about her adventures and hear about his, and he went on down to the smithy fire with Bazil's hacked-up shield.

CHAPTER TWENTY-FOUR

The forest of Tunina was a dark, haunted place. Enormous groves of hemlocks crowded the stream bottoms. On higher slopes massive oaks spread their branches beside maples and ash.

Along a winding trail through these great trees came the weary men and dragons of Captain Kesepton's command.

Kesepton had mounted all his men, and his supply wagons had taken fresh horses too, so they had made good time except for the dragons, who were close to exhaustion and had fallen some ways behind.

The dragons were less than happy with this situation. Kepabar was still suffering from a tremendous headache. Only Bazil and Nesessitas were in any way fit to march all day. The dragonboys had a difficult time keeping the dragons moving and out of the streams they passed.

To make things worse, swarms of deer flies attacked the dragons along the way and the boys were busy swatting the pesky things with their leather belts. All the dragons were at the limits of their patience and ready to commit murder.

Relkin and Bazil were in the lead by this point. Relkin had stripped to the waist to ward off the heat. For a spring day it was murderously hot and humid. And since Bazil was far too worn to carry him in addition to his equipment, Relkin had had to walk all day. His leg ached and his feet hurt and he wanted to lie down and sleep for a very long time.

The infantry and the cavalry had moved steadily ahead and were now a mile or more in front of them, at least Relkin could see no sign of them except the trail they'd left.

From occasional glimpses of the sun he knew that the afternoon was waning. He wondered how long it would be before they could stop and rest. He was sure that all the dragons, and their dragonboys, would be asleep in a matter of seconds following the command to halt.

The path ahead was bisected by a small stream, and on the far side it ran between two massive oaks. Bazil had sworn that he was going to stop and drink at the next stream and cool his aching feet in the cold water. Relkin wasn't going to say a thing in protest. Let Liepol Duxe come back and talk to the dragons himself. The great beasts were close to the breaking point.

Abruptly, slender figures appeared in that gap beyond the stream. Relkin saw them and gaped.

Elves! The wild folk of the trees. Holding bows and arrows, arrows no doubt tipped with one of their deadly poisons. The elves did not look at all friendly.

Relkin tried not to move, not to excite them. There could be an army of these grim-faced folk surrounding them.

Bazil suddenly shook to a stop. Tired as he was, the leatherback had only now noticed the elves.

"Fool boy, we have trouble. Look ahead."

"I see them, Baz. Tunina elves."

Everyone else had seen them now. Dragoneer Heltifer, who now commanded the 109th, moved cautiously to the front. "Does anyone speak the forest tongue?" he said in a very quiet voice. No one, not even Marco Veli, replied to that.

More elves were becoming visible on either side. They kept their bows cocked, with slender arrows ready to deal death to man or beast.

"Hail!" said Heltifer finally.

The elves by the stream moved aside and another figure appeared, this one clad in the feathered costume that denoted rank among the green forest people.

"What is this?" grumbled Bazil.

"Someone of great importance, that's all I know," said Relkin.

Dragoneer Heltifer rounded on them. "Quiet! Wait for them to speak."

Bazil snorted irritably and rested on his sword. "We're supposed to meet with elves today anyway, that's what I heard," he said in a mutinous whisper.

"Silence," said Heltifer.

The feathered elf approached.

"Greetings!" it said, and raised a hand, palm toward them.

"Well, at least it speaks the tongue of the Argonath," said Relkin.

"We come in peace," said Heltifer nervously.

"You come to Tunina, and you bring wyverns. You bring trouble to Tunina."

Heltifer winced at that; the elves were supposed to regard them as allies on this venture.

"Look, we're bringing up the rear on the company, everyone else is up ahead. Don't you want to talk to Captain Kesepton?"

The feathered elf came closer. He was a typical example of his kind, of medium height and slender build with the deep set eyes and long narrow jaw that always denoted elf rather than man. Relkin could see the green flecks, like little triangles, that mottled his skin.

Equally obvious was the fact that this elf lord was angry.

"No, the captain will not listen to us," he hissed. "We talk with you to tell you to take the wyverns from our sacred woods."

Heltifer looked around him helplessly. "But we are supposed to meet with the elves of Matugolin."

"I am Prince Afead. This part of Tunina is my fief, I do not agree that wyverns can come here."

Relkin spoke up. "But there are trolls coming here. Without the dragons we cannot stop them."

"Bah, leave them be and they will soon go. They mean no harm to elf folk."

"I must confer with the captain," said Heltifer with a note of desperate confusion.

"No!" said the elf in a loud voice, raising his hand. "You will turn now and go back."

Bazil and Nesessitas were growing restless. Big Vander was coming up to take a look at this. Relkin had a premonition of disaster. Bad-tempered dragons and intemperate forest elves could produce a battle right here and ruin everyone's plans.

Finally Bazil leant over Heltifer and muttered, "Tell this tree person to get out of way. I am going to put my feet in the stream."

Relkin heard that and moved to Heltifer's side.

"Baz, are you sure that's the best thing to do right now?"

"Yes."

Nesessitas was restless too. "My feet are just as hot— I too will place them in the cool water," she said.

Relkin turned to her with his voice tight. Nesessitas was usually the most reasonable of the drags in the 109th.

"And we will then be fighting for our lives with who knows how many elves. Those arrows are poisoned."

"I will get new dragonboy," said Baz calmly. "My feet come first."

"Oh thanks, that's great to know. New dragonboy. And what about dragons that get so pricked with arrows that they die of the poison too?"

"Tragedy for dragons, tragedy for boys, but right now it is tragedy for feet."

And with that all the dragons moved forward in a mass and sat themselves in the stream with huge groans of pleasure.

The astonished elf lord stared at them with bulging eyes. Then he began to rave in the forest tongue.

Relkin was on the point of reaching for his own bow

in the impossible hope of living long enough to fire back at the archers he knew were aiming at them at that very moment.

Over his shoulder he heard dragonboys grumbling.

"This is a bloody stupid way to get killed!" groused Marco Veli.

"Damned right, we're supposed to be on the same side with these hotspurs," said Rosen Jaib.

"Hot arrows is more like it," said Relkin.

And then they heard another sound, a shout from up ahead and then three sharp notes on the cornet and then several riders came cantering down the trail on the far side of the elves.

A moment later Lessis on a slender white mare and an elf riding a similar graceful, small-boned horse, had reined in beside the stream where the dragons sat, cooling their blistered feet.

This elf lord was clad in a costume of red and blue feathers, a small jacket, breeches and a headdress. He said something in the forest tongue to Lessis, who replied with something that made the red and blue elf lord roar with laughter.

Then he got off his horse and crossed the stream just above the dragons, strode up to Prince Afead and began berating him in a low, angry voice. Afead huffed and puffed in reply, but it was obvious that he was outranked and knew it.

Some more riders had appeared: Subadar Yortch, a couple of his men, and Lieutenant Weald. Their horses seemed huge standing next to the forest ponies of the elves.

Lessis had dismounted and now joined the two elf lords on the far side of the stream. Relkin watched her move diplomatically between the elf king, Matugolin, and the haughty Prince Afead. First she made the king laugh. Then she took Afead's arm and walked away with him for a few paces and spoke in a soothing voice. Afead muttered and grumbled, but when they came back to Matugolin, Afead bent his knee and kissed the king's hand.

Matugolin then embraced the prince and bellowed something. The prince seemed to take this well and embraced the king in return. Then they turned back to the waiting men, elves and dragons.

Lessis noticed Relkin close by and nodded to him. "Well met, Relkin of Quosh. Lagdalen told me you were here."

"Well met, lady," stammered Relkin, still awed by the speed with which she'd settled down the high-strung elf prince.

Now the king went down to the stream and addressed the dragons.

"Great wyverns, please forgive the foolish pronouncements of Prince Afead. I am King Matugolin and I welcome you to Tunina." The dragons were cooling their feet with gasps of pleasure. They gave little heed to the elf king. Dragoneer Heltifer was too stunned to say anything. Relkin seized the moment, moved to the front and gave a deep bow.

"On behalf of the dragons of the 109th Dragon Squadron, I thank you, oh great king."

He noticed Lessis looking at him with a pleased expression. Encouraged, he went on. "Right now the dragons are too afflicted with sore feet to reply with fair words and courtesy, but I know that they would like me to extend my thanks to you on their behalf."

King Matugolin blinked at him and looked at Lessis for a moment, then broke out into a smile and turned back to the elf archers and cried out something in the forest tongue.

The arrows went back into their quivers and their bows went back over their shoulders.

CHAPTER TWENTY-FIVE

By nightfall Kesepton's men and dragons were setting up camp in a clearing deep in the great forest. They had covered two-thirds of the distance to the old trade trail, which ran east-west through the forest of Tunina and was the most likely route for Thrembode to take.

Fires were blazing and Cowstrap the smith went to work on a mountain of repairs and welds that had yet to be done. It seemed impossible to finish it all. However, no sooner had he and his men struck hammer to steel than a half dozen elf smiths came out of the trees, staggering under the weight of anvils and sacks of charcoal.

As the men watched wide-eyed, the elves started more fires and unpacked bellows and hammers and small bags of dry weld. They had clearly come to work.

Cowstrap and his assistant Rogin were quick to recover from their initial surprise, however.

"Welcome to the firepit," said Cowstrap. "Long have I admired the skill of the elf smiths of old."

One elf, an elder with white hair and a luxuriant mustache, spoke for the others in turn. "We thank you for your welcome, and we will show you that the skills of our forebears are not lost."

A loitering dragonboy was dispatched to beg Captain Hollein for a small jug of whisky to fire up the spirits of the smiths. Hollein gave his assent and soon the smiths, men and elves, raised the jug in a circle to toast this historic occasion in the forest of Tunina.

Then the elves fell upon the work ahead with cries of anticipation. There were a dozen Marneri swords that were notched or broken. Then there were the cut shields and the damaged pieces of armor. All these pieces were made for men and were thus much heavier and more robust than comparable pieces would be for elven warriors.

"You think that is work?" said Cowstrap, and he showed them Bazil Broketail's damaged shield and Nesessitas's notched tail sword.

The elves gasped at the size and heft of these things. Then they clapped their hands together and broke into excited chatter among themselves. The bellows roared and quickly their fires grew hot.

By the time Relkin returned with Bazil's helmet, which had taken a dent sometime in the heat of the battle, he found a hectic scene.

The massive shield, the size of a door, had been heated over a pair of fires until the damaged areas were red hot. Now elves with slender hammers were at work, smoothing out the torn metal and working in one of their magical welds.

Cowstrap took the helmet from Relkin's hands.

"Looks like we'll need to hammer that out. Your dragon must have been sore under that."

"He's sore enough, but he'll fight tomorrow if we have to. Of course, whether he fights after that will depend on that shield they're working on."

Cowstrap nodded and chuckled. "I reckon that shield will be stronger than it was brand new. They're a wonder with those welds."

Relkin noticed the regimental whiskey jug. His eyes lit up. "Is there anything left in that?"

Cowstrap looked up at him, then grunted. "There is, but it's not for the likes of you. I've got a half dozen elves here and this is thirsty work." He paused and grinned. "And besides you're too young for it."

"I am not!" exclaimed Relkin, stung by this accusation. "I'm fifteen and I have seen five battles. I have drunk whiskey before."

"I'll tell you what," snorted Cowstrap, "you square it with the captain, see, and I'll give you half a mug."

Relkin turned away in disappointment. He knew better than to ask the captain. Chagrined, he strode away. He was a seasoned campaigner and they wouldn't let him touch a drop of the regimental whisky. It seemed very unfair.

"Next," said Cowstrap. Relkin saw Tomas stagger forward with Kepabar's mangled helmet.

Relkin made his way to the cookpit where they were preparing the evening noodles and waited there to take a big bowl back to the dragon lines. He was still there when Lagdalen appeared quietly out of the dark.

"Lagdalen," he called.

"Relkin. So you survived the march."

"Only just. A certain Prince Afead took a dislike to having the dragons on his fief."

"I heard about that. The elves of Tunina have a proscription on wild dragons, poisonous snakes and manticores."

"Manticores?"

"Lion-headed men—they died out long ago. At least in this part of the world."

"Now you sound like Marco Veli, who tends Nesessitas. He knows everything too."

Lagdalen laughed. "I have learned so much. Just being in Lessis's company makes you learn things, like the weight of a thrush's song, or how to spin the Birrak or the fate of the manticores in Eardha."

Relkin could not fail to notice how lovely Lagdalen became when she laughed like that. He wished once again that he was a lot older than he was. They had both grown up since Fundament Day in Marneri, but Relkin was keenly aware that he was still just a dragonboy, not even a dragoneer yet, while Lagdalen was constantly at the side of the Lady Lessis, constantly involved at the highest levels of the struggle. He felt distinctly envious.

"And do you know what we will do tomorrow?" he said.

She nodded cautiously. "We will fight, all of us. Our enemy comes—he will have the advantage of numbers."

"How many?"

"A hundred imps or more, five trolls at least."

"We don't have enough men."

"There will be two hundred elves fighting with us. Their arrows will help."

"Not with the trolls. Trolls don't care about poison."

Lagdalen nodded sadly. "The dragons will have to destroy the trolls."

"The drags are not at their best. Kepabar is still seeing double. Vander and Chektor have sore feet."

"We will be with you, and the lady will think of ways to even the odds."

Lagdalen spoke with a peculiar certainty about this. Relkin reflected after a moment that she probably knew something that he did not.

"Still there will be hard fighting—five fresh trolls, a hundred imps—we will need everything we have."

"I will be there, Relkin," she said. She pulled aside her robe and he saw strapped to her waist a short sword.

She drew it and showed it to him; it was a Kadein stabbing sword, light and sharp with a narrow blade some two feet long.

"I'll be proud to fight beside you, Lagdalen of the Tarcho. I remember the way you fired that stone at me— I expect you're good with that overgrown dagger."

She put it away and shifted as if embarrassed, which she was by this display. She wondered what had gotten into her. This was not the sort of behavior that Lessis would approve of.

"Well, I'm taking lessons in how to use it. To tell the truth I haven't wielded it in a real fight yet, and I certainly haven't drawn blood."

"Tomorrow's your chance then," he said. Then he was signaled to approach the cooks, who had a big bushel bowl full of noodles lathered with akh.

Relkin staggered away with it in his arms and lurched back to the dragon line. He found Bazil sitting alone, working on the edge of Piocar with a whetstone. The leatherback looked up with big, eager eyes and gave his chops a heavy lick.

"Ah hah, dragonboy finally bring back some food for starving dragon."

"As quick as they could dish it up, Baz. We're getting the first boil."

Bazil put aside Piocar and took up bowl and fork. First he doled out a boy-sized helping to Relkin, who ate out of his steel pot helmet.

"Less akh," said Relkin.

"Nonsense, akh good for you just like it good for dragon. Noodles boring without it. In fact noodles without akh make dragons go back to meat diet, which means end of dragonboys."

"Which would mean end of back scratches and scale rubs."

"Yes, that is true, so best we have plenty of akh, eh?"

There was no sound but the sound of dragon and boy feeding for a few minutes, then Bazil sat back and belched. He had eaten half the bushel bowl and had satisfied his immediate hunger.

"So what will happen tomorrow?" he asked the boy.

"We fight. There are five trolls."

"Damn, with Kepabar knocked silly we will be down to four tired dragons."

"Kep can fight."

"We hope—I have my doubts." Baz raked through the noodles. "Why is there so little akh? You know I like plenty of akh."

"There's only so much to go round—we don't know how long we may be marching."

"Bah, we need dragon cook. It was good in Dalhousie where we had cooks who knew how to cook for dragons."

"Why didn't you take some of those trolls you killed? I thought you were going to roast them."

"Too heavy to carry troll meat all the way up here. But if there isn't more akh tomorrow, then dragon will have to supplement diet with whatever he can catch."

At this Baz gave his long jaws a snap and Relkin finished up his own bowl in silence. The morrow was likely to be a long and tiring day, and he just hoped there would be some dragons left alive at the end of it to worry about the amount of akh they got on their noodles.

And while dragonboys worried about the morrow's battle, their captain was already fighting a battle, albeit with his senior officers. In his tent on the far side of the cookpit, as far as possible from the pounding smiths, he was engaged in a fierce argument with Duxe and Yortch, neither of whom thought they should be giving battle on the say-so of the Lady in Grey.

"We're so under strength I'm having to compress all our formations. We don't even have enough spears. And you want to risk everything in a fight for some elves on the orders of a Cunfshon witch?" Duxe spoke while giving him a stubborn look.

"Sergeant, we must fight. The woman has the rank to command it, and she says we fight to rescue the Princess Besita."

"Bah," said Yortch. "You are men! Why are you fighting to bring on the rule of women in Marneri?"

"Keep out of this, Talion," snapped Kesepton. "The succession to the throne of Marnerei is our business not yours."

"It is mine when my captain intends to throw away the lives of my men on the orders of a witch."

"You refuse to serve the emperor, is that it?"

Yortch colored. "Of course not."

"Well, the witch is from his council; she speaks with the emperor's voice."

"How can we be sure of that? How can we be certain we're not being used for their own purposes. The witches want a queen, that's natural enough—they always want queens rather than kings."

"I don't think that's true, and in this case there are special circumstances."

But Duxe was not having it. "No, Yortch has it right. The damn witches want to supplant Erald and give us that silly baggage Besita for our queen. Then the witches will be able to do anything they want in Marneri, and they'll start by raising taxes. You mark my words, they'll be taxing the water and the air next.''

"Look," said Kesepton, struggling to be reasonable, "you know that Erald is too weak in the head to be king. There's no choice except Besita, unless we turn aside from the line of Sanker and look among the noble houses.''

"And start a civil war that will destroy Marneri? Of course not." Duxe was simmering with anger and frustration. "But you want us to fight tomorrow without orders from Dalhousie. If you're wrong and this witch is playing some game of her own, then we'll all hang.''

"The witch sent for orders.''

"So you told me. She talks to wild birds and animals, she probably talks to the trees as well, and this is the person you think is fit to give orders to the Thirteenth Marneri?''

"She is of the council, Sergeant.''

"Damn the council, I'm talking about our lives.''

And at that very moment the guard pulled open the entrance to the tent to announce the Lady Lessis.

"Send her in," said Hollein after a long moment of silence.

Duxe snorted. Yortch muttered a charm against witches under his breath.

Lessis was as bright-eyed as ever, unassuming, clad in plain grey, slight and yet filling the tent with her presence.

"Greetings, gentlemen. I believe you are discussing the curse of women's rule." Her smile had grown slightly frosty.

Duxe colored; Yortch stared at her with insulting disdain.

"Something of that sort," said Hollein after an uncomfortable silence.

"No offense, my lady," began Duxe.

"No offense taken, Sergeant Duxe. You want what's

best for your men, I understand that. It is not my choice that we fight this battle tomorrow. But if we are to rescue Princess Besita, then we must fight and we must win.''

"But is Besita any improvement over Erald?'' said Duxe. "Why must we have the rule of a silly woman over that of an addled boy?''

Lessis nodded as if recognizing that there was something to these arguments.

"Of course, of course, such questions must be faced. Besita lacks the will of King Sanker perhaps, and she has made many questionable decisions. However we feel that she will be more susceptible to good sense once she is queen. She responds well to responsibility. Alas, young Erald does not. We fear a disaster for Marneri if he should mount the throne. He speaks for instance of coming to the frontier with his entourage to take control of the Marneri legions to fight with them as a separate army. How would you and your men fare then, Sergeant Duxe?''

Duxe had paled. "I never heard of this.''

"No, of course not, you have better things to do than to sit around in Marneri sifting through gossip of the court. But that is our task, Sergeant, we of the Office of Insight. We watch over the courts of Argonath and we attempt to prevent the excesses of princely rule.''

"Bah, interfering female busybodies!'' snorted Yortch. "We have no truck with them in Talion.''

"Yes indeed, Subadar, Talion is the least cooperative of the cities of the Argonath, and Talion is also the most heavily infested by agents of the enemy. Talion is also the city ruled for six generations by the increasingly feeble Matulik family. If you think King Fildo has been a troublesome monarch, wait until his son Esquin takes the throne.''

Yortch's face clouded. "The king is troubled in his mind, all agree, but he is the king.''

"And Esquin is an irresponsible savage who will steal the Talionese blind.''

Yortch screwed up his lips but made no reply. In truth

the city of Talion already dreaded the day when the haughty Esquin would mount the throne.

Lessis held up her hand. "But all this concern is unnecessary, gentlemen. I came here because I am about to receive the orders for Captain Kesepton from Dalhousie that we sent for yesterday."

"How can you know that?" grumbled Duxe.

"It is my business to know these things. Come, Chinook will not enter the tent, we will have to greet him outside."

"Now this is foolish," groused Yortch. "We are to wait outside for your trained bird to find us out here in the middle of the woods?"

"Chinook is not trained, far from it."

"Even better, we are to wait for a wild bird to find us."

She smiled sweetly. "If you wish to put it that way, then yes, we are to wait for him. He will come, you will see."

Still grumbling, Yortch followed the others out.

Outside the tent she cupped her hands and produced a loud hoot that echoed off the trees along with the banging from the smiths.

Silence fell, the wind sighed through the trees. The moment stretched itself out as the men fidgeted, wondering how mad this hag was.

Then suddenly a larger pale shape detached itself from the dark masses of the trees and fluttered down to land atop Kesepton's tent pole. The great owl confronted them with its huge eyes.

Yortch emitted a startled oath at the size of the bird and took a step back.

Lessis made another of the eerie calls and encouraged the great owl to hop down upon her upraised staff. A message was tied to his leg. In a few moments she had removed it and passed it to Hollein Kesepton. He stared at it for a moment.

"It is from General Hektor himself. See, here is his seal." He held it up for Yortch and Duxe to see. They grumbled together but they could not deny it; the seal was official.

"He orders us to fight tomorrow and to obey the Lady Lessis implicitly until she no longer requires our service."

Duxe sucked in a long breath. It was Hektor's seal, no doubt of it, and thus he and his men were given up to the command of the witch. It was either that or mutiny and complete disgrace and the end of his career.

Yortch screwed his mouth up and then spat eloquently to the side. "We can just hope that we survive the fiasco, then."

Lessis was imperturbable. "Oh, I think we will survive, Subadar, and perhaps we will surprise you too." She pressed her palms together. "Now here is my plan of action. In the morning we will set off early and cross the Thun at the Trail Ford. But we will not set our ambush there—there is a better place that Matugolin knows, just a couple of leagues further to the west. Our enemy will expect an ambush at the ford, and not finding one will perhaps become overconfident and less wary when he reaches our place of choice."

"And where is that?" said Duxe.

"A place called Ossur Galan, where the giant Ossur is said to have cut the rocks with his axe, long ago."

"A giant, eh?" muttered Yortch as he left. "And tomorrow trolls will cut our men with their axes?"

CHAPTER TWENTY-SIX

The next day, however, dawned grey and cloudy. Before long a drenching cold rain began.

It was evident to Lessis that not even Thrembode would

get much movement out of the imps and trolls that were his escort through Tunina on a day like this. Accordingly she told Kesepton to rest his men and dragons during the morning. Then with Subadar Yortch and Lieutenant Weald, Lessis and Lagdalen rode along one of the trade trails to the site recommended by Matugolin for the ambush. They crossed the river at a shallow ford where the water was still high with melted snow. Throughout the journey they saw no sign of the enemy, no tracks at all. Lessis was increasingly confident that they were in time.

After another hour's ride they reached the spot. A jagged sill of volcanic rock formed a north-south ridge here. Through this ridge was cut a single pass, the great gash called Ossur's Galan, or axe cut.

Here the trail narrowed to a point where it was barely twenty feet wide. A perfect bottleneck. With a small force, protected on both sides of the rocky ridge, they could easily trap their foe and then destroy them from above.

A wave from the rocks above told them that King Matugolin was waiting. They climbed to meet him. The rain hissed down again and everyone was cold and wet, except for the elves who had forsaken their feathered costumes and were clad instead in drab green cloaks with pointed hoods that seemed to repel the rain and remain perfectly dry. Matugolin rubbed his hands briskly as they drew close. He was bubbling with his news.

"I have word of the enemy this hour," he said to Lessis, who alone understood the forest tongue. "They are moving very slowly today. There was a struggle in their camp this morning, and two men were hanged before they left."

"Good, it is as we hoped. They'll not reach this spot today."

Matugolin waved to the rocks behind them. "We shall set our forces on the heights above the pass. When they are stuck in the canyon we will destroy them with rocks and arrows."

Lessis paced around the site, examining it carefully. It

was the last choke point before the high pass over the saddle north of Mount Ulmo.

Later, when the rain slackened, Captain Kesepton rode up to join them. He had set the men and dragons to march over the ford and come up to Ossur Galan that afternoon, and thus ensure that they would get there ahead of the enemy.

However, Yortch had been less than eager to keep his men on patrol behind them. They were tired, they needed a rest and everyone was wet through. And indeed some of the men were very slack about watching the flanks of the moving column.

Thus they missed the rider in black who approached Ossur Galan from the north and spotted the advancing column in the late afternoon.

By the time the Talionese returned to patrol, this rider had already slipped back to the east, to the crossing of the river, and was gone.

At length the rain ceased and the clouds cleared in time for the sunset, which illuminated Mt. Ulmo and turned its white crown into a glory of purple and gold.

Kesepton ordered an early evening meal and the dousing of all fires immediately afterwards. Cooks were told to prepare foods to be eaten cold for breakfast.

At length some elves brought word of the enemy force. It had crossed the river and made camp. The trolls were reportedly cooking and eating some men they had captured along the Argo. This news went around the camp very quickly. An angry buzz soon edged the cookfires.

Lessis ordered vigilance through the night with constant patrols. She feared that Thrembode, realizing the nature of the obstacle at Ossur Galan, would discover her trap and leave the trail, going north around the rocks.

But the enemy camp was quiescent during the night; only at dawn did a pair of patrols go out and neither of them were particularly aggressive. Lessis began to hope that finally she would snare the wily Thrembode and recapture the princess.

It was such a bright clear morning that everyone's spirits soared to join the occasional white cumulus cloud that floated across the vault of blue. The men and dragons were in their positions shortly. The dragons were to hold the pass while the men and elves controlled the ridge above them. Once the battle was joined Lessis had agreed to send Yortch and his men around to attack the foe from the rear and snap shut the trap.

Now they waited. From Matugolin's elves they had reports of the enemy's progress, which was slow but steady and continued straight along the trail.

Another hour passed and more elves came in to report that the enemy was close. Within twenty minutes the clank of metal and the throb of heavy feet upon the ground confirmed this.

For several long minutes the men and dragons peered down the narrow pass. They could hear the enemy's approach, but still there was no glimpse of imp or troll.

Then at last a mass of imps appeared at the eastern end, moving in a defensive phalanx with black shields serried behind a forest of spear points.

A mounting concern gripped Lessis.

"He suspects something," she exclaimed. "We must change the plan."

Kesepton was unconvinced. "But lady, he will know that this place is dangerous. He will seek to investigate it before trying to cross."

"Which he has not done, Captain. I'm afraid we are discovered."

Kesepton continued to study the phalanx of imps at the eastern end of the defile. They had not moved forwards. He began to share Lessis's misgivings.

Lessis sniffed suddenly.

"Quickly, Captain, order the dragons to join us on the ridgeline."

But it was too late. Almost as soon as these words were spoken, the forest to the east of the ridge came alive with a huge shout and more imps, with men leading them and tall purple trolls stalking behind them, came surging out from beneath the trees.

The elves of Matugolin turned about, but they were taken in the flank, and though they sent volleys of arrows whistling into the enemy masses they could not halt them.

And then the two forces closed and everything became a confusing whirling chaos of men, elves, imps and trolls.

On the south side of the pass a dozen elves were knocked over the edge of the cliff and fell screaming to their deaths when the charge drove home.

A troll got in among the men of Marneri and cut down two with a sweep of his great sword. Others gave way in near panic. They were on the point of breaking in a complete rout.

Kesepton clashed with an enemy officer, a man with the dark face and slanted eyes of the Hazog. Their swords rang on each other for a moment, but Kesepton was the swifter and his short blade cut inside and struck home. The officer went down and Kesepton rallied the men around him. They stiffened for a moment until a swarm of imps came in around them.

The pressure was too much and in moments they were all falling back, men and elves pressed together too tightly to fight, while their enemies hewed at them like standing wood.

But fleet-footed Lagdalen had already reached the dragons with the news, and now they split into two groups and pushed themselves up the slopes, huge reptile claws digging into the rocks for purchase, stentorian breaths venting from their nostrils.

The trolls hammered men and elves to the ground and strode over their bodies, crushing them to pulp. Imps pressed in with stabbing blades seeking unguarded eyes and chests. The men fought back with desperate energy, but their swords were too light and their shields too slender for combat with trolls.

At one point Sergeant Duxe was knocked headlong and saved only by burly Cowstrap's quick thinking when he seized the sergeant's collar and yanked him out of range of the troll's lethal axe. Kesepton lost his shield to another troll's axe and would have been mown down except that he slipped in slick blood and fell under a wrestling heap of imps and elves.

Troll axes rose and fell and the slaughter grew terrible. It seemed they were doomed.

And then when all seemed lost the dragons arrived on the scene and, with scarcely more than a deep breath, threw their weight into the struggle.

Their arrival broke the death spell of the trolls and rocked back the mass of imps until there was a cleared space before them, on which were strewn the bodies of dozens of dead and wounded.

For a moment it seemed they had witnessed the worst, but then drums thundered and horns brayed and out of the woods came another host of imps with more long-legged trolls on either side. Keseption knew with a sick feeling that the dragons were outmatched.

"Form the hedgehog!" he shouted to the men scrambling up beside the dragons.

The elves were giving ground, on the verge of breaking and running. Only the presence of Matugolin, fighting side by side with Lessis herself, who had taken a sword from a fallen soldier, was keeping them standing against the shock of so many imps and trolls.

Just then a troll smashed five elves to the ground with a terrible blow from a mace that bore a ball the size of a man's head. The line wavered, and suddenly Lessis was there, alone in front of the troll.

With a shout of "Lessis!" another slim figure in grey pushed through beside her. Two small blades thrust at the troll as it swung its mace. The two Sisters ducked beneath the hurtling iron and ran in and stabbed the monster in the thighs.

It snarled in rage and batted at them with a heavy hand and caught the second small figure a glancing blow that sent it tumbling head over heels.

Lessis threw up a hand and said something in a voice of cold power. The troll snarled, momentarily distracted, and the great mace missed and slammed into the ground inches from its target.

And then Bazil the Broketail was upon him. Piocar sang down with a shriek of steel and the troll flung up the mace convulsively to save itself.

With a flash of sparks Piocar cut the handle of the mace in two. The troll stared stupidly at the broken shaft, and Bazil stepped forward smartly and smashed the troll in the face with his shield and knocked it spinning around, completely off its feet.

As they danced over her, Lagdalen had had the wit to crawl away from the giants and avoid being crushed beneath their massive feet.

For a moment the leatherback, still puffing for breath from the climb up from the canyon floor, was face to face with Lessis.

"Thank you, Sir Dragon. Rarely have I seen a blow so powerful and so well struck."

Bazil let out a breath and recovered his balance. "We'll need some more of those, lady. Here they come."

And the shriek of charging imps resounded again.

But now the men were moving forward in the dense phalanx of the hedgehog position, with spears facing outwards in a ring of steel points. With a loud crash of steel on steel the hedgehogs bit into the dense mass of imps.

This sight, and the presence of the dragons, put new heart into the elves, and they swung around and returned to the attack.

Lessis found Lagdalen and pulled her back from the fighting. A quick examination showed no serious wounds, although the girl's head was still ringing from the troll's head slap.

"Can you fight, girl?" said Lessis.

"Yes, lady, I think so."

"Good, but get your breath back first. We need every blade today and you need your wits about you."

And indeed the clash was intensifying swiftly on both sides of the canyon. Once again the trolls came forward, surging through the imps as if they were wading through a flood.

Each dragon faced three trolls. Impossible odds, but

with the men in hedgehog position on either side of each dragon the trolls were only able to come at them one at a time for the moment.

Bazil engaged the first. He feinted with tail sword and then dropped his left shoulder and hooked the troll's round shield with his own and pulled it away. The troll responded with a textbook mistake, jerking backwards and losing balance so that its chest was exposed. Bazil hewed it through the waist with Piocar and it collapsed with thrashing limbs.

The next was already upon him, a bulky maroon with a square shield and a sword of its own: a sword troll. They'd heard of them, a new breed with the intelligence and skill to wield a sword, but they'd never seen one yet.

"There's a first time for everything, right?" shouted Bazil over his shoulder.

Relkin dodged around behind the dragon, snapping arrows past him as fast as he could load them. He saw the troll with the sword and whistled.

"Sword troll, beware his blade!" he shouted.

Two men in the nearest hedgehog thrust at the brute with their spears and it slashed at them, turning aside their spearheads on its shield and then hewing down the nearest of them.

Relkin got an arrow into its shoulder, and it roared with pain and rage, turning back on Bazil in time to meet Piocar with its own blade.

Steel struck shards from steel and Piocar was turned. Baz was still surprised by this when the troll swung in an overhand strike that Baz took on the shield. Tail sword flashed and struck on the troll's helm but caught only a glancing blow. The troll danced away from Piocar's sweep.

The troll was quick! It slipped to one side and thrust with that heavy sword. Baz only just avoided the blade in his belly; his tail lashed reflexively and knocked Relkin sprawling.

A brave fellow in the hedgehog to Bazil's right ran in

and got his spear into the monster's thigh. It responded by emitting a weird scream, and then it clipped the man with its shield and knocked him to his knees. Then its sword came down and clove him from neck to crotch.

Imps surged in around it to protect it from the men, and a great clatter went up as spears struck aside spears and sought to stab through to the shields beyond. Behind these imps came a third troll with the dragon lance, its yard-long tip gleaming.

Bazil exchanged more hammer blows with the maroon sword troll, pieces of their shields flying in odd directions under the terrible impact.

Meanwhile the troll with the lance waited for the right moment and then hurled itself forward behind that glittering point of steel.

Bazil jerked aside just in time, but the lance pierced his shield and lodged there. He flung himself backwards and swung Piocar out to deflect the maroon's next sword thrust, but with the shield pinned he could not maneuver freely.

Relkin was back on his feet, and he saw with a sinking heart that the maroon was surely going to score sooner or later. The men in the hedgehogs could not help now; they were fighting twice their number of imps. Relkin drew his own sword and ran in.

He got under the troll's shield before it was even aware of him, and his sword was in the monster's leg a second later. Black blood flowed thickly as he pulled it free, and the maroon gave an anguished grunt before it struck with the inside rim of the shield and shoved Relkin towards its sword arm.

The sword flashed in, but he leaped high and it passed under his toes. However, he tripped on landing and rolled directly between Bazil's stamping feet.

"Fool boy!" roared the dragon, staggering to avoid trampling him. His feet tangled, and with a sick groan Bazil lost his balance and toppled. The dragon lance snapped beneath him and he wound up holding the business end of it with his shield hand.

The maroon swung at him but Bazil deflected the blow with a blind swipe of the dragon lance, which was knocked away with a whine of hot metal. Bazil shoved back and rolled away, missing Relkin by a hairsbreadth.

But the maroon was on him now; Bazil was flat on his haunches, sword trapped behind him, shield down. The maroon's blade rose, death looming, until suddenly the slender figure of Relkin rose unsteadily in front of the troll and with a cry of rage and despair thrust home with his own small sword once more, right into the troll's belly. Still screaming his war cry Relkin ripped upwards, his sword point searching for the monster's heart.

The maroon's sword stroke withered; it gave a great moan and black blood gushed from its mouth in a sudden torrent, covering Relkin from head to foot. With a second, deeper moan it clutched its ruined stomach and fell backwards with a crash, its enormous sword toppled to the ground.

Bazil got to his feet in time to meet the charge of the remaining troll. Piocar struck aside the troll's axe and Baz met its charge with a knee up into its belly. The troll stopped dead with an explosion of foul breath. Then Piocar flashed and the troll's head flew away to land among the imps.

The dragon's eyes were flaming and his nostrils were dilated enough to make flames like his terrible ancestors.

The other dragons were doing almost as well—they exchanged shouts in their own tongue and clashed their weapons on their shields and dared the enemy to come on against them.

The trolls moaned in panic like cattle tormented by thunder and lightning. They put down their heads and turned and ran.

The trolls were broken. They fled back down the ridge and with them went the tide of imps, maddened beyond the power of the commanders to control them.

One last maroon troll stood at the edge of the cliff, snarling defiance and waving its heavy axe. Nesessitas exchanged blows with it, and then used her tail sword to hammer it senseless and topple it into the gorge.

Nesessitas turned back and showed her teeth.

"Count three for me!" she said in triumph.

"Two!" roared Bazil.

"Two also!" bellowed Kepabar.

"And one for me!" shouted Relkin Orphanboy as enormous dragon hands seized him up and lifted him into the air.

"And one for damn fool boy!" roared a huge voice in his ear.

CHAPTER TWENTY-SEVEN

For the moment the enemy was driven from the field, leaving a heap of dead strewn before the victors. What had begun so disastrously had been retrieved from complete rout and destruction.

But still Lessis's heart was heavy. The casualties were terrible, and while they fought she knew Thrembode was escaping past them into the west. He would be over the high pass by nightfall and she would have failed once again to close the net. The Princess Besita would be removed to the evil embrace of the Doom in Tummuz Orgmeen, and the future of the white city of Marneri would be left in the hands of the cretin Erald.

Lessis cursed herself for foolishly listening to an elf in matters of war. Elves were notoriously bad at warfare, the major reason for their sharp decline across the world.

At one point she found herself face to face with Kesepton; she winced at the look of betrayal in his eyes.

"Thank you, Captain. You and your men fought like heroes today," she said quickly.

Kesepton did not reply, and after a moment she turned away.

There were more trolls out there. How many of the damned things did Thrembode have with him? The enemy must have rated the successful abduction of the princess very highly to send so many. And sword trolls, too! That was an ominous precedent. The Doom had been working hard for several years to improve the intellectual capabilities of the maroons. Now it appeared to have succeeded.

More men were marching up the slope and behind them came the other two dragons, Vander and Chektor. Kesepton was consolidating his small command on the south side of the pass.

Meanwhile the elves were grieving for their dead. Matugolin was wounded; Lessis paused beside the place where he lay. The elf king had taken a sword thrust in the side—he would not fight again. Prince Afead would be the next king, and that in itself would not help the alliance of elf and man. Lessis could do little for the king, who was already drifting into a revery of his own. She tried speaking to him, but either he did not hear or could not respond. The other elves stared at her with eyes filled with shock and sorrow. After a few moments she rose and went on.

To make herself useful she joined young Lagdalen, who was assisting the surgeon. A screaming man, slit across the belly, was thrashing on the ground. Lagdalen was trying to hold the man's innards inside him.

Lessis knelt beside her. The man was doomed. There was nothing to be done for him. She took Lagdalen's hands and pulled them away.

"Tend to the others, girl. Leave this one for me."

Lagdalen's eyes were filled with the sights of war, things she had seen in these last few days that were enough to break the heart of anyone, much less a girl not yet out of her teens.

"So many, my lady, so many."

"I know. Go to the surgeon, help him."

Lagdalen left. Lessis laid her hand on the brow of the dying man. She closed her eyes and summoned the power, and after a while her hand became warm and his struggles slowed. The cries faded and died away as his agony was replaced by a slow heaving bliss, the sweet prelude to his departure from life.

Nearby a man shrieked as the hot cauterizing iron was pressed to a wound. Lessis shivered; she had seen enough battlefields for one lifetime, and for the moment she wished she were far away from here, tending sheep on the Rehba hills with none of this pain, horror, blood and death which now oppressed her spirit.

A cornet blew. Sergeant Duxe was running through the position calling the men to arms once more. She saw Kesepton with his sword out and his arm waving.

"More of them. They're coming!"

Lessis got to her feet with a groan. The wounded man was dead now. She drew her short sword; it was crusted with blood. Would this day never end?

"Form hedgehogs!" came the cry.

"Dragons to the front!"

Now the enemy horns were blaring and once more the foe stormed out of the forest and came up the slopes, and everything dissolved into a flurry of slamming blows, fragments of shield and helm whining off the giants in the midst of the struggle.

Bazil and Kepabar fought side by side now while Nesessitas guarded the right flank and Vander and Chektor held the other. Dragonboys danced around behind their great charges, their bows snapping as they sent their arrows flicking into the enemy.

Once again the tide of imps rose around them and the clash of steel reverberated amid screams and roars of rage. But there were fewer trolls now, and with all five dragons grouped together the enemy could make no impression on the center. The hedgehogs held and the elves poured their remaining arrows into the imps from the side.

The remaining trolls were disheartened, however. They

pressed their attack with much less fervor, and after one of them was chopped down by Kepabar the others turned once more and moved back down the slope.

Seeing how things went, the men in the black of Tummuz Orgmeen blew their horns and swung their whips, but to no avail; the imps continued to give ground.

Now the men of Marneri set up a shout and pushed harder, driving into the retreating mass of the enemy with the dragons to the fore. Bazil and Kepabar shoved forward, knocking the trolls back, and now it seemed that the enemy would be broken and sent hurtling away in flight.

And then, just as the imp formations were dissolving, Bazil looked up and saw a line of men on horseback charging out of the woods towards them. In a desperate bid to stave off a rout, the enemy troopers were engaging.

"Look up, Kepabar!" he called. There were dragon lances on those horses, but Kepabar was too busy with the trolls to notice.

With a heavy shock the horsemen drove into the hedgehogs and halted them. The mass of men, imps, trolls, horses and dragons was squeezed too tight to fight for a moment. And now the horsemen at the rear lowered dragon lances, couched them and spurred their mounts forward.

Bazil caught the first lancehead with his shield and turned it aside and flailed ineffectively with Piocar at the rider. Nesessitas stopped another lance and broke its haft and threw the rider to the ground. But old Kepabar was unlucky. His shield was pinned between his belly and the men of the hedgehog; he could not free it in time and could only attempt to knock the lance upwards with his sword.

The blade caught the lance a slight blow but did not deflect it sufficiently. Instead it ran smoothly into Kepabar's throat and pierced it through and through.

The great brasshide dragon emitted a squawk of dismay and slowly toppled, still skewered on the lance. The lance was pulled from the horseman's grip, but it was impossible for Kepabar to dislodge it.

Before Bazil's horrified gaze, Kepabar thrashed and died while red dragon's blood poured onto the ground. The Broketail gave a great cry of rage and grief and shook himself free from man and beast.

A horseman spun past him and he took the man from the saddle with a vicious cut from his sword that spread the fellow far and wide. The horse plunged and bolted, kicking a pair of imps onto their heels as it charged into the trees.

A troll staggered into him and was caught the next instant as dragon's teeth snapped shut across its face. Piocar pulled back and drove home and the troll was down, and Bazil had broken through and was moving on in a red-hued frenzy, killing anything that came his way.

At the sight of him the imps broke and ran like rabbits and he pursued them into the forest with the men of Marneri, the other dragons and the elves at his back all yelling at the top of their lungs and hewing down the defeated enemy.

So caught up in this slaughter was he that he missed the notes of the cornet blowing recall and went on, pursuing a large group of imps that ran from him all the way to the banks of a wide stream.

The imps forded the stream, throwing away their weapons in their panic. Bazil plunged in after them; they would not get away! They would all die for poor Kepabar!

On the other side they scattered, and he raved through the forest behind them until at last, lungs heaving, he noticed that he was alone—the men and the dragonboys had fallen behind the dragon! Still he did not slow his steps; as they said, there was a first time for everything!

The forest on the far side of the stream changed character quickly, and Bazil soon found himself in a stygian gloom beneath a mature forest of hemlock and spruce.

He came upon an exhausted imp, lying sprawled on the mat of needles that covered the forest floor. Bazil stood over it, sword poised, when a gleam to his right startled him and he dodged, slamming his head into a massive tree trunk as he did so. He heard a heavy thud and saw a dragon lance bury itself in the side of the same tree. By the Ancient Drakes, that was a close call!

A pair of imps and a man on foot in the black uniform of Tummuz Orgmeen sprang at him. Freeing himself from the tree Bazil rasped at them, "Much better you stand and die rather than make me chase you all day!"

Piocar swung like a great scythe; one of the imps was slow in leaping away and was cut in half in a spray of blood and a shriek that cut off in an instant. That ended the others' resistance, and they scattered and ran in different directions.

Bazil gave chase to the man who'd thrown the lance but lost him in a maze of deer trails through the hemlocks. For a while he ran on, venting his rage on the trees around him, Piocar leaving huge slashes in the hemlock and spruce.

At length he stopped, suddenly unsure. He listened carefully but heard nothing except the wind in the hemlocks. He was alone and he had definitely lost his quarry.

The red rage cooled a degree or two and allowed more rational thought.

Where was everyone? For that matter where was he?

Under the dense mat of hemlock branches the light was dim—it was impossible to even work out the sun's position in the sky. He turned about. Which way would lead him back to the battlefield and the rest of the unit?

After careful consideration he set out in what he thought was the right direction. Shortly he came to a stream, but it was not as wide as the stream he had crossed earlier. Did that mean it was a different stream, or was he further upstream from where he had crossed before?

After agonizing for a while he shrugged, crossed over, and went on into the trees on the other side.

CHAPTER TWENTY-EIGHT

The hemlocks gave way to a birch forest, then to pines and oaks, and then quite suddenly Bazil realized he had climbed a considerable distance and the way was getting steeper.

The trees were less dense now, the blue sky was visible and with it the sun, which was far down in its course and close to the western horizon.

A few moments later he emerged from the trees onto an upland meadow, not that different from the one on Mt. Red Oak that had become a battlefield two days before.

Bazil looked around himself with wild eyes. Where was he? And where was everybody else?

He saw Mt. Ulmo's great snow-covered dome behind him with late afternoon sunlight striking on the nearest face. Immediately he realized he had come a long way and that he was hopelessly lost.

In front of him was spread a narrow valley that widened out towards a bright blue lake fringed with trees. Beyond the lake stood another, smaller mountain, with trees marching right up to the crown.

Towards the sun the land seemed dreary and flat, and he knew that he gazed upon the endless expanse of the Gan. In the other direction the view was cut off by an outlying ridge of Ulmo.

Somewhere back there, in that vast expanse of forest, was Relkin and all the others. How was he ever going to find them? It seemed impossible. He pushed it out of his thoughts.

He had a more immediate problem: his feet were sore.

He cast about and found a likely boulder and sat down on it, planted Piocar's scabbard into the ground in front and sat there, resting his arms on the sword's pommel.

He took some deep breaths. He was weary enough for three days sleep and his hind legs ached. Two solid days of marching and fighting, coming on top of twenty days travel up the river, and Bazil was ready for a good long rest.

On the other hand he noted how tight and smooth his body had become. The winter campaign, and now this Argo fighting, all had transformed the slightly plump leatherback that had entered the legion last autumn into a lean fighting machine with hard muscles and a tight belly. He slapped his midriff and was rewarded with a drumsnap.

He was a battle-hardened dragon, alright. Even the ancient drakes would be proud of this dragon!

Memories of the battles came rushing up, and with them came the grief for old Kepabar. Old Kep was gone forever, along with Sorik. They'd never hear one of Kepabar's funny monologues again, never hear his jokes. And without Kep's sense of humor the squadron was going to be a grim one—both Nesessitas and Vander were inclined to dragonish dourness. Baz was going to miss old Kep, no doubt about that.

He sat disconsolate for a little while, and then his nostrils caught a trace of a fragrance that raised his eyebrows in an involuntary snap.

His head rose, he sniffed the air again. There it was, a sweet, musky perfume, very faint but definitely wafting to him on the wind from higher up the mountain.

A few moments later he was on his feet without having made a conscious decision, and he started on, heading upslope and into the breeze. His feet were killing him, but he ignored them.

The woods thickened into a scrub oak jungle, but he forced his way through. A patch of thick brambles blocked his way, but he drew Piocar and carved a path through them. A stream-fed bog lay on the other side and he waded through it with mud up to his belly.

And then he came upon the clearing, in a patch of pines on sandy soil. In the clearing a great mound of branches had been woven into a nest. As he watched, the nest moved. Something large lurked within. A curious rhythmic hissing sound came from the midst of the movements.

Bazil crept closer until at last he could peer over the edge of the wall of branches. A lively, dark green dragoness was at work weaving the branches together. Bazil felt his eyes widen.

She was simply gorgeous. Her skin was a glittering green on top and her movements were precise and graceful. He watched with total absorption as she wove boughs of pine into the walls of oak and alder. She was the most beautiful thing he'd ever seen. Her skin was one shade or other of dark green everywhere except along her folded wings which were as black as soot. Her underside was a lighter shade and the scales there were small and tight. Down her spine she wore a crest of larger scales, and these were darkened almost to black. Her talons both fore and aft were a lustrous dark grey and longer than those of battledragons, who let their boys clip their talons to make it easier for them to wield a sword.

"Greetings!" he said at last in the gutturals and hissings of the wyvern tongue.

The green female, who was almost as large as Bazil himself, jumped at the sound of his voice. Then her head snapped around and her huge yellow eyes focused on him. All living things, except perhaps for particularly large bears, would promptly have run for their lives. Bazil remained where he was, his right forepaw resting on the hilt of Piocar.

"By the blood, who, or what, are you?" she said suddenly.

Her accent was like that of the oldest dragons, with long vowels and heavy sibilance. Bazil wondered briefly if this was a dream he was having about the ancestors, and then decided that if it was it was a damn fine one and he would just go on with it.

"My name is Bazil," he replied.

She rounded on him; she had immense wings, like all wild dragons, and now they unfolded and seemed to fill the sky. She seemed to bore into him with those brilliant yellow eyes and dilated red pupils. Her teeth flashed, long rows of saber-sharp white curves.

Bazil felt a thunderbolt of dragon love.

"Bazil!" she mocked. "A slave name for a slave dragon. You are one of them! One of those crawling, ground-bound worms that fights for the humans."

"And you are a most beautiful sight, the most beautiful I have ever seen," he said humbly.

"What?" The eyes flashed. "Did you not hear me scorn you?"

"When you are angry, your eyes get very big. Did you know that? It is lovely to watch."

"I—" She stopped. She blinked; he was ground-bound, he had no wings, but he was impressive in a large, heavyset way. These human things, the helmet and the immense steel shield, they gave even more bulk to him.

And he did seem to know how to charm one. It was quite remarkable, this creature actually had some manners!

But he was wingless! There were just some disgusting nubs on his back and shoulders to suggest where wings should be. She knew she could never love a male who had no wings. She drew herself up to her full height, and noted that she was definitely half a head shorter than he and certainly less massive. This was quite disconcerting.

"What, in the name of the ancestors, is a freakish mutant like you doing way up here? This is the time for the calling for drakes, not mutants!"

Bazil did not understand her term for mutant, but he knew she scorned him and he cared not.

"There was a female in my village with whom I would have mated if I had stayed. But she was not as beautiful as you."

"Dragons in a village! What perversity is this?"

"None at all, it works very well. Everyone eats plenty."

"Ah yes." She inspected his leatherback girth again. "I can see that you're used to that. But what else would I expect from a slave! You're a kept animal, fed and watered and told what to do."

Normally Bazil would have felled anyone or anything that dared to say such a thing to his face, but in this case it was as if he could not feel the words. She was simply ignorant, he knew, and once she was acquainted with the facts she would stop saying these dreadful things and all would be well.

"I am battledragon. I fight so that all dragons can be free."

"Bah, what care we for their endless wars? They cannot harm us!"

"You do not understand. The enemy can breed a million trolls if they want, and then they will exterminate all dragons and crush all humans beneath their heel. That is certain—I have heard much concerning the enemy and it is a terrible foe of all dragonkind. That is why the ancestors agreed to join with the humans of the Argonath in the first place."

"All humans are beneath contempt, why be bothered with them? Crawling things, they infest all the warmer parts of the world, but we rarely see them in Dragon Home."

"Ah, Dragon Home. Often I have heard it described but never have I seen it."

She gave a small strangled shriek of amusement.

"Of course not, for it lies at the end of the North Mountains, and since you cannot fly it would take you a year just to walk there."

"Someday I will. When we retire, Relkin and me, we will go there so that I can see Dragon Home."

"Retire? Relkin? Who is Relkin and what kind of name is that, anyway?"

Baz made a small dismissive gesture with his forepaw,

a gesture he had adopted from humans. The dragoness stared at him with incomprehension.

Baz spoke softly. "It does not matter, beautiful one. There is a wide world out there, I have seen some of it and you have seen some of it, and we could talk about these wonders and those marvels for many hours and still not exhaust our memories. But I have a better idea."

"Oh, you do, do you?"

"Yes, tell me why you are building this great nest of boughs and leaves."

"I am in my prime, and I await a mate. Is it not obvious?"

"Well, yes, but I wanted to hear it from your lips."

"Well?" she said with half slitted eyes. "Now you have."

"Do you already have a mate?" he said.

"Not yet, not yet, but I expect he'll be along very soon."

Bazil puffed up his chest.

"Might I suggest that he is already here, in the shape of one damn fine battledragon?"

"Oh really! You propose yourself as a mate for me, do you?"

"I do!" said Baz happily.

She looked up at the sky. "Well, we'll just have to see about that, for a much more suitable mate for one such as I has just appeared. Look! It's the purple-green from Hook Mountain—doesn't he look wonderful?"

Bazil looked up and saw an immense winged dragon soaring above the slope of Mt. Ulmo, circling down into the clearing. An age-old eruption of emotions took place in his breast. With a swish of steel he drew Piocar from its scabbard and unlimbered his shield with a clang.

At the sight of Piocar the dragoness blinked in astonishment. Such a weapon was beyond any sword she had ever seen before.

"What do you do with that?" she said.

"I fight."

She emitted another snort of amusement.

"You? Fight the purple-green? Think again, in fact run away while you still can. The purple-green rules the skies; he will smash you and trample your remains into the dust. Run away now and you might live to tell your tale to the other slaves in your village, wherever it is."

"I stay and I fight."

"Run while you can."

But it was too late for running.

With a dozen huge wingbeats that bent the pines double, the purple-green landed.

He was a handsome sight, blazing purple scales covered his underside while green colored his top. His wings were like vast draperies of black velvet shot through with yellow veins. His eyes had black pupils and these now blazed with a peculiar intensity at the sight of Bazil.

"What are you?" he hissed in an enormous voice.

"Battledragon!" said Bazil, who flashed Piocar between them. The purple-green leapt forward in a great bound.

"Battledragon? You are human slave? What do you want?"

"This is my female, begone."

The black pupils dilated.

"Your female! You dare to interpose yourself between this female and myself?"

"Go away."

The wild drake roared with amusement.

"I will destroy you!"

Bazil made no reply except to gesture with Piocar once more. The purple-green roared again and raised himself to his full height. Bazil noted that the wild drake was several inches taller than himself and considerably heavier. Then he swung his shield into position while Piocar swung loose in his hand.

An astonishing sense of calm had come over him. This was not like fighting trolls with their axes and shields. Despite the presence of the female, Bazil felt no red rage descend over him. Nor did he feel any fear; he had the weapons, this wild drake was virtually defenseless in his terms. Such a combat could only end one way.

Then Bazil realized he could not slay the wild dragon, precisely because it was unarmed and did not know how to fight. It would dishonor Baz, his ancestors, even the village of Quosh to kill such a foe.

He chuckled to himself—what a pickle to be in! He could not bring himself to kill his foe while his foe could certainly kill him!

The drake pawed the ground in front of it while the dragoness watched them with wondering eyes. Indeed, she seemed quite excited by the thought of having a battle fought over her.

That shining blade in Bazil's hand drew her gaze again. She knew how sharp these things could be. Once she had had a painful disagreement with a knight in a far-off land who had wielded one. She had eaten the knight and his horse, but only after a fierce battle. A tiny frisson of doubt passed through her.

With a roar the purple-green attacked, leaping at the hunched figure standing on its hind legs and cowering behind its shield.

The purple-green cannoned into the shield but did not bowl the wyvern over, and then he received a hefty whack from the flat of the sword which staggered him momentarily. He roared with renewed rage while stars flashed in front of his eyes.

The wings half opened, he sprang again and seized the shield in both forepaws and gave it a hard tug.

Bazil was pulled off his feet. As he crashed to the ground, he reflected that not even maroon trolls possessed this kind of brute strength.

He rolled over and over to get away, but the purple-green sprang on him like a lion on its prey. Bazil had just managed to get to one knee and bring the shield up when the purple-green slammed into him and both were knocked over onto their backs.

They lay there for a second, dazed by the clash of multiton bodies. Bazil was the first back on his feet, and he brought Piocar over in another flat-of-the-blade strike that rang on the purple-green's heavy skull.

That slowed him up! Baz noted with a degree of satisfaction as the wild drake crawled away slowly on all fours.

But a moment later he was bowled over again as the purple-green drove in low and rammed his shoulder into Bazil's knees.

Then the wild drake was on top of him, huge teeth snapping together just short of his throat. Baz gave a great heave with his upper limbs and thrust the growling drake away from himself. Then he cocked a fist and planted a straight right on the purple-green's nose.

The drake gave out a huge bellow of woe and rolled away, clutching his wounded proboscis. Bazil regained his feet once more, and after a few deep breaths, advanced with Piocar in hand.

The purple-green scrambled back out of the reach of the gleaming length of steel.

"I would not kill you, dragon," growled Bazil, "because you are at a disadvantage. But I will cut you if I have to."

The purple-green roared with rage and defiance and sprang at him once more, but the sword sliced the space between them. He ducked back and circled, wary, just out of reach of the blade.

Bazil advanced. The purple-green stepped into the dark green female's nest and fell over backwards. He emitted a wild roar and struggled to his feet. In the process a section of the nest was shredded. The female scrambled out in the other direction, hissing curses on the pair of them.

The purple-green launched himself once more in a huge athletic pounce that should have borne down the impertinent wingless dragon and pinned it to the ground, except that Bazil sidestepped smartly and swung the sword backhand and low to catch the purple-green across the legs and trip him.

The purple-green crashed to the ground with a snarl

and slid across the meadow. He arose frothing in rage and charged again.

Baz sought to sidestep, but this time the wild drake was prepared and jinked at the last moment, then crashed into Bazil and bore him down.

His hind claws came up for the disemboweling stroke but caught on Bazil's heavy leather joboquin and stuck. Baz twisted and dislodged him, and they disengaged momentarily.

Bazil spun around, unable to see the wild drake, and then with a thud he felt the wild one land on his back. The great forepaws fastened on his head and started twisting it backwards. It was hard to breathe, his neck felt as if it was going to snap and the drake was trying to get those terrible teeth on his throat.

"I didn't want to do this," grumbled the Broketail dragon, "but you leave me no choice."

There was nothing for it; he wrenched himself backwards to bring up his right arm, and then hewed down hard upon the purple-green's exposed flank.

Piocar bit deeply; he swung again and cut the shoulder muscles above. The purple-green lost the use of one arm, and Baz dislodged him and shoved him away with a final swat of the flat of the sword on the back of the head.

Baz staggered onto his feet. The heavy leather of his joboquin was shredded down the front. A few talons had gone through and cut his skin, dragon blood was pooling on his belt buckle.

But the purple-green was in much worse shape, stretched prone upon the meadow with dark blood welling from the shoulder wound in particular. After a moment it awoke and struggled upright.

It gazed up at him with expressionless eyes. It could not comprehend defeat. Such a thing was unimaginable. But the arm was useless and blood ran thickly upon the ground.

A sob behind him turned his head. The female dragon was there, staring in horror at the purple-green.

"He dies!" she said.

Bazil said nothing. There was little wrong with the wild one except for the bleeding in his shoulder—Piocar had gone in deep and severed a vein. The purple-green could bleed to death if he did not receive help.

If only there was a dragonboy!

The dragoness crouched beside the drake. "He is beyond any poultice I can make," she wailed.

Indeed he was, only a tight bandage, drawing the severed flesh together, could hope to stem the loss of blood.

Then Bazil recalled the bandages wrapped around his own shield arm, where he'd been cut by a troll in the battle of Red Oak. His wound had hardened under a crust of dried blood, and it had not been as severe as this, anyway.

He peeled off the bandage. It was a little worn, sweaty and even stained with mud, but none of these things mattered so much as that with it he could bind the dragon's shoulder tightly and press the sides of the wound together.

The purple-green hissed as he approached.

"Don't struggle," said Bazil. "I have a bandage, a thing of the humans to help heal wounds, even wounds as bad as this."

The purple-green did not understand. Nor did the female. But the fight had gone out of the wild drake and he did not resist.

Still it was hard work for thick, clumsy dragon fingers, but Bazil worked the bandage around the purple-green's shoulder and tightened it hard until the flow of blood was stopped to a trickle that gradually clotted. Finally he stepped back and admired his handiwork.

"I think it will do. You rest now, and do not use the arm for a few days."

The dragoness moved closer. She was actually touching Bazil alongside. Her tail curved up around his own.

"I will come back and feed him," she said. "The purple-green will live."

She looked at Bazil, and there was a completely different expression in those huge eyes now.

"The nest I built is useless now. I will use it to cover the purple-green while he recovers. But first we will go away, you and I—we must find a high place where we can be together, alone."

Her tail rubbed along his own.

"Alone, yes, that good." Bazil had never felt like this before.

Her neck curved against his, entwined. She hissed something in his ears and then slid away.

He followed.

CHAPTER TWENTY-NINE

It was full night and the moon rode high above the western Gan. From Mount Ulmo a cool wind brought a hint of ice on its breath.

They stood outside the tumbled walls, the young captain and the two women. The broken towers were like so many ruined teeth in the moonlight, while the dead city before them was like some fossilized beast from antiquity, exposed by erosion on its mountain ridge.

Kesepton was uneasy. This place was haunted by cruel spirits. Even though the drawbridge had been thrown down long ago the ruins still glittered with a malign presence.

"Lady, I would prefer that you not enter this place. It is a pit of evil," he said.

She wore that familiar grave smile, so maddeningly superior. "Thank you for your concern, Captain, but we have an important errand here. We shall not be long."

"I will send guards with you, but it will not be popular duty."

"No need, there is nothing here that would harm us. Unless there is a bear that I do not know about."

He was shocked, despite everything.

"You have been here before?"

"Yes, but never on an errand like this."

Kesepton found his mouth quite dry. He himself would much prefer not to go into that dreadful place, for this was Dugguth, city of the Demon Lord. Long dead, but still remembered, the builder of this place was Mach Ingbok, renegade Master from Padmasa. His vile memory still lingered here.

"What errand could possibly make one want to enter Ingbok's citadel?" he wondered aloud.

She smiled again but did not reply for a moment. When she spoke she looked away over the ruins.

"This is bear country," she said. "But even the big brown bears dislike this place. We won't have to worry about any wandering bruins."

The lady seemed to take his concern very lightly. Kesepton was moved to anger.

So there was nothing to fear, was there? Then why did the eyes of the younger Grey Sister betray such anxiety?

And with a furtive glance at the girl he felt another painful tug at his heart. What was going on? This girl was dangerously beautiful! So well born, so lovely, and yet serving in this most dangerous duty alongside a Great Witch. It seemed unnatural somehow.

Clearly she was not like most of the young women in her social class. And now he felt ashamed of his own cowardice. He was a battle-hardened veteran of five years service in the legion, and he was not willing to go into Dugguth, and yet she was.

But when he caught her eye, he saw how unsure she was and indeed how terrified. The dead city of Dugguth was no place to enter lightly, for truly was it said that the legends of Mach Ingbok had been written in blood and horror.

Lessis was looking at him again; he dragged his eyes away from the girl. The witch was so keen, so perceptive. Did she already know of his infatuation? How could he possibly hide such a thing?

And the terrible thought plucked at him again. What if the witch trailed this girl before him to gain his acceptance of her orders? It was such an easy thing for them to do, to rule a young officer through his passion for a girl. Such officers were frequently in the field for months at a time and denied the company of women. How easy to arouse one and turn his head and thereby gain his allegiance.

Perhaps that was exactly why the witch had the girl as her assistant. Men could not help but want to love this girl; she was fully in the ripeness of young womanhood and irresistibly pretty. By force of will he wrenched his gaze away from the girl and kept it there.

He shivered. What had the woman done to him?

"Farewell, Captain," said the witch with a slight amusement in her voice. "We'll see you at breakfast, I expect." Lessis turned her pony towards the ruins. The girl went with her.

He watched them go and thought how sweet it would be to be alone with that Lagdalen of Marneri for an hour or two. Just to walk under the stars, or the sun, or the moon, or any damn thing. To talk and sing and maybe even make love.

It was dangerous to feel such things on campaign, far beyond the frontier, but it was impossible to stop them while he watched her departing back, with her hair blowing in the wind.

Then they were out of sight in a gulley. A trooper was standing watch; he knew he had to get back to the men, but he stayed until he saw them climb the far side of the empty moat and pass through the shattered gate, atop which once upon a time heads had rotted by the thousand.

When he reached camp and dismounted he managed to grab some hot polenta and pickles at the fire and then withdrew with Weald to consider the situation. Weald had a full list now of dead, wounded and the remaining effectives.

They sat together and went over it. It was a terrible conversation. There were barely forty men left fit to fight in his whole command. Back at Ossur Galan they'd buried twelve more men and burnt the body of another dragon.

The wounded included big Vander, the other leatherback, and several troopers from Yortch's command who'd fought their own fight under the trees with the enemy's cavalry and barely held their own.

Kesepton's first command had become a catastrophe. Already he was sure in his heart that they would never give him another. There was a growing emptiness there, which combined with his lovesickness for the girl was unsettling, even nerve-racking.

And so Hollein Kesepton struggled to keep control of himself. This situation could make shreds of his authority with the men—a calm front was essential. By the goddess, this was not a situation he would have sought after in a million years!

But while an anxious Hollein Kesepton went over the situation with Weald, the two Sisters in grey strode softly through the ruins of the once mighty city.

Moonlight struck harsh shadows off ruined walls and shattered spires. These truncated towers and tumbled stones were infected with evil remembrances. In this place malice had known no restriction, power no check, and cruelty no rein.

Almost silently they stole down the dead avenues, passing smashed statuary that lay where it had been thrown by the victorious armies of Argonath, nearly two centuries before. They paused before an arch, left standing by the conquerors to emphasize the collapse of the rest. A monument to the mad mentality of the Demon Lord, this arch consisted of two tetraclusters of pillars, wrapped in carved serpents, that supported the upper part on which the terrible visage of Mach Ingbok glowered down with triumphant glee. A goblin mask, the human shape distorted by the passions of greed and lust and unbridled power into a crazed caricature with bulging eyes and loose-lipped mouth.

The figures in grey stood and gazed upon this face for a few moments. In the moonlight its harsh features were rendered even colder and less sympathetic than were those upon which it was modeled. Once it had glowered down upon captives as they were driven beneath it to the slaughters and tortures of the dungeons beyond. Now it glowered in futility at dust and moonbeams.

Lessis gave a sigh after a while and they passed on, leaving the great Master of Dugguth to stare down forever at the ruin of his ambitions.

At length they entered a tumbledown structure of collapsed galleries and roofless rooms. Outside it, resting on the pedestal from which it had been broken, were the ruins of a symbol of horror, a blank stone sphere from which a fanged mouth projected like an open eye.

The younger of the two produced a small lantern and twisted the mechanism to light it. Immediately shadows chased away down a long gallery at the center of the structure. In places the roof had fallen in, but for the most part the floor was still level and flat. They moved down this wide corridor and came to a broad set of stairs that descended to a deep place where the unholy had once been worshiped.

Here they found a smashed altar stone, flung down beside a circular pit, like an obscene baptismal built on a heroic scale. In the pit a darkness twitched softly.

On this altar many young people had ended their lives in shrieking horror; the whole place still screamed on the psychic plane. Lessis was forced to blunt her awareness on the higher planes to dull it.

The lantern was held over the pit. Beneath was a void, a nothingness, and in that void there was a liquid shifting of surfaces. This was the syphon of a dead Thingweight, that horror which had once been celebrated here with ritualized feedings on human victims before crowds of fanatical worshipers.

The older woman pulled back her cowl and then pulled from her cloak a spoon with a heavy handle and a deep cup. She pulled on the handle and it telescoped out until it was four feet in length. She tested it carefully for strength and then removed a small bottle that she unstoppered and set on the brink of the pool of nothingness.

She knelt beside the lip of the pit and composed herself. Lagdalen held the lamp high and closed her eyes.

Lessis muttered a long incantation and made a number of passes over the spoon set on the stone before her.

Then she pulled up one sleeve, took up the spoon, leaned over the edge of the pit and plunged the spoon deep into the central spot, where the glims and glitters spun in the nothingness.

The center of the pit became more active, thrashing and tumbling as the spoon was thrust into the roiling murk.

The spoon shuddered and shivered in the woman's hand, but she moved it vigorously for a while before withdrawing it. A moment later she poured a small amount of a black dust into the little bottle. Twice more she repeated this act and then stoppered the bottle tightly and sealed it.

She collapsed the long spoon, replaced it within her cloak and put the bottle in an interior pocket. The two women turned and padded quietly away into the night. Darkness returned, but the glistening center of the pit shuddered and shook for a long time before growing still.

Outside the ruins, the trooper posted by Kesepton was suddenly joined by three men on horseback.

Trooper Sarne was surprised to see Sergeant Duxe riding beside Subadar Yortch, along with a third rider, Trooper Harkness.

"Sarne," said Yortch as he pulled up, "you can stand down. Get some food while it's still going."

Sarne didn't question any further; he kicked his horse into a canter and rode down to the glittering campfires he could see on the lower slope of the ridge.

Yortch, Duxe and Harkness exchanged a long look.

"No turning back now," said Yortch. He showed the gleam of a cavalry dirk in the moonlight.

Harkness grinned back. He was ready whenever the Subadar was. Liepol Duxe was not so happy, however.

"I still don't like it. If anything goes wrong, we're finished."

"Damnit Marneri, stop letting these women control you!" Yortch was impatient. The men of Marneri were like puppets sometimes. "Look you, if we don't kill them they are sure to get us killed. Don't fool yourself, man. None of us are going to make it back from where they're taking us."

"We don't have to do this. We could arrest them, or drive them away."

"Ach, they'd have you around their little fingers in no time. See how the hag uses the young wench to distract the captain? That's how they work their wiles, damn them."

"We Talion men, we don't listen to the damn witches anymore," said Trooper Harkness, emboldened by the Subadar's intensity.

Duxe could not shake his dislike of the plot, but he could think of no alternative. They had to get rid of the witch Lessis. The captain was under a spell of some kind; he obeyed the witch's orders without the slightest protest. As a result they'd taken seventy percent casualties and been destroyed as a military unit. There was almost nobody left; Duxe had twenty men still able to fight. Back at that accursed elf trap in the rocks they'd left twelve more bodies. The men were on the edge of mutiny.

And now Liepol Duxe was on the verge of committing murder. Harkness showed a gleam of teeth as he elaborated on his boldness and ventured a thought that had been close to his heart for days.

"I say we take our pleasures with the little one first."

Duxe turned on him with a venomous look.

"You try that and my blade will be in your heart before you touch the girl!"

Harkness scowled. "Come on, why waste that? She's

the only good thing on this damned wild goose chase. I have dreamed of taking her for days. If we plan to kill her then we should take those pleasures with her first.''

Duxe would not hear of it.

Yortch broke in. ''Trooper, this is a military operation. You will keep your damned lecherous thoughts to yourself. We kill them, that's all, and we make sure their bodies are never found and then we get back to the camp before dawn. That's the job, and that's all we will do. Understand?''

But Harkness saw a glint in Yortch's eye and divined the Subadar's real intent. What if they disposed of Duxe as well? And then had their pleasure with the little wench? Duxe was already a pain to deal with—if they got rid of him then they would be the only witnesses to the deed.

''Yes, Subadar,'' muttered Harkness. Duxe relaxed a trifle.

Trust old Yortch not to miss a thing, thought Harkness. And then Harkness felt a little shiver in his spine. Of course, the subadar would want to go first. And while he was occupied upon the wench, Harkness would be free to kill him from behind. One thrust would do it.

And then, well, since the story would have to be that they were surprised by imps, Harkness and the girl would just disappear. Up into these mountains somewhere—and who knows? The girl might last him quite a while before he killed her and returned to civilization, claiming to have escaped from the clutches of the enemy. No one would have lived to tell tales on Harkness, and he would have had the best of the situation.

He grinned to himself at the thought. How rich! What a perfect end to Subadar Yortch!

''Look, it's simple,'' growled Yortch to Duxe. ''You heard her, she plans to make us follow her across the Gan. Then it'll be Chazendar and the White Bones, there's no end to it. She's out to kill all of us.''

Casting around in desperation for some excuse, Duxe

grumbled, "Anyway, I don't see why we have to go into that hellhole."

Liepol Duxe normally had little truck with witchcraft and was largely unimpressed by what he'd seen. But this was Dugguth, and even he was afraid of what it stood for.

Yortch grew impatient. "None of us wants to go in there, but we have to. Anyway, nothing lives there, and the demon has been dead two hundred years. It can't hurt us."

"So you say."

Duxe noted that Harkness had sobered up considerably now that he understood where they were going. Damn Talionese were so ready to stoop to rape and killing; he hated having to work with them. Duxe shivered. He hated the whole thing, but there was no other way. Not with Kesepton completely bewitched.

The moonlight glittered on the dead city. He could feel something cold and inhuman in those stone hulks. A horrible place where he would be drawn into committing an infamy, something that would damn him forever. He wished he could find the courage to say no to the damned subadar, but it seemed he was in too deep to back out now. He shivered and nudged his mount forward.

CHAPTER THIRTY

The same moonlight that fell upon the ruins of the dead city also illuminated a pathway through the pine forest on the mountain above. Down this path came a weary dragon that hummed a happy tune despite considerable fatigue.

Occasionally it paused to slash away some restricting

vegetation; the path was generally used by smaller animals than dragons.

The tune that it hummed was an odd one to human ears, but it concerned a race between aerial dragons and the bets that were placed on one of them, which had great odds against it, and how those bets were recouped by the heroic efforts of the underdog dragon which won the race even though it broke a wing in the last flap.

Bazil Broketail reached the chorus anew and gave it an especially heavy hum. As he did he thought of her, the mother of his children, and he wondered what she was doing at that moment.

Flying on the night air, he decided, somewhere over Tunina as she hunted. They had agreed that she would stay and hunt for the wounded wild drake until he was able to fly again.

Then she would fly north and find a good place to nest and hatch her and Bazil's young. Of course that would be far away, and those young would quite possibly be unable to fly. Bazil was not sure what the union of a wingless wyvern and a flying dragon would be like, but he had told her that if they were wingless they were to be sent south and he would see that they were raised for the legions of Argonath.

And that brought up another thought, even more unwelcome. Would he ever see her again? She of the slinky green skin and lashing tail and velvet wings?

It was impossible to say. The humming ceased.

The best that could be said was that she would return to Mt. Ulmo the following year. If he could get there at that time then they would be reunited.

And how was a battledragon to be sure of returning to this region at that time? That was a problem, but he resolved somehow to get back here and win her once again. And that brought on euphoria and happy memories and the humming began once more, louder than ever.

Until it was most rudely interrupted by a heavy growl from the forest ahead, somewhere to his right, but close to the trail.

With the growl, simultaneously, came a host of smells. Raw meat was the first, with blood overtones predominant. Then came the stink of a big mammal, a peculiar mixture of musks and muddy odors. Bazil searched his memory; it was unlike anything he could recall, certainly not dog or cat, nor ox or cow or horse or pig. By the Ancient Drakes, what was this? And then he had it, surely this was bear!

Bear!

Bazil slowed his tread and peered into the dark. Dragons have good eyesight in the dark, not as acute as that of cats perhaps, but better than that of most creatures, and he most definitely wanted to see this bear. There were some species of bear that became monstrously large, and they could be very aggressive too. Not even a leatherback battledragon wanted to stumble into a bear like that.

A few moments later he'd picked it out of the darkness, a heavy blotch of blackness within the more general gloom under the pines. It was close, and it was angry and surprised and it was getting ready to charge, and it seemed very big.

Meanwhile the smell of meat had started Bazil's stomach rumbling. It had been a long time since his last meal. Indeed, when he thought about it he realized he was starving.

But hungry enough to eat raw meat? As if he were a wild dragon himself? He was torn; raw and wild meat did not appeal to his civilized side, conditioned to human norms. But he was a starving dragon, and dragons ate anything they encountered, if they felt like it.

Hunger won out over caution. He edged closer, and pulled his shield down from his shoulders and slipped his left forearm into the grips. He wouldn't take the whole thing; he'd leave this bruin some of his kill.

Of course it was always possible that this might not have been the bear's own kill anyway. Bears were more known for driving other predators off their kills than for running down prey themselves, he seemed to recall from the stories they'd told him at the village school in Quosh.

Then the bear lunged out onto the trail with a roar and stood up on its hind legs and roared some more. Baz whistled to himself. This bear was huge alright; it was as tall as himself and it looked as if it might weigh a ton or more.

The bears he'd known before had all been the black bears of Bluestone province, none of which grew much larger than a man. Those bears were no threat to a dragon and shy of man, fearing his arrows and spears which had taken a terrible toll on them.

This was a very different proposition, a giant brown bear, and since it was roaring its challenge to him from just ten feet away now the stink of it was appalling.

The bear was worked up into a killing rage by a mixture of fear and hate. It roared its challenge to the strange-smelling thing that had come up on it out of the night.

The bear was seven years old and in the prime of life, but right then it was in truth a little puzzled, even alarmed, for the first time since cubdom. Never, except in nightmares, had it seen anything as large as Bazil Broketail.

Nor did the thing smell familiar in any way. There were man scents, of leather and metal, and there was a serpent-like odor and an odor like blood, but no blood that this bear had ever tasted.

Again it roared its challenge.

Bazil heard the anger in that challenge, but he was not deterred.

"You got more meat there than you can eat, friend bear," he said in as placating a tone as he could manage. "This dragon will take just half, if you don't mind."

The bear reacted badly to this little speech, perhaps understanding the intent if not the words. It dropped to its four paws and charged up the trail snarling in rage.

"Ah," said the dragon. "You do mind."

Bazil met it with Piocar swirling and shield ready.

The bear slammed into the shield, then gripped it and

shoved Bazil back a couple of steps. The shield stayed between them however, and with a roar of frustration the bear slapped it with a roundhouse left.

Bazil felt himself lifted almost off his feet by that blow and he gave up another step. The bruin had an almighty great punch—it had to be as strong as a maroon troll, maybe stronger. But it was unarmed, and about to get a lesson in humility.

"Silly damn bear," muttered Bazil, and then he moved to his right and swung Piocar in a flat slap that echoed hard in the dark woods as it connected with the bear's rump.

The bruin yelped with shock and pain.

Piocar swung again and connected once more, though not quite as solidly this time. The bear jumped and almost fell over as it scrambled back. Baz let out a dragon roar and charged it, bringing his sword overhead for another swat with the flat of the blade.

This blow rang on the bear's head. It went down for a moment, then rolled over, crushing small trees and came back up snarling for more.

Baz met the charge, got his shield down to occupy the bear's claws and walloped it on the rump and flank again and again.

It tried to swallow the shield—great gobs of saliva flew into Bazil's face. He shook them off and then was shoved backwards by the brute strength of the beast.

They paused. The bear stood up on its hind legs again and considered the situation. It didn't seem to be getting anywhere with this and its rump was smarting from some tremendous blows. It looked back at the monster it was fighting. Was this really worth it? Getting whacked all over the body by an opponent that you couldn't seem to get a grip on?

The bear was unsure about this.

Suddenly Bazil let out a dragon scream and charged. The bear was spooked; abruptly it turned about and crashed off into the thickets at high speed.

Staying around to fight this monster for the remains of

that old elk he'd killed was not something the bear wanted to do anymore. It was time to go elsewhere. He'd never run from anything in his life before, but clearly there was a first time for everything.

Bazil wasted no time in appraising the carcass of the elk. It was an elderly animal with thin limbs and gaunt ribs. It had been simply too old to outrun the bear once it got close.

It was going to be tough and very, very chewy.

With a sigh he divided the elk carcass in two and then took up the front half and carried it away.

He butchered it crudely with the sword and then wiped the blade before sheathing it once more. He sat down on a rock and applied himself to the elk and devoured it, with a lot of chewing and a lot of saliva. The biggest bones he tossed into the bushes, the rest he chewed up and swallowed.

Noodles with akh it was not, or roasted salmon, or any of the more sophisticated foods he had grown used to living among humans, who had elevated cooking and foodlore to a point far beyond that of any other race. But chewing the tough, gamey-flavored flesh of the old elk brought out something wild and primeval in Bazil's heart. This was something he was meant to do, just as he was meant to fight for a female and win her and lie with her on a mountaintop. The taste, which had been sour and rich at first, gradually became acceptable, even enjoyable.

He was finishing his half of the elk when he heard a new noise nearby. Vicious snarls and growling echoed through the trees.

A look back showed that several smaller animals were at work on the other half of the carcass. By the snarls he identified a group of coyotes in conflict with something else that was keeping them very busy.

Bazil moved closer, surreptitiously. Like most dragons he had the ability to move quietly if need be in the woods, and now he shifted to within fifty feet of the fracas around the elk remains. The wind was blowing toward him quite strongly and thus the warring little animals were unaware of his presence.

Crouched over the elk was a small dark creature with a big mouth and oversized teeth. It kept snarling and snapping at the trio of coyotes that surrounded it and driving them back. Whenever it charged, however, another would rush in and nip its rump or tail.

Bazil watched the contest for a little while. Three coyotes didn't seem to be quite enough for this indomitable little fellow.

Abruptly the wind began to shift, taking his scent to them. Bazil moved into view and gave a loud hiss. The coyotes almost leapt out of their skins and disappeared in a flash. The small animal in possession of the kill remained in place, however, and continued to snarl defiance.

Bazil stared down at it; in the moonlight it was hard to see clearly in detail but after a few moments he understood.

"Ah, a gulo," he snorted. No wonder—this most fierce of all beasts would rather die than surrender anything, especially a kill like this.

Bazil examined the wolverine briefly and prodded it with Piocar once or twice, eliciting howls of fury but no retreat, and then with a chuckle he left it and went on down the trail.

The place where he'd eaten his half of the elk was already the scene of vigorous scavenging by weasels and mink.

Far ahead in the moonlight he could see the dark, wide-spreading Gan, with great rivers glistening where they weaved across it.

He intended to descend to the Gan, find the Argo and move along that until he reached Dalhousie, then he would get across the river somehow and report for duty. This seemed a more likely bet than searching in the vast expanse of Tunina for the small force under Captain Kesepton.

The thought of his dragonboy roaming around out there

with no dragon to look after him brought a twinge of worry and guilt. He'd never forgive himself if something happened to that boy while they were seperated. What had got into him to run off like that and get lost in the forest? He was supposed to be a trained military dragon and he'd lost his wits when poor old Kepabar was killed.

Well, at least he knew better than to try and search Tunina for Kesepton's force. From Dalhousie they could be reunited, eventually. In Tunina he might blunder around for years, tormented by elves and forced to live wild on elk and bears!

The pine woods thinned out suddenly and he found himself on a deer trail that passed along one side of a ridge that jutted out from the mountain. On the far end of the ridge something caught his attention. The suggestion of walls and towers, a human-built fortress!

He hadn't known there was a legion post out here, but if there was then things could be simplified considerably. Somehow a message would be sent, and he would be reunited with Relkin and the rest of the 109th in a matter of days.

He picked up his pace, dipping down into gulleys that cut through the side of the ridge where pockets of oak and birch survived. Finally he came out of the last gulley and found himself standing at the edge of a dry moat. It was then that he made a discomforting discovery: the walls of this place were in ruins.

Jumbled stone covered the bottom of the moat, glinting in the moonlight. Jagged towers were broken down along the wallfront. The ruins had the look of great age about them. Intrigued, he stepped forward, climbed the moat and found a breach through the masonry wall to reach the city within.

CHAPTER THIRTY-ONE

Set less than a mile from the city, as close as the men were prepared to go in fact, was the camp—a huddle of tents and shelters, with three fires blazing and a corral for the horses to one side.

It was a quiet camp; the men, survivors of two hard battles in the past three days, were shocked, bruised and exhausted. They'd fought too much and seen too many friends die to even think about celebrating around the fires. This was a good thing considering the likely topics of conversation.

Even the smith, burly Cowstrap, was too weary to repair damaged weapons, of which there were many. After the evening meal, washed down with a measure of whiskey released by the captain, everyone laid themselves down and slept except those unfortunate enough to have pulled watch duty.

But underneath the exhaustion there was a pulse of something uglier, for the men were close to mutiny. After the fight at Ossur Galan the rumors had begun about what lay ahead of them. It was being said that the witch was going to lead them onto the Gan. There were enough horses now for every man to have a mount, and with them they would ride to hell under the witch's command.

The captain, it was also said, was besotted with the witch's beautiful young apprentice and helpless as a result. No one wanted to follow that witch out onto the Gan, to be lost forever in the sea of grass until they were slain by the nomads, or worse, taken as slaves and sold in Tummuz Orgmeen.

It had barely been articulated yet, but it was there, and

if the captain ordered them to ride out onto the Gan he was going to be slain, along with the witch and the girl. Furthermore, anyone else who didn't go along would also be killed and the survivors would tell the authorities they had died in battle. The question of what they would do if the surviving dragons wouldn't accept this had not yet come up.

At the campfire of the 109th dragons, the boys discussed the rumors briefly. They were grieving for Tomas, killed beside old Kepabar, and Kalstrul, Sorik's boy, who had been found dead after the battle, slain in a thicket during the victorious pursuit.

The trio of dragons that was left, Chektor, Vander and Nesessitas, slept like dunes around the fire. The surviving boys lay back against the dragons. Relkin and Marco Veli huddled against Nesessitas, but Relkin did not sleep, lost in misery at the thought of his dragon wandering somewhere out there in the unknown forest.

No one knew what had happened to the Broketail dragon. Bazil's wild charge at the end had completed the enemy's rout, there had been a wild pursuit through the forest, and afterwards the leatherback from Quosh was gone.

Somehow Relkin was certain that his dragon was not dead. If Baz had died he was sure he would have felt something, and he had not.

Which of course left him wondering if Bazil was out there somewhere with a broken leg or a wound too serious to let him move. Would his dragon die alone, perhaps starve to death?

It made tears well up in Relkin's eyes even though he was fifteen now and hardened by experience of war. His dragon was lost and anything might have happened to him.

He was exhausted, but he could not sleep. He heard Rosen Jaib talking in a sing-song voice to the sleeping Vander on the other side of the fire. Vander had a nasty leg wound; he could not keep up with the rest of them and would have to be sent down to the Argo as soon as he was able to move.

Behind him Nesessitas snored, softly and gently as usual. Marco was asleep, Heltifer was asleep in his blankets, too. Even the elves, trackers sent from Matugolin's army, were asleep in a row beside Heltifer.

There was nothing to keep Relkin from his dire thoughts about his lost dragon. He tossed and turned a while, and then got to his feet and wandered away to visit the other fires of the camp.

He considered disobeying orders and going out into the forest to search for Baz. There were elves out there tracking, but Relkin mistrusted the forest folk when it came to dragons. Would they report a wounded dragon unable to move, starving to death alone?

Relkin wandered over to the biggest fire, where they had cooked the evening meal. Rosso was the surviving cook and he was asleep. So was Cowstrap the smith. The Marneri men were laid out in a row, asleep in their blankets.

Still restless, Relkin went on and came to the fire of the Talionese troopers, lodged away from the rest, with their horses pegged nearby.

A few of these men were still up. They had augmented the rum ration with a flask of black spirit, picked up on the battlefield. The black drink of Tummuz Orgmeen was sweet and fiery, and tainted with the dark magic to feed the urge to battle. The most faint-hearted imp could be made a lion by just a half cup of the black drink forced down its unwilling throat.

Now the troopers' eyes were lit up with the dark energy of the black drink. Their long hair was sticking out wild and unkempt. Their coats were opened despite the cold night air because they were hot from the energy within. Their voices were loud, their conversation uncouth.

Relkin squatted nearby, ignored by the young men, who passed the flask around once more. Their talk turned back to complaints against the witches. This had become something of an obsession with one of them—Trooper Jorse, a thick-bodied fellow from the city of Vo. When Trooper Menster passed the flask and said, "And damnation for all the witches!" Jorse roared in response, "Damn right, damn 'em all to hell."

But then Jorse remembered something.

"Except one, we'll keep that little brown-haired wench from Marneri. Eh? Eh? We'll keep her."

Jorse tugged on his long, ragged mustachios as he said this. The others laughed and slapped their palms on their thighs.

"Right, Jorse got the idea. We keep that one."

"A beautiful little slut. By the gods where do they get them?"

"Exactly, my frien', now there's a tail worth keeping aroun'."

"And a chest worth explorin'?"

"Ha, ha. Now that would be worth an evening or two."

"Anyway, I already had her," said Jorse.

"What?" the others were openly incredulous. Jorse was a boaster, but this was unusual even for him.

"Yeah, had her in the woods that night we camped with the elves."

"Oh really?" said Menster with exaggerated care. "How did you keep the elves off her? They go crazy when they smell a woman in heat."

"I had a deal with that prince of theirs, after I'd had her he could have a go, too."

"I bet he jumped at that."

"He did. Anyway she was sweet, so sweet, and so enthusiastic. What they teach those witches to do, why it's almost a crime!"

"I don't believe it!" hooted Menster with glee and just a trace of concern. Could this be true? Had this oaf Jorse actually had his way with that delicious girl? Menster couldn't stand the thought.

He wasn't the only one present who couldn't.

Jorse was shaken out of his jovial mood by a sudden stinging slap to the face.

"What the hell?" he roared, starting up.

In front of him he found a dragonboy, with a dirk shining in his hands.

"You befoul the name of Lagdalen of the Tarcho. Take back what you said and admit it to be lies, or you must answer to me. Now!"

A damned dragonboy, talking to him like that?

"Answer to you, is it? Well, I'll be . . . glad to!"

Jorse pulled out his own dirk, a heavier, wider blade than Relkin's.

"And I'll be equally glad to cut out your liver, you little reptile pup!"

The others were up on their feet.

"No, Jorse," said Menster loudly. "He's only a boy. Just slap him around, no cutting." But Jorse wasn't listening. In a drunken rage he went for Relkin.

Relkin dodged his lunge, slipped to his left and got a knee up in the man's crotch. Jorse gave an explosive grunt, stumbled and went to his knees. He doubled up coughing and spluttering.

Relkin stood there, praying the man would not get up, anxiously watching the others. They seemed about to rise and attack him.

Jorse was recovering, however; he was a seasoned trooper and had seen more than his share of fights.

"Why, you little bastard!" he snarled, and then he sprang forwards onto his feet, his dirk slicing the air just a hairbreadth away from Relkin's nose tip.

His fist came around in a powerful punch that caught the boy on the shoulder and sent him staggering past the fire.

Jorse fought down the nausea from that kick in the balls and hefted his dirk.

"By the gods of men, I'll cut his witch-loving tongue out of his head!" he roared.

The other troopers got to their feet, but none wanted to intervene other than to tell Jorse to be merciful. To kill the boy would only earn old Jorse a court martial, but with the man intoxicated by the black drink none wanted to cross blades with him. The boy got himself into this, it was up to him to get himself out of it.

On the far side of the camp, sitting by a small fire, Captain Kesepton and Lieutenant Weald discussed their situation. It was not good. Not good at all. Even Weald, the most stable and good natured of men had reached his limit.

"But Captain, the woman wants us to go marching off into the Gan with no orders from Dalhousie. I agreed that we had orders to meet up with King Matugolin and to engage the enemy, but to vanish into the Gan? That will make renegades of us all. We'll face a hanging after court martial."

Kesepton nodded helplessly.

"I'm afraid you may be right. But the orders she showed us were open-ended. You saw them. The lady says we go on, if we say no then we are open to charges of mutiny. We'd certainly hang for that."

"So either way we're going to hang, you and I, Captain." Weald had a habit of putting his finger on the worst case in most situations.

"Looks that way, Weald, unless we can somehow succeed in catching this fugitive she wants. Then perhaps we can get someone to overlook the fact that my entire command has been destroyed in one week of fighting."

"Against overwhelming odds, Captain. The men fought like tigers—we killed twice our own numbers. The dragons slew twenty trolls."

"Unfortunately that's never the yardstick that Dalhousie uses. They will look at the casualty list and then they will send me to court martial."

"What if we can catch this man Thrembode?"

"Well, that will depend on our horses and on his. We lost contact with them after the battle, but we know they had to go north and probably had to climb Mt. Tamarack. That will have slowed them up a bit. We had scouts here all day and we had no sighting of a party heading north.

Unless he starts tonight, we will be ready to match him stride for stride to the river.''

"The way things are going, I expect he will have fresh horses somewhere.''

"That may be.''

"And fresh trolls, too. I've never seen so many trolls attached to such small parties of imp. You know there's normally only a handful of the damn things with a regiment, but we've had more than a dozen each time sent against us.''

Unsaid, but in both men's thoughts, were their poor battered dragon force.

"I know, I know. We can't give battle against such a force again. We're down to thirty-five effectives and it's just not enough.''

"We've lost Vander, old Kepabar is dead, and the Broketail is either dead or lost in the forest. We can't expect to fight trolls again with only Nessie and Chektor.''

A loud yell interrupted them. A pail went clanging away on the other side of the fire. Steel rang on steel.

"What the hell?'' said Hollein, getting to his feet, noticing that his legs were hellishly sore.

"A fight among the Talionese,'' said Weald. "Let Yortch handle it.''

But Kesepton had seen something. He was already in motion. With a groan Weald followed.

They found a dragonboy backed up against a boulder, his dirk knocked away, his mouth bloody. Trooper Jorse, twice the boy's size, closed in, his own dirk shining in the firelight.

Suddenly Jorse lashed out with a boot and caught the boy's leg and sent him sprawling. Another boot caught Relkin in the midriff and turned him onto his back with a gasp of pain.

Jorse leaned over him.

"Alright, little drag-rat, now comes the sticking time!'' Jorse sneered and raised his dirk.

And stopped, transfixed.

A wide swathe of steel, worn but well-burnished, had

suddenly slid in front of his face. He could see his own face clearly reflected in it.

A big voice spoke softly behind him.

"Yess, man has won the fight against the boy. Fight is over now, unless man want to fight me."

It was a relatively soft voice for a dragon. He looked up into the eyes of the freemartin, Nesessitas.

He gulped and gasped, fighting the dragon-freeze.

"Man want to fight me?" purred the voice.

Dragon-freeze overcame him. Impatiently she poked him with her tail tip. He came out of the freeze and backed away, trembling.

The other troopers had their weapons out, but none was inclined to start anything with an aroused dragon armed with one of those long swords.

The next moment Kesepton and Weald arrived on the scene. Kesepton moved aggressively between them.

"Alright, what's going on here?" he demanded.

A silence fell on the scene. Then the dragon spoke, still softly.

"Nothing very much," she said. Jorse had recovered from the dragon-freeze, his blood was up again.

"Damned reptile, I was only chastising him for his own good!"

"And if I fought you, it would only be for your own good, man."

"We're allies, don't you know that?"

"And so is boy, so why kill him?"

Kesepton waved a hand between them.

"Enough! Trooper, drop that weapon. Somebody tell me what started this."

Trooper Menster spoke up at last.

"We were just sitting around the fire, sir, then this damn little hellion came in and punched Trooper Jorse in the face. Jorse sort of lost his temper with him, I'm afraid."

Relkin was back on his feet now, his ribs hurt and so did his leg, but his anger was still hot.

"I did hit him and I don't regret it. He befouled the

name of the lady Lagdalen of the Tarcho, and no one does that when I'm around to hear them.''

Kesepton turned to the boy.

"Ah hah, it is Relkin of Quosh. I might have known you'd be the one to try and fight a trooper twice your size. What's all this about Lagdalen of the Tarcho's name?''

"I will not repeat what he said, but I will make him take it back.''

"Now, now, you'll do nothing of the kind.'' He turned to Jorse, who shifted uneasily on his feet while Hollein glared at him. "Because I will.''

Jorse glared back at him.

"Come, trooper, tell me what you said of the young lady.''

"It's a lie, sir. I said nothing about her at all. I'll leave that for her swains and lovers, sir.''

Kesepton colored; he knew that was aimed at himself.

"I find it hard to believe the boy would strike you and get himself killed on a whimsy.''

"He's a little liar, sir. I gave him no cause to strike me, and then he pulled steel on me. No one does that and—''

Nesessitas shifted weight on the periphery of his vision. He bit the rest back.

Kesepton gave him a long, cool stare. Jorse fidgeted uncomfortably but remained defiant.

"I want no more swordplay in this camp,'' said the captain in an iron voice. "And anyone who does pull steel here will answer to a court martial. You understand that?''

Jorse nodded eventually.

"Good.'' Kesepton spun on the boy. "And you get yourself out of here and go to sleep.''

As the captain left he turned to Weald. "And where the hell is Yortch, anyway?''

Weald shrugged. Subadar Yortch was an unpredictable presence.

In the other direction Nesessitas walked Relkin back

to the fire and the other boys. They were still asleep; so was Chektor.

"You see what dragonboys should be doing now?" she said. He nodded. The blood on his lip was sticky and drying. His ribs hurt something awful, but the worst of it all was the sense of aching loss.

"Where is my dragon?" he said.

She sucked in a big breath.

"Well, boy, the Broketail is a big dragon. He can look after himself."

She lay down and felt the boy sobbing against her ribs. Nesessitas curled her tail about him and hoped she was right about that Quoshite; she missed him and had an idea they were going to need him before long.

CHAPTER THIRTY-TWO

It was rare for a dragon to feel fear, and yet Bazil Broketail could not shake a strange feeling of discomfort that seemed to emanate from the ruins around him.

The moon lit up the tumbled towers and fallen galleries. A few buildings gaped like skulls into the night, their open windows like the empty eyes of the dead. He found himself walking stealthily as if he feared detection.

Massive walls, mounds of rubble with dwarf trees growing atop them, all were illuminated in white moonlight. The sense of foreboding only became more intense.

Then he came onto a broad avenue, stone flagged. Above it loomed the arch of Mach Ingbok. For a long moment he gazed up into the mad face carved in stone.

There was only cruelty and an insane lust for power in that face. He turned away with revulsion and promptly got lost in a maze of ruined courtyards on the far side of the avenue.

He decided to turn back. There was nothing here but rubble and an omnipresent sense of evil. As he worked his way back to the central avenue, near the arch, he heard something to his right, coming from deeper inside the city.

He paused and then heard it again, clearly—the sound of voices. He listened and discerned that there were two women talking together, and there was something familiar about at least one of them. Something tugged at his mind.

And then he saw three men, with drawn dirks and swords, stalking through the ruins towards the voices. Their intent was plain; they were about to kill the speakers.

One voice laughed, and he looked up in surprise and dismay. It was the laugh of Lagdalen, dragon friend of Marneri.

The men with weapons were about to kill her!

Bazil moved, slipping quickly down a sloping alley and around a pile of stone.

The men were close, and he could see the women, Lagdalen and Lessis, in their cloaks of grey with cowls up against the wind. The men were familiar, too; he saw the symbol of the Sixth Talion Light Cavalry on their coats.

Did they really mean to kill the ladies? But why else did they draw weapons and crouch there? What mad treachery was this?

The two figures in grey were very close now. Bazil drew Piocar in silence and stepped forward.

For a moment he thought one of the men had seen him. He was only a dozen paces away, standing in the shadow on the same side of the avenue. The man's head had turned towards him, then turned away. But the man had noticed nothing.

The women passed Bazil's position, went on, and the men sprang out of concealment in front of them.

Swords flashed. The girl screamed and tried to run but fell, twisting her ankle. Lessis sprang back, her own knife glittered in her hand. Three men with dirks drawn set against a single woman, caught by surprise.

And suddenly Bazil stood among them with Piocar drawn. The men gaped, their eyes bulged. Baz saw Sergeant Duxe's earnest features contorted in astonishment. And then despair overtook the surprise.

"What goes on here?" said the dragon in a loud voice.

Subadar Yortch was the man in the center, his face a picture of surprise.

"Why, it's the Broketailed one, and the lady!" he said.

"By the old gods, we almost slew them!" exclaimed the trooper beside him.

Lessis held her knife in front of her, her eyes glittered as dangerously as the blade, perhaps more so.

She raked them across the men—Duxe wilted.

She knew what they had planned.

"The Broketail, we thought you lost for good," said Yortch with a slight sob as if he were under great stress.

Bazil looked to Lessis—should he kill them?

"Stay your sword, Sir Dragon," she said. "There must be an explanation for this. A mistake, I'm sure."

Yortch was still struggling to compose himself. "There was a report of imps, lady. Imps here in the city. We came to ambush them."

"Imps?" she said.

"Ah yes,' said the trooper. "I saw them, crystal clear—they were climbing along a wall. I told the subadar and he suggested we take a look. When we heard you coming along, we thought you was the imps."

"Of course," she said with a smile. "Well, if there are imps you had better carry on, find them if you can and dispose of them. I will tell Captain Kesepton that you will report back when you find them."

Duxe had the look in his eyes of a rabbit mesmerized by a weasel. Lessis was dispatching them into the depths of the city to hunt imaginary imps. But they'd already claimed that was their mission; there was no escape.

Duxe stifled a great groan. He was ruined. He knew the lady understood what they had intended. Now she would destroy his career.

Coolly Lessis helped Lagdalen to her feet and walked away. The men were too paralyzed to help. The girl's ankle was tender at first but gradually the limp ceased.

With a long, searching look at the men, Bazil sheathed Piocar and strode off behind the two figures in grey. He caught up after a few strides.

The lady turned back to him.

"Tell me now, Bazil of Quosh, how came you to be here at such a fortunate moment?"

"Ahum, yes! Well now that is a long story, but let us just say that I was lost and now am found."

"Found, yes, and in the nick of time." Lessis reached out and pressed one talon with her hand. For some unknown reason this made his heart seem fit to burst with pride.

They went quickly out of the city and climbed up to the path through the rocks that led to the camp. At the sight of the campfire, a scattered handful of small lights, Bazil felt tremendous relief.

He had barely reached the camp when he heard an excited voice behind him, turned, and a dragonboy slammed into him and wrapped young arms around his leathery neck.

CHAPTER THIRTY-THREE

By the fire, before she went to sleep, Lagdalen finally articulated the worrying thoughts that had been churning inside her since they'd left the dead city of Dugguth.

"My lady, how can we travel on with those men? They

meant to kill us back there. So how can we trust them from now on? They will surely fear condemnation and will have to kill us to avoid court martial.''

Lessis had merely nodded. "Of course. But we have not intervened yet. In the morning I will speak to the men.''

Lagdalen noted that jut to the lady's chin. She knew that was a signal that a supreme effort was about to be made. The woman was a Great Witch, a sorceress of the highest quality. Lagdalen wondered if it could be possible to change these men's minds. But then, she reflected, Lessis could produce the most amazing effects in people.

"They did mean to kill us though, did they not?''

"Yes, my dear, I'm afraid they did,'' Lessis said mildly, "and we shall have to watch those men carefully. It may be hard to dislodge the evil in their hearts now, for exactly the reason you spoke of. The fear of punishment will act as a mirror for their fear of destruction on the Gan. But, I will be thinking of them too.''

"Why do they want us dead?''

"Because we lost the battle at Ossur Galan. And because they fear we will lead them to their deaths.''

Lessis paused to consider something. "And of course they're probably right. The difficult thing to communicate to them is that we have to recover the princess, and that if we must forfeit the lives of all the men and dragons, then we must if by that we can free her.''

"The princess is that important?''

"Yes. All forecasts of Marneri under the rule of Erald show a terrible corruption and eventual collapse of the morale in that city. We cannot allow this to happen. Marneri is the most vital, the most valuable of all the nine cities.''

"What about Kadein? It's so much bigger.''

"Ah, Kadein. If only they knew how to work in Kadein. But they are a great trading city and they are blessed with the wealth of the Minuend. No, Kadein is a great metropolis, alright—someday it will rival Ourdh in size, I think—but Marneri is more vital. Our best generals and sea captains always come from Marneri and Talion. Unfortunately, those from Talion are so difficult to get along with that they alienate their men and sailors, and so it is Marneri that we turn to for the very best.''

"So we must find Besita."

"We must find her and bring her back alive, and untainted by the arts of the Power. Once that dreadful stone in Tummuz Orgmeen has had time to work on her, she will become more dangerous than even Erald."

Lagdalen gulped—were they going all that way? To that terrible place?

Lessis was looking at her carefully, reading her thoughts precisely. "We'll catch up very soon, and then we'll find a way. We won't have to go that far."

Lagdalen accepted this. The fear of the grim city of the Doom faded a little.

"There is something else that troubles you, child. I can sense it."

Lagdalen blushed.

"Come on, my girl, you can tell me. In fact you must, I insist upon it."

There was nothing for it but to confess.

"Oh, my lady, I fear that I am in love."

"Love?" Lessis said the word softly. Unsurprised, however.

"Yes."

"I'll bet it isn't the first time."

Lagdalen was startled.

"Well, no. I'm afraid not."

Lessis was smiling. Lagdalen felt a surge of relief.

"When I was your age I fell in love about once a week, I think. I eventually married a man as well, a great man."

Lagdalen was awed to hear such personal information from the Great Witch.

"What happened?"

"To Hujo? Oh, we are great friends still, although we have not lived together as man and woman for many years. Our work separated us. He is still the leading man in the village and will be until his death."

Village? Was the great Lessis just a village girl? Lagdalen was used to thinking of the village folk as being ignorant, crude, inferior to the city folk. To think that Lessis had come from a village was upsetting to a lot of deeply held prejudices.

"Who is the lucky man?" said Lessis.

Lagdalen licked her lips.

"Captain Kesepton. I know that he looks at me with strong feeling. I can read it in his eyes."

Lessis clapped her hands softly together once.

"Ah, youth! How could I have left this out of the projections? Lessis, you're getting too damned old!" She turned back to Lagdalen.

"I had noticed the young captain's eyes upon you, my dear, and I should have known you'd be aroused to him. He's a good-looking young devil, that's for sure. But—" She raised a warning finger, then checked herself.

"Well, you're young, although I feel a wisdom growing swiftly within you, my child. Soon I will be unable to call you "child" at all. However, in the affairs of the heart wisdom is a difficult thread to pull forth. You must of course realize that the captain is a soldier, he has at least ten years to serve in the legion. So you will be a soldier's wife, living on the frontier here, for at least that long. You won't be living in Marneri, surrounded by your kith and kin."

Lagdalen was clearly ready to sacrifice for her heart's sake. Lessis smiled again; the girl was such a good-hearted sort. She knew she'd made the right choice with this one. And it was equally impossible to guess how someone would come through the turmoil of early adulthood and the attractions of the opposite sex. Or the same sex, for that matter. Lessis knew that her predecessor on the Imperial Council, Great Witch Fyine, had preferred the company of women to men all her life, in bed as well as out of it. It had not prevented her from giving great service to the empire.

She shook her head. There was no way to know how

this would go. Perhaps she would soon need to find a replacement, perhaps not.

"And you should also remember, my dear, that young Kesepton will be seeing a lot of combat in these next few years. He may not survive long enough to support a family."

Lagdalen knew this risk too well. She had seen what battle was like now; never would she forget the screams, the grunts, the clash of steel and flesh and helmet and club. Never.

And her beloved would be going into that hell again and again, for years. Sometimes she thought she could not bear it.

"I know," she said. There were tears welling in her eyes. "Is it wrong, my lady? Is it wrong for us?"

"Not at all, and if you and the captain decide you love each other, then I will be glad to wed you. But not until we are safely back in Dalhousie or some other fort with our mission accomplished. Our duty comes first here, our hearts must obey and we must concentrate on our mission. We cannot allow ourselves to fail. You understand this, of course."

Lagdalen nodded. "Yes, of course." She relaxed. Her secret was out, if it had been a secret at all, and with Lessis one could never be sure. She leaned back into her blankets.

"My lady, I am so relieved that you approve."

Lessis shrugged her shoulders. "Approve isn't quite the word I would choose, my dear. But this old woman knows better than to try to get in the way of love." She chuckled as if recalling some other situation in some other time.

"Oh no, nothing could be more foolish than that. It has its own tides and times, times and tides." Lessis reached out and stroked the girl's face with a gentle hand.

Soon afterwards Lagdalen slept. Lessis removed the small bottle containing the dust she had taken from the syphon in the temple and examined it.

It glittered in the glass. She shook it and watched the

grains sparkle and tumble, literally stuff from beyond the world. There were many uses for such strange material, and in the imperial laboratory back in Cunfshon the researchers were waiting for her to return with this sample.

She put it away and stared into the fire. She had to compose a little speech for the following morning. These men had taken a beating. Of course they'd won a victory, but at too great a price. It had been such a desperate thing, and they were hardly fit to continue the campaign. Certainly not in their own minds after two battles in three days and losing two-thirds of their number in casualties.

But they were all she had at her disposal, and so they would have to be convinced that they must make a great effort. And she resolved that she would have to lay her ambushes more carefully in future.

Ossur Galan had seemed the correct choice. Matugolin was so confident of it that she'd allowed herself to be swept up by his enthusiasm. Alas, the good king was dead, a victim of his own mistake. It was such an obvious place, where the trail could be blocked so easily. The enemy had scouted it and seen them and turned the tables on her. She sighed. It was hard, but she could not allow herself to wallow in guilt—what was done was done. They had to go on.

She returned to composing her address to the men in the morning. It was almost completely worked out in her head when a light touch on the ground beside her woke her out of revery. Her hand flashed instinctively to her dagger's hilt, but then she saw that it was just an elf.

The elf greeted her with a little bow. It was young, but already accomplished enough to wear a necklace of weasel skulls. Clearly it was an exceptional tracker.

The elf spoke quickly in the Tunina tongue, which Lessis understood, though not as readily as the elf tongues of the coastal forests.

When he had finished she rose and dismissed the elf with thanks and sent him to the fire where the other elf trackers were asleep. Then she went to Kesepton's tent and woke the captain.

Five hours of uninterrupted sleep left Kesepton befuddled at first, but under Lessis's gaze he struggled to clear his mind.

"Our foe has emerged from the forest just to the north of Mt. Tamarack."

"Tamarack?" he muttered. "That's about a dozen miles from here."

"He has been met by a tribe of Baguti, the Redbelts."

"A tribe?" Kesepton was aghast. "I don't think we have enough men to fight a tribe."

Lessis was undeterred. "Baguti are superstitious people, they can be panicked sometimes. Perhaps we will be able to surprise them."

"The men may mutiny. The idea of attacking an entire tribe, it's just, uh, excessive perhaps."

"The men will not mutiny." She said it with extraordinary certainty. "But we will have to get across the Oon before our enemy. Then we can set an ambush in one of the canyons on the far side. I know where he will cross—the Baguti always go to the ford at Black Rock."

"How many Baguti are there?"

"Many, perhaps three hundred men and five hundred women and children. They have their flocks and herds with them, to feed on the fresh grass here south to the Oon."

"Three hundred! We'll be massacred. The Baguti do horrible things to prisoners, didn't you know that?"

"Of course. But we will pick our spot very carefully this time."

Kesepton didn't care to argue. It looked as if Duxe was right—the witch intended to kill all of them in this futile pursuit of the magician Thrembode.

"So we must make good time tomorrow, an early start."

"The men will mutiny."

"No, I will speak to them in the early morning. They will go on, you will see."

He didn't see, but he didn't argue either—he knew it would be pointless.

CHAPTER THIRTY-FOUR

The Princess Besita who had once dwelt in Marneri would scarcely recognize herself, but this lean young woman with hardened features and blank eyes was the same princess who had been abducted on that cold night, so many months before.

The changes were many. Instead of her regal ermines and silk she wore just the simple shift of a nomad woman and carried three big waterskins over her shoulder as she strode down to the stream nearby.

The heaviness in her body, which she had fretted about in Marneri, was gone. Along with any chance to overindulge in fattening foods.

They had arrived the night before, finally emerging from the dark depths of the forest onto this open plain. It was a vast place, a flat immensity, broken here and there by low hills that stretched away to the west.

The Gan, the men had called it. Especially Gasper, rider Rakantz of Captain Ushmir's detachment. He had been telling her about the Gan for days, ever since they'd entered the forest in fact.

According to Gasper Rakantz, the Gan was a cruel wild place, where men like Gasper killed their prey without hindrance and had their way with any women they met. The Gan was a desert of grass ruled by nomads, and the nomads were ruled by men like Gasper.

On the Gan, came the hint from Gasper Rakantz, anything might happen. Even the sudden murder of a bad-tempered magician with more arrogance than was warranted in any man.

On the Gan she might be free of Thrembode. . . .

For some reason this idea did not excite her as it once might have.

The stream ran almost straight down a gulley lined with white rocks. The water was high, and she did not have to do more than hold the waterskins down under the surface to fill them.

The water was cold, too, a chill that mimicked the deep freeze that had settled on her heart. She no longer understood herself. And that was not entirely the fault of Thrembode the magician.

At first her abduction had been a thing of wretched confinements, bound and gagged, smuggled in a carpet aboard a merchant ship, hidden in a coffin one night in a mortuary in Ryotwa.

Then in Kadein things had improved. There'd been a luxury suite of rooms in a grand hotel plus Thrembode's impassioned lovemaking and their mutual pursuit of the muse of art and music in the great city.

Something had changed in her heart. It was so romantic, living an underground life of luxury. Thrembode had friends everywhere, or servants, it mattered little. Agents of the witches sought him out, but he evaded them with ease and they never penetrated the secret of the hidden suite of rooms in the Hotel Tablor.

She'd stopped thinking about escape. She'd stopped resisting his advances, had in fact grown to relish them again.

Was it love that she felt? Could she actually love this man of cruelty and harshness, who was also capable of such sweetness that she willingly surrendered to him?

But, she asked herself, how could she resist him? The knowledge of his power, coupled with his wit and intelligence, overawed her. He was so far beyond all the men she'd known it was almost as if he were another kind of creature altogether. In fact she was his slave. And she seemed happy to be so. It was just hard sometimes to understand why.

Not that he beat her, often, at least not since the time at the pink villa outside Kadein. That time she'd fought back and he'd gone wild. Gone a little too far, leaving her crumpled on the floor.

He'd checked himself then, livid with fury but aware of the value of his prisoner. His life lay in the balance and he needed her. His Masters would not accept failure, and her death would be a most grievous failure.

She had realized her hold over him. He could not harm her too seriously, no matter what she did. And yet she did not push him too far; she was content to serve.

Perhaps, she'd thought, she was making amends for the shallow, comfortable life she'd lived. Now she was tasting the hard side of life. Oddly she felt more alive than she had ever felt before.

Staggering under the three full waterskins, she made her way back up the slope to the camp. It never ceased to amaze her—here was a princess of royal blood, carrying water for her master like any common serving wench, but she felt no real sense of outrage. She had no wish to complain.

They'd pitched the tents in a grove of foragebush on top of a slight rise. The Gan lay flat and open on all sides, except to the east where the trees thickened quickly into the forest that cloaked the higher ground of Mt. Tamarack.

Further south, dominating the scene, was the massive dome of Mt. Ulmo. She stared at the mountain and its white snow cap. Somewhere far beyond that mountain, beyond other mountains, lay her home.

Home—there should have been more feeling behind that thought but there wasn't. Home did not seem to mean what it had once. She was puzzled by this lack. She loved Marneri, where else could she want to be?

Then she thought of Thrembode lying stretched out on a bed in Kadein with the winter light on his tawny skin. He was her home, he was her god. She felt the heat begin again in her loins. She needed him, desperately, nothing else mattered anymore but this violent need she had for his body.

The water was heavy, but she bore it up the slope and into the camp. She was getting better at this. In the early days she'd been appallingly weak and helpless.

Even as she set the water down, her master's voice came from his tent.

"Here—wash me, woman."

She poured water into a small basin and took up a clean pair of rags and went in. Thrembode sat on a small camp stool, wearing his boots and little else.

She trembled. He was ready to take her once again.

It was this that she lived for. She got down on her knees and removed the boots. Then she began to wash his legs and feet. His hands tousled her hair; she moved closer. And stopped.

There was someone outside the tent, coughing loudly.

"Uhh, Master Thrembode."

Thrembode's eyes bulged. If this was more impertinence from Gasper Rakantz he'd make the fellow regret it. He'd had enough of these riders. They were nothing more than an elite group of arrogant nincompoops, as far as he could see.

"What is it? I don't want to be disturbed."

He needed the woman's attentions just then; she was the only pleasant thing left in his life. This endless riding in forest and steppe was not Thrembode's idea of a good time. Thrembode was made for more sophisticated worlds, great cities, high societies.

"The Baguti are here. The chieftains want to see you."

Thrembode's eyes opened dangerously for a moment. Then with an oath he pushed the woman's mouth away. God she was becoming quite beautiful, now that she'd lost the soft flesh of civilization. He had trained her well.

It would be a pity to lose her, but in Tummuz Orgmeen she would be required by a higher power.

And all that training would go to waste, for the Doom was merely a spherical stone, a black monster buried in

the city of the steppes. It had no fleshly desires except
an urge for revenge on all living things.

Such a waste. "Alright, I'll be with them in a moment."

He turned to Besita. "My apologies, princess. While
I am engaged with these men, why don't you see what
sort of food Captain Ushmir and his men are preparing
and bring me some."

It was the gentle Thrembode, he was being kind to
her. She loved him for it.

"Yes, Master," she said, and pressed her face to his
boot.

Thrembode pulled on his breeches and jacket and went
out to greet the Baguti chieftains. The woman ducked
out ahead of him and headed for the tents of the riders.
The Baguti eyed her and then one of them whistled. She
did not look back.

Thrembode's eyes narrowed momentarily, then returned to the Baguti. They were short men, with the classic bowlegs of the steppe, nomad peoples. It was said
they were born in the saddle, and it was certainly true
that many of them learned to ride before they learned to
walk.

Clad in dust-colored shirts and leather trousers, with
metal pot helmets atop their heads, they stood there with
eerie false smiles on their round weatherbeaten faces,
while their eyes flicked about nervously examining the
scene, and most of all examining him, whom they had
come to meet.

They could sense the power emanating from him. He
was indeed a servant of the great ones. They could tell.
They would have to go carefully here. He must be delivered safely, along with the luscious wench he had brought
with him. Which was rather a pity.

Women like that were a great rarity on the steppes.
Baguti women were short, bowlegged and ill-tempered,
much like their men, whom they resembled in other ways
as well, including a predilection for knives and for drinking the black drink.

"Welcome to the Gan," said Pashtook, chieftain of chieftains of the Redbelt Baguti. Pashtook had the look of a wily horse thief, which in fact was pretty much what he was.

Thrembode nodded to the Redbelt chief.

"Greetings," murmured Dodbol, spear chieftain of the Redbelt. Dodbol had the warrior's contempt for other men. He wore brass knuckles and carried a heavy quirt that he slapped idly against his legs.

Thrembode felt the challenge in the man, but he restrained himself from launching a spell and instead settled for a cold stare without any nod of recognition for the warrior chief. If there was to be trouble it would most likely come from this one, who was young, heavily muscled and filled with too much pride.

The third chieftain was Chok, horse chief of the Redbelts. He was older than the others, with wiser eyes. He said nothing at first but nodded in turn to Thrembode, who nodded very slightly back.

"Sit," said Thrembode, indicating the rugs laid out before his tent.

The chieftains crouched, they never sat except on horseback. Thrembode set up his stool once more. He pulled a flask from within his jacket, opened it and toasted the Baguti.

"To the brave and the free—long may you roam the steppes and call them your own."

The Baguti struggled with some of this, since their knowledge of tongues beyond their own was limited, but they eyed the flask eagerly enough.

"Good black drink, you bring?" said Dodbol, the warrior reserve broken all at once.

"The best, I make it myself. Very strong. So be moderate."

"I like that, sound good."

Dodbol took a heavy swig.

Fools, simple nomadic fools, thought Thrembode.

The flask moved among them.

"And now, tell me, what conditions lie ahead?" he said in his most diplomatic voice.

Chok handed back the flask.

"Fresh grass all the way to the river. On the other side new grass, too. We can make good progress."

Thrembode had a sudden premonition. "How many are there in your party?"

"Whole tribe. We graze horses here and collect slaves for the market."

Thrembode felt his temper twitching again. Why couldn't anyone get anything right?

"I am supposed to meet with a small party, for a very quick transit to the city."

Chok spat on the ground. The city was an evil place, a place that destroyed men, at least as far as the Baguti were concerned. It was not good to hear it mentioned.

"We not go all the way."

Thrembode nodded. "Of course not. Just to the Fist. But I need only twenty or so men. My pursuers are reduced to very few now. We ambushed them in the forest."

Thrembode enjoyed a warm feeling of euphoria at the memory. Such a victory he had wrought. Of course it had all depended on Gasper Rakantz's sharp-eyed scouting at the Ossur Galan, but still it had been a victory to spice his report when the time came.

He just hoped he didn't have to go on, into the Hazog beyond Tummuz Orgmeen. The city was the nearest he liked to go to the heart of the Great Power. It was always so insufferably cold and disciplined there. Everyone was so paranoid, and the secret police were so ubiquitous.

The Doom could tell Them anything they might want to know. Surely They did not have to interview him personally?

The chieftain of chieftains spoke up. "Whole tribe is going same way you need to go. We take whole tribe, then you really safe."

By the dark gods why did it always have to happen to him?

Thrembode felt accursed. First Captain Ushmir, then a collection of defective trolls that couldn't fight their way through a silk sheet let alone a pair of battledragons, and now these mad Baguti, who were going to make him amble along in their stinking, dusty column for days. But there was little to be done about it. With only five men left he didn't have the resources to risk crossing the Gan on his own.

He'd mauled the enemy at Ossur Galan, but they had won the field of battle and annihilated his force of trolls and imps. The enemy still had a couple dozen effectives left and they had horses. So he needed an equal force, at least, for a swift passage across the steppes.

"I would be perfectly safe with a small group. Then your tribe can remain south of the Oon and feed your animals as much as they like."

The chieftains nodded at this. Chok chuckled and said something in Baguti. Then he said to Thrembode, "You must like Bagut to speak this way." He chuckled again. Thrembode did not get the joke.

No one in the whole world liked the Baguti, and with damned good reason.

Chok controlled himself. "We have to go soon anyway, we have good slaves for the Power. So we go now, quickly and then we return for another visit south of the Oon."

So that was it. They had more slaves than they wanted to feed, and they wanted to get them to the market as quickly as they could.

Damned greedy nomads! Thrembode seethed, but internally. He still needed them.

Dodbol suddenly spoke up. "We travel together. You lend us your woman. We lend you ours. This is ancient custom of our tribe."

Thrembode strove to keep his face from betraying any emotion. "We travel together, but we may not exchange women."

Dodbol leaned forward, his squat features contorted in sudden anger and suspicion.

"What? You insult men of Bagut?"

"Not at all, not at all. But this woman goes to the Doom itself. To be interrogated, you see."

"So what?" said Dodbol with a shake of his shoulders. "Doom is just big rock. Power live in rock, but it no need woman."

"You don't understand, do you? The woman is a very important prisoner, the Doom might even want to breed her with selected men. She must be in condition to breed."

Dodbol scowled.

"Why does big rock want to waste good woman?"

Thrembode licked his lips and looked to Pashtook—could he not see the impossibility of this?

Pashtook could see. He knew that the Doom might never forgive tampering with such a prisoner. But Pashtook was equally sure this magician was tampering with her, and besides there were ways to pleasure that did not involve her power to have children. But Pashtook had lived to rule because he was a careful man, and so he ruled against Dodbol with a chopping hand gesture that silenced the spear chieftain.

"It not matter why. If the Power want woman then no Bagut will get in its way."

Just then Besita returned, swayed past them and went inside the tent. The Baguti looked at her like wolves watching a chicken.

Thrembode cleared his throat. There was potential trouble in the spear chieftain's eyes, but before anyone could say any more there came a loud interruption.

Shouts from the perimeter of the camp and the thudding of hooves.

The Baguti were on their feet in a flash. Thrembode peered over their heads. Two Baguti came riding in; they had someone tied over the saddle on the third horse.

They drew up, with flashing teeth and lots of exclamations as they explained themselves to the chieftains. Then they got down and threw their prisoner to the ground at Thrembode's feet. It was an elf, a young male, still alive.

"Spy, we catch him in forest, about a mile from here."

"A spy, good, well done." Thrembode was pleased with this interruption. "We will question him now, and see what moves our enemies are making."

The elf was seized up onto a rude wooden cross and brought to the fire while Thrembode got out his instruments.

Time during torture often seemed to stand still, everything waiting on that moment when the victim would break and confess all. On this occasion time passed very slowly—the elf gave up very little.

They had worked on the elf with hot irons and had peeled much of the skin off his limbs, and still they knew very little about him or where he had come from.

His name was Barritook, and he lived in the Grove of Gavulon, this much he had told them very early on. He claimed to have been sent out by King Matugolin to search for them. He also claimed that he knew nothing of Lessis or a Grey Lady or where she and her forces, including the surviving dragons, might be.

Thrembode was actually coming around to believing the elf. He decided to give it one more try. Using a hot iron he began to blind the elf, first in one eye.

Inside the tent Besita heard the gasps and squeals of the dying elf. For some unknown reason they meant nothing to her. She seemed devoid of feeling, as if a rock had replaced her heart. She wondered what she was becoming that she could be so cold to such suffering.

Still the elf volunteered nothing.

"Stubborn, unimaginative breed," muttered Thrembode. And so resistant to the Power! If men were like elves, the Masters would rule no more than their freezing vaults in Padmasa.

He put out the other eye. The elf made no noise this time. Thrembode dropped the hot iron in disgust. The blood of the elf was pale and green; it smoked in the fire and smelled like burning apples.

"Kill the damned thing and bury the body," Thrembode snapped to Gaspar Rakantz, and turned back to his tent.

CHAPTER THIRTY-FIVE

The Gan, here in the north, was not as flat as Kesepton recalled from previous experience in the southern stretches. Nor was it the same semi-desert, dotted with acacias and home to antelope and lions. Instead, tall prairie grass predominated, while in the hollows grew thickets of alder and occasional aspens and pines. The spring had brought fresh green to the short grasses, but the longer types were still covered over with the dead stalks of the previous year.

The first day it had been cloudy with a cool breeze blowing into their faces from the west. That night they camped on a low hill surmounted by rocks. Nearby was a hollow with a small lake where they could water the horses and refill their canteens. No fires were lit, and they ate cold rations boiled up the night before.

Almost as soon as darkness had settled over the land a lion to the south of them started roaring. It was soon challenged by another lion somewhere to the north. The two cats continued to roar to each other every so often for hours.

With no fires the men felt a primeval fear of these animals, and they huddled together as close to the dragons as they dared to get.

The lions were bad enough, but the smell of the men and the horses soon drew a gang of hyenas. The horses grew increasingly nervous. Kesepton was forced to rouse the men and send them out to patrol around the horses and keep the hyenas away.

The hyenas showed precious little fear of man; they had to be speared and struck repeatedly to make them retreat. In the dark, it was a nightmarish business. Then the moon rose and it became easier. Lessis conjured a spell that made the hyenas jittery, although it could not drive them off.

Then the dragons were asked to help. They heaved themselves up, three sudden bulks against the sky and charged out at the hyenas. While the hyenas were unafraid of men, they did have all their kind's terror of the giant reptiles, and at the sight of the monsters bearing down on them they panicked and fled and did not return.

The lions however continued to roar at each other, and the one to their north moved closer and then drifted westwards. It had got downwind of them and smelled the horses, the men and other—the reptiles. While the horses smelled like food, the men smelled like trouble and the great reptiles were things, like elephants, that lions always avoided. The lion passed on, seeking easier prey.

Slowly the exhausted men sank into slumber except for the watch and Captain Kesepton. Thus Kesepton saw the two figures in grey that slipped away from the camp under the moonlight.

Hollein started up. The girl was out there with lions and hyenas and who knew what else and without any man to protect her. He wanted to go after them, and would have except that he knew the witch would be amused at his presumption.

What the hell did they do out there? he wondered. The night before it had been the city of the Demon Lord, now it was the trackless Gan. Every night they went off on some secret mission. Maybe she was talking to more birds and animals. Perhaps there were types that were too wild to approach a group of men.

Unlike the birds of the day, which had flown up to them as they rode and visited quite openly with Lessis. All day long they had come to her, and then depending on their size they had landed on her shoulders or her head or wrist, where they sang to her and ruffled their wings.

After the owl in Tunina, Kesepton realized he should not have been surprised by anything. She was a Great Witch; the birds evidently knew this as well as anyone. Such a witch had enormous powers.

The hours passed, eventually the women returned and Kesepton let himself relax enough to sleep.

The second day was much hotter, without a cloud in the sky or any breeze to ameliorate the conditions. Under the sun they were much bothered by biting flies, until Lagdalen pointed this out to Lessis.

The witch immediately summoned one of the flies to her. Even Lagdalen, who had seen Lessis work her will upon all creatures great and small, was startled when one of the big grey flies buzzed in and sat obediently still on the back of Lessis's hands for almost a minute while a spell was woven. Then it flew away.

Shortly thereafter the flies ceased to bother anyone in the entire column, all the way back to the dragons. Kesepton saw this deed and felt a chill run up his spine. Birds, flies, did she control men as easily?

He recalled how she had won over the men in the dawn light on the first day. There had been no evidence of witchcraft, no spell casting, no magic dusts, no flames or smokes. Just a simple speech by a woman sitting on a calm white mare. But that speech had had such a power of truth and a beauty of words that it opened their hearts to the witch and bound them to loyalty.

The men had been ready to mutiny that morning. The command had been destroyed in three days fighting. Two-thirds casualties, twelve more dead men buried at Ossur Galan. The witch was responsible for at least half the slaughter, making them march into Tunina and fight again after they had taken such a hammering on Mt. Red Oak.

Now the witch was going to tell them that they had to go on, to ride into the Gan to who knew what horrible fate. And the men had been determined to say no; the witch would have to understand that the men could be pushed so far but no further.

And then she had spoken to them and they quietened. She painted a picture of heroism, citing the battles they had already fought. She had seen each of them perform some act of courage and skill, and she mentioned every name. Each man felt pierced to his heart by her words.

They would be sung of in the Argonath forever, heroes to match those of the wars against the Demon Lord. This was certain, just from what they had already accomplished. But what they were going to do next, she told them, would send their fame around the world. They were going to go on, into the Gan, in pursuit of a deadly agent of the enemy. They were going to track him down and seize him and thwart his evil designs. It was a blow that would save thousands of lives in the near future, it was a task that they had to perform—all the Argonath depended on them.

The words were pretty, and so heartfelt and correct that they were all beguiled. By the time she finished, they gave her three cheers, thrust their swords into the sky and swore to keep on to the death in pursuit of their quarry.

Lessis thanked them all, and they swept into their saddles and were underway. They rode out with their hearts high and their collective will red hot and smoking. It still had not cooled. They were still buoyed up, still ready for anything. Kesepton was amazed; no soldiers he had ever known had gone that long without complaining.

Were they just like the flies? So easy to control?

Perhaps they were all just sleepwalking, mere puppets controlled by some subtle enchantment. Would she sacrifice all of them if she had to? Somehow Kesepton thought she would.

He shook his head to clear it of these gloomy thoughts but others surfaced in their place. Such as his future in the legions. It seemed likely that his career as an officer was over.

The battles at Red Oak and Ossur Galan had destroyed

his small command. On the legion's record of honor it would appear disastrous. They would probably call this the "Doomed Patrol" or some such rubric. He was headed for a court martial and expulsion from the legion.

Unless they hanged him.

Nobody came back with only a fifth of their command intact. It was very bad for morale. The future looked grim.

Of course there was one aspect of the situation that he wanted to consider, but he had to force himself not to look that way, not to consider how she rode her horse or anything else about her.

Lagdalen—it amazed him how swiftly his interest in her had grown. Every time he glimpsed her now, he felt the tension begin within him. Her beauty, her grace, they riveted him every time.

He had never felt this way about a girl before. Oh, there'd been girls, plenty of them, since he was fourteen at least, but never one that had struck him like this.

And to cap it off, the object of his love was the assistant to a Great Witch involved in a mad quest into enemy territory. In addition to which, he himself was on the same quest and he was many miles from the end of the journey, in pursuit of an overwhelming enemy force, and he had a lot more important things to think about than the swaying walk of a girl! Except that it was damnably hard not to slip up in this resolve every time Lagdalen's form came into view, riding ahead of him on a brown mare beside the lady. Every movement, every curve in that young body made his heart yearn. He had to make himself turn away and stare at the horizon above the waving grass.

A flicker of yellow announced another bird. A small thrush with a brown spotted front. It fluttered up to rest on Lessis's wrist a moment and then sped away.

A few moments later another bird flew in. A bluebird with a stiff little crest. It fluttered its wings as it rested on her wrist for a moment, and then it too flew away.

It was too uncanny to watch, but already he half ac-

cepted it. After all there'd been that owl—who could forget that? His eyes glazed over. All this witchcraft, it was
beyond him, it had no place in military thinking. He
turned his thoughts elsewhere.

But within moments he was thinking of Lagdalen
again. What were his chances with the girl? He tried to
think rationally, to work it through point by point.

If he survived, which he realized was a big if considering how things had been going on this mission, then
there might come a time when they would be together
privately and he could ask her if she looked upon him
with favor. He thought she did; she'd looked at him several times in a way that made him think she had to be
interested in him.

Perhaps when they returned to Dalhousie, they could
walk out together along the river promenade where court-
ing couples went.

But then a critical voice took over in his mind. Who
was he deceiving but himself? He was not high born.
She was.

True, his grandfather was a famous general, but his
father had retired from the military and was a grain merchant in the Blue Hills. His mother came from an old
family with ties to the Cunfshon Isles, but compared to
the Tarcho they were merely peasantry. No, he was a
commoner and she was nobility, and for that reason alone
his love was doomed.

Of course, he told himself, the girl was not very representative of the high born, from his own experience of
them at least. Why would she have become assistant to
Lady Lessis if she was like the rest of her social class?
Why forsake a life of comfort and city excitements for
hard duty on the Gan?

And so the thought gnawed at him; perhaps she was
not destined to be the bride of some rich man, perhaps
she was unusual enough to consider Hollein Kesepton,
soon to be an ex-captain of the legion, if they didn't hang
him.

The thought that she might, that she was a rebel seeking to escape from the society she'd been born into, gave him a shred of hope, and with hope he was tormented.

To evade the torment he deliberately set himself to make plans for the event that he was discharged at the end of this mission.

Among his other options was that of taking some frontier land and beginning a farm. With a couple of mules and the right tools, he could clear the forest and plant his crops and grow prosperous in time.

And with Lagdalen he would have a family and they would grow up as sturdy young frontiersfolk. With Lagdalen. He rubbed his eyes for relief. By the goddess, this was a hell of a time to fall in love!

He tried to clear his thoughts again. Ahead lay the Oon, a tricky crossing with the river rising to its spring peak. On the far side the land rose abruptly to the further stretches of the Gan. There were cliffs and only occasional breaks in them. These breaks in the cliff wall matched the only pair of fords within two hundred miles. Other fords existed but only to stretches of the far bank where the cliffs stretched unbroken.

Lessis had informed him that she knew of a way up the cliffs. And once they were across Lessis intended to set another ambush. Only this time their prey would be an entire tribe of nomads! Kesepton's imagination failed at that point. How were twenty-five men and a handful of dragons going to upset hundreds of nomad warriors?

The lady swore she had a plan. Hollein just hoped it had not been hatched by the birds.

Finally a pair of horsemen appeared ahead and ended this gloomy revery. The men rode down the slope towards them, through a meadow sprinkled with spring flowers. Soon Kesepton could see that it was Lieutenant Weald and Trooper Jorse, who had been out on forward reconnaissance. They reined in beside him.

Lessis had halted ahead, tactfully out of earshot.

"The way's clear to the river, sir," said Weald. "No tracks of anything other than some antelope."

"The far side of the river's lined with cliffs, about

sixty feet high I'd say. We couldn't see any way up them.''

"Good," said Kesepton. "We go on. Estimated distance to the water?"

"About three miles, sir. Once you're over this next rise the ground slopes all the way down to the river. Then there's the cliffs.''

Kesepton shrugged. "Don't worry, Weald. I expect the birds have told the lady a way to get up those cliffs.''

"The birds have, sir?" Weald was looking at him strangely.

"You've seen them scouting ahead for us. I mean, what else are they doing?''

"Well, I don't know, sir.'' Weald's voice dropped to a whisper. "I expect we're all in a trance, maybe we're seeing things that aren't there.''

Kesepton nodded. "Well, maybe you're right, Lieutenant, but until we find out for sure we'll carry on. Right?''

"Right, sir.''

"Trooper Jorse, tell Subadar Yortch I'd like another two-man patrol out front, right away.''

Jorse grinned quite insolently. "Sir, if the birds are helping us surely we can forget about running patrols of our own?''

Kesepton was in no mood to be amused.

"When I want your advice, Trooper, I'll ask for it. Until then, keep it to yourself. Now get along and pass on my message to the subadar.''

Jorse nudged his horse and they moved away; Kesepton kept his eyes on Weald.

"You don't trust the birds, sir?" Weald said softly.

"Damn right I don't, Weald. Now tell me about the water—how deep and how swift is it?''

When they reached the top of the rise and finally had the river in view ahead they halted to allow the dragons to catch up. From Weald's account Kesepton knew they'd need the dragons to help them get across.

The water was running waist deep in places, and it

was cold and moving very fast. It wouldn't sweep away dragons though, and they could keep the rest from slipping downstream.

The dragons caught up and sat down, demanding a short rest. Kesepton was uneasy, thinking they might need every second.

Then a small hawk began circling above their heads, and after a couple of turns it swooped down and settled on Lessis's wrist. After a minute or so there it lifted again and flapped away, building altitude as it went.

Lessis rode back to Kesepton. "Good news, Captain. Our enemy is moving slowly, encumbered by the baggage train of an entire tribe of nomads. We have time to cross and take up positions above the ford the enemy will use."

Kesepton raised his eyes to the hawk, now just a dot in the sky.

"If you say so, lady," he said softly.

Had the bird delivered his death warrant?

CHAPTER THIRTY-SIX

To the dragons, crossing the river came as a welcome relief after the long march. The chill water was wonderful to overheated reptile bodies. They made a great show of splashing out to the deep water and forming a chain to prevent the men and horses from being taken downstream in the swift current.

In the meantime a line was taken across by Marco Veli, who was the best swimmer among them. With the aid of the line and the dragons in the deep places, all twenty-five men and the fifty-odd horses were got across quickly and efficiently.

In the end the dragons were quite reluctant to leave the bracing stream and come onshore again, but were persuaded with offers of cold noodles and plenty of akh.

Everyone ate while Lessis and Lagdalen scouted the cliffs for the secret trail. They found it in less than half an hour, set in a cut-back on the cliff face that hid it from view. It was just a narrow gulley, but there were convenient rocks, like crudely cut steps, every few feet that made it quite navigable for man, horse and dragon. For the dragons it was still an ordeal however, since the gulley was only just wide enough for them to squeeze through, particularly Chektor. Perhaps it was fortunate that Vander had been sent south to the Argo with his leg wound since the big brasshide would have been a very tight fit indeed.

Finally they were all up on top of the cliffs with the river behind them. Far away in the east could be seen the snowcaps on Mts. Ulmo and Snowgirt.

When they looked in the other direction they could see the White Bone Mountains, a line of serried white peaks running parallel to the river's course and ending in the north in a single massive mountain, broken into five distinct peaks.

"The Shtag," said Liepol Duxe to Kesepton. "Tummuz Orgmeen is just the other side."

"I know, Sergeant."

Duxe gave him that searching look again. Ever since they'd set out across the Gan, Duxe had been withdrawn, as if waiting for some blow to fall.

"Sir?" Duxe began.

"Yes, Duxe."

"I, um, I . . ." Duxe swallowed.

"Come on man, spit it out." Hollein had never seen Liepol Duxe so hesitant.

"I just hope we're not going to end up there."

"Where, Sergeant?"

Duxe waved to the Shtag, the "Fist" Mountains that ringed the dread city of the Doom.

Kesepton glanced that way and shrugged.

"Unless we do our part in this everything will be ruled from there, or so the lady tells me."

Duxe was giving him that look again. "You've spoken to the witch then, sir?"

"Yes, Sergeant, of course."

Duxe struggled with himself briefly but said no more.

"Carry on, Sergeant," said Kesepton, spurring his own horse forward.

By the time the sun began to set behind the White Bones they were several miles upstream and in sight of Lessis's destination, a wide canyon where a small river joined the Oon just above a much-used ford across the great river. Several side canyons opened into the main canyon, all had steep sidewalls and bottoms filled with boulders.

Lessis sat her horse and viewed the scene with considerable relief. There was no sign of the Baguti. The birds had been very reliable guides. The nomads were traveling slowly as their herds fed on the new grasses of spring.

For the first time in days Lessis felt her spirits rise a little. This had become a harrowing mission. She felt her prestige, even her position at the imperial court, was hanging in the balance here.

This damnable magician had given her the slip all over the Argonath. First at Marneri, then for months at Kadein, and then in Pennar and Bea and Talion, again and again she'd missed him and his prize, the princess. In Talion she'd come close, and would have had him but for treachery in the Talion Temple.

Once again she'd recovered by riding for five days and nights to reach the Upper Argo in time to find Captain Kesepton and his small force and whisk it north to Tunina.

At Ossur Galan she'd been completely outwitted and almost destroyed. A galling defeat from which she could take nothing but blame.

Still she could not give up. The princess was too valuable to the enemy. Without her Marneri would weaken dramatically at a time when both Kadein and Talion were also ruled by weak men, ineffective leaders who tolerated corruption and a considerable amount of trafficking with the enemy. Such a course would bring disaster upon the entire enterprise of the Argonath.

But now her hopes were renewed. After his victory at Ossur Galan surely Thrembode would have dropped his guard somewhat. He must know that her force was small to begin with and quite disabled by that fight. He would also know that the elves would not leave the shelter of their trees. So realistically what could he fear from her now? He had three hundred Baguti horse archers around him on their native territory.

And so she would make one more try for him. Her means were slender, but armed with the powder from the Thingweight's siphon she had an opportunity to yet recover from the abyss. The Baguti would arrive here sometime late on the morrow. They would find no tracks, no sign of her waiting ambush.

She sighed. It was the best she could do, considering. She just had to pray that it would be enough this time. Failure was unthinkable.

Captain Kesepton came riding up to meet with her while his men fell out and rested. The sun was gone from view but in the twilight the canyon could still be seen clearly. The captain had a wary look. She'd captured him along with the others with her little speech, but she knew that he was made of sterner stuff than most, and besides must be wondering if his infatuation with young Lagdalen was the result of some witch's work.

It was not; Lessis had felt no need to secure his loyalty with such deviousness. Indeed since the desire on his part was matched by that of the girl, Lessis faced the unwelcome possibility of having to find another young assistant all too soon. Still, the captain harbored his suspicions—it would be inhuman not to.

She pointed to the second of the small side canyons on the south side of the main canyon wall. Its entrance was particularly narrow while the side walls were very steep.

"That is where we will build our barricade," she said.

Kesepton could not keep his dismay from showing. The box canyon she pointed to was a perfect death trap.

"I don't understand," he murmured thickly. What was she doing? Did she intend for them all to be killed? So there would be no witnesses to her bungling at Ossur Galan? Kesepton was vaguely aware that even a Great Witch would have to account to someone for the loss of so many men and dragons.

"Of course you don't. Why would we set ourselves in a trap like that? And it would be a trap, except that we must keep in mind the fact that the Baguti will be in a chaotic state after they have crossed the river. At that moment they will be vulnerable."

His forehead creased in puzzlement.

"You've not dealt with the nomads before, have you, Captain?"

"No, my lady."

"They're a disorganized force, with little discipline. We can take advantage of that lack."

"By the goddess, we'll need something to even the odds."

She smiled. "When they cross the river their formations will be bunched up on the banks at first. They will be anxious to ensure that their families and their own animals get across. Everyone will be milling around down there for an hour or so. That is when we strike."

Kesepton stared at her. How were twenty-five men and a few worn-out dragons going to strike three hundred Baguti horsemen?

"First we send the troopers down the canyon on a slash and run raid." She saw his eyes bulge.

"A dozen troopers?"

"We topple a few of them from their saddles in the surprise and cut out a few horses, make the women scream a little."

"This will certainly focus their attention on us."

"Indeed. The troopers will then ride to our barricade, dismount and join us inside."

Kesepton tried to imagine Talionese troopers willingly

abandoning their horses and consigning themselves to a death trap. It was not easy.

"Then the Baguti will follow, not all of them but enough. They will attack our barricade and we will repulse them and cause them some more casualties. They will stand off and fire arrows at us while a few ride down to the riverbank and tell the rest what's going on. As I said, discipline will be at its most lax. Many, perhaps all of the riders will spur their mounts up here to take part in a fight against a small party of Argonath men. It's an irresistible prize for a tribe of scalp and skull wearers."

Kesepton found it too easy to visualize his own skull shrunken over the fire and added to a necklace for some Baguti firstwife.

"So we will be facing three hundred of them here."

"Right, and they will eventually dismount—most of them—and try to storm the barricade."

He nodded. The nomads would be driven by pride and the fear of showing weakness to one another. In this they were like the Teetol.

"We will have to hold them then, but it will be a fight on our terms on our ground and we will hold them."

He gulped. "For how long?"

"Not long, enough to get them worked into a frenzy. Then we will send up the signal to the dragons."

"Oh, and where will they be?"

"Down in the river, upstream from the ford. They will float down once the Baguti are across, but they must not be seen too soon. When they get the signal, though, they will storm out of the river and fall on the baggage train and the horse herds."

Kesepton's eyes widened. "That will upset the Baguti alright."

"At the same time I will unleash some fireworks. We must have it worked out with all our men that when I signal they must shield their faces and close their eyes tightly."

He stared at her, still puzzled.

"Fireworks?" he began.

"Yes, I think that's the best word to describe it." Then she explained and Kesepton's eyes grew wider yet. This was either going to make history, or their skulls would be decorating Baguti necks before much longer.

"With just a little luck, I think we'll be able to reach the forest before they can catch up with us," she concluded.

He knew it was futile to question the plan, and certainly he had no alternative to offer. Still there were things that troubled him.

"What about the horses, where are we going to place them?"

"Lagdalen and some of the dragonboys will ride herd on the horses and keep them within reach when we need them."

At the thought of Lagdalen fending off lions out there on the Gan, Kesepton found himself bestirred with fresh anxiety.

"Lagdalen?" he said.

Lessis had a level smile. "I know, young Captain. Your heart is involved there, I know. But you must remember that the girl is resourceful and brave and she will not be alone. I would not risk her otherwise."

"My heart?" he stumbled.

"Yes," she said. "But it is not my doing, you can trust your feelings. It is no witchcraft except that of the Great Mother herself."

With an effort he composed himself. Well, that at least answered some questions while it raised others. Was he as easily read as that?

It seemed he was.

"If the Baguti pursue us back across the Gan, we will lose the dragons—they'll never be able to keep up," he said.

Her face had become very grave and her jaw had tightened.

"Then we will lose three brave dragons, but we will have to if we are to reclaim the princess."

Kesepton left her then and rode back to confer with

Weald and Duxe. As he rode up to his men, he passed a group of boulders against which the dragons were reclining, resting very sore feet.

Dragonboys were down at a small stream filling waterskins, and while they were gone the dragons conversed among themselves in a quiet mutter of dragon speech.

"By the Egg, I am tired of walking. No dragon was meant to come so far so fast," said Nesessitas.

"My feet are too swollen to walk anymore." Chektor was holding up his hind legs to inspect his troubled feet.

"Don't talk about feet. I am trying to forget that feet exist," growled Bazil.

"What about stomach, then? You forget that too? That not like you at all."

"By the Ancient Drakes, you are a pain in the tail—you know that?"

"Yes, tail hurt too. Too much fighting with tail." Chektor could be implacable.

"Maybe we'll eat soon," said Nesessitas. "Looks like we've reached wherever it is we're going."

"Hope so. Can't keep dragon marching all day without feeding him."

"Or her."

Baz looked up at Nesessitas. "Right." He shifted his back and scratched at an itch under a scale. "You know, Nessi, I need to say something. While boys are not here."

"Say?"

"I owe you a great debt, Nesessitas. You save skin of worthless boy. I heard about what you did. Boy means a lot to this dragon."

"Worthless boys, no good. Boy fight because trooper insult the young witch."

Bazil looked up. "Trooper insult Lagdalen, dragon friend?"

Nesessitas shrugged. "Human sense of honor, you know that." But the Broketail had puffed up his chest and his odd-looking tail was standing up straight.

"Worthless boy did right to fight. Trooper is lucky that it was you who was there and not me."

Nesessitas bared saber-like teeth in a dragon smile. "My thoughts exactly, Broketail."

CHAPTER THIRTY-SEVEN

For Thrembode the magician it had been a difficult couple of days. Being on horseback all day long was bad enough, but the company was stretching his nerves to the limit.

The Baguti men were simply insane on the question of women, particularly attractive women from beyond the steppes. There had been a stream of pests, all trying to speak to Besita, sidling their horses up beside her or cutting in quickly to separate her from Thrembode and the other Tummuz Orgmeen men.

Thrembode had used spells; when they failed he and the others had used cudgels, and then finally they had drawn steel and threatened to cut Baguti heads.

Old Pashtook gave orders that the princess was to be left alone, but such orders were eventually ignored by the young hotheads. Pashtook had little influence now with the young men, who all followed Dodbol the spear chieftain.

Dodbol had let it be known that he was in favor of killing the magician and taking the woman and sharing her with the men for a while until she died, too. Thus Pashtook was put in the position of thwarting the wishes of the young men of the tribe.

Dodbol had added that when the magician was dead they would send a message to the Doom in its dread city and claim that Thrembode was killed by elves at the edge of the forest. Thus emboldened, the young men had become relentless.

For Thrembode and Besita the worst moments had come during the long night they'd spent on the Gan in their tent. Thrembode had barely slept a wink while his men stood guard in turns to keep watch for the young Baguti bucks.

Three times young men hit the tripwire and had to be driven away with blows. On the third occasion there were six of them, and a fight developed that actually crashed into Thrembode's tent. Thrembode had been forced to dispatch one young fellow who was about to drag Besita into the night.

He sent back the young man's head and a loud complaint to Pashtook. It brought an ominous silence.

Dodbol and a group of warriors rode by in the morning and glared at Thrembode and his six remaining horsemen. Pashtook was nowhere to be seen. Since then Thrembode had found his nerves stretched taut as wires, expecting a treacherous attack at any moment.

Indeed two of his men, Siurd and Joab, had managed to detach themselves from the column and vanish into the Gan during the morning. They saw how things were going and had no wish to add their skulls, suitably shrunken, to the necklaces worn by Baguti women.

At long last the scouts came back and the Baguti became excited. The river was ahead; they would cross this evening and make camp on the High Gan.

Within an hour or so a line of low cliffs became visible, breaking the smooth flatness of the Gan. Gradually they drew closer and soon they could see the river, a slate grey curve of hurrying water.

Thrembode had not concerned himself much with the crossing, assuming that the Baguti chieftains knew what they were doing. After all they did this twice a year, every year of their lives.

But to Thrembode's dismay the crossing quickly became a disorganized rout. The Baguti were quite undisciplined about the process and groups of animals were

started over with no clear control. Then a string of pack
animals was knocked off its feet and almost washed
downstream, and fights broke out among the women over
who was to blame for this.

Then a wagon, which carried the worldly wealth of
Pashtook's own clan, broke a wheel in the middle of the
ford. Everything was held up while men struggled to repair the wheel and drag the wagon out of the flood.

When the Baguti were finally across, Thrembode and
Besita crossed on horseback, despite warnings concerning the strength of the river flow. Their horses swam
strongly and well; Besita almost lost her position at one
point, but the horse recovered itself in time and then they
were over, soaking wet and already shivering but safe on
the opposite shore.

Complete chaos ruled on that bank as the tribe sorted
itself out. There were lots of loose horses mixed up with
the pack animals and the wagon train. Baguti women
were everywhere, untangling lines and pulling animals
free. The noise was deafening.

Thrembode turned back to the water. His men were
crossing, except that instead of four horsemen he saw
only three.

When they caught up he rounded fiercely on Rakantz.
"Where is Streik?"

"Gone south I think," said Rakantz.

"Damned traitor—the Doom will have his head from
him."

"Only if we live to tell the tale. From my experience
in playing cards with him I'd say that Streik is usually
one to bet wisely."

"Mmm." Thrembode was not amused. There were a
hundred miles to go or more, at least four days without
a change of horses. He needed the men if he was going
to survive the Baguti with the girl intact.

What his fate would be if he arrived without the girl
or with her damaged by the Baguti he did not want to
think about. The Doom could be very cruel indeed to
those who incurred its wrath.

With an effort Thrembode banished these thoughts, turned to Besita, but found she was already breaking open the watertight pack on the packhorse for some dry clothes. He sighed to himself; at least he could take off these wet things and get warm again.

He and his men grouped as far upstream as they could in the confines of the canyon's mouth. Here they dismounted while the men tried to dry themselves as best they could. Thrembode and Besita put on their dry clothes, sheltering behind some rocks at the water's edge.

Finally Thrembode emerged, feeling a little more comfortable and looking forward to a meal of some sort. He had decided they would camp right where they were and build their own fire. The Baguti would be sorting themselves out for a long time yet, and with the way things had been going with Pashtook, Thrembode didn't want to have to ask the tribesmen for food again.

Furthermore, with the canyon wall at their backs and the river on one side they were protected from the Baguti youths on two sides, which would help if the coming night was to be as active as the preceding one.

Maybe he should go and see Pashtook. Possibly Pashtook did not realize that the Doom knew he was with them, and would know whom to punish if he and his prisoner were not delivered alive and well.

Suddenly these thoughts were interrupted by an even louder outburst of noise, up the canyon on the other side of the mass of horses, wagons and people.

The noise grew louder, there was the sound of hooves thundering, and for a few moments Thrembode could see a handful of horsemen in Talion grey go coursing through the Baguti baggage train slashing at everything within reach with their sabers.

Thrembode felt his heart freeze for a moment. Had the witch been reinforced and managed to get ahead of him? How? It seemed impossible. After the fight in the forest her forces had been smashed beyond repair. Then Baguti riders went past, the shrill yelling of dozens more cutting the air.

Besita climbed back into the saddle to get a better view. She saw a small group of riders heading up the canyon pursued by about fifty or sixty of the younger Baguti men.

Thrembode had followed her example. He was nervous, casting around them for any threat. The witch was at work here; he could almost feel her presence, a formless threat just beyond immediate perception.

"What are they doing?" said Besita.

Thrembode wasn't sure.

"They've dismounted," said Rakantz. "There's some kind of fortification there at the mouth of one of those canyons."

Thrembode pulled out a spyglass, but he found it hard to keep it trained on the distant scene while he sat astride a horse made skittish by all the chaos. Eventually he got down and scrambled up onto the nearby rocks. From there he could see reasonably well.

Across the mouth of a side canyon the fools had built a wall of rocks. The Baguti were attempting to assault this wall in groups of ten or twenty at a time, rushing in and climbing up to be met by a solid line of men with bright steel in their hands. Thrembode watched seven Baguti braves fall to the Argonath blades.

Then more warriors rode into view. Thrembode pulled the glass aside. A stream of horsemen was heading up the canyon to the site of the small battle.

"Now they're all going up there," he exclaimed. "Would you believe it? They've no more wit than their horses."

As Thrembode watched helplessly, the Baguti rode up to the mouth of the side canyon, dismounted and formed up into a huge mob that ringed the wall. Then they rushed the wall, fought their way up it, and went belly to belly with the defenders.

Thrembode was appalled. At least a dozen men died in the first charge, and now he saw blades rising and falling and men staggering and going down.

"They are the most incredible pigs!" he exclaimed. "Look at them going to the slaughter there!"

The whole thing seemed too stupid to be possible. Why were the men of Argonath bringing down the whole Baguti force upon themselves? Why were the Baguti throwing away their lives in this impetuous attack?

Thrembode's skin crawled. The witch; she was out there somewhere, this was part of some dreadful scheme of hers. The hairs on the nape of his neck were rising. The sense of her presence was hanging like a mist around them.

He examined the surroundings. Horses still milled in dense confusion, penned in by the river's edge. A solid mass of wagons was grouped in the center with dozens of women at work moving and maneuvering horses, oxen and the long lines of slaves, mostly hapless Teetol villagers. Whips cracked while the harsh voices of the Baguti women began to bring some order out of the chaos.

Still the witch was up to something. Thrembode looked back to the fight at the wall. It was reaching a climax of sorts as the struggling mass fought on at the top of the piled rocks.

And then there was a chorus of shrieks nearby, including one from just behind him that almost made him lose his balance and plunge to his death.

He whirled about. "What in the name of . . . ." He felt the words die in his throat.

Enormous monsters were rising out of the river and splashing ashore. Battledragons, with those terrible long swords gleaming in their hands. He felt his eyes widen.

Then the dragons were ashore, right among the baggage train. The screams of the women were joined by a new sound as huge swords rose and fell.

Thrembode watched in awe as the roof of a wagon was torn up and hurled into the air by one of the huge beasts as it ploughed through the Baguti. He made up his mind in an instant.

"Back! We will cross to the east shore and get away from this."

A trap! A filthy trap!

The obvious explanation flashed into his brain. The

battle in the forest had been a ruse. This was the real trap set by the witch. No wonder it had been so easy to flank her and destroy her force. It had all been part of this elaborate scheme.

He gritted his teeth and urged his horse back into the river. Well, damn her eyes, she had miscalculated.

Unless there was another side to this that he had yet to grasp. He stared across the stream with sudden terror in his heart, but there was nothing to be seen there on the flat shore.

What if there were Talionese cavalry over there, waiting for them? What if the witch had calculated his every move and was now waiting for him just over there?

Thrembode halted, torn by indecision.

By the black gods, there were perils everywhere. Thrembode felt his mind shifting uneasily on its balance. He struggled to keep control.

The dragons were getting closer—no time to waste! He pushed on, seizing Besita's bridle and pulling her along behind him. The water was just as cold the second time, rushing past in the near dark.

His horse was tentative about the river bottom. Impatiently he urged it on, and it rose on its hind legs and then suddenly lost its footing and fell into the water.

With a curse Thrembode went down, tumbling head over heels, and simultaneously there was a terrific flash of light that lit up the water around him as if it were directly beneath the sun. Clearly, starkly, he saw the muddy bottom, a fish in the distance, crabs and rocks on the mud.

And when he came back up for breath, everyone and everything around him was blind.

CHAPTER THIRTY-EIGHT

It was a desperate fight in a desperate place. Twenty-five men, a few boys and one woman, set against hundreds of Baguti warriors. Their only defense a crude wall of rocks they'd piled there during the morning.

But the Baguti were without leadership and they rushed in armed only with their scimitars. While these were great weapons for fighting on horseback, they were seriously flawed for such tight-pressed work as this.

The first rush was dealt with easily enough. The Marneri men formed into two lines, with swordsmen in the front rank and spearsmen behind them. To either side were grouped the Talionese troopers and the dragonboys. Kesepton, Weald, Subadar Yortch and Duxe were ranged behind this line, ready to move in to plug any gap that might appear.

Kesepton and Weald had their short stabbing swords out, as did Duxe, but Yortch held only his cavalry saber, a weapon of limited value in a tight press.

Behind the wall, over a low fire, the witch was crouched, her face taut with concentration. In her lap was a disemboweled rat, for the magic of the enemy was always rooted in the loss of life. In one hand she held a tiny pouch, packed tight with the alien stuff of the Thing-weight retrieved from the well of horror in dead Dug-guth. In the other she concentrated the spirit of the dead rat. From her lips ran blood, for the taste of blood was also important in this sorcery.

With these things she wove a harsh spell, a cruel spell that could mean the death of everyone present. She was well-versed in the lore of the Masters, perhaps better than any other Great Witch of her time, but in this case she knew less than she would have liked. In particular she did not know how violent the reaction she would unleash might be. It might simply serve her purpose, or it might equally destroy half the Gan in a fireball that would rock the entire world. Unfortunately, she had no choice but to try this desperate strategem.

The Marneri men caught the first rush of Baguti, held them off with their shields while the scimitars flailed away and then worked inside with their stabbing swords.

Seven Baguti were down in a matter of moments, arrows from dragonboy crossbows took down two more and the rest, about fifty strong, ran back panicked by the sudden loss.

They regrouped about eighty paces away. The boys held their fire, not wishing to waste their arrows on distant shots. The Baguti resumed their chanting and hoarse battlecries. A few rode back to tell their comrades and enlist more support. Others pulled out their own bows and began loosing arrows into the canyon.

Crouched behind the wall, Relkin watched Lessis as she worked by the fire. He could feel it now, the magical fury. The hair on the back of his neck was raised; there was an eerie energy source growing there, something vast and terrible, unholy and cruel.

Swallowing hard, he looked away and along the line of men. They were afire for battle, their eyes positively glowing. Swords quivered in eager hands. In that first clash they'd barely taken a scratch—they were eager for more.

Sergeant Duxe stood back from the wall a step and started the war chant. "Argonath!" he roared.

"Will not falter!" they shouted back.

"Argonath!"

"Will not fail!"

"Argonath!"

"Will stand in victory!"

"Argonath!"

More arrows sang overhead and ricocheted off the rocks at the far end of the little box canyon.

The Baguti were fighting like the Teetol fought when they had no war chief. The men of the Argonath felt confident enough in such a clash.

"Argonath!" they shouted.

A thunder of horses hooves announced the appearance of more Baguti. With harsh screams they leapt from their horses and ran towards the barrier. As they came they cursed the men who had broken off the attack and called them cowards and slaves.

The fifty or so braves involved in the first attack were galvanized by these insults, and they too ran forward. The scuffle of feet on rocks was the signal to the men of Marneri and they surged back up to the top where they met the Baguti, shield to shield.

Now the numbers involved had changed the game, but for the Baguti it was still not much improved. As fast as they came forward they were killed, and the bodies of those in front were held up in the crush, hampering Baguti arms trying to raise those long scimitars. Baguti shields were wedged awkwardly and even pulled from their wearer's arms by the dead weight of the men in front of them as they sagged to the ground.

And through it all the Marneri swords and spears stabbed again and again, flicking through the crush of bodies to find exposed necks and bellies and spill their owners' lives to the ground.

But sheer numbers did begin to tell on the left flank where the Talion troopers were not as adept at this kind of fighting. A couple of them were knocked down in the rush, and Kesepton and Weald moved to the left to plug the gap.

Then another heave from the Baguti broke the right side open. Lessis looked up in alarm; Baguti were breaking through and the spell was not quite done.

Relkin looked back and saw her, followed her urgent head motion and ran to the right side with the other dragonboys. He glimpsed bowlegged men with bare chests gleaming with oil; a scimitar flashed at him and he caught the blow on his shield, almost knocked off his feet by it while his arm went numb. Mono burst onto the man and forced him to defend against a jabbing short sword.

Relkin was already occupied. A screaming face, contorted in rage, rose up in front of him. Relkin ducked a slashing blow and managed to get his shield up in time to stop another.

He brought up his own sword in an instinctive thrust. The Bagut was pressed forward from behind and could not dodge the blow which went home and pinned him against the shields behind him. With a sick groan he went down, dragging Relkin's sword out of his hand.

Relkin fell back, stunned and horrified. He turned aside a ringing blow from the next Bagut on his left and stumbled over the body of a Talion trooper and almost fell.

Another trooper rocked back with a shriek as a Baguti blade cut deep, and his body toppled and almost crushed Lessis beside her fire. She did not even blink but spat the rat's blood into the fire and whispered the last words of power. The thing in her hand was jumping and quivering, eager to be born into horrid life.

It was almost done. But the last process was the most tricky, for it took the life of the infant Thingweight and converted it into simpler energies. She concentrated again, fixing the pouch with a gaze so intense it began to smoke.

But now the men of Marneri were now flanked on the right. Relkin was spun aside by a powerful youth, a glancing blow rang off his helmet and he stumbled to his knees.

A swordsman was down, a Baguti knife in his belly. Another Bagut was dying, stabbed through the heart, but more were pressing in behind him.

Then Kesepton was there, and another Marneri man, and Subadar Yortch joined them with a wild yell and their swords flicked out into the onrushing Baguti. Men fell, a pile of bodies began to form and Kesepton led the others, smashing forward and driving the wavering Baguti back and off the top of the wall.

Kesepton was breathing hard, even his strong arm was growing weary from the heavy work. He saw Relkin and bent down and picked up a sword, which he tossed to the dragonboy.

"They come again on the left, sir!" said Weald with a gasp.

Kesepton looked up and sprang to it.

Yortch eyed Lessis. "We will all die in this place, I think," he said.

"I think not, Subadar," said Kesepton. "I think not!"

The Baguti came again and once more broke through with their initial push. A trooper was pushed over, and one of the Marneri spearsmen was hamstrung from behind and then beheaded as he fell.

Relkin was thrown back by a powerful Bagut wearing armor plate on his shoulders and chest. A scimitar flashed in the next second and met Relkin's blade to blade. Relkin felt his wrist go heavy with the crunch of the blow.

The scimitar came again; Relkin could not get his shield up in time. He ducked and felt the blade ring a glancing blow off his helmet.

He staggered—the Bagut moved to open his belly, but a spear lanced in and caught the man in the throat.

He put his hands to the spear and pulled it forward. The spearsman got a foot up on the Bagut's thigh and pressed home the spear and toppled the nomad.

Moving by instinct while his head rang, Relkin got his shield up in time to protect the spearsman from the man to his left and took another heavy blow that sent shocks through his arm and shoulder. Relkin's shield arm felt like lead, his head hurt and he could scarcely think. When he tried to swallow his dry throat rasped.

And suddenly there was an uproar away down by the river. Shrill screaming broke out among the Baguti women.

The Baguti men quieted, and wavered. More than thirty had already paid with their lives for this ill-considered assault. This was not their kind of fighting. But the spear chieftain was there and he bellowed and shrieked and drove them forward once more.

"The drags are at 'em," shouted one of the spearsmen.

But the Baguti were coming and the men of Marneri were spent; they could not hold the enemy any longer. Then Lessis bounded to the top of the wall while blowing frantically on a cornet. An arrow missed her by less than an inch.

"Down!" screamed Kesepton, and everyone threw themselves to the ground as Lessis raised an arm and opened her hand and shouted the final word.

The world shuddered, the ground seemed to heave.

Relkin fell off the wall with a crash. All the breath was driven from his lungs with a single explosive grunt, but he kept his eyes screwed tight as commanded.

And the darkness became light! The world was filled with a blaze so intense that it was brighter than any sun and then it was gone and all seemed darker than it had ever been.

He opened his eyes, there were red and green spots floating on his vision, as if he had stared at the sun too long.

But he could see, while the Baguti could not. From the nomads now came wails of terror mingled with screams of outrage.

The captain was back on his feet.

"Now men, let's to work," shouted Kesepton.

Lessis was scrambling over the wall.

Relkin dropped his heavy shield and got to his feet, lungs heaving with the effort to get his breath back. He crawled up the wall.

The Baguti were in chaos. Some men fell from their horses and crawled on the ground, others rolled here and there wailing like wounded animals.

The men of Marneri stumbled past them, following Lessis who was running down the valley as fast she could go. They followed and went past the shrieking Baguti women and the panicked horse herd that was streaming up the canyon in blind flight.

By the river they found the dragons sitting beside smashed food wagons, helping themselves to horsemeat sausage and whole sides of dried salmon.

Nearby, standing in a dazed group, mostly blinded, were about a hundred men and women, chained together at the ankles. These were the slaves bound for a grim future in the works of the Blunt Doom.

All bore the marks of the lash.

"Poor devils," said someone.

"Free those people!" ordered Kesepton.

The men surged forward and began to free wrists and organize the cutting of the chains between them. A fire was started, and burly Cowstrap brought out his hammer.

Now Lagdalen and Rosen Jaib rode up with the horses, which had been kept in a distant canyon to preserve their vision. Eagerly the surviving Talion troopers swung into their saddles. The Marneri men followed suit, and so did Lessis who climbed aboard her white mare and galloped down to the river's edge.

Here she moved back and forth, scouring the place with anxious eyes. Where was the magician?

They had captured a handful of the black-shirted troopers of Tummuz Orgmeen, but the magician and the princess were not with them.

Lessis rode to high ground and cast about her for some sign of them, but there was nothing to see in the gathering dark. They rode back, Lessis in a storm of impatience driving her mare harder than she had ever driven her before.

"Search the wagons!" she called, her voice cracking with anxiety.

The man had to be here—he couldn't have escaped again!

CHAPTER THIRTY-NINE

Thrembode counted himself among the fortunate, despite his sodden clothes, his loss of all the troopers and his now uncomfortable loneliness on the steppe.

He was fortunate indeed, because despite all this he could still see with both of his eyes. Furthermore, the horses could still see and were able to pick out their way across the steppe. The horses indeed had found the hidden pass that got them off the riverbank and up onto the Gan. So luck had not abandoned him entirely.

Besita, on the other hand, was partially blind. The flash had struck while her right eye had been closed, just as she plunged into the water as her horse fell. Her left eye had caught the flash. She could see nothing with it, and barely comprehended what might have caused it. She seemed bewildered, almost witless, and on a couple of occasions he had used his whip on her out of frustration with her stupidity.

Besita might not be able to understand what had happened, but Thrembode could and he knew the source of the problem.

It had been the witch, damn her! And she had used something enormously powerful for an Illuminant, something so powerful that it was far beyond anything he knew of.

He had seen that flash, while underwater and with his eyes closed. The world had gone as bright as day for a moment. Anyone in the canyon with their eyes open would have been blinded, perhaps for life.

He caught himself marveling at the audacity of it. She could not have more than thirty men, plus a few dragons.

The moon was high now and very bright. The steppe was transformed into a grey velvet flatness beneath a dark vault in which the stars gleamed like jewels on velvet. It was cold though, damnably so, and their clothes were soaked and would have to dry in the wind. There was no time to waste.

Thrembode thanked the dark gods again for the fact that he had escaped the witch's trap. But for those dragons and the panic they'd raised, he'd have been there with the rest of the poor fools, completely blind, helplessly awaiting the pleasure of the witch.

Instead he was giving her the slip once more, cutting west across the High Gan to the land of ash canyons that he knew lay a day's ride away. Once in those canyons he would be able to lose his pursuers.

And then it would be a flat out race to the north, to the gates of Tummuz Orgmeen. The witch was sure to find his trail, but she would be hours behind them. She would have to choose between following it into the canyon land or cutting her losses and heading north to try and get ahead once more and take them in ambush somewhere in the lava lands.

He nodded grimly—that's what she would do. She would go north and work up an army of spying birds and animals and try and take him in the night. Well, there were precautions he could take against that!

And being alone meant he could make good time, at least as long as these horses held up. And he was free of the immediate worry about the damned Baguti. Another night with hot-eyed braves circling them, lusting after the princess, would have been impossible. Tension like that could only lead to a horrible incident, most likely a massacre.

Yes, it was better to be free of Dodbol and his braves and to be able to make their own pace. Thrembode just wanted to reach the Shtag in safety and hand over the wench. Then he wanted an assignment in some other part of the world. He cursed to himself—it was a wretched business being so wet and cold!

Far away, floating in the dark with an ethereal light, the ice atop the White Bone Mountains formed a mocking palisade above the horizon. Thrembode had had enough of ice and cold and witches. He would head for warmer climes just as soon as he had completed the task at hand.

The Princess Besita was also miserably cold and wet. The half-blindness was horrifying; she was terrified that it might be permanent. She thought again and again about that bright light, that incredibly vivid flash.

Thrembode just said it was witch magic, and she supposed it was. And it had blinded her.

It seemed awfully unfair.

Dimly she stared at the distant mountain ice. She tried not to think about her destination, there, in the far north, beyond the ice mountains, where lay the city of the Doom. All her life she had lived with the vague terror of that entity and now she was going to be taken to it. When she looked north her heart quailed and she felt as cold inside as she was on the outside.

And then she looked at Thrembode and felt her heart warm in the fire of her infatuation. She hoped they would stop soon so she could give herself to him, even wet and cold, under the stars; she would writhe with him, do anything he wished. None of her many loves had ever been as intense as this! With Thrembode she lived at a higher level of mortal tension.

Of course it had been her handsome magician who had found her, who had plucked her from the water. He was a good swimmer; like everything that he did, he did it well.

He had found the horses and managed to walk them out of the torrent and onto a sandbar that connected on the shore. And of course he would not let her lie on the sand and weep and moan about her half-blindness. No, he had driven her mercilessly on down the riverbank, stumbling through the rocks and now out onto the Gan, into this cutting wind.

When the moon slipped behind the mountains, Thrembode dismounted and urged Besita out of her saddle as well.

In the dark they would walk, leading the horses and being careful not to let them step into a coney hole. Without the horses the damned witch would still be able to catch up with them.

And though Thrembode was cold, he still felt something much colder pass through him when he thought of the consequences of being captured.

CHAPTER FORTY

The men were subdued around the campfire. They ate provisions stripped out of the Baguti larders and drank some whisky and passed out, exhausted.

The dragons lay down after the meal, dragonboys perched amongst them, and dragon snores soon reverberated through the camp.

Lagdalen, however, did not sleep immediately. She relived her own memories of the day, of waiting with the horse herd a dozen miles to the west until the sky above the river went white suddenly in an enormous flash of light. Then they'd ridden hard for the canyon and arrived to find the men of Marneri and Lessis down by the shore, completely ignoring the shrieking Baguti who were stumbling helplessly around on the canyon floor amidst their blinded horse herds.

Lagdalen still had spots before her eyes from that flash of light. Brighter than any lightning, brighter even than the sun, indeed she was still awed.

Lessis had explained it to her in a matter-of-fact way as they were helping to build the wall. She was going to liberate the energy in some of the Thingweight matter

that they had taken in that grim place in the city of Dugguth. To do so had required the witch to commit blas-
phemy and use the techniques of the enemy, for the Rose
Magic of the Isles would not affect the matter of the
Thingweight, an entirely alien substance.

The result of the flash was that the Baguti would be
blinded for a few days, some for weeks, a few for years.
They were no longer a threat.

It was so fantastic that she wondered briefly if she was
really living this life, or whether it was all a dream. To
think that just a few months earlier she had been confined
to the Novitiate, scrubbing floors and learning catechism
day after day. All that seemed like someone else's life on
another world somewhere.

But after so many days of living in the saddle, Lagdalen was unable to continue this revery for long and
soon slipped into the oblivion of slumber.

Lessis, on the other hand, spent the night in a turmoil
of nerves. She interrogated the troopers from Tummuz
Orgmeen, but they knew very little. The magician had
turned back into the stream when the dragons had burst
out, but then the light had flashed and they knew no more.

Lessis had ground her teeth. The man's wretched luck
was endless! He must have floated downstream, possibly
not even affected by the flash. Despite everything the
damned man had got away again, and he had the princess
still. It was insupportable.

Worse of course was the fact that they'd taken casualties in the fight at the wall, and she knew that it had been
a much closer thing that she'd anticipated.

The thought that it had all been a waste of lives and
effort made it irretrievably bitter. When this was over she
would beg for a sabbatical. Perhaps she could herd sheep
on an upland farm, perhaps it was all she was good for.
When dawn finally broke she roused Lagdalen and went
south to hunt along the riverbank.

Her worst fear, of course, was that she would find the
princess dead, drowned and washed up on the riverbank.
But by mid-morning they reached the hidden pass to the

Gan without seeing any bodies, not even a dead horse. Lessis dared to hope that Besita was still alive.

She dismounted and went over the ground with a careful eye. It was difficult to pick out the trail from that of the fifty horses they'd brought through there the day before, but eventually she was sure the man and the princess had been there and walked up, leading a pair of horses. Their tracks were just a bit sharper, almost clean in comparison to the others.

At the top, amidst the chaos left by their horses and themselves the day before, it became more difficult, the ground was harder, the tracks innumerable.

When Kesepton and his men caught up with her she sent them to track around the edge of the trampled area and find the trail. It took a while, but eventually they found it. Two horses had gone down a rocky streambed and then climbed out and gone west onto the short grass steppe.

Lessis felt her heart sink. The magician was heading for the canyon lands. They would reach the ash plain tonight and be in the canyons by morning. The chance of finding them there was slim.

It was just as she had feared, a total disaster.

The men were waiting in a tense group, standing by their horses on the edge of the cliffs. A fire had been made to brew some tea and warm some porridge. The dragons were sitting on the cliff edge with their boys alongside.

Lessis felt her heart breaking. They had fought so well and come so far, and all for nothing.

Captain Hollein Kesepton strode up, leading his horse behind him. The lady seemed more pensive than he had ever seen her. And the girl was standing about fifty feet away, holding the horses with an averted face, a sure sign that Lessis was thinking hard. He had to tell the men something; he would have to intrude on her solitude.

"Lady, what are your conclusions?" he asked.

She seemed calm, almost unconcerned.

"A beautiful day is coming on, another beautiful day."

And indeed it did seem as if the good weather was to continue—there was not a cloud in the sky.

Kesepton waited, staring at her.

They all want their orders from me, she thought. Well, she had taken charge of them, she did owe them that much.

"West," she said at last. "He's gone west. Are you familiar with the ash country, Captain?"

"No, my lady, I was in the southlands until this command. Indeed I have never crossed the Oon before. In the south the Oon is the border with the Teetol."

"And therefore a border to be respected. Well, to the west lies a plain of volcanic ash, which stretches much of the distance to the Fist. This ash is much cut about with canyons, a maze of hiding places and false turns."

"You mean you can no longer detect him?"

She sighed. She hated to admit this.

"Not at such distances, although I will send out birds to look, but by then I expect he'll be safe from us."

Kesepton was crestfallen.

"Then we have failed after all," he said in a low voice.

She heaved a great sigh. There was still the chance they could snatch victory from the very jaws of defeat.

"So far we have failed. But we cannot give up. We will go north. We can still trap him when he enters the lava land closer to the Fist."

"The lava land?"

"The black land, where water boils in the rocks and steam erupts from holes in the ground. It shudders still with the death throes of the mountain that made the Fist. Of course we must be careful—we will be close to the ramparts on the Fist, patrols will be out, that land is always watched."

"And we will try and catch them there?"

"We will do more than try. This time we will have them."

Kesepton felt a great weariness. Not only was his career destroyed, along with his command, but now he was going to his death, leading his men to the margins of

Tummuz Orgmeen, the heart of the enemy's power. But he let none of this show in his voice.

"I will pass the orders, then. We go on to the black land."

CHAPTER FORTY-ONE

Seven days later they were spread out on a crest of black lava, hidden among the fractures and hummocks of a black land where little vegetation grew.

Frowning down upon this desolation were the five peaks of the Fist. Each of these mounts was ringed with forts and riddled with tunnels, for behind them lay the city of Tummuz Orgmeen, the dark star that now reigned over the interior world of the High Gan.

Directly in front of their position was a flat expanse of bare rock covered in a dark grey sand. This expanse stretched for a mile or so before the younger lava began again. Only the occasional, stunted pine broke the barrenness of this harsh world of plane and shadow.

Relkin had thought the ash lands were bare enough, but in those canyons and hollows there were shrubs and trees, patches of grass even for their horses to graze. Here there was nothing but black rock, still warm in places from the horrific eruption that had destroyed the great mountain and left the fingers of the Fist in its place.

Through Lagdalen, Relkin had learned the names of the mountains. Feiger was the ash cone on the left, a smooth-sided triangle of dark grey. Directly ahead was Mor, a jagged crag, coated with lava around its base. To the left were Mor's companions, Lo, Bazook and Mik.

Beyond these clawlike hills lay the great city. At night they had seen the lights, reflected up against the clouds.

The energies that were controlled by the Doom were very great—they provided free illumination for the entire city.

Relkin had been awed by the sight on the first night that they had become visible. He and Lagdalen had ridden away from camp, up to a high place. To talk and to get away from the older people.

Lagdalen told him that she was in love with the captain. Relkin regretted this but saw that it was inevitable. Relkin knew that he loved Lagdalen but also knew how impossible his love was. She was the older by several years and she came from a great family, whereas he didn't even have a family other than the 109th Dragons.

It was the age gap that made the difference, though; he would have dared anything else. But being younger than she and still but a youth, while she was already a woman, made him hold back the words he'd dreamed of telling her. He knew she would think him foolish, even worse, childish for saying them.

He'd listened to her with half a mind from then on while looking at those fantastic lights, silhouetting the distant mountains and casting a glow as if a huge fire, or indeed an ancient volcano, blazed within. The lights had somehow helped to neutralize the pain of her words.

Even worse perhaps than Lagdalen's confessed love for the captain was the sight of Kesepton back in camp. For Relkin had nothing but admiration for the captain who had demonstrated his prowess on the battlefield again and again. Relkin could never hate him, just as he could not stop loving Lagdalen.

But all these thoughts had to be pushed out of his mind now. They were trespassers in this realm of lava, and out there were many spying eyes searching for the slightest sign of movement.

Relkin returned his keen-eyed gaze to the further lava field; Lessis wanted it watched carefully. Their quarry could try to slip by at any moment.

While Relkin hunched there he heard the captain moving along the line behind him. Down below on the far side he heard the two remaining dragons grumbling to each other. Chektor had been left behind on the banks of the Oon. His feet were too swollen for him to continue, and he certainly never would have made it this far through the rough lava lands.

Further away he saw a small hawk circling. Relkin knew the bird was descending to report to Lessis, who was in the hollow there with Lagdalen.

The lady was certain that Thrembode was coming up the canyon nearest to them and would emerge onto the plain at any moment. Once he was in sight the plan was that they would move quickly to cut him off and surround him and take him. Then would come the desperate part, for the plain was watched from the mountains, and troopers and imps would be sent forth at once to hunt them down.

To prevent this Lessis planned to split their force in two. She would take Thrembode and the princess south at once, with an escort of two men and Lagdalen. The rest would move along the lava ridgeline and draw off the pursuit. With the two dragons in their midst they would be strong enough to beat off anything except a large force aided by trolls. They would have to move quickly and try to lose the pursuit in the canyon lands.

When Relkin had heard this plan the first time he felt a hollow feeling. He realized it was almost certainly a death sentence for all of them.

But that was why they were here, wasn't it? They were heroes, so Lessis had said, and they would have to die as heroes so they could be immortalized by the bards and sung of for ages to come.

Captain Kesepton had seemed so calm, so fatalistic when he told them; Relkin had seen that the captain accepted death. It was preferable to the probable court martial and disgrace that awaited him if he ever returned to the Argonath.

The dragons were silent for a long time and quite morose. Now they grumbled about silly things, like the heat of the sun on this clear spring day. Neither Baz or Nesessitas had mentioned the plan again.

Everyone knew they were going to die here, except for the lucky ones, Troopers Jorse and Hooks, who had been selected to ride with Lessis and the captives.

At least Lagdalen would probably survive, thus Relkin consoled himself. He visualized her grown to matronhood, wed to some noble in Marneri. Would she remember them? The handsome young captain? The Broketail dragon? And the boy?

The hawk had finished its business in the hollow and now rose and circled lazily before flying away to the east. Lessis and Lagdalen appeared soon afterwards and joined them on the ridgeline, watching the mountains and the plain.

They waited. Thrembode was late in his appointment with destiny. Lessis fidgeted. She had only bird reports: two horses with man and woman, heading down the canyon. No human eye had seen them.

She trusted the birds but knew that they could not tell her if the people they had seen were really the ones she sought. What if Thrembode had doubled back?

The man was tricky and he'd foiled her a dozen times already—why shouldn't he try again to make a nice odd number? Bitter thoughts like these kept recurring. These men, these heroic men and dragons, they were all going to be sacrificed to capture the damn magician and recover the princess. They had to be, it was essential for the cause of Argonath, but knowing that didn't help Lessis feel any better about it.

And then came the catastrophe!

Out of nowhere came the sound of a horn, a long low note, echoing across the plain from the dark mouth of a canyon on the far side beneath the cliffs of Mt. Mor. A few moments later a squadron of horsemen appeared there, at least eighty strong. They rode directly across the plain, red pennons snapping from their lancetips.

When they were halfway across a pair of riders emerged from the canyon below them. A man and a woman, wearing cloaks, riding slowly on tired horses.

Thrembode and Besita, no doubt of it. And safe from

Lessis and her plans; there was no feasible way of capturing them here and holding them against eighty troopers on fresh mounts.

Complete and utter disaster!

Kesepton slipped into place beside Lessis. His face was filled with concern.

"What now, lady? Give the word and we'll take them."

"And we'll all die uselessly. No. We will have to think of something else."

Kesepton gave a worried look to the sharp peaks of the Shtag, or Fist.

"We'll have to get inside there."

She set her jaw. There could be no turning back now.

"I think so. I wish there was another way." She looked up, her eyes opaque, staring.

"We have no choice, captain. We cannot fail in this— we must succeed, too much depends on it."

Kesepton stared at the five ominous peaks. Each one crawled with thousands of enemy troops, safe within high battlements and massively built fortresses. He did not see how it could be done.

"Of course," was all he said.

CHAPTER FORTY-TWO

And so it came to pass that they stood in the shadows with a ruck of lava beneath the flank of Mt. Mor. Fifty feet above their heads stood the gates of the Lower Fortress on the mountain. Great ramparts surmounted the rocks above the gate. Turrets bristled over the ramparts. Lights shone from dozens of slits and narrow windows.

Within the mountain, tunneled into the rock, lay most

of the actual structure. All of it built by slaves, driven by the lash to build a fortress for the Doom that now sat in Tummuz Orgmeen.

Day and night parties of mounted men and marching imps went in and out of this gate, the tramp of their iron-shod feet ringing off the rocks. Lessis could see that the Doom was drawing to itself a great army, preparing the blow it planned to launch against the Argonath.

As dusk drew on she conjured up a mist, and under its protection they crossed the last stretches of the plain to this pool of dark shadow, hidden at the foot of the mountain. By riding on the rutted path leading to the fortress they had disarmed the attention of the spies.

Now everything rested on their skill at creating an illusion. They were but twenty men, a handful of boys, two dragons, a girl and an old woman. In the fortress of Mor, Lessis estimated there were at least two thousand troops and perhaps that many imps as well.

Accordingly, Lessis had asked only for volunteers from the men. Somewhat to her surprise they had all stepped forward, even the surviving Talion troopers.

Despite the fact that she had failed them again and again, they were ready to throw their lives behind this last desperate gamble. There was no need even for an uplifting speech or a spell; they were under their own spell now, and they were prepared to go to the ends of the world if that was what it took.

Thrembode and Besita had passed within the gates hours before them, but Lessis was sure they would be kept in the fortress here overnight and taken to the Doom the following morning. Important as the capture of the princess was, she knew that the Blunt Doom was constantly busy with thousands of such operations and schemes.

Now Lessis went forward to the edge of the gulley in the lava and detached the three small bats she had been wearing in her hair. With urgent little noises she sent them whispering into the night.

The fortress was huge; she hoped the bats' tiny minds

would be able to cope with all the information she sought. It might take too long for them to find Thrembode if she was wrong in her notions concerning the general layout of the place.

While she waited she sought to dispel her anxiety by going over the plan in her mind.

Everything was balanced on a single certainty. Thrembode would most likely feel perfectly safe now. Inside a fortress guarded by thousands of troops he would think that only a great army could reach him and he would know that no such armies existed on this side of the Oon.

Naturally he would be very glad of the opportunity to wash and shave and dress in clean clothes.

Lessis knew his habits—the magician was a man of the great cities, a dandy fond of elegant appearances. He would be as anxious as the princess to abandon the sweat-stained garments he had worn across the steppes. His first act would be to take a long, hot bath.

Then he would dine with the High Warden of the Gate. It would be expected of him, and Thrembode would no doubt be starving and ready for some wine. And he would have much boasting to do, to an avid audience since the officers of the Guard and their wives would be all agog to hear of his adventures in the glamorous cities of the south. Life in Tummuz Orgmeen was not exactly joyful for these women and their families. And then on the morrow he would go for an audience with the Doom.

She smiled grimly.

The first bat returned and hung squeaking in her hair for a few moments before flying off to hunt for moths to renew its energy. It had little worthwhile information; the fortress was a confusing place and the bat had become quite lost inside it.

Lessis pressed her lips together tightly, hoping against hope.

A few moments later the second bat returned, this time with some better news. This bat had negotiated a stair-case and reached the uppermost level of the fortress inside the mountain. There it had flashed through upper rooms that were crowded with people.

A reception for Thrembode, of course. The bat had been chased out a window then and had returned to her immediately. She stroked its fierce little head while keeping an eye out for its needle-like teeth. They were hardworking little souls but quite liable to bite. Their eyes met and it squeaked something meaningless to her and lofted away to hunt for its food.

Abruptly she turned, Sergeant Duxe had crept up behind her. She tensed and her hand was about to fly to her dirk when she saw that his sword was sheathed and his demeanor was unthreatening. At the same time his face was fixed in a funereal expression of utmost gloom.

"Is everything ready, Sergeant?" she said.

He came closer, his eyes burned with a strange light.

"You never said anything did you?" he whispered. "To the captain, I mean."

"No."

His face did not change but she sensed a wild leap within.

"Why not?"

She smiled; in the near distance she heard a bat chittering on its way back to her.

"Sergeant Duxe, you have great heart and strength. I believe you were simply led astray by the hotheads from Talion. I expect such things from men like them. You were under strain, that is all."

"Is that what you will say in your report? If we return."

"I will not even mention the incident in my report, Sergeant. If I survive to make one."

"I do not understand."

"The legions need men like you, Sergeant—it is not my place to destroy your career. The incident is done with. I have forgotten it, can you?"

He stood there shaking his head, the anger still burning in him.

"You bewitched us, all the men, they are in a daze."

"They are heroes, Sergeant, just like yourself. They will be remembered and sung about for hundreds of years."

He grimaced. "Ach, but we will all die here. The Talions were right about that much."

"Not if I can help it. Not if we pull together. Our enemy will relax his guard now. He thinks we are already fleeing south, pursued by the black troopers."

Duxe plainly wished that he was.

"All that I ask, Sergeant, is that you play your part when the time comes, which will be soon."

The third bat returned and flew directly into her hair, where it squeaked out its tiny report.

Duxe shuddered at the sight and turned away.

But Lessis stroked the little creature's forehead and then let it loose to hunt in the sky. Now she knew not only where to find Thrembode but even a way to escape once she had him.

It was time for the final throw of the dice.

After a check of the road which showed it empty, Lessis and Duxe moved up onto it and started forward to the gates. Behind them came ten men, dressed only in tunics and leggings, with their heads shaved like Teetol braves. These men were bound together with Baguti thongs, neck to wrist, like any other slave gang wending its awful way across the steppes to this gateway to hell, except that these thongs were loose.

Behind these men came two soldiers on horseback, stripped to the waist like Baguti, with their sabers sheathed at their sides.

Duxe was also clad like a Bagut, and he carried a whip which he cracked over the heads of the "slaves" while he barked some choice insults at them in crude Baguti.

Lessis ran a careful eye over the assemblage. It was as close to perfect as she could hope to achieve. Duxe did look just like a slave driver; he had that same hardness in the face even though he was too blond and pale for a real nomad of the Gan.

In the horsemen's saddlebags were a dozen short swords, ready for the right moment.

She was instantly aware of a number of eyes watching their progress as they climbed out of the mist. Everything depended on the sentries being slack enough not to raise an alarm. Parties like this came in frequently enough, even though this one had not been sighted before now.

At a single bugle call dozens of archers could appear on those ramparts and then they would all die swiftly. As they walked along Lessis tried not to imagine the arrows and how they would feel as they sank into her back.

But no bugle blew.

They reached the gate at last, and after Duxe hammered on it with the stock of his whip, a voice bellowed from within.

"Who goes there?"

Lessis replied in the harsh tongue of the Teetol.

"Slaves, good strong slaves for the Doom. Open up."

There was a shouting match going on inside.

Among the men standing outside the gate the tension was rising to an unbearable level. If they were detected here they would be slaughtered in a matter of moments, or worse by far, captured.

The watch was back. "It's past the curfew, the gates can only open to a warrant."

"I have a warrant, you fool, from the magician Thrembode himself."

"Ah hah, more of the gallant Thrembode's work, eh? They are making a fuss of him tonight! He came in only a few hours ago, whole place has been in an uproar since."

Lessis shrugged. "These slaves are his, although he has yet to pay for them."

The small, inset door in the gate was opening with a squeak of dry hinges.

"Hush yer complaining mouth, woman! None of yer Baguti complaints about the gallant Thrembode now!"

"The gallant Thrembode owes good gold for these

men. If he wants to buy on credit again from the slavers of the Gan he'd best pay me.''

"Oh, he'll pay you alright." The watchman had emerged. He was a short but massive fellow with the look of an imp about him. His eyes were overlarge and seemed to protrude from his skull while his mouth and teeth were also too great for his jaw.

"Well, let's see 'em," he snarled, unloosing his whip.

The men in the thongs kept their eyes lowered, mute and submissive.

"So what have you got here then?" said the watchman, and he pulled out a young man with a very light shade of skin.

"Renegade from the coast," said Lessis, who ducked her head inside the gate while the watchman was busy poking the youth.

"Hah, bet he wishes he'd sailed away to somewhere else, eh? Bet he wishes he wasn't coming in here, eh? They'll take his manhood off and put him in the bilges here. It kills them in half a year but the Doom don't mind, he wants to depopulate the coast."

Lessis had noted the other guards were playing a game of dice in their guardroom, none were paying attention.

The watchman pushed the pale-skinned soldier back into the line and then exchanged a long slow glare with Duxe, who had moved forwards to shove the man away from the ''slaves.''

For a moment their eyes burned into each other. The watchman spat loudly, then turned to Lessis.

"Alright, let me see the warrant you have from the excellent Thrembode."

Lessis was reaching into her cloak, but instead of a scroll she brought out a shining dirk that slashed through the watchman's throat and reduced his noise to a gurgle. Duxe finished him with a heavy blow to the back of the head that dropped him to the road.

The ''slaves'' crowded round the horses, there was a clink of weaponry. Cowstrap, the burly smith, bent down and took the watchman's sword; others were already pressing inside.

A brief fight erupted in the guardroom. The guards were still concentrating on the dice when the men of Marneri burst in on them. The surprise was complete, and fatal, and then the guards were down and their weapons were taken.

Lessis's force fanned out around the gate area, keeping out of sight. Things were quiet at this hour on this, the lowest level of the mountain fortress. Only the occasional guard keeping to his lonely rounds was to be found.

Lessis was gratified to see that her bats had reported quite accurately concerning the layout of the place. Behind the main gate a wide passage with a curved ceiling drove deeply into the mountain. Along this passage were many doors of wood with steel fittings. Lanterns every fifty feet were the sole illumination.

Lessis sent Lagdalen back outside the gate to signal to the rest of the men and the dragons, waiting below.

They emerged from their hiding place and charged up the pathway to the gate, which swung open to admit them.

At the last moment someone above looked down and saw the dragons; instantly a wail of alarm went up.

Inside the gate Lessis led them to an open passage, which ran to the base of a wide stair. A door opened and an imp emerged, bearing a tray of goblets. From the room behind the imp came the sound of many imps at their feed. The imp stood rock still, eyes bulging in its flattened head, then it dropped the tray with a crash and started to scream.

A bolt from Relkin Dragonboy's bow took it in the throat a moment later and dropped it to the stone-flagged floor. Lessis gently closed the door on the feeding imps, who never looked up from their plates.

But above them the alarm was definitely raised; they had to keep moving quickly. Softly they sped up the stairs to a landing and then to the second floor.

On this floor there was the sound of many occupants. Doors were opening and closing down the passages, voices murmured. Above them they heard feet thundering on stairs and voices raised.

And then someone below found the dead imp on the floor. There was a bellow of rage and then more noise and then uproar.

"Quickly," said Lessis, running up the stairs to the third level as fast she could go.

She was tiring. After such a long and exhausting pursuit she was reaching the limits of her strength.

"Gazak! Dragon!" shrieked a voice, and more doors crashed open. A roar of voices was coming from the first floor now.

"Gazaki! Dragons!"

At the third level they were met by a pair of wide-eyed guards who turned and ran at the sight of Lessis surrounded by Kesepton, Weald and Cowstrap, steel glittering in their hands.

A door burst open and another man emerged; he saw Nesessitas coming up behind Cowstrap, and bolted back inside and locked the door from within.

Lessis paused—to make a mistake here would be fatal. She looked both right and left and then chose the right side. At the first turn in the passage, where it split again in two directions, they were met by five imps and a guard, gibbering in fear. The other guard was gone.

Swords flashed, Kesepton cut down the nearest imp, the others fled and the guard fled with them. Following them down the passage came Lessis and everyone else.

Another door opened, and Lessis heard the sound of festivities somewhere beyond it, many human voices raised in excited chatter.

Terrified imps in servant garb ran shrieking ahead of them. A man in the black uniform of Tummuz Orgmeen drew a sword and was slain by Liepol Duxe.

Then they reached a pair of wide double doors. From behind it came the sound of many people. The alarm had not yet reached this room.

Lessis turned to the nearest dragon, it was Bazil of Quosh.

"Sir Bazil, would you be so kind as to break open these doors?"

Bazil's teeth flashed; he stepped forward and hurled himself shoulder first into the doors. They swayed but held. Bazil uttered an oath, stepped back and hurled himself at the door a second time. This time the doors gave way. Indeed, they exploded open and Bazil's great body surged in, tripped and crashed to the floor in front of four hundred pairs of horrified eyes.

There was a guard holding a ceremonial pike right over the prone dragon, but the man was so surprised he fell down in a dead faint before anyone could kill him.

Pandemonium broke out. Two hundred wives of the ranking guards in the fortress rose with a collective shriek. Their men either shrieked with them or tried to draw steel and defend themselves.

At the head of the room was a table, and behind it was Thrembode the magician. Thrembode, to his credit, was not surprised for long. Within a second he had realized the peril, understood the incredible risk the witch had taken to catch him, and rose and hurled himself towards the nearest exit, seizing Besita and forcibly lifting her in front of him.

The princess screamed in shock at being torn from a conversation with the wife of the High Warden about the fashions in Kadein and borne away without a word by Thrembode.

Then she glimpsed a dragon and saw a girl with a determined face and a small sword in her hand leap onto a table and jump across Thrembode's path. The magician cursed and dropped her; Besita fell roughly to the floor.

The girl's face was faintly familiar to Besita, from Marneri, a high family, serving in the Novitiate. As she lay on the floor trying to get a breath, she watched Thrembode lash out at the girl with his dirk and then attempt to kick her.

The girl ducked the dirk and parried the kick with her own, inside the magician's poorly aimed blow. He had to dart aside to avoid the next thrust with her sword.

A woman trying to escape tripped and staggered into Thrembode's side. He seized her and shoved her, spinning, into the girl with the sword. They fell over together.

And then Besita was jerked to her feet and dragged through the serving door at the rear of the chamber.

As the princess disappeared, Lessis was only a few yards behind her, struggling to push a way through a throng of panicked wives. Lessis was on the verge of screaming with frustration. They were so close this time! She pointed to the serving entrance—Kesepton was there, he had seen them.

"Through that door!" she shouted.

Kesepton shoved the ladies of the fortress out of the way, ignoring the ripping of gowns and lace.

Lessis broke free of a clinging fat woman who was screaming frenziedly at the top of her lungs. Others were breaking through to join them. A table went over with a crash, and plates and cutlery flew through the air.

Steel rang on steel all around them as those guards with the presence of mind to remember their weapons drew their swords and engaged the invaders. Dragon swords were out, however, and everything, including the tables, was being cut to kindling in the process.

On the far side of the room there was a screaming mass of men and women clustered beneath the windows. Several were attempting to climb through.

Lagdalen was at Lessis's side now as they darted down the service corridor and entered the main kitchens through a large doorway with the doors propped open.

More chaos greeted them. Imps and pot boys were climbing the walls. Chefs were crouched beneath the tables.

At the far end Thrembode had opened a low set door that led to the wine vault. First he pushed Besita through, then he slipped in and closed the door with a mocking wave to Lessis.

She reached it a second later and heard a heavy set of bolts sliding home. Her attempt to hold them with a spell was thwarted; the magician broke the spell as she said it and hammered the bolts down.

Her heart sank, the locks inside the door meant that the vault had another exit and was designed as a bolt hole. She looked around herself with desperate eyes. No magic could loosen those bolts in less than an hour or more now. They would have to break the door down with physical means.

The dragons were there. Unfortunately, the door was too low for a dragon to really get a shoulder to it. The Broketail made one intensive effort, but the door was either too stout or he was simply unable to bring enough force to bear. Nesessitas tried a kick and raised some splinters from the surface but little else.

Then Relkin gave a shout from the butcher's block. He slid two enormous cleavers across the floor to the dragons. These cleavers just fit into the huge forehands of the dragons, and now the wood chips flew fast and furious.

From the main entrance to the kitchen came the sound of the pursuit. A horn blared and a dozen armed imps burst in.

The men of Marneri met them with drawn steel and the battle renewed itself. More and more imps began pressing in and Lessis realized they would overwhelm them unless they were held.

"Nesessitas," she cried, "block the doors!"

The green dragon dropped her cleaver and picked up a long kitchen table and used it as a ram to catch up a dozen imps and hurl them bodily back into the service corridor through the door. Then she jammed the table into the doorway. There it remained, forming a barrier to the kitchens.

Over it the battle was rejoined, but the men of Marneri with Kesepton and Duxe at their head were in a much better position now. Their swords rose and fell as they hewed down the imps and troopers that were pressed up against the table outside the door.

Meanwhile Bazil had broken through the vault door,

the timbers were fairly splintering under the cleaver in his huge hand.

A trumpet was blaring in the corridor again. Voices shouted in excitement. Lessis knew that some dread reinforcement had arrived for the enemy.

She signaled Bazil to stop, then reached through the broken door and undid the bolts.

The little door swung open.

A voice beyond shouted, "Make way for the Hogo!" and she felt a chill go down her spine.

She grabbed Lagdalen and drew her in after her. Relkin followed.

"Hurry, girl!" she snapped to Lagdalen as she stepped into the wine vault.

At the front entrance to the kitchen a group of imps wearing elaborate face masks pushed a metal box on wheels up to the overturned door.

Kesepton and Duxe exchanged puzzled glances. Lieutenant Weald shrugged.

"What the hell is that?" said Subadar Yortch.

"Leave it, follow me through this door!" shouted Lessis, but she knew it was already too late. Relkin hesitated and Lessis shoved him roughly inside.

"Run!" she hissed, and began to sprint down the length of the wine vault.

At the front entrance to the kitchen the metal door to the box popped open and a stumpy thing, like a black pumpkin with vertical red striations, crawled purposefully forth.

The men stared at it in amazement.

The head was narrow and curved back over the shoulders like a cucumber. A green tongue flicked in and out of a wet looking hole at the front. Red eyes glowed like glossy buttons on the top.

"Disgusting!" said Cowstrap in a loud voice.

And then the thing's pumpkin body swelled suddenly to twice its previous size. The skin grew taut like a balloon and then it burst with a weirdly soft thud.

A grey cloud of vapor emerged that seemed to flow

into the kitchen like a living thing. And with it came the most incredible stench any of them had ever had the misfortune to smell.

It was a combination of the foulest things imaginable and it struck with a stunning force. Men toppled to their knees, gasped, retched uncontrollably, and lay still.

Bazil gazed on all this with amazement until the smell reached him a second later. Then his eyes opened wide as his nostrils were seared, and he became conscious of a roaring sound in his ears. Relkin was looking back at him through the door as he sank to the floor, and a blackness swelled up and overwhelmed him.

CHAPTER FORTY-THREE

The secret exit from the wine vault was through a false barrel. Fortunately, Thrembode had been in too much of a hurry to shut it properly behind him. It fell open as Lagdalen went past and brushed against it.

Lessis gave a prayer of thanks, the Mother of them all was indeed keeping an eye on her servants. With the way things had been going lately Lessis had begun to have doubts.

"Quick now, into it. Relkin, don't breathe!"

The youth's eyes were troubled.

"Please, my lady, what was it back there?"

"Get in, we've no time. 'Twas a Hogo—everyone out here is done for, they will be taken."

"The box for it seemed small, I don't—"

"Will you get on, Master Relkin!"

He went through and she scrambled after. Imps were already coming towards them with torches and drawn steel.

The barrel masked a narrow door which lead to an equally ungenerous passage with stone walls and floor. Lessis forced the bolt across to shut the secret door. It was difficult to get it through the hasp, the reason no doubt why Thrembode had failed to close it. There were imps pounding on the inside of the barrel; someone started to try and pull it open.

Relkin had seen the difficulty, the lady was not strong enough to force the bolt home. He pulled her aside and slammed the heel of his hand against the bolt.

It rammed home and the barrel stayed shut.

Lessis was fighting down the shaking she felt in her whole being. Another moment and they would have faced imp swords and pikes.

"Thank you, Master Relkin, that was well done."

He was clutching his hand, bruised by the bolt, and trying not to cry out with the pain.

"It was my fault—I was slow before. I didn't understand."

She got her breath back and examined their surroundings. There was no time to dawdle.

It was pitch black and cold, and smelled of damp. Lessis lifted the ring on her right hand and muttered the words of power. A small light was ignited within the small blue stone and their shadows were thrown down the long dark adit. There was just enough light to see their way.

"A Hogo, my lady?" said Relkin.

"A new deviltry from the Doom's laboratories. It emits a stench so foul it causes most men to faint. Dragons will not be proof against it either, although trolls apparently are."

At the look on Lagdalen's face Lessis grew impatient.

"No time now to explain. A most awesome responsibility has now fallen upon the three of us. It is up to us to catch the magician."

"We're all that's left?" said Relkin, still questioning the obvious.

"I'm afraid so."

Lagdalen knew better than to say anything. But she was wondering how they alone were going to overcome the massed power of Tummuz Orgmeen.

Behind them they heard the sound of axes working on the hidden door. The imps were after them.

"This way," said Lessis with what sounded like complete confidence, and she headed down the pasage.

Relkin and Lagdalen followed. They came to a junction with another corridor. The sound of axe on wood behind them rose to a crescendo.

"Hurry," said Lessis.

They turned at a corner; after a second to consider, she led them on down another passage.

Somewhere ahead they heard a woman's voice raised in pleading. A harsh male voice responded loudly.

Lessis's heart lifted.

"It is them." Lessis quickened her stride. They rounded another corner. The voices were nearer yet.

Behind them there came a loud crash and a triumphant roar of brutish voices.

Then they turned another corner and saw a man in a white shirt and black tights forcing a woman in a green evening gown up a ladder and through a trap door from which yellow light flooded down.

Even as they ran for the foot of the ladder, Thrembode gave the woman's posterior a mighty shove and she disappeared with a shriek.

Lessis jumped onto the ladder and scrambled up it, her dirk clenched between her teeth.

The magician would not escape her this time!

But he was already halfway through the trap door. He looked down and saw her and went white with terror. He jerked his shoulders up and began to lever himself through the trap.

With a little shriek Lessis grabbed the dirk from her teeth and stabbed him through the heel of his boot.

Thrembode gave a cry of agony and lashed out with his other foot, knocking Lessis off the ladder and almost falling back through the trapdoor himself as he lost his balance. For a moment he teetered there, and then his scrabbling fingers found Besita's ankle and he held on to her long enough to get his other hand back on the ladder.

A moment later he slammed down the hatch and sat on it while clutching his leg and howling with pain.

In the passage below Lessis fell heavily atop Relkin and they both slammed into the stone floor. Neither was seriously hurt however, and in a second or two they had regained their feet with Lagdalen's help. Above they could hear Thrembode's cries.

It meant only another failure to Lessis. She felt a dangerous sense of confusion closing in around her. This was becoming an exceedingly tight spot.

"They are coming," Lagdalen said.

It was true, there were a great many imps somewhere close, their terrible cries echoed down the stone passages.

Lessis had heard the hatch slam and with it had gone most of her hope. Thrembode was forewarned that she was still after him and yet he was safe from her. The entire mountain would awake in pursuit of a Great Witch known to be trapped there. How could she hope to escape?

She would kill herself before she'd let them take her—she could not countenance surrendering her secrets to some horror like the Doom, or worse, to its creators in their chill cloisters far away. But she was not alone; she had two young people, virtually children, in her custody and she could not simply abandon them to die.

They fled on, Lessis leading with the faint light of the ringstone. Behind them the sounds of the horde of imps drew steadily closer.

They reached a junction and were about to turn right when a door exploded open a few yards ahead and light burst in. With it came a couple of men with drawn swords.

"They're here!" roared one of the men, and several imps came through the door with cutlasses held high.

"Run!" shouted Lessis, pushing Relkin in the opposite direction.

They ran, but the imps were close behind when the passage curved suddenly and descended slightly, then ended at a short rail and a precipice that fell into a dark abyss.

"Trapped!" groaned Relkin, turning back with his sword out.

Lessis stopped by the rail with her heart sinking towards that abyss. She felt ready to give up. It was an impossibly strange feeling. She had never been so completely defeated before.

"Jump!" said Lagdalen. "Must be water down there."

The girl was right. Hope flashed in her heart, small hope but hope nonetheless.

"She's right." Lessis prepared to climb over the rail. Relkin was still looking back with his blade in his hand. "Lagdalen is right, young man—we jump."

But then the imps were upon them, and Relkin's sword flashed against a cutlass, parried another and raked across its owner's neck. He felt another imp at his side, and he dodged out of the way and slipped and fell backwards over the rail and down into the abyssal dark.

As he fell he retained the image of the Lady Lessis being cut down by another imp whose sword was buried in her side. Then darkness swallowed him up until with a terrific blow he landed in deep, cold water.

He went down a long way, feet first, and then struggled to the surface. It had been a hard landing, his body ached.

On the surface he gasped and spluttered for several seconds before he could heave a breath of air into his tortured lungs. Suddenly a hand fell on his shoulder and he struggled around. It was Lagdalen.

"Where is she?" she said.

He couldn't speak; he was still fighting to get breath into his lungs.

But Lagdalen had seen something—the light from the ring; it was coming to the surface nearby. She turned away from him and swam towards it. In a moment she was holding Lessis above the surface. The lady was unconscious.

Relkin finally had enough breath to speak.

"I saw her cut down, she must be wounded."

Lessis gasped. "She is bleeding, badly. From her side." Lagdalen held her up. "We have to get her out of this water."

Suddenly there was a tremendous splash nearby.

"The imps, they're throwing down rocks."

"Follow me." Relkin struck out in the direction of a ring of faint green luminescence he had spotted about fifteen yards away.

More heavy splashes sent waves washing over them from behind as they pulled slowly away from the foot of the cliff, towing the lady behind them.

High above, lanterns were being lowered, and when she looked up Lagdalen could see many figures clustered on the narrow ledge. But before the lamps could expose them to the watchers above, Lagdalen felt her heel ground on something solid. Then she was standing on a slimy stone floor and Relkin was helping her pull Lessis out of the water and into a circular passage that was filled with a faint phosphorescent glow from a slimeweed that grew thickly on the walls and ceiling.

By the pale light of the weed they could see that the floor of the tunnel was covered in sand with large things half-buried in it here and there.

Behind them the lamps had been lowered almost to the water level now, and they threw a brighter light down the tunnel ahead of them. It stretched away, curving slightly to the right until it disappeared.

"We must go on," said Relkin.

But Lagdalen shook her head; she was examining the lady's side, using the light from Lessis's ring to get a better look.

"She cannot go far—look."

Indeed, Lessis was bleeding from a six-inch gash across her lower ribs.

"Can we staunch the blood? She'll die if we cannot."

Lagdalen did not answer but tore off her sopping wet robe and began to rip it into strips.

The lights outside the tunnel were withdrawn. The watchers above were satisfied that the fugitives were not swimming in the deep pool.

Lagdalen had learned much in the lore of wounds during the past few days. She had seen Lessis bind up those of many men. Now she went to work to recreate what she remembered. With Relkin's help she was able to shut the wound and bind it tight in just a few minutes.

Her robe was destroyed, of course, which meant she was down to a thin cotton shift, still soaking wet. She hugged herself but couldn't stop shivering.

Relkin had taken off his shirt. He wrung out most of the water and now put it around her shoulders. She protested but he insisted.

"You're shivering enough to drive me crazy. Put this on."

He still had his leather joboquin and his leggings; when they dried they would help keep him warm. If they would ever dry in this clammy place.

"Now, we must move," said Relkin.

Relkin lifted the wounded Lessis. She was surprisingly light, weighing no more than a child. Then with Lagdalen leading they went on into the tunnel beneath the mountain.

CHAPTER FORTY-FOUR

The heel of Thrembode's foot throbbed horribly. Even worse for his precious sense of dignity, the bandages made it impossible to wear a boot and so his foot was encased in a grotesque slipper from the surgeon at the Gate of Mor. But despite the pain he endeavored to stand straight and to walk without limping overmuch. The Doom was notoriously impatient of human failings such as painful wounds.

A few years back some poor fool of a junior magician had sneezed in the Presence. He had gone into the Abyss, to lose his ears and tongue and become the Eyes of the Doom. This story had many companions, and thus did Thrembode do his damndest to ignore the lancing bursts of pain that shot up from his ruined heel.

Damn the witch!

A man slammed a heavy hammer down on a slab of steel. The huge double doors opened in front of him. Unsmiling guards, giant men with something of the look of trolls to them, waved him through.

The main chamber was lit from high above through tall, narrow windows. Those same windows offered views of the city and the amphitheater. Ahead, dominating everything, was the metal grille that surrounded the Doom's Tube.

There it was. A lump rose in his chest, but it was not from love. A perfect sphere, a black marble, thirty feet across, within which dwelled the malignant intelligence that was the Blunt Doom. Created by the Masters in their dark citadel, the Doom was a projection of themselves, subordinate only to them, designed to extend their dominion upon the world.

The Tube was open on one side, to allow those humans that the Doom wished to interview to come close to the side of the great mass.

Within the Tube the rock was suspended in a web of steel cables that gathered together above it and rose to the pulleys and tackle that hung on the great hook in the ceiling of the Tube.

In front of that opening in the Tube a handful of men, clad in black with gold stripes down their fronts, stood murmuring together. As Thrembode passed them he felt their eyes on him and imagined their calculations, their intrigues.

With a jangle of chains the Eyes of the Doom were pulled up from the Abyss. In a narrow cage stood a gaunt, naked man with large protruding eyeballs.

A red spot had appeared on the front of the black rock, now it pulsed slowly.

Thrembode came to a halt. He set his heel down, although it hurt so badly he had to grit his teeth to keep from crying out. The Eyes were gazing down at him from the narrow cage.

Thrembode knelt and made submission to the Doom.

More chains rattled, the Mouth was swung up.

"Ahah!" boomed the Mouth. "You have returned to us, Magician Thrembode, after a long sojourn in the cities of the enemy. You have sowed confusion there and sent us many useful reports. And now you have brought us a most interesting captive. Yes, this is very good."

The Mouth was a huge man, now blinded and deafened and confined in another narrow cage. Sometimes he boomed, at other times he purred and hissed when the Doom moved him to some degree of nuance.

"But of course, we must balance all this against the knowledge that you were supposed to remain in Marneri and ensure a swift and peaceful succession for the Crown Prince Erald."

Pulleys squealed above and the Ears, a woman of enormous girth who virtually bulged through the bars of her narrow cage, was swung into position.

Thrembode cleared his throat, he hated this feeling of helpless terror, but what else could one feel in such proximity to this thing, this monstrosity of the Masters.

"Yes, that is true."

His voice sounded weak, almost hesitant. He paused and gathered himself. "But circumstances became difficult. The imperial organs were also involved in Marneri. I was detected, possibly by treachery on the part of our agents there."

The red spot flared a moment.

"Or possibly by your own clumsiness, magician."

"I do not think so. I am always careful. But in those hag-ridden cities the slightest thing can trip one up."

"Indeed. And in my city, too, or so it seems."

Thrembode kept silent. This was dangerous territory. The Mouth went on. "In fact an agent of the enemy accompanied by a handful of soldiers actually invaded the Gate of Mor and almost reached you and our prisoner. You know the identity of your ardent pursuer?"

"Indeed, it is the great hag herself, Lessis of Valmes."

The Doom paused here, the red spot pulsing; the Mouth in his cage gripped the bars while drool ran from his mouth. Finally he spoke again.

"Yes. So it has been claimed. But we have no body. Lost in the abyss under Mt. Mor."

"I was not in charge of the search, oh Great One."

"No. You were incapacitated, they say."

"A wound, nothing more."

"You are sure you are able to continue?"

"Certain."

There was a pregnant pause.

"Good." Again the Doom paused while the obscene puppet show went on and the Ears and Mouth moved and stabilized.

"I want the hag, either dead or alive. We know she was not alone—at least two companions fell into the abyss with her."

"I'm sure your security forces are tracking her down even as we speak, Great One."

"Possibly, but I doubt it. Instead I am appointing you to a special commission with the task of finding the hag or her body and bringing it to me."

Thrembode paled. Hesitated. Then he realized it was useless to try and avoid this duty.

"Of course, Great One."

"Do I detect a hesitation in your voice, magician?"

"It was only a throb of joy, oh Great One. I will dedicate myself to the task."

"Good, because if she is not brought to me within three days I shall want to know why."

"Yes, Great One," said Thrembode, making submission once more. Then lifting his head Thrembode offered another thought, shifting away from his unpleasant prospect.

"In addition to the Princess Besita, I would point out that we have also taken a good haul of other prisoners."

"Yes," said the Voice more quietly. "Two dragons, that is excellent. And the princess will be most useful to us, I believe. However," the Voice shifted from warm to cold in an instant and Thrembode became most uneasy, his foot was throbbing and his knees were aching, "we cannot overlook the fact that we lost a great many trolls, a great many imps, a great many men. Indeed, I am informed that the Baguti of the Red Belt have been completely disabled. There is now a great gap in our surveillance of the High Gan to the river. And my force in the woods of Tunina has been reduced to a negligible level."

Thrembode said nothing; the Doom went on remorselessly.

"General Erks was here to report not long ago. He had many comments to make upon the generalship that was shown in your campaign, magician."

"With respect to the general, he was not there. At Ossur Galan we took them in the flank and destroyed their force."

The red spot pulsed.

"Destroyed their force?"

The Voice was loud, angry again.

"Well yes, they were left with a handful of men and a few dragons."

"Then what happened to the Baguti of the Red Belt?"

Thrembode shrugged. "It was the witch. She created a blinding light, brighter than the sun at midday."

The Doom's red spot pulsed.

"Ah, then it was not of this world. She must have

entered Dugguth. The syphon of the Thingweight still exists there.''

''I do not understand.''

''This is a secret beyond your level, Magician.''

''Well, it is a powerful weapon. By good fortune I was looking away when the light came, but the Baguti were not and they were blinded and rendered quite useless.''

''It is troubling to me to hear this. Somehow the hags have penetrated to the secrets of the Eighth Level. They must have a mole well-hidden in the upper hierarchy.''

Thrembode shuddered at the thought. A hag spy well-placed in Padmasa? It was unthinkable.

The Doom paused, as if mulling over this new intelligence.

''Anyway, your mission is finished and it has cost us much. But if you can find the hag for me, preferably alive though her body will suffice, then you will be redeemed. I have a mission requiring a magician to go south to the Friendly Isles.''

Thrembode willed himself to get to his feet without screaming from the pain as he was dismissed. The rock swiveled and suddenly descended, the chains rattling around it as the slaves below paid them out through the pulleys.

He went past the men of the Doom's court once again. He lived, his authority was if anything greater than before. In their eyes was new respect, plus concern for their own positions should Thrembode succeed in capturing the hag alive.

Damn the witch! But if her capture led to a voyage to the south seas and the Friendly Isles, then captured she would be. Thrembode vowed it.

CHAPTER FORTY-FIVE

The tunnel led on and on, the walls coated with luminescent slimeweed in which cavern snails and rock weevils moved busily. Their luminous trails made patterns criss-crossing the tunnel walls.

As they went on it grew warmer, and they crossed patches where warm water had flooded the tunnel floor. The air here was redolent of a swamp and echoed with the scritching of weevils as they fought and mated all around them.

Relkin eventually had to halt for a while. The lady was not heavy, but after a mile of tunnel he had to rest his aching arms. Lagdalen carried her for a while, then Relkin took up the burden once more.

Eventually the tunnel widened into a cavern with a pool of water in the center. The air here smelled of sulfur and the water in the pool was hot; gas was bubbling to the surface in the middle. Rocks had fallen from the ceiling in several places. They found a slab that was as flat on top as a table and here they set Lessis down.

Relkin sagged against the rock, his arms throbbing, and concentrated on simply breathing. The sweat was running down his face and neck—he was slippery all the way to his feet.

After a while he noticed that the wall of the cavern was punctuated with dark fissures that ran from floor to ceiling. Some of them were wide enough for a boy his size to slip into.

Lagdalen meanwhile examined Lessis with the aid of the blue stone ring. What she found was both encouraging and depressing.

Her bandage had held up, and the worst of the bleeding had stopped, but the lady was still unconscious and her pulse seemed weak. Lagdalen was terrified that Lessis was going to die here in this dank and dismal place. This concern so dominated her thoughts that she barely considered her own peril.

And on the occasions when her thoughts did turn away from Lessis it was only to the agonizing realization that Hollein Kesepton was dead, or worse, taken for the amusement of the Doom.

There was no relief. She was caught up in the vortex of a terrible disaster. She knew how important the Grey Lady of Valmes was to the efforts of the empire. In her six months of service with her, Lagdalen had learned much of the true strength of the Empire of the Rose and equally much of its weaknesses. The loss of the lady would be a disaster of the first rank. Beside such a loss her own misery over the fate of the handsome young captain was too trivial for consideration. But that thought did not help her accept his death any more easily.

Relkin, meanwhile, gradually regained his strength. He was dying of thirst, but the hot water in the pool was laced with chemical salts and the taste was bitter.

"Got to have drinking water," he said.

"She is dying, Relkin."

He swallowed, his mouth and throat dry. They had to do something.

"Have to go on, we can't stay here."

"We can't carry her any further—she probably shouldn't have been moved in the first place."

"Need water and food."

She nodded.

"One of us stays here with her." He pointed at Lagdalen. "The other goes on and tries to find a way out of here."

"And some food and water."

"Right."

He gathered himself up. Lagdalen gave him the ring. "You will need this more than I will, I expect."

He nodded and she changed tack.

"Where do you think we are?"

"Under the mountain." He shrugged. "Marco Veli said it was a volcano and that there would be hot waters underneath it."

"He was right about the hot water."

Relkin took their only waterbag and a kerchief of Lagdalen's, then adjusted his boots.

"Don't go too far, Relkin. Hurry back."

He grinned at her suddenly, all doubts forgotten.

"I wish I were old enough to tell you that I love you, Lagdalen of the Tarcho."

She snorted. "Fortunately you are not, so get along with you. And don't forget that our mission is more important than our feelings for each other."

Her face softened, however, even as she said this; she could not be angry with Relkin for long.

He laughed. "You wish I was the captain now, don't you?"

"No. You wish you were the captain. Go on, we need water."

He was still looking back.

"I'm too old for you, Relkin Orphanboy, and I won't wait for you to grow up either." She was smiling. "Besides it doesn't look as if we're going to live long enough to grow up anyway."

Still he lingered.

"Go away!" she snapped. "And find some food if you can."

He had located another tunnel mouth, dark and ominous, on the other side of the cavern. Inside this tunnel the gentle luminescence of the slimeweed continued, and with the addition of the blue stone ring's light Relkin was able to make much faster time.

Still the tunnel seemed endless. For a mile or more he went on into the dim light. This tunnel was not as straight and broad as the first. In places the floor had collapsed into a mass of boulder-sized chunks of lava. Small side passages and holes opened up in the walls and ceiling.

And then he noticed another light, a warmer, redder light coming from somewhere ahead. And with it came dim, muffled sounds. In particular, the sound of metal ringing on metal.

Eventually he found a patch of reddish light on the floor of the lava tunnel. The light was coming in from a hole in the wall high up near the ceiling. Tumbled rock beneath the hole indicated a way to climb up high enough to reach it.

He scrambled up and looked through the hole.

It was a vent into another world. The passage above was cut and fashioned, with a tiled floor. The light came from one direction, as did the noise. The passage was not in good repair. Tiles and bricks had fallen from the ceiling. Rubble was piled knee-high in some places nearby.

Relkin pulled himself through the hole with a great effort and then recovered by lying on the floor for a few minutes. The air was hot in this passage, with a sulfurous smell.

Slowly Relkin pulled himself to his feet and went on, towards the red light. Soon he turned a corner and the light grew much brighter and the sound grew thunderous.

Then ahead he saw an opening to one side of the passage—this was the source of the light. A minute later he emerged onto a tiny gallery, carved into the rock, high above the floor of a vast chamber.

Below blazed the fires of the forges of the Blunt Doom. With astonished eyes he saw several great trolls at work hurling gigantic shovel loads of ore into a small lake of molten metal. At another point a gang of men, naked but for leather aprons, worked at casting swords and pikes and axes. Smoke rose in clouds from the sizzling steel as it flowed across the sand into the molds.

Beyond this were arrayed dozens of benches on which other men hammered the steel, and then sharpened it and placed it on wagons that took the new weapons to be fitted with hasp and hilt and shaft and made ready for the new armies of the Blunt Doom.

Huge doors crashed open, and from another great chamber came a long wagon laden with ore and dragged by a team of sweating slaves. An imp of evil countenance cracked a long whip over their heads.

The wagon rolled to a halt beside the trolls with their shovels. The slaves ran to tip the wagon over and dump the ore on the pile from which the trolls fed the lake of metal. The whips cracked over them as they were sluggish in righting the wagon once more and turning to pull it back out of the forge.

In the crush Relkin saw a man stumble and fall. The imps began beating him. He rose to his knees but then collapsed once more.

The wagon rolled out, but the imps continued beating the fallen man for a minute or more. Then they seized his limp legs and dragged him to a hole above the fires of the mountain. A thin, constant trickle of smoke rose from this vent. Without hesitation the imps threw the man's body into the hole. There was a momentary flash of light, Relkin imagined the smoke grew a little thicker, and the imps turned away and followed the wagon out of the forge.

The great doors slammed close again.

Relkin shivered.

One of the trolls turned its head and its red eyes seemed to be looking directly at him. Relkin crouched low, his heart pounding.

But no alert came, and after a few seconds he peeked back over the edge of the natural rock wall of the gallery.

The troll had resumed shoveling ore, another great bucket's worth splashed into the frothing white hot metal. Workers positioned below opened a vent and released another stream of liquid steel. It roared and hissed as it poured into the sand.

Relkin crept away and returned to the passage. He understood that he had seen the heart, in a way, of the power of the Doom. To manufacture weapons on this scale would allow the Doom to arm such a horde of imps and men that it would overwhelm the legions of the Argon-

ath. Once more the cities of the Argonath would be surrounded by a sea of enemies.

A little further on from the gallery the tunnel opened
into three passages. One went straight along, one went
downwards and one went off to the right.

He decided against the descending passage, in case it
led to the forge and those trolls. The passage ahead went
on into darkness, the passage to the right had a faint light
somewhere down it.

He chose the light and quite quickly came to a slit
window in the wall illuminating a narrow stair that wound
downwards out of sight.

Through the slit window Relkin could see another great
space, but it was lit very dimly—a sort of grey-yellow
twilight though which drifted a reek of smoke and stench.

With some trepidation he went down the steps and
found himself at the bottom of a well facing an empty
wall.

The only break in the smooth wall was where a pair
of bricks had been laid on end to purposely project from
the surface.

Relkin touched them and then pushed on them. Nothing happened. He tried pushing on them one after the
other, still nothing happened. He was about to give up
and return up the steps when he tried pulling on them
instead.

Immediately a narrow section of the wall pivoted in-
wards and he found himself standing in a storeroom, lit
only by the light that entered from an opening about thirty
yards further along.

On one side were barrels of fresh water. On the other
were bins filled half full with oats.

With a prayer of thanks to the goddess, Relkin opened
a spigot and let fresh water gush into his mouth. When
he had drunk his fill he loaded his kerchief with the oats
and tied it up and stuffed it inside his joboquin. Then he
filled the water bag from the nearest butt.

He pressed on the bricks and went back through the
door to the hidden staircase where he cached the food

and water. Then he passed back through the door to the storeroom and continued his exploration of the place.

He found, in fact, a series of storerooms of different sizes and purposes. One was quite small and filled with the reek of rum, which was stored here in hundreds of small barrels.

There were men on guard at this room, too, tall men of sober mien, dressed in black and carrying pikes and bows. Relkin turned back at the sight of them and tried another.

This contained wax, in blocks three feet long and one foot wide and deep. Another was filled with tubs of pitch, and he had to hide while a party of slaves was driven in by some imps and made to load a cart with a heavy tub of pitch and then tow it away.

Eventually Relkin decided he had seen enough; Lagdalen needed water and food too and he had been gone a long time. He found the storeroom with the oats and water and worked the hidden door again.

He slipped back down the long tunnels, past the forge and then to the hole in the floor that lead to the lava caverns below. He climbed through the hole with the food and water and scrambled down the rocks into the slime-weed light of the lower tunnel.

He did not observe the yellow eyes that watched him from the darkness and which followed him, keeping always to the shadows.

CHAPTER FORTY-SIX

Bazil awoke from a deep dreamless sleep. It was like a slow climb up a vertical well from a deep dark pit. Eventually his eyes opened. There was light but it was dim. There was a foul odor on the air.

He tried to move; metal clanked all around him and he felt pressure at wrist and ankle and all along his tail.

He let out a great groan of woe. He remembered now. The desperate fight in the kitchen doorway and then the Hogo, the black thing that exploded like an unwholesome balloon, a sausage loaded with corruption.

He was chained to a wall, each limb encircled by five great steel bracelets, locked and welded to heavy chains that were sunk into the wall on metal pins. Even his tail was restrained, with more chains and cuffs.

"Ah," said a dragon voice from nearby, "the Broketail wakes at last."

"Nesessitas!"

"The same."

At least he wasn't alone.

"Where the hell is this?"

The green dragon was chained nearby, spreadeagled against the wall.

"No idea. When I woke up I was already here, like you."

"What about the others, Captain Kesepton, dragonboys?"

"You know as much as I do, my friend. It's been pretty boring in here, until now of course."

Bazil snapped his jaws together. This was a damned terrible situation for a dragon to be in.

"What can we do?"

Nesessitas's voice grew weary. "Nothing very much. I suggest we wait."

So they waited, for what seemed an eternity to Bazil but was just a day and a night, judging by the slow waxing and waning of the light that entered from a single small window high above.

And then the door crashed open and a group of imps in black uniforms trimmed with gold and scarlet came bouncing in with an arrogant air.

They used tin whistles to summon a quartet of heavyset

trolls, but these were trolls unlike any Baz had seen before. Their skins were milky white and their hands and ears and feet were bright pink. Their eyes were pale, colorless, and in their mouths bristled heavy tusks.

Behind them they had a heavy two-wheeled cart.

The imps strode about the cell, examining the chained-up dragons with an exuberant display of insolence. Then they grouped around Bazil and gesticulated among themselves while keeping up an intense gabble in their thick-throated tongue.

"Looks like you're to be first course, Broketail."

"I have news for them. This is one lobster that won't go in their damn pot alive."

Nesessitas chuckled. "I don't think you'll fit into a pot anyway. Maybe they eat you raw."

"Damn tough meat to chew. Old dragon here, been in the wars."

The huge trolls lumbered forward and began to work the locks on the cuffs. This was difficult for them; their fingers were too clumsy for such keys. Bazil felt the cuffs loosening, one by one freeing his legs and arms and finally his tail.

As they released his cuffs the trolls seized him by the arms and legs and lifted him smoothly off the floor. Two imps seized the tail and gripped it under their arms. Without his feet he was helpless, or almost.

"They tell me dragons hiss a lot when they go into the boiling water," said Nesessitas.

"They haven't got me to the pot yet," he shot back.

He tensed and then tried to break free from the grip of the four albino trolls.

He heaved and shook, and for a moment took them by surprise with his strength, but then they held him again. The imps gripping his tail, however, were not prepared for the unusual strength in that twisted and broken end piece. With cries of woe the imps flew through the air and slammed into the wall with dull thuds.

With his tail free, he grabbed a troll's ankle and tipped

it onto its side, bringing down the whole group in a tangle of heavy limbs and stocky bodies.

The dragon was the first on his feet. The rest of the imps in the cell let out shrieks of fear and jammed in the doorway.

Bazil grabbed the first troll that got to its feet and swung it head first into the door. Imps flew out the door and the troll was stuck fast in their place. The other trolls were up now, and while Nesessitas urged him on, Bazil the Broketail gave them the fight of their brutish lives.

The odds were in their favor, of course, except that they were slow. He battered them, knocking loose tusks and opening up long gashes on their heads and shoulders. Their pale blood, as colorless as the rest of them, soon made the floor wet and slippery while the air filled with its peculiar sweet-salt smell.

In the end they cornered him, slowly wrestled him down and kicked him in the guts to subdue him. By this time two fresh trolls, also albinos, had come in to aid them and the narrow cell was packed with the hulking creatures.

Swathed in chains once more, Bazil was lifted up and carried out to the waiting cart. The cart was then wheeled through the great underground city of the Doom.

Bazil observed the stone walls and ceilings, the wide prospects and narrow adits. On the wide thoroughfares there were well-lit spaces on either side, shops and work places. A constant traffic of rickshaws and small carts went past, all pulled by human slaves chained between the shafts.

Riding in the carts were men and women for the most part, a people self-selected as servants of the Doom. They were of all races and types but shared a common hardness of the features and a certain arrogance.

Then his troll escort came to a huge black gate. This opened for them and they went on into a darker area with much greater rooms and corridors. Another gate, and another until at last they entered a large hall dominated by a great black sphere that hung from the ceiling like a spider the size of a house. On three sides the space in which the black ball hung was surrounded by a filigree of steel. On the fourth side it was open.

Braziers burned with a hot light along the walls. Armed men stood beneath them.

The trolls wheeled the cart across until it was almost beneath the black sphere. Baz could raise his head slightly, and when he did he noticed that the cart was at rest on the edge of a deep black abyss, a pit that went straight down.

Then he heard a rumbling of chains and pulleys and the sphere of blackness was descending.

Down it came, rattling the chains that it hung in until at last it loomed over him, huge and menacing.

Now he saw that it was nothing but a rock, a piece of black lava, polished and smooth, and held in a lacework of steel chains. He had heard much concerning this bizarre creation of the enemy but had somehow never accepted its existence as real until now.

This was no ordinary piece of rock. There was such a palpable presence in this stone that even an ignorant dragon could feel it—vast, implacable, malevolent. A great intelligence was now focused on him.

A red spot about the size of an apple was emerging on the stone. It pulsed and suddenly there was a rattling of smaller chains and three tall, narrow cages rose from the pit to hang in front of the great black rock.

In the center cage was a gaunt man with no ears or eyelids. He clutched the bars and stared with bulbous eyes at Bazil.

In the cage to his right was a monstrously fat woman whose flesh bulged through the bars. She was blind and her mouth had been sewn shut, but she had large, prominent ears.

Suddenly the large man in the third cage grabbed the bars and spoke in a loud voice.

"Welcome to my city, Master Dragon."

The Eyes of the Doom were suddenly dropped and

swung to dangle very close to Bazil. The Mouth ceased to boom and purred instead.

"It is a rare pleasure to be able to welcome one of your race. Seldom indeed have we been so honored."

The Mouth became suddenly querulous. "Indeed, usually dragons die rather than accept the opportunity to come before us in my city."

The Mouth calmed. "But now you are here and that is wonderful, even if we do have to put you to death."

Bazil tried to see what mechanism controlled the cages in which were held the Eyes, Ears and Mouth of the Doom. He peered down into the pit.

Far below he made out shadowy movements and heard the crack of a whip. Great trolls organized slave gangs there to toil over the ropes and blocks.

"You are interested in the workings of our apparatus, Master Dragon?"

Bazil looked up at the rock but said nothing.

"Well," it went on, "no matter. You are here and we shall have a great deal of fun with you, unless of course you are sensible and see reason . . ."

The Eyes jerked away and the woman with the ears was swung close to Bazil. A response was clearly required of him.

Play for time, said a small voice in his head.

"What is all this? Who are you?" said Bazil.

The Eyes were back, bulging close.

"Who am I?" boomed the Mouth. "You do not know? Can this be possible?"

Bazil felt his anger stirring.

"Yes, who are you? All I see is naked man in cage. Naked dirty man."

The voice laughed, a horrible sound.

"You see nothing, reptile. These are *my* eyes." Chains rattled and the gaunt man with bulging eyes swung up.

"And these are *my* ears!"

The cage with the fat woman rose and jerked to a halt.

"And this is *my* mouth!" and the big man was jerked up and down.

Baz let a moment of silence pass.

"So you live in rock, that's what you say."

The voice laughed horribly again.

"For a reptile you are quick on the uptake at least."

Baz bristled. "Reptile" was a human word that most dragons disliked intensely.

"But dragon, you should listen to me. Listen, my friend."

"I am not your friend, rock. You release me and I show you that pretty damn quick."

Again the laughter.

"Oh yes, I can imagine, but fortunately you will not get the chance to do me harm, oh no. That is inconceivable. However, you will get one chance to save your miserable hide and continue to live. In fact, your conditions could improve immensely."

More time.

"How?"

"I will set you free and set you up in splendor if you will promise to obey me and fight for me."

This idea was so preposterous that Bazil felt his rage rise at the scale of the insult.

"You kill dragons, kill people, make slaves. I have nothing to do with you."

The voice was back to the purring tone.

"Oh come now, don't waste this opportunity. You will not get another. Think about this: you can either die miserably for the entertainment of a crowd, or you can have more life as my servant, proud and protected."

Bazil's throat had become hard with hate.

"Since I hatch from egg I know that you and your Masters are evil. I never serve you. You waste your time, rock."

But the Doom was not quite finished.

"I certainly hope not. Come now, reconsider this. I will make you a general of troops, we will gather an army of dragons to fight for our cause."

Bazil erupted at that and almost heaved the cart over.

"Dragons never fight for you. You think we fight

alongside trolls you breed to kill dragons? Never, stupid rock, never!''

There was a long silence, the red spot pulsed. Then the Mouth jerked back to life.

"Well, in that case I must accept that you are as stupid and pig-headed as they said you would be. Well. So you will die for our pleasure. Good, the crowd needs a new thrill."

The Mouth lifted its head with a snap.

"Take him away!" it roared.

CHAPTER FORTY-SEVEN

They sat together in the darkness and chewed the oats that Relkin had brought back. It was hard work, but it was the first food they had had in a long time.

Lessis was a slender shape lying across the rock. She was dying and there was nothing they could do about it.

Lagdalen was fighting the urge to weep. The situation seemed utterly hopeless and terribly sad. Relkin had tried to comfort her, but she had recoiled at his touch. Since then they had sat close but not touching and concentrated on chewing.

For some unknown reason Relkin was filled with a strange sense of hope. His journey through the underworld of Tummuz Orgmeen had given him the mad idea that they could somehow escape this place.

Beyond that he could not bring himself to think much. There was too much pain waiting there. A lost dragon, possibly dead, possibly in agony. He had to find him, somehow.

Of course this led to further unwelcome questions. What if he did find him? How was he going to rescue a dragon that if it lived might well be badly wounded? That might not be able to walk?

Relkin sighed inwardly. He would concentrate on simply getting out of this place. That was the first step. He chewed and swallowed and took a little sip of the water. From the corner of his eye he noticed that something was moving in the darkness.

He looked up and felt the blood freeze in his veins.

Eyes! By the million, all around them, glinting like evil little gems.

Lagdalen had seen him stiffen, she glanced up and a little shriek exploded from her. The cavern was now carpeted in fur. Thousands upon thousands of rats had appeared silently out of the dark around them. A solid, living mat of rats that was creeping in towards them.

Relkin's mouth and throat were dry. He drew his sword and slowly got to his feet although he felt his knees shaking. This would be a terrible way to die, no doubt of it. Devoured by an army of rodents.

The silence was broken by the harshness of his and Lagdalen's breathing, and out there, a susurration of rat feet on the stone.

"Oh Mother, help us now," said Lagdalen.

The rats crept towards them, silent and implacable until there was a sudden, explosive interruption. With a shriek of feline anger, a black cat leapt down from the rocks at the side of the cavern right into the midst of the rat horde.

The rats scattered back, leaving a clear space for the cat, a tom, which while still heavily muscled was clearly old, with white around his mouth and many scars upon his head. But with those ears flattened and those eyes blazing rage and fierce yellow teeth exposed, he was still a cat to respect. This was no plump house cat, no pet for human hands to gentle.

He yowled again and rats scurried out of his way, but not quickly enough, and the cat's right paw smacked out six times in the blink of an eye and sent rats flying in all directions.

Relkin noticed another odd thing, the cat did not use his claws and no blood was spilled. The rats that were struck landed safely and dove into the protective mass of their fellows.

The rats crowded back and the cat moved towards the young man and woman standing in front of the body of Lessis the Great. There it hissed, ears flattened, body tensed as if ready to spring on the youth.

Relkin stared, amazed, but he hefted his sword in front of him. This was a fearsome cat, but still it was only a cat and Relkin was no novice with a blade. If it came at him, it was going to be a dead cat.

As for what the rats might do at such a point, Relkin didn't want to imagine. But what were they doing now? It was all quite inexplicable. Was this cat a king of rats? Why were such implacable enemies behaving like this?

The cat hissed and darted in, he swung the sword at it but missed, and it was past him and up on the stone beside Lessis in the next second.

Relkin raised the sword. The cat crouched there and hissed at him but made no move to escape. He hesitated.

The cat let out a long mournful wail. Lagdalen suddenly squeezed his arm.

"No. I don't think it's a good idea to kill this cat."

He let the sword drop. "Alright. It's not harming her, but what the hell does it want?"

Lagdalen had no answer to that.

"And what about them?" He gestured towards the rats. She shook her head. "I don't know, Relkin."

The cat now turned from them and focused its attention on Lessis. It sat near her shoulder and appeared to study her carefully, settling into a position of feline immobility.

"I don't understand," said Lagdalen, looking back at the massed rats. She was shaking like a leaf and her insides felt strange. She didn't think she had ever been this scared in her entire life, not even when that troll turned on them in the cellar of the Blackbird Inn.

Relkin reached out and took her hand. For once she

did not pull away. Relkin was shaking too, but somehow holding her hand helped to steady him.

"Don't know, don't know what to think," he mumbled.

The cat turned back to them, hissed and flattened its ears again, then it leapt from the rock and yowled and struck out at the rats around it, smacking them hard and knocking them about. But there was no blood, the cat's claws were still retracted. Nor did the rats who were dealt with like this protest or attempt to defend themselves.

A wave of tension built up in the air, and then it broke and all at once the rats moved; the entire horde flowed forward around them, through their legs and up onto the rock where Lessis lay.

Lagdalen sucked in her breath.

"No," she said.

But the rats took no notice. They burrowed under the lady, hundreds of them, forcing themselves underneath her body. In a few seconds she was lifted up and carried to the side of the slab of rock.

Thousands more rats were mounded there to receive her body. Gently she was shifted onto them and then the mound subsided, carrying her forward.

The black cat snarled and struck out again, and once more rats were tossed in the air but not killed. No rat did so much as snap back at the cat, and those that were struck simply picked themselves up and went on with their business.

The lady's body was borne away on a river of rat backs.

"No," sobbed Lagdalen.

Relkin was on his feet. "Come on, follow them. I don't think they intend to harm her, or us."

Lagdalen stared, could this be possible? Lessis had many friends, especially in the animal world—but all these rats? Still, there was nothing else to be done and Lessis was being carried away from them.

She stumbled after him, and together they followed the horde of small brown figures that moved across the cavern floor and vanished into a narrow cave.

Here the cat paused to rake the two of them with those blazing yellow eyes again. Relkin approached slowly, carefully. The cat made no movement, gave no growl of warning.

When Relkin was within a sword's thrust, the cat gave a series of small, plaintive miaows, turned and ran on into the narrow little side cave. Relkin and Lagdalen followed.

After a few yards they came to a place where the cave dwindled to a hole just two feet high and three wide. The cat slipped through this and miaowed from the other side.

"It wants us to follow—come on." Relkin crawled in. It was a close fit, but after about six feet of narrow tunnel he emerged in a wider space. The same pale luminescence was at work here from the ubiquitous slimeweed.

The rats had placed Lessis on a pile of hay that had been brought there by unknown hands.

Rats were grouped up around Lessis in a sea of little bodies, but none approached closer than the edge of the straw. Their discipline was extraordinary, even when the cat leapt in among them and lashed out, again without using its claws. They merely darted away from it and made no attempt to retaliate.

The cat moved close to Lessis's face, sat down and gazed at her in the most solemn way.

Relkin and Lagdalen exchanged startled glances. There was a long silence, and around them they could feel a rising sensation, a power that emanated from the horde of small animals. The air seemed to tingle and the hair rose on their hands, arms, the back of their necks, and all the way down their spines.

"Can you feel it?" asked Lagdalen after a moment.

"Feel it? It's almost lifting me off the floor!"

"It's for her—they are doing it for her."

"But what is it? What are they doing?"

Before Lagdalen could reply her thoughts were frozen in her mind by the sight of Lessis suddenly waking and raising her head.

"Lady!" she exclaimed, thinking that perhaps she was having an hallucination.

Lessis blinked, looked at Lagdalen and smiled. "So we are not dead yet! I'm glad of that."

Then Lessis looked at the cat. "Ah, old friend, you are still here in this place of death. Well, I am glad to see you and I know you have come to repay your debt. I'm afraid I must ask you to pay it in full because our peril is great and I am close to death, and though I would accept my death, I may not. The cause we serve still has need of me and thus I must live. You understand, old friend, I am sure."

The cat was unperturbed. The rats, however, were restless.

Lessis noticed. "I see all of you, and I see that you have done very well for yourselves. There are many more of you than there used to be."

Relkin felt his skin crawl; the rats milled about. The rats were pleased! There was a feeling of rodent exhilaration rising all around him. Well, there were a hell of a lot of them, that was undeniable. Lessis spoke again.

"But I am getting ahead of myself. I will need a few things. I have lost a lot of blood and there is little time."

Relkin edged forward.

"What can we do, lady?"

"Ah, Relkin Orphanboy. I should have known you would have survived. Along with my Lagdalen. Well, there are some things I need and I must ask you to go forth and fetch them."

Relkin jerked his thumb up. "From the city?"

"Yes."

"I can do that—I already found a way to get there."

"Of course you would. When I first laid eyes on you, boy, you were stealing something, do you remember?"

He swallowed. "Yes, my lady."

She smiled. "Now you have to steal again, but you cannot allow yourself to be caught this time."

Relkin vowed that he would not.

"Good, because you must go to the Magicians' Garden. There are certain mushrooms that only grow there. What I must have is a golden cap; it is a little thing, no more than the size of a button on your shirt. The magicians use it for many things, but it is crucial to what I must do here. I need that, and I need a candle and a means for lighting it.''

"Where will I find the Magicians' Garden, my lady?"

"Describe to me what you saw on your previous trip."

Relkin quickly did so.

"Good, then we are close to the forge, and that means we are underneath the vault. You will have to find a window and climb the wall to the first battlement. From there you will be able to see the Magicians' Garden. You will see a blue pagoda that stands at one end of the garden.''

Relkin leapt to his feet.

"Wait," said Lessis. She coughed, her eyes were unnaturally bright.

"There will be difficulties. At the wall to the garden— listen closely.''

Relkin bent over to hear her words.

CHAPTER FORTY-EIGHT

The most difficult part was not at the gate to the Magicians' Garden, as Lessis had predicted, but getting from the interior of the keep, which surrounded the vault of the Doom, onto the exterior wall and back again.

The only way Relkin could find was through a recessed slit window that would allow him to jump across to a place on the outer wall where he could see a group of potentially useful handholds. It was a five-foot gap between the walls. Below the handholds was a sixty-foot drop to certain death.

Relkin decided that getting across to the wall was possible, even relatively easy. What was going to be impossible was getting back without help.

Thus Lagdalen had to be placed at the narrow window with a rope or a belt or something that he could cling to for long enough to allow him to get a leg through and hoist himself back inside.

This meant that Lagdalen had to accompany him on his way back into the labyrinth of passages that honeycombed the vault and also had to remain there, hiding in a storage closet and coming to the window to look for Relkin every fifteen minutes or so.

The recessed window was at the top of a stairway that connected the southern dungeon complex to the midlevel of the keep where the guard force was concentrated. It was a quiet spot at the head of this stairway—apart from an occasional guard, nobody passed this way. Still the risk was extreme and what remained completely unknown was whether Lagdalen would have enough strength in her arms to hold the leather belt while Relkin hung on it and scrambled to get up to the window.

Once he was on the outer wall things grew simpler. Relkin crept along the wall to a gate tower. There he found good handholds and went up and across the wall below the gate tower turret. There was a guard in the turret, but he heard nothing as Relkin skulked silently past just ten feet below.

The outer wall of the keep was covered in rough stone with many handholds; for Relkin it was relatively easy to descend while remaining in the shadow between the wall and the gate tower.

He reached the ground without incident after passing over the roofs of a couple of storehouses that were built very close to the gate itself. He dropped eventually into a dusty little alley that ran down to the broad avenue that led to and from the Gate. The blue pagoda in the Magicians' Garden was clearly visible, not far away.

He hurried through the streets of Tummuz Orgmeen. Close to the keep they were not crowded. Further down in the lower valley of the city lay the ancient quarter, and here the crowding was immediately noticeable, but around the keep were the Guard barracks and other structures of the Doom's rule, along with the magicians' temple and their garden.

At the garden he thrust himself into a line leading to the entrance. About half the people in the line were boys, some older than himself, some younger. Most were raggedly dressed, a few wore velvets and silk with white hose and purple garters. These youths even wore white wigs and rouge on their cheeks. Such affectations marked them as senior apprentices to important magicians. However, all the boys in line were magicians' apprentices of one level or another, and none looked twice at Relkin in his scruffy, travel-worn garb.

At the gate each boy was questioned briefly by the guard. Relkin said what he had rehearsed with Lessis, that he was the apprentice to Spurgib, magician of the Fifth Advent. That he was to collect a golden cap mushroom for the good master Spurgib. When asked for Spurgib's password, Relkin said "Ralta!" and he was waved through after a check in the guard's code book.

How Lessis knew a password for a magician actually resident in Tummuz Orgmeen was something Relkin could not do more than guess at—truly the Lady in Grey had friends in many strange places.

The garden was a maze of tiny pathways and small plots of ground filled with bright flowers, dingy fungi and numerous esoterica of the plant world.

Relkin saw a pair of wizened old men tending to a group of shrubs with maroon-colored leaves and black stems. Carefully they brushed the leaves with milk and patted down the soil around the stems.

Beyond them a burly fellow in a black suit was harvesting "death's fruits" from a tall tree with white bark. The fruits resembled tiny skulls and each contained enough poison to kill twenty people.

From another old man Relkin got directions to the patch of golden caps that was being harvested for that day. He joined a short line of apprentices being served by another old man with a protuberant nose.

When his turn came he received a single mushroom and wrapped it in a twist of coarse paper. Then he returned to the street and made his way back to the alley. From there he climbed back over the roofs and onto the outer wall.

He soon reached the top of the wall and stood there for a moment regaining his breath. He was on the point of moving on when a door, not twenty feet away, opened with a crash.

Relkin dove for cover around the side of the gate tower. Two guards strode out onto the wall. They were coming his way. Quickly he slipped back over the wall and climbed down to a buttress where he clung, perched high above the city on the outside of the wall.

His handholds were poor, his feet were barely able to keep some purchase on the slope of the buttress. He couldn't stay there for long, even if he wasn't seen from below.

The men came to a halt just above him and remained there while discussing a bonus that had not been paid and for which they were waiting with some anxiety.

Relkin gave up on getting back to the little window where Lagdalen was waiting.

He had to find a way down this buttress, or at least to a lower level where he could find better holds. Carefully he eased himself sideways and then down, groping for toeholds. When he was fifty feet further down, he found a narrow but serviceable ledge that ran along the wall. It marked the spot where the walls had been raised with the advent of the Blunt Doom in Tummuz Orgmeen.

On this ledge he made rapid progress, heading for the next tower set into the wall. He reached it and continued to descend, now protected by shadow from prying eyes below. Soon he was back in the maze of alleys. He began to circle to the far side of the keep, which stood on the eastern margin of the old city of Tummuz Orgmeen. Ahead, looming above the old quarter was the outer wall of the great arena built by the Doom's slaves for the amusement of the populace.

He passed into the ancient soukh and was soon lost in the dust and noise of the great market. Here was the heart of the city, a place that had been a great city long before the coming of the Doom.

But though Tummuz Orgmeen was a trading city, astride the natural trade route into the Hazog, it was a city that had always been steeped in a cruel reputation. It was a city of old evil, a place where the savage nomad tribes of the great steppe turned to corruption and decadence. Upon these old patterns the Masters had merely imposed the iron rule of their terrible creation.

Around him nomad traders haggled with the city folk over everything from horseflesh to rugs to fruit to metals. The din was tremendous, but to Relkin it was no more distracting than the hum of activity in the cities of the Argonath. Marneri was like this, too.

Then he passed through the slave market and understood at once the great difference between the cities of the Argonath and their enemy. In the Argonath no one was a slave, all were free albeit hampered by economic bonds to city, village and clan. As Relkin understood this he saw anew just why he was here, why he had been caught up in this titanic struggle.

On the auction block an attractive young woman was being disposed of to an audience of wealthy folk. She was stripped naked for them while the actioneer gestured to her sexual charms with lewd gesture and leering tone of voice. Her face betrayed no feeling whatsoever; it was as if she was carved in stone. She could have been Lagdalen. The thought chilled his heart.

He passed on. There was a group of young Teetol warriors; they still had traces of their face paint. They were chained at the neck, their eyes still blazing with the fury of their forests. Examining them were a group of paunchy contractors in need of fresh hands for moving stone and brick. Relkin pitied the poor braves, torn from their lands and deprived of their freedom, now doomed to a short and brutal life as overworked stone carriers.

Then he saw an elf in a cage like a wild bird. The despair in the elf's green eyes was so palpable that Relkin's heart was struck anew with sorrow.

He wrenched his eyes away; there was nothing he could do about it, nothing he could do here and now about any of it, except to return to the Lady Lessis with the mushroom he carried in his pocket.

He passed a large pen full of old women, worn-out slaves put up for sale to the magicians for their cruel experiments.

A whip cracked, someone screamed in pain.

He went on with his face drawn unnaturally tight, his teeth clenched to prevent him venting the curses that bubbled up in his heart.

There was a corner—he ducked around it, leaned against the stone and stood there breathing slowly until his heart stopped pounding and the sweat on his temples cooled.

An old man with a slaver's cord in his hand was sidling up to him. Relkin darted away, but not before the old man's hand caught his arm.

"Well, my pretty, what are you doing here?" he cackled, and his noose was lifting towards Relkin's head in the next moment. His breath stank and his eyes were merry, and Relkin punched him in the nose and evaded the leather noose with a lunging jerk.

The old man shrieked insults as he held his nose, but he retained a grip like iron on Relkin's arm at the elbow. The pressure increased and Relkin twisted and struck out again, this time knocking the old man off his feet. Still the grip was retained; the slaver would not let go. In desperation Relkin kicked him and managed at last to pull his dirk. He set the steel to the old man's throat.

"Release me or die," he whispered harshly.

The grip on his arm relaxed and Relkin pulled away.

The man let out a yell and started calling for guards. Relkin moved backwards quickly, slipped out of the mar-

ket and cut through an alley between buildings stuffed
with pigs—the smell was very strong—and came out at a
shallow ditch. He turned and walked along the ditch with
an occasional glance behind him to see if there was any
pursuit, but none appeared.

Less than two hundred yards from where Relkin paced,
consumed in fear and rage, Captain Hollein Kesepton
stood in a dugout inside the great arena and clenched his
fists in anger.

In front of him was the flat sand floor of the amphitheater. Above and all around was the vast spread of the
crowd, roaring as the combat before them reached its
climax.

Only Trooper Jorse was left of the three men that had
been thrust out to fight with the champion imps in black
armor.

It was three imps to one man. The imps were armed
with bullwhips and stabbing swords. Jorse had a clumsy
axe, almost too heavy for him to use at all.

The imp whips snapped and cracked around him.

Jorse swung desperately and was pulled off his feet by
the momentum of the blow. Bullwhips cracked and he
lost control of the axe. The imps kicked and whipped
him while the crowd roared in delight.

Kesepton looked away. Thus it would be for all of
them, cut to ribbons on this bloodsoaked sand for the
delight of the mob in Tummuz Orgmeen.

"Come on man, get up!" growled Subadar Yortch.
Yortch's angry eyes crossed Kesepton's for a moment then
moved on. Yortch would not speak to Kesepton now.

As if inspired by his subadar's call, Trooper Jorse did
manage to stagger to his feet one more time by catching
a bullwhip with his hand and hauling himself up with it.
He punched the imp that held it in the face and drove the
others back with the whip. They were afraid to face him
now.

The crowd grew quiet.

A horn sounded.

The imps drew back and the crowd noise changed to a concerted "aaah."

At the far end of the amphitheater the great double doors had opened and a chariot had rolled out, pulled by a team of four white horses. Holding their reins was a beautiful young woman, clad in white silk pajamas with a silver helmet capping her long golden hair.

With a sharp cry she urged the four horses into a charge and thundered down on Jorse.

Jorse was past running, he could barely stagger, and besides there was nowhere to run to. He took up the clumsy axe again and awaited the onrush.

The horses ran down on him, veering to his right.

The woman had a rope twirling above her head with one hand while she guided the team with the other. As she came she let out a wild, maniacal scream.

Jorse looked into the cold killer eyes of the girl and lost concentration, then he seemed to snap out of it and moved to swing the axe, but it was already too late and his swing missed.

The blonde valkyrie in the chariot did not miss, however, and Jorse was plucked off his feet the next second as the rope settled around his shoulders and tightened across his upper arms.

The rope was turned about a pommel on the side of the chariot's rim and the lovely Valkyrie, blond tresses flying, was able to ride on while waving with one hand to the crowd which rose to give her an ovation, while Jorse's dying body was dragged through the sand, flayed and torn, leaving a long bloody streak behind.

After a second lap of the arena the young woman pulled her horses up and cut the rope loose. The gates at the far end boomed open, and she whipped up the team again and ran them toward the gate and out of sight at top speed. She did not even look back at the corpse stretched out on the sand.

Slaves, old men and women almost too weak to move, were driven out across the floor of the arena now. To these ancients was allotted the grim task of removing the dead and dying. Their decrepitude led to many bizarre incidents, a source of constant hilarity to the great crowd. To urge the fun along clowns, mostly imps but with a human or two among them, would often join in, using jokes and jests and an occasional blow with a club or whip to produce more general amusement.

But this was to be all that Kesepton's men would contribute for that day. Doors at the end of the dugout suddenly banged open and imps with whips appeared.

The survivors of Captain Kesepton's little force were driven down the steps and back into the labyrinth of the dungeons once more. Finally the door to their cell slammed shut behind them. Kesepton found Liepol Duxe staring at him with angry eyes.

"So Captain, pretty Captain, this is what your command has come to. A line of victims set up to be slain one by one for the pleasure of a mob of bloodthirsty fiends. And all because you were bewitched!"

Kesepton shrugged. What of it? What else could he have done? Duxe was too angry to stop now.

"You were too busy chasing that girl! You were not fit to command—I said it all along."

Hollein felt his own anger stir, but he kept it under tight rein.

"We had orders, Sergeant, if you recall."

Weald was watching him warily. The other man in the cell was Flader, a swordsman from Marneri. If they fought he would side with Duxe and Weald would side with Kesepton, it was understood.

Duxe's head was nodding, his mouth was slack, the words tumbled out thickly coated with hatred.

"Always you were preferred, because of your grandfather. And because of that you were there for the witch to play her game and destroy all of us."

Hollein balled up his fists but kept them at his sides.

"That's a lie, Sergeant, and when this is over I'll see you over drawn swords and we'll settle it man to man. But until that happy moment you will remember your rank and position and you will concentrate your mind on efforts to improve our situation here and make an escape.''

''Bah.''

''Did you hear me?''

''Your mind has gone, burnt out with too many dreams of that girl the witch trailed before you. Never have I seen such calf eyes.'' Duxe grinned somberly at Flader. ''Our captain was like a schoolboy chasing his first piece of ass.''

Flader grinned back. Weald tensed, ready to fight if he had to. The tension rose; they stared at each other, ready to kill.

There came a sharp rap on the door and a cranking of keys in the lock. It was the imps with the evening meal, another bowl of barley gruel served with a chunk of black bread.

The tension evaporated for the moment. Grimly they took the food and moved apart to eat.

In another cell, no more than one hundred yards away from the one Kesepton shared with Duxe and Weald, Bazil Broketail from Quosh woke out of a doze when the door banged open.

The huge albino trolls were back, with Nesessitas, following her interview with the Doom. Bazil watched dully as they chained the green dragon to the wall. She seemed unusually subdued.

The trolls slammed the door behind them again.

''So?'' he said in a quiet voice after a few seconds.

''So I saw the rock, it was just as you said.''

''Stupid rock.''

''No, you're wrong there, it is not at all stupid. But I did see how it moves up and down.''

''Ah.''

''There is a gallery below on which teams of men and trolls haul the ropes that pull the chains up and down.''

''As we thought, then.''

''Very much so.''

Baz looked up at the slit window in the wall that let in the only light.

"This place is big, I have that feeling."

"Very big, bigger than Marneri."

"The rock is big too, eh?"

"Very big, impressive."

"But any rock no matter how big can be broken into smaller rocks, eh?"

Nesessitas laughed lightly at that.

"True, but even dragons would need hammers and their hands free to do it.

"Not if we cut the chains that hold rock up."

Nesessitas chuckled. "Good idea, except we can't even get out of our own chains."

Bazil nodded. "That is problem. I haven't worked that out yet."

"Well, when you do let me know. But you'd better hurry because we're due to be the chief entertainment tomorrow. They're putting us into the arena to fight for our lives."

"Just what we expected."

The door crashed open again and a group of imps in stained and filthy white smocks pushed in a trolley laden with bowls of raw meats.

"You are to eat well, great monsters, for tomorrow you die and the Doom would have you be strong in your death throes."

The imps dug shovels into the chopped meat and raised it to the dragons' mouths.

"Eat, eat, eat," they chanted in a weird, shrieking song.

"What is this meat?" said Bazil. There had been no meat in their meals before, only a pablum of tubers and grain.

"Eat, eat, eat!" shouted the maddened imps.

Bazil looked to Nesessitas.

"It tastes like pork, but I'm too hungry to care much what it is."

Baz looked back to the imps.

"What the hell is this?" he roared.

"Man meat, oh dragons, man meat from the arena," shouted the imps. One imp leaned close as it screamed at him.

With a snarl Bazil snapped his jaws shut on the imp's shoulder.

It gave a shriek of pain and horror and struck him furiously on the side of the head, desperately trying to gouge an eye, anything to dislodge the teeth sunk into its flesh.

Bazil tossed him with a sideways jerk of the neck, and the imp sailed into the nearest wall and then slid to the floor of the cell.

The imps fled, taking their unconscious leader with them.

"Do you believe them?" said Nesessitas.

"I don't know, damn them, damn them all."

They lapsed into a gloom-ridden silence. Could it be that the captain and all the others were dead? Had they really been innocently eating them?

It was a nauseating thought, even for creatures that in the wild would unquestioningly eat men as well as anything else they happened upon.

Time passed; Bazil saw the light fade from their narrow window and the gloom of the late afternoon begin. He wondered if he would see the sun ever again, or would he die in this dark pit, lost in this evil city?

Some time later he noticed a tiny movement at the window. It was repeated, then a round shape appeared there. After a moment a human leg was thrust through the narrow gap. After another few moments there were two legs and part of a torso as the daring fellow squeezed through the slit window into the cell. There was something oddly familiar about those legs, clad in dirty brown cloth.

"Very good, whoever you are," said Bazil. "Now you have to get down from there without breaking neck."

There was a drop of twenty feet beneath the window. However, the owner of the legs did not slip down the wall, he climbed down—there were several handholds in the cracks between the stones.

Bazil gaped, so did Nesessitas, then he roared.

"Fool boy! How did you find us here?"

Relkin scrambled over to his dragon, then took a look at Nesessitas.

"I've been getting some things for the lady. She still lives, but she was wounded and has lost a lot of blood. We fear that she may die, but at least she is hidden in a safe place, deep beneath the city."

"Who else is with you? Who is we?" said Nesessitas.

"Lagdalen of the Tarcho, the lady's assistant."

"No one else?" the green dragon was disappointed.

"No, Nessi, I do not know where Marco Veli is. I fear he was taken with the others."

"What happened to us? What was that damned thing?" said Bazil.

Relkin went back to his dragon and hugged the huge, rough-skinned body.

"The lady called it a Hogo, that is all I know."

"Fool boy, you should not have come here."

"I was climbing the wall and I heard dragon voices. I knew you were here then."

"So tell me what you know, you who have been outside. What was a Hogo?"

"A beast made by the Doom, a thing of evil."

"It make stink, we fall over."

"Yes."

"How do they make these strange creatures?"

Relkin shrugged. "Some evil process."

"What is outside?"

"A high wall—you're on a midlevel floor of the central keep in the city. An outer wall runs around the keep, and that's what you would see. Beyond that wall is the city—it is very large, very squalid. It is . . . terrible."

"Where are the others?" hissed Nesessitas.

"I do not know, nor do I have time to search for them. I must return to the lady."

"Well, goodbye then, boy, because tomorrow we die."

Relkin turned a stricken face to his dragon.

"How do you know that?"

"They tell us that we fight in the arena tomorrow."

Relkin licked his lips anxiously.

"Something will happen, don't worry. The lady will not fail us."

Bazil chuckled.

"Good, I'm glad you said that—it will help me to sleep tonight."

Nesessitas gave dragon smile, without mirth in her eyes. But Relkin had stiffened.

"I mean it." His voice grew harsh. "We will stop them, you'll see. Be ready for the signal. I must go."

Then he scrambled up the wall again and squeezed out of the narrow window and disappeared.

"Fool boy," growled Bazil.

He and Nessi looked at each other somberly.

"At least he lives," she said.

CHAPTER FORTY-NINE

This was the third time the Princess Besita had been called to a long private audience with the Doom. Such meetings took place in an intimate interview chamber set above the hall of the Doom, on the topmost floor of the keep.

Besita was rather flattered by the attention. She liked the excitement of such proximity to power. No one had treated her like this back in Marneri, certainly not her father.

The interview room was a gem, a luxuriously appointed little box, lined with fur and equipped with ivory furniture. One end of the room was open to the Tube, a black emptiness which was filled entirely with the mass of the Doom during an audience.

For the occasion she had been dressed by five hand-maidens in a beautiful suit of black silk and white silver fitments, topped off by a simple, round helmet, also in silver.

She felt like some fantastic barbarian queen when she saw herself in the mirror with the flared silk pantaloons and the glittering silver buckles and clasps.

And indeed, since her arrival in Tummuz Orgmeen she had been treated as a queen. Even Thrembode had become quite deferential to her, bowing low, offering help instead of giving orders. In fact, even taking orders from her!

Besita had found it all very enjoyable. And with her body newly honed by months of hard travel, she felt more physically alive than she had ever felt in her adult life.

Then there was Tummuz Orgmeen. This was a true metropolis. It made Marneri seem so pinched and provincial, so limited and unexciting. There were broad avenues lined with the villas of the elite, graceful squares and rotundas, and a wonderful carriageway that wound back and forth on the hillside of the Thumb. In many ways it even rivaled Kadein in size and splendor.

And then there were the soukhs and bazaars of the old city, packed with life, teeming with multitudes drawn there from all over the world. Here one met people from every faraway land, all sorts of exotics from all sorts of distant climes. And they talked of such exciting things, of trade to the Friendly Isles or to distant Ianta and the cities of the Palasae. And best of all, they accepted her! They wanted to hear all about her adventures on the Gan.

The men at the dinners and parties were hard-faced and exciting. Their women were clever and sharp and wonderfully deferential to Besita, always calling her princess and always speaking so respectfully.

And now there was the Doom which, far from being the terrifying monstrosity that she had always believed in, was in fact a fascinating "person" with so many problems and so much work that one had to feel pity for it.

Or was it a he? She had not yet entirely made up her mind about this—how could a mere "it" show such sympathy, such understanding of one and one's problems in life.

And it was an orphan in a way, a natural object of pity. It had been created and then just cast off and told to work for the rest of time to bring peace in the region and end the aggressive warlike expansion of the Argonath cities. One had to feel sorry for the poor thing.

She sat in a comfortable chair made of bones from the recently extinct mammoths of the Hazog and cushioned with stuffed foxes and martens. On her feet were the most fascinating shoes, made of lizard skins and decorated with butterfly wings pasted on with a clear lacquer.

The great rock filled one side of the room and the red spot glowed on its front.

Three cages, draped in black velvet to hide their occupants, were hung in a row to one side. All that could be seen of them were eyes glittering through holes in the velvet in the central cage.

She had become accustomed to their presence; they hardly registered to her as human beings anymore. Instead, she focused on the red spot—it was the "active node" according to the Doom, where "it" was located at that moment.

The audience began, as had the others, with a long monolog from the Doom. It had much to say concerning the long war with the Argonath.

The Doom was taking her into its confidence. She was very important for the near future of the entire region. She and the Doom together would have to share the burden of administering it and bringing the war to an end.

It was enormously flattering to be addressed like this.

"You see," murmured its Mouth, "the present situation cannot be allowed to continue. Too much bloodshed and destruction is the result of all this stubborn clinging to imperial pretensions and designs.

"You, my dear, are the answer to this. You shall be the greatest queen in history, and if you so desire Thrembode shall be your consort."

She nodded. Yes, having the handsome Thrembode as her consort would do very nicely. She would be the ruler though, not the dashing magician—oh, how he would hate that. She smiled to herself.

The Doom continued. "Once we have seen you placed on the throne of Marneri, we shall be able to expand our trade and there will be wealth enough for everyone. The people of the Argonath will benefit immensely, of course. Taxes will be reduced, the towns and villages will grow rather than the graveyards. Can you see it like I do? This near future of peace and plenty."

The red dot pulsed. She struggled. In fact she was seeing herself and Thrembode, living in utter luxury and ruling over Marneri, but she made herself think about villages and farms and common people instead.

"Yes, I think I can. I think it will be wonderful."

The Doom was pleased.

"My dear princess, who shall be queen in Marneri, I do feel we have come to a very useful meeting of minds, do you not agree?"

"Oh yes," she gushed.

"I would ask of you a favor, a simple thing."

"Oh anything, I'd be glad to help."

"I am but a rock, trapped here immobile, built to serve the world. Yet I live in a sense, I am someone and I have feelings nonetheless. Can you understand that?"

"Oh yes," she said.

"I want you to touch me. Put your hand on the red spot where you see it glowing."

She was moved—the poor thing was reduced to this when it needed intimacy! And at the same time she was revolted, while at the back of her mind ancient proscriptions shrieked uselessly.

Abomination, they cried. Evil!

She clasped her hands together on her bosom, unsure.

"It will not harm you in any way." The Doom sounded just slightly unhappy.

"Is it hot?" she said.

"Not in the slightest. What you see is not caused by any energies known to you. Come, I hunger for your touch, Queen Besita."

She giggled and reached out and put her palm on the stone. There was a faint tingling, a sense of presence in her thoughts.

"Can you feel me?" said the Mouth.

"Yes, at least I think so. There is a tingling, a sense of something other."

"Good, we have made contact then."

"Yes."

"We shall do this again." The Doom's Mouth had grown husky, quite emotional.

"We shall?"

"Yes, and in time we shall perfect the contact. We shall know each other well, my princess."

"I—I think you're right." She felt a weird excitement. This was a strange magic, indeed. She was so privileged to witness this, she felt as if she had been plucked from an undeserved obscurity and taken to the heights.

"In time we will be able to speak without the need for words and voices."

"Oh, how, uh, amazing," she said.

"Yes," said the Doom.

The hook was in her, and in time she would be his, as open to his will as any of his human "operatives."

And now it was time to depart. The Doom bade her farewell and made apologies, but a conference was scheduled and it had to be dealt with.

With a rumble of tackle and the steady clanking of chains the Doom stone rolled away from the great window and sank down the Tube. Sliding doors slid across the opening to seal the Tube once more. The small door by which she had entered opened and smiling slave girls beckoned her to follow them.

Fifty feet below her the Doom halted above the main

audience floor. There, assembled beneath it were the executive officers of its hegemony.

The generals of the armies, clad in black leather and burnished steel were in the front. Beyond them stood a group of senior magicians, all in the black robes of the Padmasans. To one side a phalanx of senior administrators, to another chieftains from the savage tribes that bent the knee to Tummuz Orgmeen and the power that sat in it.

"Welcome, all of you," said the Doom's Mouth.

The men and women in the audience were from all races and all parts of the world, but they shared a certain glitter in the eyes. They were a people intent on satisfying their greed for power and wealth. In the depths of their collective heart was a boundless hatred for the rest of the world.

They murmured salutations to the Doom while bowing low to it. After a moment it continued.

"As you have been informed, we have shifted our strategy for the coming campaign. Our enemy either deduced what we were going to do or learned of it from a traitor in our ranks."

There was a pause.

"Believe me when I say that if it was treachery then that person will be found out, and then . . ."

There was a slight collective shudder at the thought of what would happen to such a person.

"Anyway, we are as flexible as our enemy—we have changed our plans. The Teetol will be of little use to us this year, the enemy struck the northern tribes hard in the winter. Wishing Blood cannot rouse them now.

"But we have had great success with the new breeding program. Imp production has increased to a thousand a month. Our agents in Ourdh are to be congratulated for securing so many females."

A couple of the magicians nodded tightly to the others, acknowledging the polite applause.

"And so we have the augmentation of force needed

for the coming season's work. General Erks will outline the strategy we have agreed on.''

General Erks stood forward and climbed the dais set to the right of Doom's mass. He was a tall man with grey hair and cold eyes, a renegade from the kingdom of Kassim far away. He had served the Doom Masters themselves in Padmasa for many years, and they had sent him to the new Doom in Tummuz Orgmeen to lead the new armies.

Erks cleared his throat before speaking. His voice was low and harsh.

''We have enough force available this year to mount at least three diversionary assaults before we throw in our main army. The enemy will have to respond to our feints, however, because each one will be large enough to threaten devastation to large areas. Then when their forces have been scattered up and down the frontier, we shall cross the Oon with thirty thousand imps and attack them in Kenor. We expect to take an advantage of two to one into the battle.''

The audience nodded and murmured.

''We shall crush their main force and then move in to destroy their smaller forces. Ultimately we will move across the Malguns and into the coastal provinces. By midwinter I expect to have Talion and Marneri under siege.''

More murmuring and nodding followed.

The Doom rattled the cage of the Mouth.

''And by next summer we will be masters of the Argonath!''

They raised their right fists and gave the Doom a great cheer.

CHAPTER FIFTY

It was evening before Relkin finally found his way back to the place on the wall opposite the narrow window. He waited nervously crouched beside the turret, eyes glued to the window.

For a long time he saw nothing. He began to wonder if something had happened to Lagdalen. The window was in a quiet part of the keep, but that was no guarantee of her safety.

Feelings of despair were beginning to grow in his heart and the sun began to sink into the western horizon before at last he saw something move within the window.

He waved and looked again. It was Lagdalen at last.

Quickly he slipped over the wall and descended, taking extra care with the handholds now. He could not allow himself to fall when everything was so close to success.

He stopped when he was slightly above the position of the window on the opposite wall. Now came the hardest part, the likeliest place for failure.

Lagdalen had dangled the end of the belt out the window and was braced on the inside with the other end wrapped in her hands.

There was a dark emptiness beneath him, a symbol of the death waiting to collect him. He jumped, for a moment he was flying above the abyss, then he slammed into the stones of the keep, slipping, his fingers scrabbling at the hard surface; he was falling, and then the leather was under his hand and he caught frantically at it and it held, right at the utmost end.

Lagdalen was pulled hard against the window but she

held on. He dangled for a moment there, then he got his other hand on the strap and his feet against the wall.

He walked himself up, testing Lagdalen's strength to its limit. She had both hands gripped together and her feet braced against the window, but she could not hold him for long.

Just as she reached that point, with the strap finally slipping from her numbed fingers, he flung out a hand and caught the edge of the window.

A few moments later he was inside. Lagdalen was standing there, sobbing with relief, her hands livid with the marks of the strap.

He grabbed her and held her tight and noticed that they were almost exactly the same height. In Marneri six months earlier she had been the taller by a fraction.

"Lagdalen, you did it," he hissed, keeping his voice low.

She sobbed again, then cleared her throat.

"Did you get it?" she asked.

"Yes."

"I've been hiding in a storeroom down there, there were imps here earlier. But I waited for hours—I thought something had happened to you."

"There were guards on the top of the wall for a while. I had to go back and hide in the city."

"I was going crazy with worry. I almost went back to the lady."

"I thank the goddess that you waited, and for that I am in your debt, Lagdalen of the Tarcho." He took her hand and bent and kissed it.

She balled it into a fist as if she was going to punch him, but in the end merely ground it against his chest and pushed him away.

"You are silly and too young for me. Come on, let us get back. I pray the lady is still alive."

"So do I," he murmured, while his thoughts ran on to the hope that he would live long enough to be old enough for Lagdalen of the Tarcho.

They returned, sneaking through the public halls until

they could reenter the secret passage and make the transition to the underground world.

Once more they crept through the forge and heard the cracking of whips and the hammering and boiling of metal. Then they had to go back through the hole into the deep tunnel. For Lagdalen this was almost beyond her strength and she nearly fell, but Relkin was there, and he steadied her at a critical point and she reached the tunnel floor a few moments later.

They moved down into the zone of luminescent slime. They had gone perhaps halfway back when they heard sounds coming from in front of them: a clank of steel, a rumble of voices and a sharp bark of command.

"Search party," hissed Relkin, turning and pulling Lagdalen after him back down the tunnel.

Small lights had appeared now, much farther down the tunnel, and fortunately too far away to illuminate them. They ran back until they found another tunnel opening. This they entered and continued their flight.

Eventually this tunnel began a steep descent and turned sharply to the right. Relkin was not sure, but he suspected they were heading back beneath the keep and the vault.

Then they emerged onto another hidden review gallery above a large chamber. This one was filled with women, poor wretches chained in pens along the walls where they existed while their bodies brought forth imp after imp, one a month until death brought them merciful release.

Lagdalen felt the hair on the back of her neck rise. Relkin's throat had gone dry. Hundreds, thousands of women pregnant with imps, chained like animals and supervised by other women who wore the black uniform of Tummuz Orgmeen.

"How could anyone participate in this?" he said in a choked whisper.

Lagdalen had no answer to that. The people of Tummuz Orgmeen were a fell folk with cold hearts. They had flocked here to serve the Doom, hoping to benefit from its triumph.

In another huge chamber the Doom's eugenics masters were experimenting. Relkin saw a cow, doomed to die in giving birth to the enormous thing that had been grown within her. The image of the poor cow, her belly bloated obscenely, stayed with him as they went on past the hell-holes and into further tunnels.

Eventually they came to a stair that returned them to the first level of tunnels, and from there they soon came to a junction they remembered from their trip to and from the higher floors of the keep.

They returned to their earlier path once more. This time they found no patrol on the upper level of the deep tunnels. But deeper still, on their way to the hiding place, they heard more noises, very distant but undoubtedly on the same level as themselves.

They reached the chamber where the cat and its horde of rats had come upon them. It was not easy to locate the cleft in the wall and then find the low passage into the hidden chambers. The rats had nibbled away the slimeweed here to keep it dark.

But after they had fumbled around in the dark for a while they heard sharp squeaking sounds, and then with the soft light of the blue stone ring they saw rats darting around the cleft beside them.

Some of the rats then ran under the rocks and disappeared. Relkin bent down and found the low-set passage once again. Shortly after that they were back in the secret chamber.

The black cat was there, staring gravely down upon Lessis's body. As they approached it turned to regard them with big, solemn eyes. There were a handful of rats there, but of the living carpet that had filled the place before there was no sign.

Relkin nodded to the cat and showed it the mushroom. He didn't know why but he felt he had to, as if to ask the cat's forgiveness for being so tardy.

The cat blinked once and looked back to Lessis. She was deathly pale; in fact, she seemed quite dead to Relkin.

"What?" He turned to Lagdalen, horror rising in his heart. Were they too late?

Lagdalen crouched by the frail figure of the Lady.

"Lady, we have returned. We have what you requested."

The cat gave a sudden call of complaint. It turned around and called again and arched its back. They looked at it, but it returned to staring at Lessis's face as if it were a lamp illuminating her eyes.

"I don't know. Sometimes she goes into a trance that lasts for days. She speaks to beings we cannot see. I have seen things, Relkin, things that I cannot explain."

Relkin felt that eeriness again. The small, pale woman lying there on the mound of hay was at the center of a whirlpool of forces and events—she was the tiny pivot of enormous actions. It made him giddy to contemplate them at all.

"But is she still alive?" he murmured, for she did not seem to be breathing.

"Her heart beats, but slowly," said Lessis.

"How is the wound?"

"Still clean, there is no rot."

"Then we must try to wake her."

Lagdalen was uncertain. "I do not know if that is wise. Let us wait a little while."

"But does she not need this mushroom?"

Lagdalen shook her head. "It is not medicine, Relkin. She must harbor her strength in order to be able to work with it. We had best wait a while. The lady has always told me that patience is the first and greatest virtue in these things."

Relkin shrugged. "Then we wait, while they search the tunnels."

"We wait."

Time passed. Relkin didn't think at first that he could sleep, but he chewed some more oats, drank some water, rested his head on a rock, and awoke only to a shake from Lagdalen.

"Wake up, Relkin. Something is happening, they're back."

Groggily he sat up, wiping his eyes.

Rats were returning in great numbers. He looked over his shoulder and saw many more streaming in from small holes and crevices around the chamber.

The hair on his neck rose again at the sight, but in his heart he also felt a strange sense of relief. For some reason it was damned good to see all those rats coming back.

CHAPTER FIFTY-ONE

The rats were gathered around them once more as if they were an audience come to hear a concert recital from the woman, apparently dead, who lay on the hay.

The old black cat had greeted the rats with its familiar display of ill temper, knocking them flying with swats from his paws, but as before the rats made no attempt to fight back. They flowed around the cat and formed up in a dense mass, covering the entire floorspace of the cave. In the dim greenish light Relkin saw a sea of little beady eyes, all intent on Lessis.

Once more that force built up, slowly growing in intensity, until with a gasping intake of breath Lessis awoke. Her eyes opened first, and then slowly, very slowly, animation returned to her face.

The slowness of it chilled Relkin, for it suggested to him that she was indeed very weak and close to death. But at length she was looking up at them, breathing and clearly alive.

She moistened her lips, then spoke. Her voice was very soft now, remote, little more than a whisper.

"Lagdalen, my dear, this is going to be more difficult than I had expected—my strength is failing. You, my dear, will have to cast the spell and weave the magic numbers. If you have the candle and the mushroom it should be possible. I will tell you what to do."

Lagdalen felt her heart freeze in her chest. The responsibility for this was to be hers? It was too much; she was so bad at declensions. What if she made a mistake? What if the lady were to die because of an error?

But there was no escape from it. No one else was there to take this burden from her. Lagdalen cut away the remains of Lessis's clothing. Numbly, she watched as her hands crushed the mushroom into a small ring of crumbs on the center of Lessis's chest.

How thin and worn the lady was; her breasts were withered, her ribs gaunt. Lagdalen had never seen her naked before and now the sight of her flesh made her want to weep.

She steadied herself and placed the candle, which Relkin had laboriously lit with flint and stone and the little pile of straw shavings, into the center of the crumbled mushroom.

Lessis awoke once more, again with the deadly slowness.

"Now, my dear, we need to begin the declensions, and we must hurry for they have to be completed before the candle burns out. Are you ready?"

Lagdalen shrugged. "I am ready, lady."

"Recite the seventh and ninth redactions from the Birrak."

Lagdalen knew those from memory, but she also had the lady's small pocket Birrak for the more difficult sections. The trouble was reading it; the characters were tiny and the light was poor.

Slowly her voice strengthened and the words of power filled the chamber with resonance. Carefully, brick by brick she built the spell; the curves of magical power began to harden in the air.

The very weft of the world was in play here now, and

Relkin stared at Lagdalen with amazement as the long strands of poetry rolled from her lips and caressed the magic from the fabric of the world itself.

As it went on, Lagdalen felt herself being subsumed into the play, her essence dissolving into the words as they built up the outlines of the spell.

She had to make haste with it, the Lady Lessis was clinging to a black wall that was itself sliding into eternity. Her fingers were weakening and if they gave way she would be gone, lost forever. But Lagdalen could not afford to make a mistake, and despite the need to hurry she had to be letter perfect.

There was sweat running down Lagdalen's back and sides now; she was working into the high passages, using cadenzas *creata* and *voluminate,* modes she had never used on her own.

These words were hard to say; they caused physical discomfort in the mouth, especially the *voluminata,* which she did not know how to control. At one point the breath was sucked from her body and she was left gasping for air when a volume formed a fraction too soon, before it had even left her lips, for she did not know the techniques for shaping the mouth and lips.

Fortunately this slipped volume had no effect on the curves of the high power since there was a tolerance there now, as the weight of the spell had now formed.

Relkin's hair was on end as he heard the strange growls and roars of the volumes as they were expelled. This was more witchcraft than he had ever imagined being witness to.

The candle was burning low—a long time had passed. Lagdalen's tongue moved thickly in her mouth, the words were less well-pronounced, but the rats were still there, as intent as ever on this moment of strange drama.

At last it was almost done. Lagdalen set down the Birrak. Her tongue and the roof of her mouth hurt, her throat was sore, her eyes were prickling, she was exhausted.

But she was filled with a sense of exultation. Lagdalen of the Tarcho, so terrible at declension in Abbess Plesenta's classroom had made it all the way through a spell of the greatest magnitude without a mistake.

A hundred lines of cadenza! And forty volumes!

She recovered her wind. Lessis was looking up at her.

"No time to lose, my dear," whispered the witch. "I can barely hang on any longer."

The cat moved, miaowed plaintively.

"Take him. He is ready," said Lessis.

Lagdalen reached out to the old tom cat and picked him up in her arms.

His body was hard and stringy, his claws sank into her forearms with instinctive reaction. She winced but did not drop him or release him, and in a moment he relaxed a little with a sad miaow and retracted his claws.

She said the final words of power and then held the cat above the small flickering flame of the candle. There was a vortex of invisible pressures flowing in; the whole cave seemed to shake on the primordial level.

The flame went out, there was a seething hiss in the room as if from a wave washing back out through fine sand, and a slight smell of ozone stung their nostrils.

Gradually their eyes readjusted to the murk without the candle. The cat lay on Lessis's chest; Lagdalen reached out to touch him and found that he was dead, already stiffening.

And then Lessis opened her eyes with a snap. Life blazed within her and she rose in an instant, cradling the dead cat to her bosom. She broke into a low-toned song with words in an unknown tongue.

As she held him her body seemed to inflate slightly, and her skin took on a glow of health while the lines and creases that had been so evident in near-death were banished.

Her song came to an end and she laid the body of the black cat down on the hay where she had lain.

She looked to Lagdalen and Relkin and held out her arms.

"I am different now—I am very fierce, filled with a rage like nothing I have known for a long, long time."

"The spirit of your friend, lady?" said Lagdalen looking to the cat.

"Yes, the spirit of Ecator, a prince of cats. I made him, long ago, and now I have taken him into me, forever."

The rats were now milling around the body of the cat. In a moment they had borne it up on their backs and were carrying it away.

"Tend to him well, little ones, for I love him still and he has repaid his debt in full."

She stretched again, from corner to corner of her body, with a grace that seemed at once quite feline and yet very human. Lessis seemed abruptly much younger now, although still of an indeterminate age, but perhaps in her thirties or forties rather than her sixties as before.

And where her wound had been there was now only a livid scar, a long pink line along her side.

"I am hungry, and I want to eat rat," she said. "I hope such desires will not last for long."

"We have some oats and water."

The witch made a face.

"I suppose it will have to do."

CHAPTER FIFTY-TWO

The deep tunnels were on no maps. Not even the Doom knew all the ways of this warren.

Increasingly frantic, Thrembode led the search for the witch. She was down here somewhere, he could feel it in his bones. But although they had found some traces of the fugitives in the tunnel beneath Mt. Mor, they had discovered nothing since.

What would the Doom do if he was unable to find the

hag? Thrembode came close to panic when he thought about this. The Doom had a passion for cruelty. It was said the thing did not enjoy its existence. It was trapped forever in a rock, a thing of mind alone, and yet it knew the bitterness of envy and the pain of desire for what it could not have—life itself. In rage at this fate it fed on cruelty and power.

There was a secret laboratory somewhere in the depth of the Doom's Tube; the rumors of what went on in there were stark and terrifying.

To die as an experimental animal for the Doom was a horrible fate indeed. Thus Thrembode drove on his imps and troopers, sending parties to work through the entire warren.

Still nothing was found.

Thrembode went out himself with a crew of imps and men and worked down the passages, level by level. His desperation was becoming obvious. The men knew well the sort of pressure he was under—they became surly, difficult, and slow to obey. The imps would know eventually, and he would be left down there staggering up and down after the witch alone, until the Doom sent a patrol to collect him and bring him to the Tube.

And then, in a deep place, he suddenly felt the tension of a power field. A great spell was being said, and the world itself was warping under the influence of the highest magic. Thrembode felt it at once and understood the strength and quality of it, and he knew it was her, the hag, very close by.

She was doing something on the greatest scale and this perturbed him, for what could it be but the destruction of the Doom and the city. She had to be stopped!

Frantically he ran back and forth, tracking the power he could feel. It was to his right, low down but on this level.

He ran until he came to a cavern that the imps had explored several times. The source was behind the rock wall, close. He searched up and down the wall but found no entrance.

There was no time to waste. He pulled back the imps and sent messengers to fetch mine trolls with pick and drill. But before the trolls arrived, the power rose sharply to a crescendo of pulses and the air seemed to wobble and then it was finished.

The power disappeared.

Thrembode listened intently. Somewhere back there he heard a faint singing. He tracked it to a wide crevice that ran into the wall for a couple of yards. He bent down since it seemed to be coming from somewhere below him.

There was a narrow adit, only just large enough to admit a small man. Thrembode was not about to enter it, but the voice was in there. The singing ceased. He felt his skin crawl; he had been listening to witch magic, the black gods alone knew what horror might have been visited upon him.

Did she know he was out here? He licked his lips and moved back very cautiously until he was well out of range.

The mining trolls arrived, but he held them back and instead sent a party of imps to push through the passage.

An imp was inserted into the hole. It was met by fifty of the biggest buck rats from the horde. They tore into its neck like small tunneling machines and the imp was pulled out with throat and chest torn open.

Another imp was chosen and forcibly inserted. It met the same fate. The remaining imps were unhappy. They danced back down the passage, and after some hesitation they ran away.

The sergeant of imps approached Thrembode. ''They won't go in, sir. There's something in there that just about cuts off their heads.''

Thrembode saw that it was hopeless; he urged the trolls forward. Hammers and picks came down upon the wall, and soon there were slabs of stone falling to the floor of the cavern.

Not long after that they broke through into a low side chamber to the main cavern. A search revealed a pile of hay, some drops of congealed wax and a lot of rat droppings. There were also a dozen or more rat-sized passages leading away from this place, and three of them were just large enough to accommodate a small person.

Thrembode knelt and peered into the passages. He smelled rodents; there were a lot of rats down there. Equally clear to the magician was the fact that the damned witch was moving through a rat-infested tunnel just ahead of him somewhere.

He ordered fresh imps brought up and thrust into the narrow holes. They crawled in to between twenty and thirty feet when they were attacked and slain by packs of waiting buck rats.

More imps were thrust in, but they became fearful and would only move if jabbed with spears from behind.

The witch and her friends were getting away!

Thrembode ordered the trolls to resume their work— he would carve a larger passage if he had to.

The hammers and drills crashed home and Thrembode gritted his teeth. It was dawn in the world above, but if he did not apprehend the hag it would be everlasting night for him. He had to have her, and he had to have her soon!

CHAPTER FIFTY-THREE

The dawn's light was filled with portent for other unhappy denizens of the great city.

As he watched the light swell dimly from the narrow window in his cell, Bazil of Quosh wondered if this was indeed to be his last day in the world. He would miss the world; his life had had its shares of triumphs as well as of defeats, and the tastes and sounds of life were dear to him.

Nesessitas awoke early as well. Neither dragon had slept more than fitfully. Soon the imps came, bringing them the usual oatmeal mush for breakfast. There had been no resumption of the attempts to feed them human flesh, for which both were grateful even if oatmeal mush was not exactly to their taste.

The imps left at last.

Nesessitas said, "I will not fight you for them, Broketail. I will not fight any dragon for them."

Bazil nodded energetically.

"Nor will I, friend Nessi. But they will make us fight trolls."

"Then I will fight. I will not let the trolls take my head easily."

Bazil nodded. "Damn right, kill a lot of them first."

All too soon the imps were back, and with them came the albino trolls.

One by one Bazil and Nesessitas were taken away shackled to the cart. They were pushed out through the great double doors into the amphitheater, and there they were placed in massive bull pens with movable sides that hemmed them in and kept them virtually immobile. They were able merely to peer out of the front of the pens, where the doors were made of steel bars.

What they saw was astounding, even for dragons who'd seen the world. They were familiar with the concept of the arena—every city in the Argonath had an arena for combats, either between men or between dragons. But those arenas were miniscule compared to this.

Massive tiers of seats rose around them, above a wall of smooth rock too high for a man to climb, with a wooden barricade above that to protect the lowest rows of seats. The tiers were vast, and the air was filled with a susurration of sounds as thousands of people filed in and took their places.

The pens were set in a recess about halfway down the length of the rectangular arena space. To their left was the end dominated by the keep, with the Doom's Tube

rising above the wall like a tower to allow an unob-
structed view of the arena for the Doom itself.

To the right the seats swept around in a complete curve,
tier upon tier. These seats at the end were unprotected
from the sun and the rain, however, lacking the extensive
canopies drawn over the rest of the place.

"The cheap seats are already full," said Bazil to Nesessitas.

She looked in the direction he was pointing. The seats
under the sun were filled with the bright colors of the
poor.

"Looks like a sunny day," she said.

"Sunny day to die," muttered Bazil. "Unless fool boy
come up with something damn quick."

Bazil wanted to be hopeful, but he was finding it increasingly difficult.

On the flat plain of sand, a team of animal killers were
at work. Using spear and lance, arrow and net, they were
dispatching enraged lions and leopards. Each cat would
be urged out of a cage by imps with small spears. It
would pace nervously about, seeking some escape from
this place which stank of blood and men and imps.

The men would close in, approaching the cat from
three sides. One would cast the net, and the others would
stab and kill it. These men were good at the work, and
the distracted cats were actually too terrified to put up
much of a struggle.

"You think they try that on dragons?" said Bazil.

"If they do, they'll be making a big mistake."

"Why, Nessi?"

"I will catch the net and pull it out of the man's hand.
He is not that quick with it. The cats are panicked, they
are afraid in this place, they fight with desperation."

"Hah, cats are stupid."

"Well, Broketail, they are, but there's something magnificent in all that ferocity. Look at that one!"

A tigress with more wits than her fellows had evaded
the net and escaped for a moment. She suddenly charged
towards a group of slaves, overseen by imps, who were

engaged in removing the corpses of dead lions and leopards.

The slaves panicked and ran, a horde of skinny old people, jerking their bones along as fast as they might as they headed for the double doors into the keep.

The imps cracked their whips at the tigress momentarily and then fled as she showed no sign of slowing down. She took the hindmost down and killed him with a single bite through the neck. The others picked up speed with wails of terror.

A huge wave of laughter moved through the gathering crowd.

The animal killers moved in around the tigress, who watched them come with her tail lashing and growls of rage. Suddenly she broke and fled, running down the length of the arena, growling as she went.

The killers raced after her.

She turned at bay in the corner. The netman swung again and this time succeeded. The spears drove home. The crowd roared briefly.

Bazil shrugged in disgust.

Nesessitas examined the wall of the keep and the tower of the Doom that thrust forward from it. High above, perhaps thirty-five yards up, was a dark opening, a pool of shadow.

"Look up there, Broketail. I think that's where the rock will be."

"It said that it enjoyed this."

"Sick mind in that rock."

Bazil caught sight of something else, though, that riveted his attention.

Coming out of the anterooms behind the bullpen was a line of men wearing loincloths, helmets and sandals. They carried round wooden shields and short wooden swords.

"Captain!" he shouted suddenly, and heaved at the walls of the bull pen around him.

At the bellow of the dragon the men turned. They were the men of Marneri, with the surviving Talion troopers.

"The Broketail!" they shouted. "And Nessi!"

"Where are dragonboys?" the green dragon called.

"We have not seen them," shouted back Lieutenant Weald.

Guards and imps thrust forward and pressed the men into the arena—the whips cracked.

"The lady lives yet!" bellowed Bazil, before a troll began to beat on the bars of the pen.

The men looked back in astonishment. How could the dragons know that? Was there really hope left to them?

The whips cracked over them again.

The double doors in the keep opened and a squad of imps ran in. These imps were armed with steel and proper shields.

The Valkyrie, her long golden hair streaming out behind her, rode her white chariot past the imps and swept around the arena floor, arousing the crowd to repeated cheers.

The men watched the oncoming imps with dour eyes and hefted the crude wooden weapons they'd been given. Kesepton and Duxe had already planned for this, however.

"Alright men, we'll take this like it was training school," said Duxe with his customary snarl toned down to an ugly purr. "Just like a training exercise, we fight in trios."

"What's the point? We're all dead men anyway, why give them entertainment?" moaned one of the Talion troopers.

"We have fifteen effectives, that's five trios, back to back. Officers will form the central trio."

The men looked to each other. Then the big smith Cowstrap spoke.

"We must fight because if we don't we'll be run down one by one by that bloodthirsty bitch, just like poor Jorse."

"But with wooden swords?"

"Better to die standing up than on your knees, man!"

The others nodded agreement. The trooper shrugged. "Well, then we all die together," he said finally.

At Duxe's command the men formed into four trios, ready to fight back to back. The officers formed a fifth trio in the center. Kesepton and Weald, of course, were experienced at this kind of fighting, but Yortch was cavalry.

"We fight as a team, remember that," said Kesepton over his shoulder.

Yortch nodded. "I've seen how you foot soldiers fight. I'll be with you."

"Remember to watch the other trios. When possible, we have to assist them."

"Do you really think the lady is alive?" said Weald.

Kesepton had scarcely dared to hope, because if the lady lived then so might Lagdalen.

"I would believe it. I see no reason why the dragon would say it if it wasn't true."

Yortch snorted behind him. "Bah, you are snared in the witch's spell, still lusting after that girl."

"Shut your mouth, Talion."

"Ha, hah! Brave words, Captain."

"When this is over I will demand satisfaction, Talion, sword to sword, you and me, do you understand?"

"You will get it, Captain."

"And you will rue your insults to the Lady Lagdalen."

It was out in the open, and several of the men were looking over their shoulders at their captain. Duelling was forbidden in the legions, a hanging offence for the most part, and here was the captain calling out the subadar.

A blast on the enemy horns ended all speculations. The imps halted a dozen places away and spread out into a line facing the men. The Valkyrie rode past with a naked youth, covered with gold paint, riding on the backboard behind her and blowing on a battlehorn. At the signal the imps charged with their usual shriek of battle rage.

The wooden swords were heavy and clumsy, and the

steel in the hands of the imps soon began to cut them to pieces. But the wood lasted just long enough; two, then three, of the attacking imps were felled by well-directed blows. The imps would attack head on and often were struck down by blows from the men to either side.

Then a few of the men had steel weapons and better shields, and the situation had changed slightly. The imps had fallen back. Men with whips on black horses drove them into a group again and sent them back into the attack.

Steel rang on steel now, but in one of the trios there was no steel and one man was trapped by two imps and gutted with a savage stroke. He went down with a cry of agony.

The others in the trio were soon beset. Weald and Kesepton went to their aid. Yortch, left alone, plunged into battle on his own for the moment. His wooden sword broke when he brought it down over the head of the first imp he met.

At once he was helpless, and though he staved off the first couple of blows, an imp blade soon cut into his shoulder and another sank into his ankle.

Kesepton had seen Yortch fall and was already in place in good time to clear the imps standing over him with a two-handed sweep with his wooden sword.

The imps fell side by side, and Kesepton snatched up the steel and tossed the second blade to Weald. Then he pulled Yortch back inside the ring of trios.

Another man was wounded, his wooden shield cleft through and his arm lopped off at the wrist by a giant imp as tall as a man. But disaster was averted as Liepol Duxe slammed his wooden sword alongside the huge imp's head and it went down, completely stunned. Duxe took its sword, and with the men cheering him on, he slew the next imp to face him.

Suddenly the imps were backing away, their nerve shattered, leaving eight corpses behind them.

The men re-formed. Now they were four trios, but most

of them had steel in their hands; they would not die so easily now. Their wounded they placed in the center.

Kesepton stared about him, the crowd was rising and clapping furiously.

"It seems this mob is pleased with the performance," he growled quietly.

"We'll make them remember the name of Marneri," said Weald.

"Aye, Lieutenant, that we will."

The Valkyrie rode past once again and her golden youth showered them with dead leaves, red, yellow and brown.

Men on horseback were riding out—at their front was an officer in black and silver. He drew up his horse nearby and addressed them.

"Welcome mighty warriors to Tummuz Orgmeen! You have surprised us all with your courage and skill. I am empowered by the Doom itself to offer each and any of you the opportunity to serve in the ranks of the army of Tummuz Orgmeen. All you have to do is step forward now."

No man moved.

"Come, do not throw your lives away. You are brave men, and you will be afforded respect and honor in our great army."

Burly Cowstrap spat loudly.

Still no man moved.

The man on the horse sighed.

"Well, if you are that stupid then indeed you will die shortly." He seemed to brighten. "But not yet. There are other events to come. While you watch them you can rethink your stubborn refusal to serve our great master. Go to the dugout and look on what happens here and think upon it!"

When the men stayed put, the horseman waved his right arm in a signal, and from out of the mid-section doors appeared a squad of imps with crossbows.

"If you do not obey, you will be shot down where you stand."

Kesepton waited a long second or two and then turned

and walked towards the dugout. The men followed him, still clutching their hard-won steel and dragging the wounded.

The dugout was empty now; the doors were shut tight. They were to be allowed to keep the swords and knives they'd won, but they had little likelihood of escape from this place or any chance to use them in such a bid.

"What's the point of fighting further? Why don't we just make them shoot us?" said Yortch from where he lay.

"You heard the Broketail," said Duxe. "The Lady lives. There's still a chance we might get out of this alive."

"Bah, you're mad! Nothing but some nonsense from an addled reptile. And what if the damned woman is still alive? She's hardly been a success up to this point. Face it man, we're dead meat."

Duxe chuckled morbidly.

"You are, Subadar, that's for sure. But we aren't, not yet."

Yortch stared at him. "Damned Marneris, you're all bewitched."

The men turned away from Yortch, even the troopers. There was more activity on the broad arena floor. Handlers, mostly large-bodied men, but with a few imps among them, were at work around the pens holding the dragons.

The gate to Nesessitas's pen was opened.

With a roar she charged out. Men and imps scattered and ran for their lives to the mid-section doors.

The arena was left to Nesessitas. She turned her attention to the locks and chains on Bazil's pen, but before she could get far with them the great double doors opened again at the far end and a squad of trolls marched out.

"By the egg of my mother!" growled Nesessitas. "Here they come."

She stepped out to meet them, unarmed, heaving her shoulders, lashing her long tail.

At the head of the squad of trolls was the largest troll

Baz had ever seen. It had red skin, mottled with black lumps like warts or barnacles.

The Valkyrie rode past while the golden youth used his megaphone to describe the upcoming bout.

The troll was Puxdool, champion of Tummuz Orgmeen. The combat would be with swords and shields. Puxdool drew his sword, a gleaming blade of six feet or more.

Two other trolls stepped forward. One heaved a heavy shield towards the green dragon, the other tossed a troll sword, the same size as Puxdool's, into the air. It landed point first and sank a foot into the sand in front of Nesessitas. She wasted no time in seizing it and pulling it free, then she picked up the shield.

The shield was a loose fit on her forelimb, and the sword was too small and ridiculously light, but all at once the green dragon felt halfway whole again. She flicked the sword back and forth in the air a few times.

The crowd was applauding, rising to its feet and chanting homage to the master of this dreadful place.

Nesessitas looked up to where the crowd's gaze was fixed. Under the dark cowl of the top of the tower she saw a gleam of polished rock; the Doom was there, watching.

Then, to a crash of cymbals and the booming of heavy drums, Puxdool advanced and combat began.

CHAPTER FIFTY-FOUR

After crawling for an hour or more through a series of narrow spaces no more than a foot high Lessis, Relkin and Lagdalen finally emerged into a room of sorts.

The dim light from the blue stone showed a place half-filled with rubble and discarded furniture.

The rats had worn several trails through the dust and rubble but all converged at the bottom panel of the door, made of rough-hewn wood. The bottom panel had been chewed through, however, to provide a hole big enough for a rat but not a cat.

They tried the door; it was locked. Lessis muttered a quick lock-breaking spell, and within a minute the lock took on a blue glow. With a heavy click the rusted mechanism turned and they were through the open doorway.

From the square flagstone floor and the brick and plaster walls Relkin knew they were inside the keep. But from the dust, which was deep and marked only by rat and mouse trails, he knew this area was unused and had been so for ages.

The rats had left them by now, except for a small group of the fiercest bucks who now crowded around Relkin at the door.

He shivered. It was hard to overcome the natural dislike of ratkind, but even more than that there were the memories of the screams from behind them as they crawled through those narrow holes and the enemy had tried to pursue them. It was all too easy to imagine these little horrors slicing into one's face in the dark while one was constricted and unable to defend oneself.

Lessis was peering over his shoulders, Lagdalen behind her. When she spoke he was startled by the nearness of her voice.

"This is an abandoned corridor somewhere in the deep vault."

"No one but the rats have been here in a long time," he replied.

"Good. And our pursuers are far behind us now."

"What are we going to do?" asked Lagdalen.

"Well, my dear," Lessis flashed them a fierce little smile, "we are going to raise hell. That's it in a nutshell."

"Just us?"

"No, we shall require an augmentation of our forces. So first we must find our way to the slave pens. You have seen them, I believe."

Lagdalen remembered the horror of the place.

"Yes, we did. What can we do there, with only the three of us?"

Lessis laughed. "We are more than three, my dear." She gestured to the fifty or so buck rats that were perched all around them on the furniture and piles of rubble.

Lagdalen felt a shiver of distaste.

"Are they coming with us?"

"I have the feeling that they wouldn't agree to stay behind. They're very determined."

Lagdalen recalled the shrieks in the tunnels behind them, too, and shuddered.

Lessis was examining the passage. The plaster ceiling had come down for long stretches, but although the place was half filled with rubble in places there was dim light coming from one direction. In the other there were many doors, all shut.

"This way," she said, pointing to the light.

As they went they discussed the tunnels that Relkin and Lagdalen had fled through earlier. Relkin noticed that the buck rats were keeping pace with them, a small swarm of brown bodies that shadowed them at a few steps distance.

They reached the source of the light, an opening in the ceiling of the tunnel leading to an air shaft. Far above them was a tiny circle of blue sky. Lessis paused to estimate the distance and form an idea of where they might be. She was close to certain that they were within the vault, somewhere beneath the central keep.

Lessis of Valmes had spent many hours exploring these sinister tunnels; she was no stranger to the ways of Tummuz Orgmeen. Soon she found what she was looking for, a stairwell that connected the various secret levels of the vault. There were lights high above and the distant sounds of movements, but on their level all was dark and silent.

They went down, and the stairs here were strewn with

rubbish, including a human skeleton, still clad in a few rags of a black uniform.

Eventually the stair ended and they were on the bottom level of the vault. Lessis led them on, the rats still faithfully following through a dank tunnel covered with slimeweed. The tunnel ended with a small stair that circled up to a heavy wooden door studded with metal.

This door was bolted and locked from the other side, and moreover kept in good repair. Lessis was certain now she was right about their location. With a finger to her lips to quiet her companions, she leaned her head against the door and listened carefully.

After a while she was sure there was little activity on the far side, and she set to creating the spells that would open the lock and slip the bolts.

It took time, but within a few minutes the bolts were glowing softly and the door was in her control. The bolts slid open slowly and the door gave way to her touch.

They found themselves in a public passage very near to the breeding pen, the central zone of hell in Tummuz Orgmeen where the Doom's armies were produced.

They crept forward and were soon rewarded with a view through a guarded gate of the vast slave pens. A pair of guards, in the black uniform of Tummuz Orgmeen, were stationed at the only gateway.

In and out of this dismal entrance there passed occasional small groups, mostly of women in the black robes of the Doom's breeding service who brought food and water in and pulled carts laden with corpses out. Other women, in the white robes of the creche system, emerged with infant imps, wrapped in swaddling and destined for the creche wards.

There was no time to waste and no way around this gate. Lessis whispered for them to be ready to help her if necessary, and they moved quickly down to the gate.

The guards, Relkin noticed, were women—tall, brutal-looking women with hard faces, for no men were allowed in this place. They carried spears and swords and looked as if they knew how to use them. He looked behind and saw that their rat escort had remained behind in the tunnel.

The rest would be up to him and Lagdalen, he realized.

One guard was watching a trio of women in the black robes as they dealt with a woman in one of the pens who had gone mad and was biting her flesh and those of the women chained up close to her.

The black-robed servants of the Doom struck the mad woman over the head with a heavy hammer. Then they cut her free from her chains, hauled the corpse out and dumped it into their cart.

The guard watching this chuckled to herself at some grisly private joke. The other guard looked up with instant suspicion as Lessis stepped close.

"Surgeon's party," said Lessis, who knew that such groups of trainees did visit the pens on occasion.

The guard pursed her thick lips and snarled to her companion, "Is there a surgeon's party on the board?"

The other guard glanced to the slate that hung beside her station, but before she could say anything Lessis had slipped her dirk out from inside her shift and stabbed the first guard in the throat with a speed that caused Relkin's eyes to go wide.

Lessis had absorbed much from the death of the old cat.

Lagdalen meanwhile attempted a similar act, but the second guard heard something and turned and ducked just in time. The next moment a heavy gauntleted fist had knocked Lagdalen off her feet and the big spear was coming down to bear on her.

Relkin darted in, caught the spear with one hand and stabbed with the other. His dirk went deep into the guard's hand. She grunted in pain, let go of the spear and punched him in the face. He flew backwards and slammed into the slate board and almost knocked it off its pegs.

Then Lessis had reached the guard and her knife was in the big woman's heart; she eased the body down to the stone-flagged floor.

Relkin looked up. The black-robed women with the death cart had seen nothing; they were pushing their evil conveyance up an alley between two great rows of stone slave pens and they did not look back.

Some faces in the pens were turned towards them, however; startled eyes and hasty whispers were going around.

Lessis leaned back into the corridor and whistled; in a few moments the rats were streaming along the floor and into the great chamber. Lessis whistled again and pointed, and the rats set off into the great place in small parties of ten and twenty.

"Take up their weapons," bade Lessis. "You must hold this place for a little while, let no one enter."

Relkin and Lagdalen took the heavy spears and swords and stood in the gateway. Lessis disappeared inside.

Relkin looked back over his shoulder at a sudden cacophony of shrieks. The black-robed women scattered here and there in the place were suddenly jumping and running for their lives. Quite quickly they were herded into a small group in a far corner of the vast room where they cowered. The lady's rats had done their part to perfection.

Now the chains began to rend asunder as Lessis moved from pen to pen, seeking the most vigorous of the younger women who were chained there. The power ran from her in gouts of blue fire as she broke the chains and set them free.

These women sprang up with shouts of joy and a crowd of them swelled around Lessis, trying to touch her, weeping in gratitude. Others came to join Lagdalen and Relkin—in their eyes burned a rage so deep and mortal that Relkin was afraid. He gave them the spear and the sword, keeping his dirk for his own use.

Now they had seven guards at the gate.

A pair of women in the white uniforms of the imp creche suddenly appeared at the gate. Their mouths dropped open in shock and amazement when they looked inside the pens.

"What goes on here?" said the first, and then the freed women stepped forward and struck them down. The bodies were pulled aside.

"They deserve nothing but death for what they do," snapped one when Lagdalen cleared her throat.

Lagdalen said nothing in the face of the fury in the woman's eyes. The women in black robes were similarly dispatched by other freed slaves.

Soon Lessis had freed a hundred or more, choosing the youngest and the fittest, those who had spent the least time in this chamber of hell.

She explained to them what they were about to do, and she told them that although the odds were high and that many of them would surely die it was their best opportunity to have revenge on the monster that had done this to them.

The women, many of them stolen from the land of Kenor or from the Teetol tribes, gave up a savage shout for blood and revenge and surged forward with Lessis at their head.

CHAPTER FIFTY-FIVE

Puxdool and Nesessitas circled each other. The troll was a new type—its head was snakelike, unarguably reptilian. And it moved about more quickly than any troll Nesessitas had fought before.

Their blades rang on each other occasionally as they tried a feint, a sudden thrust.

Watching, Bazil of Quosh felt a terrible fear descend on him. Nessi was a good fighter, but not a quick one. She had great technique, and used the shield as intelligently as the sword, but she lacked speed. This troll was deadly, true dragonbane, for it was as fast as any dragon, and Bazil could tell it was quicker than Nessi.

Nesessitas knew the danger. She moved constantly to her right; the troll was righthanded, like herself, and it was almost as large as the green dragon, at least as tall.

They traded blows, clashed shields and shoved at each other. Nesessitas was the stronger, despite the poor diet in recent days; she pushed the troll away and almost took its head with a slashing cut of the sword.

They circled again, Puxdool feinting, moving to the right always. Again they came together, their swords met and bright sparks flew, and they broke apart and circled.

Once again Puxdool came in with his sword swinging high to meet hers, and then he spun and shoved Nessi hard and cut low with a backhand—it was clearly a much practiced move.

Nessi danced backwards, but Puxdool's sword tip caught her across one knee and drew blood.

Disaster!

Bazil groaned in sick disbelief. A lucky blow, catching her unawares. The knee was ruined. Nesessitas ground her teeth at the pain. She could barely move now.

The troll was dancing to her right; she turned, the knee was a terrible torment.

Steel whined on steel as their blades met. Again and again, shields clashing hard enough to spend fat sparks shooting out onto the sand.

The crowd was on its feet chanting, ''Puxdool! Puxdool!''

The knee gave, she slid down.

The troll's sword lanced in; Nessi felt it slide home between her ribs. Then it was gone and rising again to chop down.

All the strength was suddenly gone from her, her blade slipped, the shield fell. She was falling. The troll's sword swung in again and half severed her neck.

She was down.

It was over. Puxdool hacked down viciously to sever Nesessitas's neck and stood with one foot planted on her prone body, then held the bloody head up to the crowd which continued chanting ''Puxdool!'' over and over while stamping its feet in unison.

Bazil of Quosh looked away, sickened, barely able to believe what he had seen.

A single lucky blow had destroyed the most graceful of the dragons of the fighting 109th. The last shreds of Bazil's temper snapped. Incoherent rage took over.

''Just let me at him!'' he roared, shaking furiously in the pen and lifting the heavy steel up and down on the stone blocks it was tethered to.

Men and imps jumped back in alarm, trolls hammered on the bars, an imp in a black leather costume lashed a whip over Bazil's back.

But Puxdool was walking away. Horns were blowing, drums booming, and the cursed troll was walking away! Bazil could not believe he would not get to fight Puxdool next.

There would be no chance for revenge? It was impossible to believe, too sickening to believe. Beyond anything he had ever felt before, the Quoshite leatherback now wished for the chance to confront Puxdool. Puxdool had fought a dragon with good technique but no speed; Puxdool had triumphed through his lucky blow, now let the damned troll take on a dragon who had speed as well as technique!

But Puxdool was gone; the huge double doors were closing behind the troll champion.

And rolling across the arena was a large metal box on heavy wheels. Pulling it was an army of slaves struggling forward with puny limbs and scrawny bodies under the lash from six heavyset imps.

The Valkyrie rode by, the golden youth tossing out double handfuls of dead leaves as they passed Nesessitas's body, which was being winched slowly into the side entrance of the arena. The golden youth picked up the voice trumpet and began announcing the next event.

The slaves hauling the box came to a halt, then they ran for their lives as one of the imps pulled the bolts on the box. As the last bolt came loose, he too took to his heels.

The pen gate was opened and Baz was goaded from behind with a sharp hook. In truth, he needed little encouragement.

He stepped out smartly, feeling exposed suddenly, the focus of the multitudes in the stadium. He was alone on the sand but for the Valkyrie in her chariot. Calmly he estimated his chances of running down the chariot.

She drove her team by with a sizzle of wheels on sand. The white horses were immaculate; he knew he hadn't a hope in hell of catching up with her in this vast space.

The Valkyrie rode back closer this time, taunting him, while the youth repeated his announcements to the crowd.

Bazil could not hear the words clearly, but even as the people sitting above him began to roar in appreciation, the door to the metal box crashed down.

To Bazil's amazement another dragon emerged, a wild drake of enormous girth and angry eyes. It vented a scream of rage and leaped forward and began to paw the ground with heavy claws.

CHAPTER FIFTY-SIX

Lessis knew that time was precious now; she had but a few minutes in which to seize the advantage of surprise. Fortunately she knew the way between the breeding pens and her destination. There was a chance—a slight chance, but enough of a chance to give her hope of salvaging a victory from the ruins of her pursuit of Thrembode the magician.

Quickly she led her small force of enraged women through the secret ways of Tummuz Orgmeen, meeting no one in the dank tunnels of the deep. Finally she halted them at the bottom of a narrow stair that spiraled upwards to unknown heights.

She checked it carefully; there were a set of marks cut into the stones at the base.

"This is it, the overseer's stair." She took Relkin aside while the women watched with mystified eyes, their hands clutching whatever weapons they had managed to liberate.

"Climb the stair for me, Relkin. At the top you will find a gallery that looks over the arena. I want a report on what is happening there."

"Where will I find you, lady?"

She pointed ahead where the passage they had been following turned right.

"When you return here go down the passage and keep to the right—I expect you will hear us at work."

"At work?"

"Yes, young man. We have a lot of hard work ahead of us."

Relkin didn't ask any more questions; he knew there was no time. He blew Lagdalen a kiss and then scampered up the stairs.

Lessis watched him go for a few seconds, then signaled to her followers and went on, almost at a run.

Relkin was already several turns around the stair by then and still climbing the steps two at a time. The stair wound into a roof and became enclosed, just stone steps ascending into the dark, around and around the central core.

After a while his legs began to tire, and then to ache, but he continued the climb. He lost track of everything except the sound of his breathing and the scuff of his boots on the stone.

And then suddenly he heard a tremendous surge of noise, the roar of a vast crowd and a rhythmic stamping of feet. The sounds and the vibrations were all around him, and he realized that the stair was now close beneath or beside the seats of the amphitheater.

On he went, and the sounds came again at regular intervals as he climbed, until suddenly he noticed a light coming in from above, and then after another turn or two he saw a glint of sunlight falling through a straight crack in the vault of stone. He reached the top and explored the ceiling above with his fingers. There was a heavy steel ring set within a pin in the center and to one side a bolt that was slid into a recessed hole in the stone. He pulled the bolt free and then pushed upwards on the ring and found that the trapdoor moved quite easily, sliding up as a hidden counterbalance moved down.

He looked out over a smooth stone floor in an open gallery space. The bright sunlight hurt his eyes, but there was no one in sight so he climbed out and set his feet on the floor.

The gallery was of stone, open on one side in a series of heart-shaped windows. At either end there was a stoutly made door.

Carefully he let the trap slide shut. He observed that it was hidden by its resemblance to all the other flat stones of the floor. To mark it he drew an X in the dust on its top.

The roar of the great crowd came again, welling up from below, and he approached the nearest window and looked out. It was an amazing sight.

To his left, at the end of the gallery, stood the great bulk of the keep. Elsewhere he looked down on a series of great tiers of seats, packed with brightly garbed people. The tiers swept around in a vast curve, surrounding the central arena. The sand below glittered brightly, and upon it there moved small figures caught up in a struggle for survival.

Above and beyond this scene was a clear blue sky with an occasional fluffy cloud, the rest of the great city was hidden from view.

Relkin stiffened—the figures below were dragons! And one of them had a bent and misshapen tail. He sucked in a breath, his heart suddenly hammering in his chest.

His dragon was down there, but even now he fought for his life on the sand of the arena!

A sound caught his attention, a scraping of metal to his left. Someone was unlocking the door.

Quickly he got to his feet and flattened himself against the wall beside the door. The door swung back and almost smashed him against the stone.

He heard heavy footsteps tramp across the length of the gallery, and then a key worked the lock of the other door and opened it.

Relkin peered around the door.

A guard had opened the other door and was going through it. Relkin slipped from his place of concealment and looked through the still open door at his end of the gallery.

He glimpsed a curving stone wall, a pair of heavy double doors that were shut, and to his left an open door. Someone was coming around the curve in the wall. There was no time to go back so he jumped through the open door.

It was a long room, panelled in dark wood and hung with trophies from the many campaigns of the armies of the Doom. Swords, banners, armor and helmets, all captured from the legions of Argonath, were nailed to the walls.

In the center of the room was a long table, and along the walls were a series of heavy chests. But it was the great sword lying on the table that immediately riveted Relkin's gaze. He would have known it anywhere; Piocar, the dragon blade forged in the village of Quosh. It shimmered there, all nine feet of it.

There were footsteps close behind. Hurriedly he dropped to his knees and crawled behind one of the heavy chests by the wall; there was just room enough for him to squeeze in. He crouched there and tried not to breathe.

Two men had entered the room; they shut the door behind them. One of them growled something in a harsh-sounding tongue unknown to Relkin, and the other replied in a smoother voice using the common tongue.

There was something vaguely familiar about that second voice.

"I think we can dispense with formalities between ourselves, magician," said the first, heavier voice.

"I agree absolutely, General."

"The fact is you have found nothing. You say you felt the witch's presence and we have had trolls cutting rock in pursuit of her for hours, but nothing further has been found. Basically, you face the displeasure of the Doom."

"General, you have known me for a long time, you know I would not stoop to lie about such a thing. I believe the witch is still alive and is loose somewhere in the city."

"Of course you do, and you want me to proclaim an emergency and put my troops all over the city and carry on your wild goose chase."

"Not a wild goose, much more dangerous."

"Hah, of course. And by this maneuver you hope to save your neck, eh? You think the Doom will overlook the fact that you have failed to find the witch yourself although you were expressly ordered to."

"It matters little what I hope for. What matters is that the hag is out there and you aren't helping us to apprehend her."

"Ah, Thrembode, always you are the same, a slippery customer, ready to get around the plainest instructions. I can't remember your ever having completed an assignment as ordered."

"General, there is no point to this. Proclaim the emergency, we mustn't waste time."

"Hah, every second we waste takes you closer to the edge of disaster, magician. For years you have been a thorn in the side of my administration. Now you will be given up to be destroyed—it is a great moment for me."

There was a silence, then the smooth voice began again but now with more edge to it.

"General, please listen to me, do not do this. For the sake of petty spite you risk the entire city!"

"On your knees, eh, Thrembode? Grovel, you dog.

Perhaps if you lick my boots with sufficient eagerness I will consider helping you.''

The heavier voice was thick with gloating pleasure.

''Thrembode, unless you lick my boots now I will have you flayed slowly, whipped by my imps to the edge of death.''

''No, General, please.''

''Thrembode, do you remember Kadein?''

''Yes, of course.''

''Do you remember a woman named Aixe?''

''She had the blue villa. I stayed there once.''

''Your bungling led to her being seized by the enemy. We lost an entire ring of spies because she was made to talk.''

The voice had filled with rage now.

''I loved that woman, Thrembode, and you killed her as surely as I will kill you!''

''No, no. You must listen.''

''Hah, what do I care for your tales? You shall go to the Doom.''

There was a sudden clink, and then a gasp and a choked cry of rage.

''You traitor, I'll gut you, I'll—''

There was a heavy thud.

Relkin could not hold himself back any further. He peeked around the edge of the chest.

The man that had come to Baz's stall in Marneri was standing there, a cruel smile played over his dark lips. In his hand was a bloodied dirk.

''No, General, I think you will not.'' He kicked a figure lying prone on the floor.

''In fact, I don't think you will be doing anything ever again.''

He knelt down and stabbed the general again, his dirk piercing the man's chest to the hilt.

Relkin watched spellbound as Thrembode got to his feet with a nervous look around himself. Relkin jerked back just in time. In two strides Thrembode was beside the chest, and he pulled the top up while Relkin cowered there thinking he had been discovered.

A pair of Marneri short swords, a shield and a helmet, all wrapped in a battle flag, were taken out and placed on top of the next chest. Then there was the sound of something being dragged across the floor and stuffed into the chest.

The lid of the chest slammed down once more and Thrembode departed, his boots echoing in the gallery as he retreated at a rapid rate.

Relkin got to his feet and glanced out the door. There was no one to be seen. He moved to the table and lifted Piocar, staggering under the weight, and then headed for the gallery.

CHAPTER FIFTY-SEVEN

The wild dragon hissed and roared and clawed the ground. Its rage was quite awesome; the very ground seemed to shake beneath it.

Bazil had stepped back in alarm, but even as he did so he felt a wave of pity wash through him, for he had seen that the wild one's great wings had been clipped—this drake would never fly again.

Still it was hissing in a vile rage and stalking after him with flashing eyes. Bazil continued to retreat, slowly, steadily. The wild dragon was possessed by a tremendous urge to kill and keep killing until either it was dead or all its enemies were no more. Such rage could not be reasoned with, and since Bazil had no sword, no shield, no helmet, he had very good reason to be afraid.

Abruptly the wild drake noticed its surroundings. It

stopped and reared up and screamed its challenge to the crowd.

The stadium was hushed, awed by this monumental violence.

It roared again and circled, eyeing the people, the imps in the dugouts and the strange dragon that stood in its path. It wanted to kill them all, again and again.

Bazil's heart sank. He had no sword and this beast outweighed him by a wide margin. If it charged him he would fight, but in his heart he knew it would be of little use and the wild one would tear his head from his body.

Then a great realization struck home. The wild one was wounded, and there were still fragments of a bandage on the wound.

Bazil lifted his forelimbs and shouted in dragon speech, "You are the purple-green from Hook Mountain!"

The wild drake blinked. What was this?

"You and I have met before," hissed Bazil. "On the mountain in the south, remember?"

The dragon speech was strange, the accent odd, but the wild one did remember. The crazed rage subsided a notch. The great head filled with glittering teeth shook back and forth for a moment, then it blinked and stared carefully at the wingless wyvern that stood in front of it.

"Yess," it said at last. "I know you. You are he who defeated me, the sword dragon of the south mount."

Bazil could still easily imagine the wild drake launching itself at him again, and he spoke up quickly.

"How did they capture you?"

The purple-green roared and hissed at the memory, exciting the crowd, which had been expecting him to hurl himself at the Argonath dragon immediately and rend it to pieces.

"I sleep on mountain. Wounded as you know. Men come with nets, ropes, tie me down while I sleep. I would have killed them otherwise."

Bazil stepped forward and raised his forelimbs.

"I will not fight you again, not for the entertainment of these people."

The drake considered this for a moment.

"I not fight either. You saved me from death, staunched the bleeding from my wounds. We fought for the female and I was defeated. Only you have ever defeated me in combat."

Baz released a long sigh of relief, then spoke up.

"She was worth fighting for, great purple-green, and you were a most terrible opponent—I have never known such strength. But now I think that we should join together and show these damned humans that it is not a good idea to kill dragons for their pleasure."

The crowd had hushed again in puzzlement. Everyone knew a wild dragon would kill an Argonath wyvern— wild dragons hated the breed created by the folk of Cunfshon.

But the dragons were standing close, grumbling to each other in their sibilant rich tongue. It was a disappointment to those who had waited for this scene for hours since the first announcement.

The wild drake could see the trail of blood where Nessi had been dragged into the side hall. He pointed.

"Dragon blood?"

"Yes."

The drake's tail lashed in fury and his huge eyes fairly glowed. Baz had seen that fury and he was very glad that it was not directed at him this time.

"Show me how to kill them," said the drake.

"Be glad to. Follow me."

Baz suddenly turned and began to lumber across the arena towards the dugout by the main doors.

There were some guard trolls inside. They had weapons.

The purple-green dropped to all fours and came after him; the crowd roared again thinking they were seeing one dragon hunt down the other.

Then Bazil reached the dugout and was joined by the drake. Together they ripped away a pillar holding up the roof at one end. The roof fell in when Bazil jumped onto it with a heavy bound.

Most of the trolls inside were knocked senseless by the collapse. The others recoiled in horror as the purple-green leaped in among them. Baz pulled away some of the bricks and rubble and reached down for the swords.

When he came up with a pair, he found the purple-green pursuing the last troll along the wall of the arena. The others had been torn to pieces.

The crowd was hushed but for gasps of horror.

The purple-green leaped on the fleeing troll, brought it down and bit through its head with an audible crunch.

The double doors in the keep were opening; a squad of trolls in armor marched in to the beat of a drum. At their head was Puxdool.

The purple-green slowed, eyeing the swords in the hands of the trolls. Baz caught up with him. The sight of Puxdool had his heart hammering in his chest.

"Here, take a sword. Try it, move it back and forth."

The drake found it hard to grasp the sword's narrow handle; it was an unnatural thing this, to pick up something and wield it like a tool. Tools were for lesser creatures, not for dragons. Thus it had been since the beginning of dragon lore.

Still the sword moved lightly enough. It was hard to believe something so light, so insignificant, could cause such devastating wounds.

The leatherback motioned to the drake to back away.

"We need the men, our men. Come on."

Men? Why did dragons need such feeble things as men? The drake was puzzled, but it moved back in step with the Argonath dragon. It knew nothing of this situation, this world of men and swords and trolls; it would follow the lead of the dragon from Quosh.

And out of their dugout came the men of Marneri, with steel in their hands and a cheer in their throats.

"To the dragons!" shouted Kesepton.

The squad of trolls came to a halt. They snarled among themselves and raged at the men. They promised to eat them later once they had disposed of the rebellious worms. Then they raised their swords and came on.

There were three trolls: Puxdool and his second, Izmak, concentrated on the dragons while the third, Gungol, protected the rear from the men.

Kesepton darted in and hacked at the rear troll's leg. A huge sword swished just over his head and he jumped to the side.

Cowstrap charged from the other side and met the troll shield to shield. Gungol dipped his shoulder and flexed his mighty arm. Burly Cowstrap gave out an odd cry as he was knocked backwards off his feet and tumbled to the sand. The crowd erupted with laughter.

"Stupid bastard smith!" snapped Liepol Duxe as he rushed in to distract the troll from Cowstrap. "Thinks he can take on a troll singlehanded, does he?" Duxe's blade flashed and the troll snarled and defended itself with its shield.

"Sorry, Sergeant, mistimed my rush," said Cowstrap as he regained his feet and moved clear.

Gungol swung his sword and Duxe dodged. Rebak of Marneri thrust in. Cowstrap moved back into the fray.

Behind them steel rang on steel with tremendous force as Puxdool and the Broketail clashed. They went belly to belly, shield to shield, and then Puxdool fell back. Bazil roared his own challenge, glad to have this opportunity to avenge poor Nessi. The troll circled.

Baz cut at him but Puxdool deflected well—the troll had skill with his sword. And for Bazil, this troll blade he held was too small for his usual heavyhanded attacking style.

The blades rang together again. Puxdool was quick, devilishly quick. He spun suddenly and Baz moved just in time to evade that knee cutter that had been used to destroy poor Nessi. He chopped down as he turned away, and his backhand deflected the troll's blade and almost ripped it loose. The shields smashed together again and Puxdool exerted all his strength against the leatherback.

Puxdool was strong, but not as strong as Puxdool thought, decided Baz, who gave ground deliberately, as if overpowered. Puxdool was a new kind of troll and quick and lethal with a sword, but Puxdool retained many of the usual troll weaknesses. Now he became overconfident. The swords came together again and again; Puxdool stamped forward swinging with a will, hand over hand, and then swung in with his shield to knock the dragon off balance and force an opening for his sword.

Bazil gave ground at first and then dug in his heels suddenly; Puxdool swung in hard and Baz deflected the weight of the blow with his shield. Puxdool stumbled a step too far and exposed his neck and shoulder to Bazil's overhand.

The troll wore heavy shoulder armor, otherwise he would have been finished there and then. Furthermore it was only a troll blade, six feet long, no dragon sword.

As it was, Puxdool's shield arm went numb and he backed away from the circling blade in the dragon's powerful fist with a wail of dismay. Puxdool had been hurt—this had not happened often in Puxdool's short, brutal life. In addition Puxdool knew that he had been tricked, and he hated that. Puxdool's small vicious mind became suffused with rage.

Beside him Izmak cut and thrust at the purple-green of Hook Mountain, who had thrown down the human-made things and returned to his normal wild method of combat.

He roared and lunged, but he was mindful of the sharp sword in the troll's hand. It gave the troll an advantage in reach—the purple-green roared and sprang from side to side while pondering the question of how to get in and kill the thing without being stabbed with its blade.

The purple-green rushed in and swung a forearm tipped with claws; the troll defended with shield and then stabbed forward with sword. To evade the point the drake had to jump backwards, and he almost lost his footing and had to stagger back a few paces. Men scattered as he crashed through their ranks.

Relieved of the pressure, Izmak leaned over and thrust at Bazil, who deflected with sword. Izmak was a maroon troll, a known quantity for the young leatherback. Maroons were strong but they lacked the speed of this Puxdool.

Baz took Izmak shield to shield, held him steady and beat down the troll's sword with a hard cut. He drove home, but the sword was too light—it slid away on the troll's chest plate and did not penetrate.

Izmak stumbled back, his chest still ringing from the blow. The dragon was very quick, quicker than anything he had faced except Puxdool.

The purple-green sprang forward again with a sudden rush, but the trolls put steel to his face and he stopped and backed off once more.

Gungol continued to duel with the men, who were keeping the other maroon extremely busy.

The crowd was on its feet, screaming anxiously at the trolls. Many could not understand why more trolls weren't being sent in.

"Why do they risk the trolls like this?" they cried, and some railed against the ring managers.

"It is the Doom's wish," said someone.

"The Doom loves the games!" cried those who heard, and they raised their hands in salute to the black sphere high above in its aerie in the tower. The cries of loyalty turned into a roaring chant of submission to the Doom from a forest of raised arms and clenched fists.

Now Puxdool came on again, shield leading and sword flicking forwards. Bazil knocked away the sword; the shields clashed, but the troll was more cautious now and backed off and went with the sword again, slamming against Bazil's shield.

Puxdool was fast, and Baz could barely keep his blade in front of the troll's. His shield was taking a lot of punishment.

Again the purple-green rushed in but was driven back by Izmak. Bazil deflected, parried and retreated. The troll swung overhand and Baz met his blade with a ringing crash. The sword in his hand was shattered, breaking above the hilt.

Bazil roared an oath and dropped the useless thing. Puxdool let out a snort of relief and surged in again.

Baz stumbled backwards.

He felt the wall of the arena at his back.

He slid to his left, keeping his shield up.

Puxdool had abandoned Izmak and Gungol, who were busy enough with the men and the worry of the wild drake that danced about them seeking an opening.

Baz got away from the wall, but kept moving backwards.

The crowd roared its appreciation and rose to its feet. Puxdool was doing the job! Puxdool was the mightiest! All was fine and well in Tummuz Orgmeen and the filthy dragon would soon be slain!

Once again Baz ran up against a barrier. He was against the doors at the end of the arena just below the keep.

Puxdool was advancing. There was no way to fight this troll without a weapon.

And then there was a flash of light, and something silver and gleaming fell past his eyes and sank quivering into the sand not ten feet away.

The crowd was hushed.

Baz reached out and yanked it from the ground.

Piocar! His own!

He kissed the hilt and swung the great sword down before him.

Puxdool had halted and was backing up. Puxdool had never faced a dragonsword before.

The blade in his hand brought renewed strength to Bazil's weary limbs. He looked up, exulting. Only one person in the world could be responsible.

There were people in the crowd pointing up at the highest gallery, which ran beside the top of the tower, where the shadows barely hid the gleam of the Doom.

A small figure stood there, waving down at the dragon.

Bazil lifted Piocar high and waved back. That boy was a good one, at least some of the time.

Then he turned and advanced on Puxdool.

Puxdool retreated but not quickly enough, and soon

steel rang on steel and the troll was defending himself desperately. Piocar swept in and then over and down, and with a crunch cut through the troll's shield and cleft it in twain. With Piocar the dragon's extra weight and power were unstoppable.

The crowd groaned.

Puxdool let out a bellow of rage mixed with fear and took his sword in both hands.

Piocar met it and turned it aside, and Baz slammed the troll with the weight of his shield. Puxdool was knocked backwards. He recovered only in time to receive another heavy buffet. He slammed into the gate and bounced back; Baz met his return with the edge of the great sword.

Puxdool gave a sick groan and went down, hewn almost in half at the waist.

The crowd was stilled. The other trolls stood back in horror.

Puxdool was slain!

From the high tower over the keep came a terrible shriek of rage from the Mouth.

Drums began to thunder.

CHAPTER FIFTY-EIGHT

Relkin flung himself down the stairs at a blistering pace. His dragon still lived! And if the goddess willed, that dragon would still be alive at the end of the day—at least he was armed properly now.

And Relkin had seen the very man they had pursued to Tummuz Orgmeen. Lessis would want to hear of that!

Furthermore, he had seen a dozen or more fighting men in the arena and they were the men of Marneri, he was certain. Even the captain, he lived. Relkin drove himself on—the lady needed all this information.

He reached the bottom of the secret stair, where a stygian gloom prevailed. He slowed his pace, not wanting to trip and fall in the dark until his eyes had adjusted.

Even moving slowly he didn't see the girl pressed into a recess in the wall until she stepped out and touched him on the shoulder, whereupon he jumped like a startled deer and reached for his blade.

"Relkin," she said, trying not to laugh at his surprise.

"Lagdalen? By the Great Mother, you scared the wits out of me that time."

"I'm sorry. I couldn't resist. What did you see?"

He nodded towards the passageway. "I have news for the lady. Bazil is alive—I found his sword and threw it down to him. And I think the captain lives, too."

She let out a heavy sigh of relief.

"Thank the Mother for that. Come on then! The lady is very anxious to hear your report."

"There's been a lot of fighting. The drags—I don't even know one of them—have busted loose. The enemy made a mistake and gave the wrong dragon a chance to fight. He's killing them."

Lagdalen drew him down the passage.

"Hurry."

The tunnel had several twists and turns before they emerged into a larger passage and stepped onto some stairs.

On the next floor up they found the survivors of Lessis's force of women. They had seen fierce fighting, and the floor of the hall was littered with their own dead, among them were twenty imps and half a dozen men.

The women had fought magnificently, but they had failed. The double doors to the Doom's Tube were guarded too heavily. There were trolls there and the doors had been shut. The women could not break through.

Lessis saw Relkin and Lagdalen and ran to them.

"Quickly, young man, what did you see?"

"Dragons are loose in the arena with some Marneri men."

Lessis accepted this with a short, deep breath.

"She has heard our prayers, that's all I can say. Thank you, Great Mother, we shall not disappoint you."

Lagdalen sensed hope bursting anew in Lessis.

"What can we do?"

"We must go up one more level and then break through to the mid-section doors to the arena. It can be done. I know the way."

Within less than a minute Lessis had led the sixty-odd survivors of her force, all of them now heavily armed with weapons taken from imps and men, and placed them below a stair that rose to the ground level of the keep. Quietly they climbed the first flight and there they paused while Lessis went forward alone, creeping silently up the next few steps.

The landing above was jammed with imps. Steel glinted in a hundred hands.

She retreated as silently and invisibly as she had appeared. Not an imp moved—none had seen a thing.

Suddenly from the dark depth of the stairwell came a ferocious bellow and the sound of heavy feet.

"Gazak! Dragon!" muttered the imps.

Another bellow, closer this time, set them close to panic.

And then the women from the pens, swords in their hands, came racing up the stairs and fell upon them, all the while screaming like banshees. The imps were paralyzed.

Swords beat down like hammers upon helmet and shield. Imps fell, were cut down and trampled. They fought back briefly and then broke and fled before the storm. The women were right behind them with swords lashing out to cut down the hindmost as they ran.

Together they all burst into the great passage to the mid-point gate. A crowd of men and imps, the handlers and haulers who worked in the arena, looked on with complete astonishment for a moment before they too took to their heels and ran down the passage.

At the gate itself a dozen heavyset guards turned to face them. There was no way past this obstacle; Lessis led them on, a sword in her hand.

But these were no imps, these were seasoned men—killers all. They eyed the onrushing mob with cold detachment; they would not flinch at witch's tricks.

Relkin was running behind the lady, and Lagdalen was just behind him.

The women never faltered. They were ready for death; their flesh tormented by the horror thrust upon them, their spirits enraged beyond measure, they came on with their swords up.

It might have been a slaughter—the guards would have killed all of them quite easily, except that as they closed Lessis raised a hand and from it flashed a blue flame that struck into the eyes of the foremost guard, who waited for her with sword ready.

He was blinded and flailed weakly with his blade, missing Relkin, who sank his dirk into the man's belly in the next instant.

Then the forces crashed together and swords rose and fell, but a gap had been opened through the line of guards, and Lessis and Relkin widened it further when Relkin engaged another guard long enough to let Lessis reach his throat with her dirk.

The women kept coming, over the bodies of their sisters, and now other guards were falling, borne down by the sheer weight of numbers, slipping in the blood that pooled on the floor.

Lessis and Lagdalen reached the doors and heaved one open.

The daylight of the arena flooded in.

Two dragons and a dozen men stood fifty feet away, formed up in a defensive position, ready to fight to the death. Marching towards them out of the double gates of the keep was a squad of eight trolls with one hundred imps. The Valkyrie was riding up and down while the golden youth led the crowd in more chanting.

The defiance of the dragons had been magnificent. Puxdool's great corpse still twitched occasionally on the sands. Other corpses were strewn here and there. The mob of Tummuz Orgmeen had seen great excitement, the dragons had been worthwhile opponents of their power, but now, now they were to be exterminated. Their defiance could only be tolerated for so long.

On came the trolls and imps.

Lessis remained within the doors, cupped her hands and blew, producing the shrill, sharp notes of the cornet of the Argonath.

The men turned, Captain Kesepton saw the opened doors and the lady in grey and barked an order. The dragons were already lumbering towards the opened gates.

"Who is that dragon?" said Lagdalen, pointing to the giant purple-green one that was approaching on all fours.

Lessis kept her voice level.

"That is a wild drake, my dear. The ancester to all our wyverns."

Lagdalen stared wide-eyed at the monster.

"They eat people, don't they?"

"They do. But right now I think this one has more important things on his mind than the menu. We'd better open these doors wider."

Relkin was also staring. Not even Vastrox would outweigh this monster. Then the gate area was crowded with them—two dragons took up a lot of space. Relkin, however, was too busy hugging his own to worry about that.

"You're alive!" he kept saying as he pounded on Baz's leathery hide.

"And so is boy!" said the dragon happily, leaning on Piocar and breathing hard.

They slammed the gates shut in the faces of the imps. Then Captain Kesepton paused beside Lagdalen.

"Well met, Lagdalen of Marneri. Even if we are to die here I will not be sorry, for I will die beside you."

Lagdalen's heart leaped even further. He had survived, they were together.

"Well met, Captain. Surely the Mother watches over us. I did not think I would see you again."

Their hands were clasped together. Kesepton leaned over and kissed her. It seemed the most natural thing in the world.

Lagdalen's eyes were filling with tears; it was all so horrifying and yet so magnificent. They had raised rebellion in the heart of the Doom's city, they had shaken the rule of the great rock, they would never be forgotten.

Kesepton leaned back. Liepol Duxe gave him an insulting look, but he refused to take the bait. Lagdalen would be his wife someday, he was certain of this now.

If they lived, which was most uncertain. Death was all around them and death was closing in, in the hands of trolls, men and imps, a horde aroused within its own foul nest. What possible chance could they have against such odds?

CHAPTER FIFTY-NINE

Thrembode had left the general's corpse hidden and gone immediately to his chambers.

To his horror he found that Besita was not there. Once again she had disobeyed his orders. She had become so filled with her sense of importance here in Tummuz Orgmeen that she casually ignored his wishes. Now he had to waste precious time searching for the trollop!

But he had to have her—she was his trump card. With her he could go over the head of the great stupid rock. He would go to Padmasa for justice.

It was a chilling thought but unavoidable. The Doom's

displeasure would soon lead to an ignominious and horrible end, or worse, conscription into the ranks of obscene sense organs hanging in those cages.

So he would flee, and he would take Besita. The Masters would like that, to be able to question a princess of the Argonath. The Masters would learn much from such an interrogation. The Masters would overrule their stone Doom in Tummuz Orgmeen.

But he would have to move quickly. General Erks was an important man and his absence would be noted. A search would soon turn up his body and the hunt for Thrembode would be on. Erks's staff most certainly knew of their meeting and probably even understood what the general was going to say to the doomed magician.

He snapped his fingers—of course! Besita was in the arena, in the magician's box. Watching the dragons fight.

He turned and ran, taking the stairs two at a time, barely pausing to identify himself to the guards at the top landing. In the box he found Besita and several other women, military wives of the high command.

Besita was stunned, almost angry at first. Had she no rights? Why did Thrembode have to ruin her afternoon? But he would not be denied, and took her arm and hustled her from the box.

"What is it?" she whispered, but he would not say.

Outside he halted briefly.

"We are leaving Tummuz Orgmeen."

"Leaving? But we went through hell to get here—why are we leaving now?"

He barely restrained himself. The trollop didn't want to go, eh?

"I have orders to go on. You are wanted at higher levels."

"Higher than the Doom?"

"Much. The makers of Dooms want you."

She swallowed. The Masters.

"I do not want to go. The Doom did not mention this. Does it know?"

"I do not know," he hissed. "I only have my orders. Come with me. Now!"

Besita did not want to come, but he would not be resisted; she was tugged through the labyrinth of the city. There was no time to waste. They but needed horses and then they would be on their way.

At the outer gate of the keep Thrembode passed through without drawing a check. No alarm had been raised yet over General Erks. Thrembode began to hope that everything would go smoothly and they would escape.

They reached the stables. Imps ran to fetch horses as soon as small gold coins were pressed into the stableman's hand. Thrembode breathed a sigh of relief. Just a few minutes now.

Before the horses appeared, however, a squad of troopers in black slipped into view and closed in around Thrembode.

He watched them with a sick feeling in his belly. He was trapped! Trapped by the Doom. The damned thing had anticipated his move. Perhaps it had even wanted the death of General Erks. It was hard to know—the thing would kill whomever it felt it needed to. It liked to kill, the magicians all knew that.

With swords to his throat Thrembode could do nothing but surrender. They put him in chains and hustled him and Besita back into the keep and up the stairs.

Eventually they were thrust into the Doom's presence, in the main chamber. Armed men, trolls, imps were everywhere. The entire place was on a maximum alert. Something was happening.

The Doom's Mouth was swung high..

"Ah, it is Thrembode. Rebels are abroad in the city, and our magician Thrembode decides to decamp. Running for safety like the coward he is. Not a pretty sight."

The Eyes rattled in the cage.

"She must go to Padmasa," said Thrembode, "if something should go wrong here."

"Are you suggesting that I could lose control of Tummuz Orgmeen?"

"It is unlikely, Great One, unlikely, but still we must not take risks with a prize such as this."

"Hah! You make a joke for me, magician. You say this girl is more important than anything else in my city."

Rebels on the loose in the city?

"Not at all, but if there is danger here I must act, and I thought that with a witch running amok I had best remove the captive and ensure her safe delivery to Padmasa."

"Ah, the witch. Yes, I remember the witch and I remember that you, Thrembode—you were supposed to have brought me the head of this hag by now. Were you not?"

Thrembode felt the sweat running down his body.

"It is not possible, this place is honeycombed with secret passages and tunnels. Your obsession with secrecy has made the place impossible to screen or even secure."

"You seek to blame me?" The Doom squeezed the brain of the Mouth so hard it choked.

Thrembode could feel the rock's anger as if it were radiating heat.

"I merely point out that there's a labyrinth down there, and even with five thousand imps you'd be lucky to find anyone. They wriggled through holes no more than a foot high."

"Incompetence!" bellowed the Mouth. "But that is hardly the gravest charge, is it, magician?"

Thrembode's heart sank.

"Yes, we have found General Erks. He has been stabbed to death. You were the last person to have seen him."

Thrembode gulped, unable to speak for a moment.

"Yes, you were, and he was going to give you some unwelcome news."

"I don't know," said Thrembode quickly. "I never met him."

"What?"

"I was too busy trying to find the captive. I decided not to attend the meeting."

"Nonsense. You lie. I will boil the truth out of you, magician, but not yet. Move him back and gag him. I will enjoy your demise later when there will be more time for it."

Troopers with leather gauntlets seized him and thrust a thick gag into his mouth and strapped it tight.

He was locked to a pole.

Besita was aghast. She stared up at the great mass of the black stone. Poor Thrembode was lost, the Doom would take his life. She could not imagine losing Thrembode completely. How would she go on without him?

She was confused. Thrembode's spell made her ache for him in one way, but in another she could not help but feel joy, for she had dreaded the idea of journeying to Padmasa, especially in Thrembode's company, serving as his thrall once more. Indeed she much preferred her life in Tummuz Orgmeen, where she had Thrembode for a lover and not a master, and where she enjoyed the favor of the Doom, to any previous period in her life.

Still, she had only seen the Doom before when it was on its most velvety-soft, best behavior. The sight of the Eyes, Mouth and Ears flung about in their cages was horrifying.

Thrembode was gagged and cuffed to the whipping post, and the Doom was about to turn to her, when messengers came in and whispered to the officers of the Guard.

One of them hurried to the Ears and repeated its message.

The Doom reacted violently. Its sensors were tossed about.

"Get reinforcements down there at once," it shrieked. "They must be stopped!"

CHAPTER SIXTY

At the great gates to the Doom Tube Lessis halted. The dragons stepped forward and struck the doors with troll axes. Their massive thews bunched with power and the axes bit deeply into the door. Soon the wood was breaking up and flying apart.

Holes appeared. The wild drake grasped one end of a timber splintered by the Broketail's axe and heaved. To his own surprise the door disintegrated.

Bazil dropped the axe and took Piocar from Relkin. Trolls rose up inside with sword and shield, dragons burst in upon them, and men and women poured in around the dragons and struck hard at the imps and troopers.

In the confined space there was a vicious, hacking fight, knives and fists were as effective as swords and Bazil found it hard to wield Piocar. The press put no inhibitions on the purple-green however, and he seized troll after troll, using his massive teeth on them.

Somehow, despite their exhaustion and their weary arms, the insurgents found a new strength, borne perhaps on the knowledge of certain death. They would die here, but they would take a great many of their enemies with them—that was all that mattered.

For the space of a few minutes the fight was more or less even, but then the men of Marneri led by Keseption and Duxe hacked their way through the troopers and fell on the imps.

The imps panicked and flowed back, and the swords of the Argonath flicked out and took them from behind.

Along the way they lost several men, however. A troll caught Lieutenant Weald with a blow from his axe. Weald was virtually cut in two and fell in front of Kesepton. Then the troll was gone, smashed to ruins by an overhand blow from Piocar, and the fighting dragon burst free of the trolls and got space to wield his sword. In an instant the great blade had scythed through the remaining troopers and cut them down like corn.

Only imps remained now and they were in terrified flight. Swords flashed briefly and then there was silence in the chamber. The victors stared down at the slaves of the Doom Tube, those who hauled on the ropes that raised and lowered the Doom and its captive "senses."

The slave masters cowered back now as the men of Marneri swept down. The swords rose and fell, for Lessis would not stop them, decreeing that justice in this case should be swift because these men who had kept other men and women in such deadly slavery deserved no further life of their own.

The place was secured. Looking up through the length of the Tube they could see the Doom, a glistening fat ebony pearl dangling high above.

"The mechanisms that move the Doom must be controlled from the upper chamber—we cannot bring it down from here," said Lessis to Kesepton.

"Then what can we do?"

"We can send someone up to the upper chamber."

Kesepton nodded.

"There is only one fit for this task and he has done much already."

"But he can do it."

Without hesitation she turned to Bazil of Quosh, who was standing nearby, leaning on Piocar and looking up the tube at the distant rock. It was a long way; he remembered how big the damn rock was when he was close.

The slaves at the ropes were staring up at him, as were the women and the swordsmen of Marneri.

"What next?" he said wearily.

"You will ride the chains," said the Lady. "We will pull you to the upper chamber. The Doom is secured from falling by a steel net. It is secured by seven strands that connect to the main hawser that lifts and lowers it. Cut those seven strands and the Doom will fall.''

Bazil nodded. ''I saw those. You are right, that is what has to be done.''

Lessis stood closer to the great wyvern.

''You must remain on the far side of the Doom. They can spin him and they will try to use the dragon lance on you.''

Bazil nodded. ''They will try to spear me while I cut cables. I understand.''

He also understood that if he succeeded, the Doom would fall and with it would fall Tummuz Orgmeen.

Bazil moved forward to the chains. Gingerly the haulage slaves helped him onto their strongest lifting pallet. The pallet was hooked to a riser and the riser run onto the blocks. Then they began to pull.

''They understand, Lady Lessis,'' said Kesepton. ''They have to get him up there before the enemy realizes the threat and cuts the rope.''

Lessis nodded, but Relkin heard these words and felt his heart freeze. No dragon could survive a fall from that height.

The slaves pulled and needed no whip cracked over their heads to give it all they had. The dragon rose into the air with a cheery wave and picked up speed until he was soaring as if rocket-propelled.

Then renewed noise at the doors turned everyone's head. Fresh imps and troopers were coming.

''To the doors!'' shouted Kesepton.

Without a word they took up their weapons once more and made ready to sell their lives dearly.

CHAPTER SIXTY-ONE

Bazil soared in the chains, holding on tight with both hands and his tail while bracing his feet on the platform. Below him five hundred slaves heaved on the rope with every ounce of strength left in their bodies to send this weapon hurtling up the Tube.

So swift was the ascent that he arrived in the topmost chamber before any effective defense could be readied.

The men and imps on the upper floors had heard the commotion of the battle for the rope room, and there were many eyes peering into the deep well of the Tube, but the sight of a dragon rising to meet them took them by surprise and many mistakenly assumed that it was a flying dragon. They turned and ran for their lives.

At the very top, securely pinned to the structure of the tower, was a complex of pulleys and gears through which the Doom's ''hands,'' men who rode forever in small cages at the Doom's equator, controlled the motions of the Doom and signaled to the slaves below when it was time to hoist or lower the great stone. From the pulleys hung dozens of lines to control the senses of the Doom as well as the great hawsers that held the rock itself in place.

Bazil rode up past the ''hands'' at the equator, and as he arrived he swung the platform on its rope so that he came close enough to the Doom itself to reach out and seize hold of one of the seven cables that supported it.

The Doom sensed him at once and knew its peril.

Shouts of alarm rose below. The Mouth was jerked around in its cage, now ominously still. The ''hands'' tried again and again to get some movement for the Eyes and Ears but found no response from the floor of the Tube.

"What are you doing here, great dragon?" said the Mouth in a strange soft tone.

"Bloody rock, I come to kill you."

Bazil had Piocar in his free forehand.

"No!" bellowed the Mouth.

The "hands" of the Doom twitched their signals in desperate reflex to have the slaves haul the stone downwards. But the slaves no longer obeyed. The Doom was trapped where it was.

"No, do not do this terrible thing, great dragon. Listen to me!"

"You like to kill dragons for your sport, rock. Now dragon kill you. Different sport."

Piocar sang and bounced on the first cable.

The Mouth shifted to the harsh, command mode.

"Quickly, destroy the dragon. Bring dragon lance."

Piocar rang on the cable again. It was of steel and thicker than a man's thumb. Worse, he was not getting enough purchase for the swing and the great blade bounced off the cable, barely nicking it.

"Hurry, you fools!" roared the Mouth.

Bazil got one foot up on the side of the rock with his claws gripping the mesh of the net of cables.

Now he swung again with more power, and Piocar cut the cable, which gave way with a great twang and then lashed back with terrific energy that sent it crashing around the inside of the tower top.

"Noooooooooo!" shrieked the Doom.

The cable whipped back with a whistle, like the lash of some demonic god, and Baz ducked and prayed it wouldn't cut his rope. Instead he heard a scream and saw one of the Doom's "hands" go hurtling down the Tube with his chain cut.

Piocar came back for the next cable, but the strike was not clean and the blade rang off the cable and struck the black stone itself. To his horror Baz saw that his sword was notched.

A catwalk had been swung out to the Doom's side and imps were approaching. Crossbow bolts began to bounce off the stone beneath him and then they began to hit him, sinking into his thick hide on back and legs and tail. The bolts stung but they could not stop him unless they hit him in the eye.

The sword swung down again, and this time the second cable parted with another loud twang.

Again it lashed around, striking the catwalk and knocking a pair of imps off into nothingness.

A troll with a dragon lance was coming. The catwalk ended some ten feet from the doomstone, the rest of the distance being bridged with ladders when maintenance was necessary. A troll planted on the end could reach the dragon and then some, enough to get the lance into his guts and finish him.

Baz saw it coming and began pushing at the stone with his foot and started it spinning slowly. It was hard work since he had nothing solid to push back against, but the stone began to move slightly after a while and then he was swept along, away from the catwalk and the troll.

Now Piocar swung again and bounced off the third cable.

Troopers on the floor of the audience chamber threw their spears, but none struck the dragon with any force and only one even stuck into the leather of his joboquin.

The turn of the great rock was taking Baz away from his platform—he could no longer keep a foot on it or hold the rope. He released them, clung to the cables, and crawled up until he was on top of the Doom itself.

The troll on the catwalk thrust at him with the lance, but he deflected it with Piocar. More arrows came, and he felt the pricks in his chest and arms and shoulders as they sank in.

"No time to waste, eh rock?" he called in a loud voice.

From his new position he could see out the hooded window atop the tower and down into the arena.

''You like the view from up here, eh? Pity about that.''
Piocar cut the third cable.

The rock shifted suddenly in its basket of steel wire.
With three cables cut, it was close to falling out.

The Mouth, the Eyes, the Ears and the remaining adjustors were hurled about. The cable whipped back and Baz
had to flatten himself on the stone as it sang overhead.

The troll jabbed at him; he moved, slipped and started
to slide down the stone.

Desperately he grabbed at the cables with his free forehand. For an agonizing second he caught nothing, and
then his talons wrapped around the last and simultaneously his right foot caught on another further down the
Doom's smooth side.

For a moment he hung there over the sheer drop, then
he slowly, painfully crawled back.

They were pushing out the ladder from the catwalk to
the Doom's upper pole. A pair of magicians were sending
imps across with spears in their hands.

Baz got his footing back once more in time to meet
the first imp's spear and knock it aside. Then he hacked
down the next couple with a backhand slice and finally
swung the sword down, cut the ladder and sent the rest
of the imps hurtling into the abyss.

The troll lunged with the lance and it sank home in
Bazil's thigh. The troll tried to turn it in the wound, but
Baz gripped the haft of the lance with his tail and jerked
it out of the troll's hands. Then he pulled it free of his
leg. The pain was fierce, but he ignored it and turned to
deal with the fourth cable.

Arrows were thudding into his back but he swung
again, a terrific blow that cut through the wire with a
flash of sparks.

The Mouth was shrieking; the great stone shifted again
and tilted suddenly; Baz clutched convulsively at the remaining wires, dropped Piocar and then hung on desperately as he was hurled upwards in violent reaction as the
doomstone slipped from the web of cables and fell down
the Tube.

Down, through the levels of the great keep it fell, past the horrified eyes of its slaves and servants, through a long second before the blink to eternity.

At the bottom it shattered with a thunderous impact that rocked the entire keep to its very foundations, while a black flame blazed up and released a choking cloud of green smoke that rose up the Tube and escaped into the clear blue sky through the hooded window at the top.

The mountain itself shuddered and shook, and from the populace of Tummuz Orgmeen came a wailing cry of terror. The unimaginable had happened. The Doom had been cut down from on high and destroyed.

Their Master was gone, and with it went their strength and purpose. They covered their heads against the sight of the black fire and ran from the arena. Within minutes the first of them began the flight, scattering from the city itself, desperate to escape the collapse of the dread power they had served.

Imps, trolls, even the black-garbed troopers ran with them, ignoring efforts by a few commanders to stop the panic. The loss of the controlling force had turned the place over like an anthill dug into with a spade. Anything that could be carried away was taken, but the exodus once begun could not be stopped.

In the confusion the forces arrayed against Lessis and her band of women survivors melted away. Lessis and Lagdalen led them up the secret stair to the high gallery and thus into the Doom's Tube at the highest level. They encountered little more than token opposition.

In the Tube they found a blackened chaos. Blinded, choking imps staggered past them into the sunlight. The women took these imps and thew them off the wall at once while the men of Marneri looked on, awed by the rage that burned in these women.

There were also a few men and women of the city, and among these they discovered the Princess Besita, alive but soot-stained and coughing from the green smoke.

Lessis plucked her up and carried her out on the high gallery to cleaner air. In the confusion only Lagdalen noticed this feat of strength. Since the death of Ecator, Prince of Cats, the Lady Lessis had grown very strong.

Besita got slowly to her feet, unhurt except where she'd breathed in the smoke. Lessis gave thanks to the goddess and hugged the princess, who immediately broke down into further coughing.

They did not find the magician, though. Somehow in the final chaos he had broken the cuffs that bound him and escaped by sliding down a cable to a lower floor of the Keep. From there he joined the rout that fled the place and disappeared into the Gan.

Finally they discovered the Broketail dragon, completely covered in soot, with dozens of arrows sticking out of his hide. He was curled up in the pocket made by the three remaining cables, still hanging there in the center of the Tube.

To rescue him they had to winch him down to the floor of the Tube, standing amidst the black rubble of the smashed stone. The place stank of sulfur and ozone, and the walls were scorched from the violence of the Doom's destruction.

The great purple-green dragon picked up the wounded leatherback and carried him out of the keep and into the sunshine. He set him down on a patch of grass near the gate that was normally used for beheadings. The lady crouched beside the limp form and placed a listening tube against the dragon's chest. Relkin had tears on his cheeks. His dragon looked virtually incinerated, grilled, covered in soot and blood, studded with arrows.

But Lessis held up a hand suddenly. "He lives yet," she said.

Relkin could hardly believe it. For a moment he stared hard at her and then erupted into a whoop and called for fire and boiling water and some tools to get the arrows out.

The Doom was smashed but the dragon lived.

EPILOGUE

It was almost three months later, in midsummer, that Bazil of Quosh, known as the Broketail dragon throughout the legions, marched through the gates of the city of Marneri once more.

The sun was shining and a warm breeze was coming off the Long Sound when, with Relkin at his side, he passed through the Tower Gate. Behind came the other survivors of the destruction of the Blunt Doom of Tummuz Orgmeen. A great crowd was on hand, indeed, folk had lined the roads for the last three leagues or more.

They were a small band, these survivors, headed by the two remaining dragons of the 109th—Bazil and big Chektor, whose broken feet had mended since the spring. Behind them came a handful of dragonboys, recovered from the slave market in Tummuz Orgmeen, and the dozen survivors of the Marneri Thirteenth and Talion Sixth Light Cavalry.

At the gate they were met by cheering throngs who showered them with petals of the white lalyx, the flower of Marneri. Every dragon in the city was lined up at the entrance to the Dragon House. Great Vastrox himself handed Bazil a new sword, since Piocar had been lost forever in the destruction of the Doom.

On that same day, Captain Hollein Kesepton and Lagdalen of the Tarcho were wed in the Temple of Marneri. Among the well-wishers were Sergeant Liepol Duxe and Subader Yortch, now recovered from his wounds.

Also present were Dragoneer First Class Relkin of Quosh and the famous Broketail dragon himself. It was the first time a dragon had entered the Temple in Marneri and the request had sent the administrators scurrying to the precedent books. Finally, Lessis had spoken with Ewilra, the High Priestess, and a special bench was set up and the dragon allowed in.

The ceremonies were conducted by the witch Lessis, who confessed that this was the first wedding she had ever performed. Nonetheless, she did it gracefully enough, except that when she released the doves that symbolized the new couple, they refused to leave the Temple through the roof aperture but perched there cooing, quite unwilling to leave her presence.

Hollein Kesepton had not been brought before a court martial as he had expected, but then neither had he been promoted. Instead, after careful consideration, the legion had given him a fresh command, a company in the Second Legion, and a posting on the frontier of the Teetol country. Lagdalen was to join him at Fort Picon.

One notable absence from the ceremony was the Princess Besita. The princess had been taken to a convent in Bea where the Office of Unusual Insight had a counseling school. The princess had suffered greatly from her months as a captive. For almost all of that time she had been gripped by a spell that had made her a willing slave to her captor. Breaking that spell and restoring the princess's sanity had become a grim and difficult task.

Of Thrembode the New, there was no word, except for a report to the Office of Insight concerning a magician who was said to have taken passage from Ourdh some three months after the fall of Tummuz Orgmeen on a ship bound for the lands of the west.

The destruction of the Blunt Doom had repercussions of great importance. In the eastern theater, the Masters found their power drastically curtailed and they went over to the defensive throughout the region. The threat of war had lifted on the frontiers.

After the wedding ceremony, the guests moved up the hill to the Tower of Guard where a feast had been laid out by the Tarcho family. Toasts and dancing began later, but after a couple of turns about the floor with Hollein and then with her father, Lagdalen excused herself and slipped down the stairs to the courtyard. There she found Relkin and Bazil sitting together on the back steps sharing a cask of ale. Relkin had a pewter pot and Bazil hefted the rest of the barrel in his huge hands.

"Welcome to the bride!" said the dragon, and shifted his tail to make room for her on the step beside him.

"I couldn't stay up there a moment longer without taking a few minutes to talk to you two. It's been too long."

The dragon chuckled. "And we've missed you too, Lagdalen Dragonfriend."

"And that's the truth," said Relkin, airily waving his pot of beer.

Lagdalen marveled at their new garments—a dragoneer's uniform for Relkin and a new leather joboquin for Bazil.

They examined the new sword, a legion blade, not quite as long or as massive as Piocar, but still a dragonsword. Since the loss of Piocar, Bazil had felt strangely naked. He'd taken the heaviest troll blade he could find but it had never felt right in his hand. Now, at last, he felt complete once again.

Lagdalen smiled. "I hate to disappoint you, but I think you may not have to use that blade now that the Doom is gone."

"That sounds good to this dragon. A life of beer and good legion food. We sit around and get fat and then retire."

Lagdalen laughed then, and marveled that they had survived to sit here in such cheerful comradeship.

"And when do you two leave for Kenor?" she asked after a moment.

"We go to Dalhousie next month, escort for the new recruits. What about you?"

She shrugged. "Soon. We are posted to Fort Picon."

Relkin gave a little sigh. "We will be far apart then."

She laughed. "Oh, Relkin, if there's anything I am sure of it is that our paths will cross again."

The dragon put out an enormous forehand and rested it gently on Lagdalen's shoulder for a moment.

"We never forget you, Lagdalen Dragonfriend."

"And I will never forget you, Bazil of the Broken Tail."

BEYOND THE IMAGINATION
WITH GAEL BAUDINO

If you and/or a friend would like to receive the *ROC Advance*, a bimonthly newsletter featuring all the newest and hottest ROC books and authors, on a complimentary basis, please fill out this form and return it to:

ROC Books/Penguin USA
375 Hudson Street
New York, NY 10014

Your Address

Name _____

Street _____ Apt. # _____

City _____ State _____ Zip _____

Friend's Address

Name _____

Street _____ Apt. # _____

City _____ State _____ Zip _____